Hocus Croakus

Just Desserts

Fowl Prey

Holy Terrors

Dune to Death

Bantam of the Opera

A Fit of Tempera

Major Vices

Murder, My Suite

Auntie Mayhem

Nutty as a Fruitcake

September Mourn

Wed and Buried

Snow Place to Die

Legs Benedict

Creeps Suzette

A Streetcar Named Expire

Suture Self

Silver Scream

Hocus Croakus

A Bed-and-Breakfast Mystery

Mary Daheim

wm

WILLIAM MORROW
An Imprint of HarperCollins*Publishers*

HarperCollins books may be purchased for educational, business, or sales promotional use. For information please write: Special Markets Department, HarperCollins Publishers Inc., 10 East 53rd Street, New York, NY 10022.

FIRST EDITION

Designed by Bernard Klein

Printed on acid-free paper

Library of Congress Cataloging-in-Publication Data
Daheim, Mary.
Hocus croakus / Mary Daheim.— 1st ed.
p. cm.
ISBN 0-380-97868-7
1. Flynn, Judith McMonigle (Fictitious character)—Fiction.
2. Women detectives—Northwest, Pacific—Fiction.
3. Bed and breakfast accommodations—Fiction. 4. Northwest,
Pacific—Fiction. 5. Casinos—Fiction. I. Title.
PS3554.A264 H63   2003
813'.54—dc21   2002038920

03   04   05   06   07   WB/QW   10   9   8   7   6   5   4   3   2   1

Hocus Croakus

$\mathcal{C}$hapter $\textcircled{\star}$ne

Judith McMonigle Flynn staggered out of the car, dumped a foil-lined paper cup of cigarette butts into a big stone ashtray, and found herself looking up at an imposing white-haired Native-American man who was wearing more gold braid than General Douglas MacArthur.

"I'm Bob Bearclaw, the doorman here at the Stillasnowamish casino," the big man announced in a deep, pleasing voice. "Welcome to our resort. May I help you, young lady?"

Judith smiled. "You can help my mother. She's in the backseat and is rather crippled. She'll need a wheelchair, if you have one available."

"Of course we do," Bob replied. "I'll get it right away." He snapped his fingers and made a complicated gesture with his hand. A young valet with a long black braid nodded deferentially before racing inside the casino.

Joe Flynn had finished speaking with a bellman who was now unloading the family's luggage from the Subaru.

"They're getting a wheelchair for Mother," she told her husband.

Joe scowled. "You mean we have to let her out of the car?"

"Don't be mean," Judith scolded. "We don't want to get off to a bad start on our vacation. I'm the one who could hardly breathe with Mother smoking her head off in the backseat."

"And bitching the whole way because there wasn't an ashtray there," Joe grumbled. "She should have thanked me for fixing that cup for her."

Judith refused to argue further. Besides, Joe had to deal with the parking attendant as well as the bellman. And Judith had to deal with her mother.

"A wheelchair is on its way," Judith said, poking her head into the smoky car.

"Don't let Lunkhead push me around in it," Gertrude Grover snapped. "I wouldn't let him haul me from a burning building."

"Don't mention that!" Judith exclaimed. "And stop calling Joe 'Lunkhead.' He's the one who had to load the car and drive for almost two hours to get to Lake Stillasnowamish."

Gertrude hadn't budged from her place in the backseat. In fact, she was lighting another cigarette. "Two hours, my foot. What was he doing, pedaling with his feet? I can move faster with my walker. It used to take us only an hour and a half to get to the family cabin. And that was before they put in the freeway."

"It was the freeway construction that held us up," Judith replied, gnashing her teeth. "Besides, we're ten miles from the cabin." She glanced behind her where the doorman was approaching with a shiny yellow wheelchair. "Here, Mother, I can help you."

"No, you can't," Gertrude retorted. "You'll pop your phony hip. At least my joints are the originals. Not that I couldn't use a few spare parts."

The reference to the artificial hip rankled with Judith. It had been over a year since the replacement surgery, and though she had to be careful not to dislocate it, Judith felt she was getting back to normal. Gertrude, however, liked to remind her daughter that she wasn't normal and never had been.

Judith felt a gentle tap on her shoulder.

"Mrs. Flynn, isn't it?" Bob Bearclaw asked. Seeing Judith give a jerky nod, he leaned into the car. "Then you must be Mrs. Grover. Wait until you see the speedy little number I've got for you. Here, let me help you get out."

A moment later, Gertrude emerged, still smoking, but far from fuming. "You're a good boy," she said to the doorman, who was probably close to seventy. "Your mother must have raised you right."

With remarkable ease, the doorman put Gertrude into the shiny yellow wheelchair and began pushing her up the handicapped ramp. Joe finished his business with the attendants just as his mother-in-law disappeared inside the glass doors of the casino. Judith took a deep breath and surveyed her surroundings.

The Lake Stillasnowamish Resort Casino was located in a spectacular setting. In early March, the cottonwood, alder, and vine maples were just beginning to bud. But the stately evergreens were reflected in the jade-green lake that nestled in the bosom of Mount Nugget. Although Judith had never visited the resort complex before, she knew the area well. Every year until her first marriage, she and the rest of the Grover clan had spent their summers at the family cabins ten miles west of Lake Stillasnowamish. In those days, no one would have dreamed of a gambling establishment in the area, let alone one owned by members of the Stillasnowamish tribe.

"Are you ready?" Judith asked Joe, who was putting the luggage and parking receipts into his wallet.

"Let's wait," Joe said. "If we stay out here for another, oh, twenty minutes, the casino might have raffled off your mother."

"Joe!" Judith exclaimed, but her exasperation was halfhearted. "Please stop making those remarks. You know I didn't want to bring Mother with us, but we had no choice since the toolshed is being renovated along with the bed-and-breakfast. She couldn't stay with Aunt Deb. We tried that once, and they almost killed each other."

"It was sheer perversity of the Rankerses to go to Palm Springs in March this year instead of January or February," Joe declared, referring to the Flynns' next-door neighbors. "Carl and Arlene actually enjoy your mother's company. I've never been able to figure out why. That's perversity, too."

"They're good people," Judith said, starting up the stone steps to the casino entrance. "Besides, they had a problem with the time-share. That's why they had to change their plans."

"Why," Joe mused, "can't they have places to board old people when their kids want to get away? You know, like a kennel. When the Steins on the corner take a trip, they always put Rosie in a boarding—"

"Rosie is a dog," Judith broke in. "Please stop. As for our neighbors, they've had to put up with a lot of inconvenience during the B&B construction. Of course it's been hell for us trying to live in the house since the fire last fall, but it hasn't been easy on anybody in the cul-de-sac," she continued as they entered the lobby. "I don't know why contractors can't keep to a schedule or at least start when . . . Oh, my!" She caught her breath as she took in the casino's glorious glitter.

The Lake Stillasnowamish complex was one of the newest and reputedly the most lavish of the Native-American-owned establishments in the state. The brochures didn't do it justice. Described as a "Wondrous Wilderness," the trees and waterfalls and streams were unlike anything else in Mother Nature's treasure trove. Fir, pine, cedar, and spruce trees were covered with gold and silver lights. The ceiling was the sky with moving clouds, twinkling stars, and an amber moon. Rainbow and Dolly Varden trout swam in gentle streams and reflecting pools. The gaming area was divided into the four seasons with artificial snow falling at intervals in the Big Buck Bonanza section. Judith was so enthralled that she didn't realize Joe had already gone to the knotty-pine registration desk.

She hurried to join him in the line of arriving guests. "It's gorgeous," she enthused, holding on to his arm. "It's every bit as spectacular as Vegas."

"They feature a magic show," Joe said as they moved up a few paces. "It must be terrific. They've already made your mother disappear."

"What?" Judith gasped, looking in every direction. "Oh, good Lord! Where *is* Mother?"

Joe was unperturbed. "With any luck, they won't be able to reproduce her when we check out Saturday."

"Please." Abruptly, Judith let go of Joe's arm and stepped out of line. She scanned the lobby, but couldn't spot Gertrude. Moving quickly, she went past the car-rental kiosk, the show-ticket booth, the special-promotions area, and the recreational director's desk. At last, in an alcove by a bank of telephones, she saw Gertrude sitting in her wheelchair and looking angry.

"Mother!" Judith cried. "I thought we lost you!"

"Lost is right," Gertrude shot back. "I've already lost money here." She clutched her purse with both hands. "You know me, I only like to play the single-nickel machines. These things want thirty-five cents. Well, I decided to get risky and put in seven nickels, but I didn't win. What a gyp!"

"Mother," Judith said, pushing the wheelchair back into the lobby, "those aren't slot machines, they're telephones."

Gertrude scowled at her daughter. "Telephones! You know I hate telephones! Why didn't somebody warn me?"

"I told you," Judith said, "you need new glasses."

"I need new eyes," Gertrude retorted. "Not to mention new ears, new . . ."

Judith didn't hear the rest of her mother's usual litany about body parts. Joe had finished the registration process and was beckoning her toward an archway that led to the guest rooms.

"Did you ask if Renie and Bill had checked in yet?" Judith inquired as they found the elevators that went to the Summer Tower.

"They haven't," Joe replied, punching the elevator button. "They're probably still at the cabin, seeing what the contractor's up to."

Judith glanced at her watch. It was almost one. The Joneses had left more than half an hour ahead of the Flynns. But Judith knew from her own recent and harrowing experiences with building contractors that dealings with them were often difficult.

The elevator arrived. Joe started to push Gertrude inside, but she waved him off. "I got a motor on this contraption. Look, I can go by myself."

Gertrude managed the motor nicely, but she forgot about the brake. Fortunately, the elevator was padded in leather. The collision was a gentle one.

"Okay, okay," Gertrude grumbled. "I need a little practice, that's all. Hey, I learned to drive on one of those cars you had to crank. If I could do that, I can run this thing."

"You'll be fine, Mother," Judith said, patting Gertrude's shoulder as the elevator purred up to the fourteenth floor. "Can you reverse?"

"Let's see." Gertrude fumbled with the controls. At last, she moved the shift to the right position. The wheelchair all but sailed out of the elevator. Luckily, this time she found the brake. "What did you say about the cabin?" she asked as they progressed down the long, lushly carpeted corridor.

"The cabin?" Judith was glad that she was standing behind her mother lest the old lady notice that her daughter was taken aback. Gertrude sometimes heard conversations that weren't meant for her deaf ears. "Oh—Renie and Bill thought they'd check things out. They haven't been up to the cabin in several years."

"Who has?" Gertrude retorted as Joe opened the door with his key card. "The place has probably fallen down by now. I blame all of you kids for letting that property go to pot," she added, zooming into the room and stopping just short of the windows. "Lazy, that's what your generation is. Your grandfather and your grandmother and your father and Uncle Cliff and Uncle Corky and Uncle Al worked every spare minute to build those four cabins on the river. Times were hard, it was the big Depression. People were living in tent cities, shantytowns. We had to scrimp and do without just to have our own summer vacation place."

Judith had heard the lecture many times. Long ago, she'd stopped reminding her mother that four hundred feet of riverfront property for the purposes of rustication had been quite a luxury back in the thirties. Not that any of the Grovers had ever been wealthy, but at least they'd been employed during the lean years. And, because it was the Depression era, the four lots they'd purchased had cost a hundred dollars apiece. Unfortunately, a flash flood had swept away three of the cabins almost fifty years earlier.

"Huh." Gertrude stopped her tirade as she gazed around the spacious room. "This is kind of pretty."

It was more than pretty, Judith thought, it was beautiful. The room's theme was Pacific Northwest wildflowers—trilliums, ginger, rhododendrons, jack-in-the-pulpit, foxgloves, and several varieties she didn't immediately recognize.

"The room is designed for handicapped guests," Judith explained as she indicated the bathroom off the entry hall. "We'll be next to you." She pointed to another door. "That leads into our room."

Before Gertrude could reply, a knock sounded on the outer door. Joe went to answer it, and let the bellman in. After depositing Gertrude's two suitcases and her walker, the young man received a generous tip from Joe.

"Shall I put your luggage in the room next door?" he asked, pointing to the suitcases on the cart.

"Sure," Joe said, all but racing out of his mother-in-law's room.

"We don't want to delay winning fabulous riches any longer than necessary."

Judith was torn. She didn't know whether to follow Joe or help her mother unpack. Joe was able to handle the Flynns' chores, but Gertrude could use some assistance. Dutifully, Judith stayed behind.

"Honestly, Mother," she exclaimed as she opened the first of Gertrude's suitcases, "how much underwear did you bring?"

"You mean my bloomers? Oh, twenty, twenty-five pairs, I guess."

"For six days?" Judith asked in disbelief.

Gertrude shrugged. "At my age, you never know."

"Mittens? Eight pairs of mittens?"

Gertrude continued to sit at the window enjoying the lake-and-mountain view. "It's early March, it's still winter, we're in the mountains."

"Do you plan to go skiing?"

"You never know about that, either." The old lady turned the wheelchair around. "Does that TV have cable?"

Judith found the remote and clicked on the set. The first screen welcomed them to the Lake Stillasnowamish casino. The second ballyhooed the Great Mandolini and his stupendous magic act. The third showed how to play keno from your very own private hotel room. Finally, Judith got to the regular stations that did indeed include cable.

"Keno," Gertrude said as Judith shut off the set. "I remember that game from the time your father and I went to Reno. He won six dollars. We had a steak dinner on that money."

A quick glance told Judith that her mother's eyes had grown misty. Usually, Gertrude was about as sentimental as a boxing referee. But the proximity to the family cabin, the memories of traveling with Judith's father, and the change of scenery appeared to have touched the old girl.

"You and Daddy had some good times," Judith said, hugging her mother's frail shoulders.

"That we did. There just weren't enough of them. He went too soon." Gertrude was silent for a few moments. Judith was afraid her mother might actually cry. Instead, she propelled herself to the bed. "I could use a nap. You go off with Lunkhead and try not to lose all your money."

"We'll be cautious," Judith promised as she helped her mother settle onto the king-size bed. "We can't be otherwise with the work we're having done to the B&B."

"What about those big bucks you got from the movie people?" Gertrude asked. "Don't tell me you've run through that already."

"No, we haven't," Judith replied, "but it won't last forever. We've already spent the insurance reimbursement for the fire loss."

"I wonder when I'll hear from Hollywood," Gertrude said as Judith tucked the floral comforter around her. "Do you think I ever will or were they just leading me on?"

Gertrude was referring to an offer for her life story as a member of the Greatest Generation. The idea had grown out of an ill-fated stay at Hillside Manor by members of a motion-picture company. An agent who had been part of the group supposedly was handling what was referred to as "the treatment."

Whether Gertrude sold her story to the movies or not, the visitors had played a fateful role in Judith's life. Not only had the movie flopped, the producer had ended up dead in the kitchen sink. Then someone had maliciously set the house on fire. Luckily, most of the destruction had been from the water used to put out the blaze, but Hillside Manor had been forced to shut down during two of its busiest months, November and December. The Flynns' insurance had paid for the fire and the water damage. But when Judith had received a check from the studio for a hundred and fifty thousand dollars in order to avert a possible lawsuit and any ensuing bad publicity, she had decided it was time to make some renovations, especially to the kitchen.

As usual with such big projects, the work had dragged on. The house was livable, but only for the family. Judith had been out of business for over four months. The only good thing—other than the money and the refurbishing—was that January and February were usually slow in the hostelry business.

But the changes in the kitchen had sent the Flynns—and Gertrude—off the premises for at least a week. As long as the main house was undergoing major surgery, Judith had opted to expand Gertrude's living quarters in the toolshed. By chance, Renie had—against her will—been forced to attend a graphic-design conference at the Lake Stillasnowamish Resort Casino. Judith and Joe had decided to tag along and make it a family affair.

By the time Judith reached her own room, Joe was unpacked and rubbing his hands together. "Let's go kill 'em," he said. "These people don't realize we're in like Flynn."

Judith was admiring the decor, which was different from that of Gertrude's room. The wallpaper, drapes, and comforter's theme wasn't wildflowers, but lush trees, berry bushes, opulent ferns, and various species of small animal life.

"Look at this squirrel," Judith said, pointing to a little furry gray fellow painted on the headboard. "He's gathering nuts for winter."

"Let's gather some money for living," Joe responded, already at the door. "I think I'll try blackjack first."

"For what stakes?" Judith asked, eyeing her husband with suspicion. "We have an agreement, remember? Fifty dollars apiece each day."

"Oh—I'm sure I can find a three-dollar table," Joe said, leading the way to the elevators. "I mean, this isn't Vegas."

"Let's hope not," Judith replied.

The elevator arrived. Moments later, the Flynns were on the busy casino floor. Coins jingled and bells chimed, and excited shouts could be heard from various parts of the casino. The players seemed to represent the entire socioeconomic population of the Pacific Northwest. Some were intense, others were laid-back, still others looked doleful. Judith, with genuine concern for her fellow humans, realized that this was a rich vein to mine for new types of individuals.

Joe started for the table games, but Judith stopped.

"I'm going to the front desk to see if Renie and Bill have arrived yet," she said. "I'm getting kind of worried about them."

"They're fine," Joe replied. "Did your mother ask any more questions about the cabin?"

Judith shook her head. "Somehow I can't bear to tell her we're tearing it down and building a B&B. But it's an idea I've had in my head for years. It's so stupid to let that beautiful piece of land sit there with nobody enjoying it."

"Well," Joe said, edging closer to the gaming area, "if that project is anything like the one at home, I'm sure it's taking Bill and Renie a while to sort things out with the contractor."

"You're probably right," Judith said. "Still, I'm going to check on them."

"Okay," Joe said, starting to walk away at a rather fast pace. "See you around, Jude-girl," he called over his shoulder.

With some misgiving, Judith watched Joe disappear among the tables. But he was sensible when it came to money—in some ways, even more than she was. With a shrug, she went to the front desk.

It was going on three o'clock. Judging from the long line of newcomers waiting to check in, the postlunch crowd had arrived. The Joneses weren't among them. All of the employees behind the counter were busy. Judith crossed the lobby to see if Bill and Renie had pulled up outside.

There was no sign of their Toyota Camry. There was a white Camry, a dark green Camry, a black Camry, and a pale violet Camry, but none was beige like the Joneses' car.

Judith slowly walked down the stairs, trying to fend off her worries by enjoying the scenery. The air smelled so clean, so fresh, so redolent of the evergreens that surrounded the resort and lined the lake. Snow still covered most of Mount Nugget, which had long ago brought gold and silver miners to the area. A railroad had gone up to the mining sites and, at one time, before Judith was born, the train had passed along across the river from the Grover cabins.

A nearby rustling noise made Judith look up. She espied a flicker, poised to peck at a tall cedar tree. The speckled bird with its reddish head let out a series of slow, high-pitched cries. Once. Twice. Three times. Then it began to peck away at the wood.

Bob Bearclaw, who had just seen off a big white limo, approached Judith. "You noticed one of our favorite birds around here," he said with his pleasant smile.

"Yes," Judith replied. "I haven't seen a flicker at home in several years."

"The city's gotten too big," Bob remarked. "And has too many cats."

Judith thought of Sweetums, her ornery pet who was being cared for by their neighbors the Dooleys. "Cats can't help but hunt. It's their nature."

Bob nodded. "You can't interfere with nature." He watched the flicker fly off to another tree. "My people have a special feeling for the flicker. We believe it has extraordinary powers, and sometimes predicts what is to come."

"Hmm," Judith said. "I wish it could predict if I can win some money."

"It usually senses only ill winds." Bob smiled kindly. "Wager wisely. That's your best bet. And never gamble more than you can afford to lose."

"Very wise," Judith agreed as three beige Camrys in a row pulled into the driveway. "Oh!" she exclaimed. "I think my cousin and her husband are here. But those Toyotas are so popular, I don't know which one might be theirs."

"I'd better get back to work," Bob said, heading for the curb. "Enjoy yourself, Mrs. Flynn."

"Champagne" was the official name according to the Toyota manufacturers, but Renie fondly called their car "Cammy." Ever since the Joneses had nicknamed their Camry, Judith had threatened to call her Subaru "Subby."

The passenger door opened in the last of the Toyota trio. To Judith's relief, Renie jumped out of the car in an excited if graceless manner. Judith knew that her cousin rarely gambled, but when she did, she got a little crazy. A moment later, Bill emerged from the driver's side, stretched his neck, and walked over to a valet-parking attendant.

"Coz!" Judith called to Renie.

Renie, who was about to open the rear door, looked around and waved. "We made it," she said, turning back to the car.

Bill opened the trunk for a bellman. The parking valet had gone inside. As Bill supervised the removal of the luggage, the valet returned with a bright-blue wheelchair.

Puzzled, Judith saw that both Bill and Renie seemed perfectly mobile. Her cousin had had shoulder surgery at the same time that Judith had had her hip replaced. She shouldn't need a wheelchair.

Suddenly, Judith was enlightened. Renie was helping Aunt Deb out of the backseat.

"Oh, no," Judith said under her breath. "Not both of the mothers. Not the two of them. Oh, my!"

It wasn't that Judith didn't like Renie's mother. Indeed, she was extremely fond of Aunt Deb. But Gertrude and Deb didn't always see eye to eye. The sisters-in-law, who had married brothers, could hardly possess more different personalities. They did, however, share certain attitudes, belonging to the same generation and coming from similar backgrounds.

Judith kept out of the way while Bill and Renie dealt with the various hotel personnel. Bob Bearclaw was placing a smiling Aunt Deb in the wheelchair. After offering him the most gracious of smiles, she spotted her niece at the foot of the stairs.

"Judith! You're here in one piece! Come give your poor old crippled aunt a kiss!"

Judith complied. "Gosh, Aunt Deb, I didn't realize you were coming, too."

The smile evaporated on Aunt Deb's face. "I simply couldn't be away from Renie for so long. Day before yesterday, I felt one of my spells coming on. Renie suggested taking me to the doctor, but I didn't want to put her out. I told her that I'd try to get through the week without her, and if I passed away before she got back, she should leave instructions for Mr. Hurley at the funeral home to keep me in a nice cool place."

Judith was spared a response by Bob, who gave the wheelchair a gentle nudge.

"Oh, look at me!" Aunt Deb cried, the smile back on her face. "I'm traveling in real style! This is much fancier than the one I have at home."

"Don't bother to explain," Judith said to Renie, who had finally finished her duties with the parking attendant. "Your mother told me. The usual martyrdom gig. Have you got a room for her?"

"Uhh . . ." Renie looked away. "Well, yes." She raised her eyes to Judith's. "They didn't have any more handicapped-accessible rooms, so we had to . . . put . . . her . . . in . . . with . . . your . . . mother."

"Oh, good grief!" Judith clapped her hands to her head and started yanking at her salt-and-pepper page boy.

"I know, I know," Renie said. "It's too awful. To make things worse, I didn't want to come to this wretched conference in the first place."

Judith was silent for a moment. "It'll work out somehow. It'll have to. After all, we can't have this trip turn into a nightmare."

As the cousins walked into the casino, Judith suddenly stopped halfway through the door.

She thought she heard the distant cry of the flicker, not the usual slow cadence, but a rapid series of shrieks. Judith wondered if someone had brought a cat to the casino.

She should have been so lucky.

Chapter Two

JUDITH had no choice but to accompany Renie and Aunt Deb to Gertrude's room. Opening the communicating door from the Flynns' side, they found Judith's mother watching keno numbers flash up on the TV screen.

"Go away," the old lady said without turning around. "I'm busy."

"Hey," Renie called to her aunt, "are you actually gambling?"

Gertrude jumped, then slowly turned around. "Serena! What . . . ?" She stopped as she saw Deb in the blue wheelchair. "What in the world are you doing here?"

"The same as you, Gert," Aunt Deb replied, "though I don't intend to spend money on foolish games of chance."

"Then shut up and let me see if I got more than three numbers on this game," Gertrude rasped, turning back to the screen. "Drat! I only got one. I lost a dollar."

"I thought," Aunt Deb said sweetly, "you never wagered more than a nickel. Except, of course, when you want to play for a quarter at bridge club. Or," she added archly, "when you can't attend Mass, but can play bingo at the parish hall."

"Bingo's always on a Wednesday," Gertrude responded. "Midweek days are my good ones. Besides," she said, pointing to the TV, "I'm not using real money. Do you see any dollar bills around here?"

Judith grimaced. "I hate to say this, Mother, but I think every time you play a TV keno game, they charge your room account."

"Fiddlesticks," Gertrude snapped. "How do they know what I'm doing up here? They got those spy-eye things in the ceiling?"

"They do on the casino floor," Renie said, "to watch out for cheating. But I don't think there's one in your room. Keeping track of your bets is probably done by a computer."

Gertrude scowled at her niece. "Computers! They're a big nuisance. And as usual, you don't know what you're talking about, Serena."

"Now, now," Aunt Deb said in gentle reprimand, "don't speak like that to my little girl. She's really quite smart."

"You couldn't prove it by me," Gertrude harrumphed. "Now my daughter here doesn't have much sense, but she's got enough brains to run a B&B. Which," the old lady added with a hard look at Judith, "is kind of funny when you think about it, because she can put a bunch of strangers in all those bedrooms, but can't find a place in the house for her poor old mother."

"Hey," Judith all but barked, "that's your choice. You never wanted to live under the same roof as Joe."

"I'm proud of you," Aunt Deb said to Renie. "Your little drawings are very clever, even if I don't always understand what they mean."

"That's because," Renie said for what she estimated was about the four-hundredth time, "sometimes they aren't really drawings. They're designs and concepts."

"At least," Gertrude declared, "when you were married to Lunkhead the First, I could live in my own house. 'Course you never let me come visit you in yours."

"That was Dan's idea," Judith retorted, "not mine. He wouldn't let any of the family or my friends visit. The only guests we ever had were his drunken cronies from the Meat & Mingle."

"The word *concept* has always bothered me," Aunt Deb said. "I understand the meaning, but people seem to use it these days as sort of a substitute for what they really mean."

Since Aunt Deb had been a legal secretary, Renie understood her mother's concern with exactitude in language. "It's an idea," Renie explained, "which takes in the . . ."

"I'm surprised you had any company out in that dump on Thurlow Street," Gertrude said. "Luckily, I never saw that place. Didn't you have rats doing the rumba inside the walls? Or did you have walls?"

"Of course we had walls," Judith said. "And yes, we had rats. But they never bit . . ."

"I honestly don't see why," Aunt Deb said in a familiar fretful tone, "when you work alone, you have to attend these conferences. They sound silly to me."

"I won't argue that point," Renie responded. "I wouldn't go if the gas company wasn't sending me. But they're one of my best clients, so I'm stuck. It's all a bunch of blah-blah, and what's worse, I have to wear a name tag. I hate name tags. If you can't remember a . . ."

"It's no wonder Dan croaked when he was only forty-nine," Gertrude said with asperity. "He was as big as a house. Maybe not your house, but he weighed over four hundred—"

"He drank too much and ate too many sweets," Judith said, a sudden pang in her breast. Dan would have loved the casino. He had loved to gamble. Unfortunately, during the times he was actually employed, he had often spent his paycheck on the last three races at the nearby track. Like Dan himself, the horses he chose were losers.

"But you get to meet so many new people," Aunt Deb pointed

out. Like her niece, Aunt Deb loved people. "I'd think you might enjoy that."

"Then," Renie said, her patience eroding, "it's too darned bad you aren't the one attending the conference." A wicked gleam sparked in Renie's brown eyes. "You know, that's not a bad idea."

"What, dear?" Aunt Deb looked puzzled.

With a sheepish smile, Renie waved a hand in dismissal. "Forget it. Let's get you settled in so that I can go out and win millions."

Gertrude's attention was caught by the remark. "'Settled in'? As in where?"

"Here, Aunt Gertrude," Renie said, her smile now as bright as a new silver dollar. "You don't want to be all alone for the next few days, do you?"

"I sure do," Gertrude retorted. "Unlike some people," she went on with a glare for Deb, "I like my own company. And I don't like having my ear chewed off."

"Now, Gert dear—" Aunt Deb began.

Judith held up her hands. "Stop. Let's make some ground rules."

"Like in hockey?" Gertrude shot back. "Get me a stick, I can bop her every time she opens her big mouth."

"Puck you," Aunt Deb said under her breath. But she smiled.

Gertrude whirled around in the wheelchair. "What was that?"

Deb kept smiling. "I said, 'poor you.' I know I can be a trial." She stopped smiling and hung her head.

A knock sounded at the door. Judith and Renie almost trampled each other to answer it. Renie, being faster afoot, got there first. A tall young waiter stood behind a cart bearing covered dishes and a coffeepot.

"Room service for Mrs. Grover," he announced.

"'Room service'?" Judith echoed. "It's not even four o'clock."

"That's not supper," Gertrude asserted, beckoning the waiter to bring in the cart. "That's my snack. You never bring me snacks at home."

Judith started lifting the lids from the plates. "Smoked salmon? Trout pâté? A prawn cocktail? Pickles?"

Gertrude jabbed Judith in the backside. "Where are the crackers? Where's the cheese?"

"It's all here." Judith sighed. "Okay, enjoy it. And share it with Aunt Deb. You can't possibly eat all this."

"I could," Renie volunteered, snatching a prawn from the cocktail glass. "Yum!"

Judith grabbed Renie by the arm. "We're going now. Get along, you two."

"Fine, beat it," Gertrude said. "Deb can get herself unpacked. And tip the kid on your way out, okay?"

After Renie had nipped into their room on the other side of the Flynns,' the cousins headed for the casino.

"Bill's unpacked everything," Renie said. "He must be downstairs, studying the table games."

"What do you mean, 'studying'?" Judith inquired.

Renie poked the elevator button. "Bill has a philosophy that he strictly adheres to when we go to Reno or Vegas or Tahoe. He believes that the only way to beat the house is to make three bets and then quit. So he always eliminates the slots because he says you never win. Instead, he studies the table games. Not just the games themselves but the players, the dealers, the stickmen, the croupiers, the pit bosses—everybody. Then, when he feels that everything is right, including his own attitude, he makes his bets."

"Does his system work?" Judith asked as they stepped into the elevator.

"No. But you know Bill—he's very methodical."

Judith did know Bill, and had for thirty-five years. A retired professor of psychology, he still saw a limited number of patients and sometimes acted as a consultant to his former department at the university. He was exceptionally intelligent and highly perceptive. Renie deferred to his opinions and was wont to repeat them like a puppet. Her cousin's attitude had always struck Judith as out of character. But, Judith figured, that was probably one of the reasons Bill and Renie had been married so long.

The elevator stopped two floors down to let in another passenger, a tall, leggy blonde with a curvaceous figure. Judith wondered if she was a showgirl. In addition to the magic act, there was also a Parisian revue and the ubiquitous Elvis impersonator.

To Judith's surprise, the young woman greeted the cousins with a cheery "Hi."

"Is this your first visit?" she asked.

Judith said it was. "But we know the area," she added. "For years, our family has had property about ten miles from here."

"Cool. By the way, I'm Salome, the assistant in the Great Mandolini's act. You should see the show while you're here. Mandolini is fabulous."

"We might do that," Judith responded. "I've always been intrigued by magic."

"Illusions," Salome said as the elevator doors opened onto the casino floor. "We don't call it 'magic.' Magic is card tricks and pulling silk hankies out of your sleeve. Mandolini is all about illusion. You'll love it." She tossed off a wave and exited on her long, shapely legs.

"It could be fun," Judith remarked as they moved toward the gaming area.

"It could be dumb," Renie said. "Bill and I avoid the shows in Nevada. It used to be different. They had real stars years ago. Now it's a bunch of retreads who're even older than we are." She stopped in midstep. "Shoot. I'm supposed to register for the conference. Maybe I should do that now."

"I'll wait."

Renie looked at her watch. "I have until seven this evening. I'll do it later. I'm hot to trot to the slot machines. Come with me, we'll win big bucks, and I'll tell you what's going on at the cabin."

Judith dutifully followed Renie through a maze of brightly colored, noisy slots. Some whistled, some played music, some made noises like pinball machines. Many had elaborate computer graphics, with colorful figures performing all kinds of antics, from landing fat fish in a boat to Cleopatra barging down the Nile. Judith couldn't help but gawk. She had never been in such a fancy gambling establishment. Unlike Bill and Renie, who had paid an annual visit to Nevada for most of their married life, Judith and Dan had never been able to take a vacation except for a couple of trips to visit her mother-in-law in Arizona. And somehow, even though Joe had a bit of the gambler in him, he and Judith hadn't spent time together at a real casino.

As always, the people fascinated Judith most. A woman sat in the dollar section with a Chihuahua on her lap. The dog was pushing the buttons with his paw. As the cousins passed by, the woman pulled the dog's ear.

"You lost again, you little twerp. I'm not giving you any more money if you don't come up with a jackpot on the next three tries."

Judith was amused, but Renie didn't seem to notice. She was moving like a running back, dodging a slot mechanic here, a cocktail waitress there, and making end runs around anybody else who blocked the aisles between the banks of machines.

Judith couldn't keep up. She would have lost Renie had her cousin not sat down at a quarter console in the Spring section of the casino where pink and white petals drifted down and dissolved upon contact. Fortunately, there was an open seat next to Renie.

"Okay," Renie said, slipping a crisp twenty-dollar bill into the machine. "Watch. I've put in twenty bucks, it'll register as eighty quarters. I play off the credits. It saves my shoulder from inserting coins every time. Always bet the maximum, which is two quarters on both these machines. If you don't play all the required coins, you can't win the big jackpot or any bonuses." As Renie explained, she pointed to the payoffs on Judith's machine. "What we've got here are two different kinds of Farmer in the Dell machines. They pay and play the same, only the animals and other symbols are different. Got it?"

Judith's head was whirling. "I think so. Maybe I'll watch you first. I didn't realize you'd been here before."

"Just once," Renie replied, pushing a button. "Drat. Nothing." She pushed the button again. "Bill and I stopped in last month when they were razing the cabin. Phooey." She hit the machine a third time.

"What were the contractors doing today?" Judith asked as a raven-haired cocktail waitress in scanty buckskin attire sauntered by inquiring, "Cocktails?"

Renie turned to the waitress. "A Pepsi, please."

Judith looked uncertain, then requested a diet 7-UP. "Are the drinks free?" she whispered to Renie as the waitress moved away.

"Yes, but tip her at least a dollar." Renie was looking not just intense, but grim. "I'm down to sixty coins. Maybe we should move on. I never play a machine that doesn't start shelling out right away."

Judith stood up. "If you move, I'll find you. I'd like to see how Joe's doing." Somehow, the idea of watching Andrew Jackson disappear into a dark hole made her nervous.

"I won't be very far," Renie said, then let out a satisfied sound. "I got twenty. Coins, that is. I'll stay here for now."

The table games weren't that far from the quarter slots. There were long rows of blackjack tables, starting with a five-dollar limit. Judith figured they must go down in amounts, but after the first eight tables, she encountered ten-dollar limits, then twenty-five.

A feeling of unease overcame her. Had Joe been foolish enough to play in a high-stakes game? Maybe the three-dollar tables were on the other side of the pit. As she turned the corner, she spotted Joe, talking to a barrel-chested man with a handlebar mustache and wearing what looked like an expensive suit.

"Joe!" she exclaimed. "I've been looking for you."

"Hey, Jude-girl, meet Pancho Green, the casino manager. He used to work in Vegas at Caligula's Palazzo."

Although Judith put out her hand, her face froze for just an instant. Caligula's Palazzo was where Joe had married his first wife, Vivian, while he was in a drunken stupor.

"Hello, Mr. Green," Judith said, forcing a smile.

"Mrs. Flynn," Pancho said with a grin that revealed dazzling white teeth. "Joe's been telling me all about you."

"Really." Judith tried not to sound skeptical. Had Joe told Pancho how he'd broken Judith's heart thirty years ago, leaving her pregnant? Had Joe mentioned that the woman he'd married in Vegas had virtually shanghaied him onto an airplane? Had Joe revealed how both he and Judith had ended up married to a couple of alcoholics and suffered through their first marriages until finally meeting again more than twenty years later?

"Yes," Pancho replied. "He told me that if he didn't win a dime here, he was still the luckiest man in the world."

"Oh." Judith wondered if that was the truth or if Pancho was merely a smooth talker. He looked like it, with his custom-tailored suit, impeccably cut silver hair, and flashing smile. But maybe that was part of his role as a casino manager.

Joe's own smile was unusually wide. "Pancho's given us four complimentary tickets to the dinner show for the Great Mandolini tonight. We won't have to wait in line. Our table's reserved. I'll tell Bill if I see him; you let Renie know."

"Oh," Judith repeated. "Yes, I know where Renie is. But what about our . . ."

"Mothers?" Joe finished for her, then looked at Pancho. "We have Judith's mother and aunt with us. They're both in wheelchairs. Would that be a problem? They wouldn't have to sit with us, of course."

"Not at all," Pancho replied, digging into a pocket inside his suit jacket. "I'll make sure their table is wheelchair accessible." He handed Joe two more comps. "I've got to go back to work. Great to see you, Joe. Wonderful to meet you, Mrs. Flynn." The casino manager moved smoothly away.

"Nice guy," Joe observed. "I haven't seen him in twelve years."

Judith looked surprised. "Twelve years? Are you sure it hasn't been more like thirty?"

Joe's expression turned serious. "That was the first time I met him. He . . . sort of took me under his wing. Then, just before we were married, Woody and I had to fly to Vegas to confer on a homicide case there that was linked to one of ours."

Woody was Woodrow Wilson Price, Joe's longtime partner in the homicide division of the city's police department. But it wasn't Woody's name that had caught Judith's attention.

"What do you mean by Pancho taking you under his wing?" she asked as they moved toward the craps tables.

"Well," Joe responded carefully, "Pancho stood up for me at the quickie wedding to Vivian. Not that I remember much about it. But when I sobered up, I told him I'd made a terrible mistake. He advised me to call you right away, explain everything, and try to get the marriage annulled." Joe shrugged. "You know the rest of the story."

Judith knew it all too well. Joe had called her several times, but Gertrude had answered the phone. She'd informed Joe that Judith never wanted to speak to him again and didn't care if he were in Vegas or on Venus. It wasn't true, of course, but Gertrude's interference had cost Joe and Judith dearly. Despondent, Joe hadn't gotten the annulment. Abandoned, Judith had married Dan McMonigle on the rebound, not because she loved him, but because she wanted a father for her unborn baby. The story didn't have a happy ending for over two decades.

"You never mentioned Pancho before," Judith said. "How come?"

"That time in Vegas wasn't exactly a highlight of my life," Joe replied with a sour expression. "I've always tried to forget it, even while I was married to Vivian." He brightened suddenly. "Hey, there's Bill at one of the craps tables. I'm going to see how he's doing."

"He's studying," Judith said. "That's part of his system."

But Joe didn't hear his wife finish speaking. He was already hurrying over to the busy craps table. Sure enough, Bill was standing just behind the players, hands in pockets, a look of deep concentration on his face.

Judith started back to the quarter slots. But she'd gone so far afield that she was confused. She seemed to be in the Summer section. There were quarter slots there, too, including a large rectangular platform with a sleek red Corvette displayed above the machines. "Who Needs a Jet?" the banner on the car read. "Win This 'Vette!" Judith smiled at the handsome car, which featured a blond mannequin seated behind the wheel, her wig blown by an unseen fan.

Judith was tempted to try for the car. Joe's beloved MG was forty years old, and it was becoming increasingly difficult to get parts for it. The MG was also red. But for now, she had to find Renie.

It took over five minutes to get back to the Spring section. Sure enough, Renie was at the same machine, engrossed in the spin of the barrels.

"Your soda's right here," she said without looking up. "This is the darnedest machine. I keep getting three chickens and three lambs, but I never get the barns. That's the big payoff. Still, I've got enough credits to keep me going."

Judith sat down and took a sip from her glass of diet 7-UP. "You never told me about the cabin."

"Oh." Renie frowned as the machine showed a lamb, a pig, and a bale of hay. "They're about to pour the foundation."

"They were going to do that three weeks ago," Judith pointed out.

"Armbuster or whatever his name is said there was still snow on the ground then." Renie smiled slightly as she got another trio of chickens. "What is he, a brother or a cousin of the contractor who's working on the B&B?"

"A brother-in-law," Judith replied. "His name is Dale Armstrong. The B&B contractor is Bart Bednarik."

"I knew that," Renie said, pausing to drink some Pepsi. "Did you find Joe?"

"Yes." Judith explained about the long-ago connection between Joe and Pancho.

"Does that mean," Renie asked, "we'll have to see the Great Mandolini with our mothers?"

"They may not want to go," Judith said. "Anyway, I'm looking forward to it."

Renie tapped her chin. "It would also mean I could skip the social hour that officially opens the conference. Okay, we'll do it. Was Joe winning at blackjack?"

"I didn't get a chance to ask," Judith admitted. "But he seemed upbeat. We saw Bill studying craps."

"Good, good." Renie turned her attention back to the slot machine. "Aha! Three bales of hay. That's twenty bucks."

"Maybe I should try this," Judith allowed. "But frankly, it makes me tense."

"Don't be silly." Renie waved a hand to take in all of her sur-

roundings. "This is a wonderland of opportunity. All things are possible. It's complete escapism from the rest of the world. Wrap yourself up in the excitement, the suspense, the drama, the wonder of
What-If-I-Win-a-Million-Bucks? Why did you come here, if not to—"
Renie stopped, pricking up her ears. "Did you hear that announcement?"

Judith shook her head. "They make announcements all the time.
I don't see how anybody hears anything with all the noise."

"I thought it was a page for Judith Flynn," Renie said, still listening.

"Really?" Judith made a face. "Could it be Mother?"

"You know she doesn't like the phone. Unless she keeled over and
my mother is trying to reach you."

"Don't say that!"

"They'll announce it again unless it was for somebody else and
they've already responded." Renie poked the Credit button again.

"I'd better check, to be sure." Judith stood up. "Where should I
go? The front desk?"

"There ought to be a house phone over by that wall," Renie said,
gesturing with her elbow. "Ah. More lambs."

Judith hurried off to find the phone. Renie was right. There was a
house phone between the security desk and the change cage. She
picked up the receiver and asked if there was a message for her.

"Judith Flynn?" the soft female voice repeated. "Yes, a Mr. Bednarik called. I'll give you his number."

"Damn!" Judith swore under her breath. "Did he say it was an
emergency?"

"Yes, I believe he did," the voice responded. "The phone memo is
marked ASAP."

Annoyed by the contractor's call, Judith remembered the pay
phones by the registration desk. Unfortunately, they were on the
other side of the casino. But the rest rooms were just beyond the
change booth, and beyond that was a row of six public phones.

After getting out her credit card and Bart Bednarik's cell-phone number, Judith went through the lengthy dialing process. Bart answered on the second ring.

"What's wrong?" Judith asked without preamble.

"It's that countertop stove you ordered," Bart answered in his lackadaisical voice. "It's an odd size, and they can't get it in stock for another two weeks. We could get the standard size right away."

"I don't want that," Judith said firmly. "I need the biggest countertop that's available."

"It's not," Bart said. "I tried a couple of other places in town. Nobody has them in their warehouses."

Judith was rubbing her high forehead, trying to determine how she could cook for the family during the week after their return to Hillside Manor. "Have you pulled the old stove already?"

"We did that yesterday," Bart replied. "It's long gone."

There was always the microwave oven, Judith thought. "How much did you get done this afternoon?"

"The fridge is out of here now," Bart said. "We should have the new one delivered tomorrow. In fact, we're knocking off for the day. There's no point in starting something right before my guys go off at five."

Judith winced. If Skjoval Tolvang had been doing the job, he'd have started before dawn and stayed until after dusk. But the octogenarian handyman wasn't on the insurance company's approved list, and was, as he put it, "Damn' glad of it, ya sure youbetcha." Furthermore, Mr. Tolvang didn't like tying himself down to big jobs, and despised subcontractors. Judith was stuck with Bednarik Builders. It didn't help that Bart Bednarik seemed to embrace obstacles, not to conquer them, merely observing, as if they were a spectator sport.

"So what will you work on tomorrow?" Judith inquired, holding her head.

"The plumbing," Bart said. "It's going to be a bitch. Some of it's pretty old."

"I had the kitchen replumbed before I opened the B&B," Judith asserted. "That was only thirteen years ago."

"Have you listened to those pipes lately?" Bart sounded disgusted. "Man, you must have done the job on the cheap."

"That's not true," Judith declared. "Is the plumbing included in your original quote?"

"Only for the hookups," Bart said. "Do you realize you've got steel pipes under the sink? Nobody uses steel anymore in a house. At least one of yours might have a leak. That's a problem."

More problems, more obstacles. Bart must feel as if he'd been awarded the Super Bowl of home renovation. It had all begun in early November, one problem after another. Too much rain to repair the roof. Too much wind to replace the gutters. Too much fog, too much frost, too little sun. Since it had been a fairly typical Pacific Northwest fall and winter, Judith wondered how Bednarik Builders ever worked on anything between October and April. When an earthquake had occurred at the end of February, she was certain that Bart would tell her the house was about to fall down and they'd have to start from scratch.

"Fix the leak," Judith said. "Frankly, I never noticed one."

"It's a slow leak. You'd be better off with new pipes, especially since you're redoing the whole kitchen."

"How much?"

"I'll have to figure out an estimate."

"You do that. Let me know tomorrow morning. Please," Judith remembered to add.

"Will do. Don't worry, we're getting along just fine."

Judith felt like saying she didn't care if they got along, they could fight like savages as far as she was concerned, just so they got the job done by the oft-postponed deadline.

By the time she got back to Renie, her cousin had moved to the other side of the console.

"Some old bat about the size of Godzilla tried to swipe my chair when I stood up to get a bucket for my coins," Renie said. "I had to step on her foot to get her to let go."

"That's why you moved?" Judith asked.

Renie shook her head. "The Farmer in the Dell finally pooped out on me, but I didn't lose all my credits, which is why I needed the bucket. I cashed out with over ten bucks. Here, play one of these baseball slots. The jackpot's three grand slams. The joker is the umpire."

"I can't afford it," Judith grumbled. "That call was from Bart Bednarik."

"Call?" Renie looked blank. "Oh, the page? What did Bart want now?"

"They can't get the countertop for two weeks," Judith began, then noticed that Renie was back at it, pressing buttons. "The plumbing's shot in the kitchen, according to Bart, and . . ." Judith was almost certain that Renie wasn't listening. ". . . and the roof flew off and is being converted into a superferry out in the bay."

"That's a shame," Renie murmured. "Ah! Three catchers' masks. I got eight bucks."

Judith heaved a big sigh. So far, her vacation wasn't off to a very good start. It was bad enough that both mothers had come along, that the contractor was already on her trail, and that she suspected Joe of going beyond his gaming limit for the day. But when Renie ignored her in favor of a stupid slot machine, that was going too far. Judith and Renie were as close as sisters, and always had been. They'd grown up together, they'd shared all sorts of trials and tribulations, joys and pleasures. Renie had always been there for Judith, and vice versa. But apparently not at the Lake Stillasnowamish Resort Casino.

To be fair, as Judith always was, this was a working vacation for Renie. She would have limited time to spend on gambling, which she obviously enjoyed.

And this evening, they'd attend the Great Mandolini's magic act. Judith was definitely looking forward to that. She'd find herself caught up in the art of illusion, and be able to forget her troubles for a couple of hours. Reality would be set aside for a fantasy world.

Judith had no idea how quickly her own illusions would be shattered.

Chapter Three

I hate magic acts," Gertrude declared. "They're phony. They never tell you how they do it."

"I've never liked magicians," Aunt Deb asserted. "They frighten me. I'm always sure something is going to go wrong."

"So," Judith said, trying not to keep the relief out of her voice, "you really don't want to go?"

Both of the old ladies shook their heads.

"At least you agree on something," Renie remarked. "What will you do all evening?"

Despite their years, Gertrude and Deb kept rather late hours. "We'll watch TV," Gertrude said. "Or play some cribbage. I brought my cards and crib board with me. I always beat the pants off Deb."

"I'll work the crossword puzzle," Aunt Deb said. "I do it every night. It keeps my brain active. As I've mentioned several times to some people," she went on with a sharp glance at Gertrude, "the brain is a muscle that needs to be exercised like any other part of the body."

"We shouldn't be late," Judith said. "It's the dinner show. I may stay in the casino for a little while, but frankly, I'm tired."

"Don't hurry on our account," Gertrude snapped. "I don't need to look at your long face if you've been losing your shirt."

"Now, Renie," Deb began, "stay away from any seedy-looking types. Keep your eye on your purse. Don't accept a drink from anyone you don't know. And for heaven's sake, don't let some fast talker try to lure you away with the promise of becoming a dancer in one of those scantily clad nightclub shows."

"Mom," Renie said with a straight face, "you know I can't dance."

Deb's eyes narrowed behind her trifocals. "They'd say they could teach you."

Judith looked at her watch. "It's almost six. Joe said he'd meet me in the room about now. We're supposed to have a drink in the Winter Bar before the show. We want you and Bill to join us."

"Fine," Renie agreed. "What, a little before seven?"

Judith nodded. "I'm going to change now. I assume people dress up for the shows here."

"If it's like our city's casual code, they just put on a better pair of jeans," Renie said. "I, however, am going to wear something wonderful."

Judith didn't doubt it. Her cousin owned two separate wardrobes. Most of the time, she was garbed in ratty old sweatshirts and frayed pants. But for her professional and social life, Renie wore expensive designer outfits. There was no in between.

The cousins retreated to their rooms. By six-twenty, Judith had changed from slacks and sweater into a long black skirt and a ruffled red satin blouse. There was still no sign of Joe.

Judith tapped on the door that connected the Flynns to the Joneses. A moment later, Renie appeared.

"What's up?" she asked.

"Joe's not here yet. Should I have him paged?"

Renie shrugged. "Maybe he's at a lucky table. We've got plenty of time. Bill's doing his neck exercises," she added, referring to her husband's chronic medical problem. "He stiffened up while he was studying baccarat. Meet you in the Winter Bar."

Ten minutes later, Judith was pacing the room. Five minutes after that, she was pacing the hall by the elevators. Maybe she should have Joe paged.

The elevator doors opened to reveal a thirtyish dishwater blonde wearing horn-rimmed glasses. She glanced at Judith, then continued down the corridor in the opposite direction from the Flynns' room. Judith kept pacing. The woman stopped walking and turned back toward the elevators.

"Wouldn't you know it," she murmured. "I forgot my day planner. This is the busiest time of night for the elevators. It'll take me forever to get down and back up here in time for Mandolini's show."

"We're going to see it, too," Judith said. "That is, if my husband ever shows up. Do you think that the Great Mandolini will be worth it?"

The blonde scowled at Judith. "Of course. He's magnificent. I work for him."

"Oh!" Judith was surprised. "You're the second person I've met since I got here who's part of the troupe. I met his assistant, Salome, this afternoon."

"Lucky you," the blonde said. "By the way, I'm Griselda Vander-behr. What's your name?"

Judith identified herself and shook Griselda's slightly clammy hand. "I'm pleased to meet you, Ms. Vanderbehr."

"Call me Grisly," Griselda said with no hint of amusement. "It's an old high school nickname."

"Okay," Judith said somewhat doubtfully. "I hope the show goes well tonight for all . . ."

The elevator doors opened on the other side of the corridor. As Griselda moved briskly to the car, Judith looked to see if Joe was among the people already inside.

He wasn't. Feeling frustrated as well as annoyed, she returned to their room and dialed the operator.

She'd just been connected when Joe rushed into the room. "Sorry. I got held up."

"You better not mean literally," Judith said, banging down the phone. "You've got ten minutes to change and meet the Joneses in the Winter Bar."

"I'll make it," Joe said airily as he went into the bathroom.

"What kept you?" Judith asked through the door.

"A bunch of double downs and more than a fair share of black-jacks," Joe called back over the sound of running water. "I won five hundred bucks this afternoon. Is that a good start or what?"

"It's great," Judith replied, her anger ebbing. "That takes some doing, given how lucky blackjack dealers usually are."

"When you're on a streak, you have to keep going," he said, coming out of the bathroom. "And you can't use a cell phone at the tables, of course. You could be cheating. Hey, you look terrific."

"Thanks." Judith couldn't resist smiling.

Joe cocked his head to one side, the gold glittering in his green eyes. "You don't suppose the Joneses could carry on without us for a while, do you?"

For once, Judith wasn't going to succumb to what she called the magic of Joe's eyes. She held out both hands in front of her. "Forget it. I'm not going to get dressed, do my hair, and put my make up on all over again. We'll miss the show."

Joe looked disappointed, but didn't argue. "We've got plenty of time. This is only the first day of the rest of our vacation."

"Which reminds me," Judith said as Joe started changing clothes, "Bart Bednarik called here this afternoon."

Joe put his hands over his ears. "I don't want to hear it. Bumbling Bart makes me crazy."

"But the latest involves spending—"

"Stop!" Joe smoothed his thinning red-gray hair in front of the big mirror over the bureau. "We're on vacation, remember? Let Bart figure it out."

Judith shut up.

Renie yawned her way through the opening act that featured Craven Raven, a once-hot grunge band singing songs Judith didn't recognize. Bill stretched his neck this way and that. Joe ordered a second round of drinks and tapped his foot, which rattled the table. Judith was getting irked.

"Stop that, Joe," she whispered.

"What?" He leaned closer.

"Stop tapping. You're driving me nuts."

Joe shook his head. "I can't hear you over this damned music." He kept tapping.

Judith reached under the table to whack Joe's leg. "Stop it!" she all but shouted.

As if on cue, the band concluded its act. The salads arrived along with the new drinks. Joe stopped tapping.

"The Great Mandolini better be great," Joe said.

"The casinos have to pull in a young crowd, too," Renie noted. "What if future generations didn't take to gambling? Where would we all be then?"

Judith looked askance. "Not broke?"

"You know what I mean," Renie said with a scowl. "Several years ago, the only place we saw young people in the Nevada casinos was up at Lake Tahoe. They'd come to ski, but they stayed to gamble."

"Speaking of the younger set," Judith said, watching Renie just miss dropping lettuce on the bodice of her bronze-and-gold sweater, "how are the wedding plans going? You haven't mentioned it lately."

Renie glanced at Bill. The previous fall, all three Jones children had announced their engagements. "What can we say?" Renie said with a sigh. "They keep changing their minds about when and where. We keep pushing for a triple wedding. Frankly, I don't think any of them will get married this year."

"Jobs," said Bill. "We'd like to see Anne and Tony and Tom all get real jobs before they get married. We'd like to see them get out of graduate school. We'd like to see them get—"

"Not out of the house," Renie said in a scolding voice. "We don't want them to feel that we don't love them."

Bill frowned at his wife. "Of course we love them. But it would be nice if they lived somewhere else before they hit midlife crises and you and I are hauled off to a home for the gaga."

Joe grinned at Bill. "For a psychologist, you have a way of avoiding professional jargon."

Bill shrugged. "Nuts is nuts."

Renie leaned toward the others and spoke in a confidential tone. "I think Bill wants to go to the Gaga House. He has this fantasy where the nurses wear short skirts and sheer black stockings with seams and—"

"You have your bosom in the salad dressing," Bill cut in. "Never mind, Joe and Judith don't need to hear it."

"I'd like to," Joe said. "In fact, I might like to go there myself."

"Never mind," Renie said, using a napkin to dab off the glob of dressing.

"I was so relieved when Mike settled down," Judith remarked as their entrées arrived. "But I worry that one of these days the forest service will transfer him. He could end up anywhere. I'd hate to see Mike and Kristin and the boys move to the other end of the country. I'm so used to having them an hour away from town."

"The kids were both so cute when we saw them during the holi-days," Renie put in. "Mac is smart as a whip and Joe-Joe is just adorable. I would kind of like to have grandchildren. It's the road to getting them that seems pretty rugged. Hey!" Renie cried as her salad plate was whisked away. "I'm not done."

"You look done to me," said the red-haired waiter. But his smile was pleasant enough.

"It's all worth it," Judith declared. "Of course, we had only one child to marry off."

Bill glanced at Judith. "Yes. One."

"And a boy at that," Renie murmured.

"Good steak," Joe remarked. "But they sure hurry you through the meal to get to the magic act."

"Don't call it 'magic,'" Judith said. "Mandolini is an illusionist. I happened to meet—"

She was interrupted by a woman whose brown hair was done up in a very tall topknot. "Excuse me," she said in a slow, deliberate manner. "You're sitting at our house table. There must be some mistake."

"I don't think so," Joe replied. "We're guests of Pancho Green, the casino manager."

"Then," the woman responded, "the maître d' made a mistake. This is the table reserved for the Great Mandolini's friends and guests." She paused to point to the table behind them, which was already occupied by two Asian couples. "That's where you should be sitting."

"On their laps?" Renie snapped. "They look like high rollers to me. I doubt they want company."

The woman fingered her pudgy chin, then looked at the watch that was pinned to her pink brocade cocktail dress. She was of medium height, but of chunky build. Her age was hard to determine. Forty, Judith guessed, but she could have been thirty-five or fifty.

"The performance will begin shortly," the woman finally said.

"You'll have to move. At least one other person is joining me, and he should be here any minute."

"We're eating!" Renie exclaimed. "You find another table."

Bill shot his wife a hard look. "Serena."

"Hold it," Joe said to the intruder. "Find us a good table and we'll move. We don't want to make trouble."

The woman's shrewd gaze seemed to absorb every nuance of Joe's personality and appearance. "Done," she said, and wobbled away as if she weren't used to wearing three-inch heels with the too-tight brocade sheath.

"I'm mad," Renie announced as Joe went off to get the maître d'. "We had a perfect view. Now we'll be stuck in some dank corner where we'll only see the illusion of an illusionist."

"We should be okay," Judith soothed. "The cabaret isn't that big. I doubt if it seats more than two hundred people."

Renie was still gobbling steak and French fries when Joe finally returned. "We're not so close to the stage," he said in an apologetic tone, "but we'll still have a decent view. The waiters will move our stuff. Follow me."

The foursome moved up the aisle between the tables, almost reaching the top of the sloping floor. The new seating arrangement seemed to be at the only vacant table in the cabaret.

"This stinks," Renie announced loudly. "Why not put us in the lobby?"

"Pipe down," Bill ordered. "It's free, remember?"

"It damned well better be," Renie said, going into her pouting mode.

When their unfinished meals and table service arrived, dessert came with it. The houselights were beginning to dim; the eerie strains of a sitar filtered through the speaker system.

Judith finished the last tender morsels of her lamb chops. Her timing was perfect. A moment later, her plate disappeared. A moment after that, the cabaret went dark and the music became louder. Then, with a crash of cymbals, a tiny blue spotlight appeared on the dark-blue velvet stage curtains.

"I can't see my dessert," Renie complained. "Are there any nuts? I'm allergic to nuts. I could have an attack."

"You may be attacked," Bill warned, "if you don't knock it off."

"Arrr . . ." Renie began, but shut up.

The spotlight kept enlarging until it was big enough for a person to stand in its center. Then the light blinked for a single second. When it came back on, the Great Mandolini was in front of the spot, sitting in an armchair, reading a book and drinking a glass of water. The audience gasped and burst into applause.

"That was pretty good," Joe commented. "This should be fun."

And it was. Even Renie abandoned her sulk as the illusionist placed a tabby cat into a large empty box, closed the lid, and opened it again to reveal a tiger on a gold leash held by a beautiful blonde.

"That's Salome," Judith whispered to Joe. "I met her in the elevator. In fact, I met another member of his troupe, too."

Joe gave a faint nod. Mandolini introduced his assistant to a round of hearty clapping from the audience. Salome was wearing a clinging silk gown that matched the tiger's stripes. As she and the tiger pranced off the stage, Judith studied the Great One's appearance. He was wearing a traditional tuxedo but with an ascot instead of a bow tie. From such a distance, Judith couldn't guess his age, but figured him to be fairly young. He looked tall and lean, with brown hair grown a trifle long in the back. His movements were elegant as well as swift.

After a dozen illusions that included suspending Salome in midair and a white rose that turned into a falcon, the curtain closed, the houselights came up halfway, and Mandolini moved to the front of the stage. He spoke to the audience as if he were in the most intimate of settings.

"Before we perform our final—and most dangerous—segment, I'd like to tell you about how I got into this rather unusual business," he began, his informal voice more high pitched than the one he used for creating his illusions. "I first became interested in magic—notice I use the word *magic* in this context—when I was about three. I had an uncle who loved to perform cards tricks and other simple sleight-of-hand stunts. My sister and my cousins and I were all fascinated, but I was the only one who thought about becoming a magician. I didn't realize that the profession involved far more sophisticated feats."

Mandolini's words became less personal as he discussed Dedi, the first magician of historical record, who lived in Egypt almost six thousand years ago. Working his way up to the medieval magicians, he recounted how they introduced dice, cards, and coins from their bags of tricks. He had moved on from the Herrmann Brothers and Harry Blackstone when Renie let her head fall onto Bill's shoulder and she uttered a bogus snoring sound.

"How long, oh Lord, how long? I'm not here for a history lecture," she griped as waiters removed the rest of their soiled tableware. "I'm here to gamble."

Judith was also growing restless, but occupied herself with studying members of the audience. "People seem to come from all over," she noted in a low voice. "Really, it's quite an ethnic mix. In fact, there seem to be a large number of Asians."

"They love to gamble," Bill said, "and they always seem very well heeled. I've noticed that in Nevada, particularly when I play baccarat."

Renie lifted her head to look around. "Ah!" she exclaimed though she kept her voice down. "I see Petunia Pig has been joined by Porky at what used to be our very nice table. They don't seem to be getting along. Maybe she ate his serving before he got there."

Judith's gaze shifted to the tables near the stage. The woman who had taken over their spot was sitting with a balding, beefy man. With heads bent and bodies rigid, they appeared to be arguing. The other two seats were vacant.

Mandolini was talking about the amazing feats of Harry Houdini.

"I should escape so easily." Renie sighed. "I think I'll disappear into the bathroom."

"I'll go with you," Judith said. "I hate to complain, because the tickets are free," she went on as they reached the nearest rest room, "and Mandolini is really very good except for the monologue. But you know me, I can sit in one place only so long with this phony hip."

"I can sit only so long with my disposition," Renie replied as they entered adjoining stalls. "That's why I like doing my graphic-design work in the basement. I can get up to do the laundry in the other room or go outside and pull a few weeds."

"Speaking of your work," Judith said when they regrouped at the sink area, "when do you start your conference meetings?"

Renie wiped her hands on a paper towel as she made a face in the mirror. "Nine o'clock. What's worse, we're supposed to meet around eight-thirty for coffee and sweet rolls."

Judith knew how much her cousin hated getting up early. Renie rarely rose before nine-thirty, and even then she didn't become fully conscious until after ten.

"That's going to be hard on you," Judith said in commiseration. "But it's only for three days. After that, you'll be free for the rest of our stay."

"If I live through the—" Renie stopped as the lights flickered and the rest room went dark.

"The power must have gone out," Judith said, surrendering the search in her purse for the lipstick that matched her red blouse.

Two other women were speaking in agitated voices as they came from the toilet area.

"Did you say the power went out?" one of them asked as they neared the cousins.

"Just a guess," Judith replied. She couldn't see either woman in the pitch-black darkness. She couldn't see Renie, either. "We're in the mountains, after all. We have property nearby, and power failures happen every so often."

An accented voice spoke from the toilet area. "What is happening? Are we in danger? Should I come out?"

"Yes," Judith called to the woman, who sounded as if she was Asian. "Just be careful." The tapping of high heels resounded on the tiled floor.

"Someone could get hurt," the foreign woman said from somewhere near Judith. "Where is the sink?"

"Just follow my voice," Judith said. "I'm close to the sinks."

More tapping of heels, then the sound of a faucet. "I do not like this," the woman said. "It is bad luck."

"It won't last long," Judith said in reassurance, though she hadn't any idea of when the power might be restored.

"Maybe," Renie suggested, "it isn't out in the rest of the complex. Let's find the door."

Judith groped for her cousin's arm. "Is that you?"

"Yes, coz," Renie replied. "We should go left."

They moved slowly, but eventually felt carpet beneath their feet. "This is the entrance to the rest room," Judith said. "We have only a few more steps to the door."

As the cousins cautiously moved forward, they heard a sound in front of them. A second later, Judith's arm was brushed by someone walking at a quick pace. There was no apology; the unseen newcomer had gone into the rest room.

Renie opened the door. The cabaret and the adjacent rest rooms were in the Autumn section, just off the video-poker slots. Except for a trio of flashlights cutting through the darkness, they could see nothing. They heard shouts, however, and what sounded like panicky voices.

Someone bumped into Renie from the back. "Hey, watch it!" she yelled. "Knucklehead," she murmured. "The whole place is out. People shouldn't run around when they can't see where they're going. On the bright side—excuse the pun—maybe they'll cancel the conference."

"What about our mothers?" Judith asked with concern. "They must be frightened."

"They know what a power failure is like," Renie replied. "Heck, we have them at home every so often. Remember, just a month ago the pole on the corner by our house caught fire and our whole side of Heraldsgate Hill was in the dark for two or three hours."

"Yes, we had the same thing happen at the end of the cul-de-sac last summer," Judith said as two workmen with Coleman lanterns scurried by. "Luckily, it was during the late morning and all the guests had left. Afterward, I wondered if it had been an omen of the B&B fire."

"Let's hope this isn't an omen of something bad," Renie said. "That woman with the accent gave me the creeps."

"Don't be silly," Judith retorted. "Do you want the casino to burn down?"

"Of course not," Renie replied. "I meant like not winning."

"Speaking of that," Judith said, "how do they keep people from stealing money and chips off the tables?"

"The dealers and croupiers put covers over the house's portion," Renie said. "I suppose there might be some petty thievery, but I've found gamblers to be pretty honest."

It seemed to Judith that they were also pretty patient. Except for the dwindling number of those who seemed upset or scared, the general tenor of voices had turned jocular. Judith supposed that most gamblers had to be good sports, and therefore, good natured.

"I suppose our husbands have both nodded off by now," Renie remarked. "After all the blah-blah from Mandolini, Bill and Joe may be in the mood for a postprandial nap."

"They'll wake up wondering where the TV remote is," Judith said. "Joe does tend to doze in front of the—"

Suddenly, the lights came on, causing Judith and Renie to blink against the brightness.

"Thank goodness!" Judith exclaimed. "We'd better get back to our seats for the rest of the show."

"Maybe it's over by now," Renie said in a hopeful tone.

"The show couldn't go on without power," Judith responded as they entered the cabaret.

The atmosphere inside the room was clearly one of relief. The cousins heard nervous laughter and high-pitched chatter as they approached their table. Joe and Bill, however, looked resigned.

"What did you do now?" Bill asked Renie in a tone of reproach.

"Huh?" Renie arranged her long taffeta skirt as she sat down. "It wasn't me, honest."

"At least," said Joe, "you missed the rest of the monologue, all the way up through David Copperfield, Doug Henning, and Siegfried and Roy."

Judith was surprised. "Mandolini kept talking?"

"Sure," Joe said, offering Bill a cigar. "Why not? He doesn't need a mike in a place this size. Even if you can't see him, you can hear him."

The houselights went down, causing a momentary stir. Apparently, some members of the audience were afraid that the power was failing again. But Pancho Green was onstage, reassuring the guests.

"We apologize for the brief inconvenience," Pancho said with a self-deprecating smile. "In the two years that the Lake Stillasnowamish Resort Casino has been open, this is the first time we've had a power failure. We've been told that a heavy windstorm has been blowing in from the west and may have affected the power lines between Mount Nugget and Mount Woodchuck. We were about to switch to our auxiliary generator, but power was restored before we could do it. Enjoy the last part of the Great Mandolini's fabulous act, and we wish you luck and relaxation during your stay with us. Thank you."

The audience applauded Pancho as he disappeared into the wings. The Flynns and the Joneses settled back in their seats as the curtains lifted on an empty stage.

"Do you think," Judith whispered to Joe, "that the flicker of lights at the beginning of the show was planned or a power problem?"

Joe gazed at Judith through a cloud of cigar smoke. "That was part of the act. For all we know, the power failure was, too. Maybe something went wrong and they accidentally turned off the power in the whole casino."

Judith frowned. It was possible, she thought, but she doubted it. Turning her eyes to the still-empty stage, the sitar music playing in the background, she had a sense of unease. Maybe, she told herself, it wasn't because the lights went out, but because of Bart Bednarik. His phone call had upset her, and Joe wouldn't allow her to share the bad news with him.

A brief flurry of what looked like snowflakes scattered across the empty stage. When the flakes evaporated, a goateed young man whose long, fair hair was tied back in a ponytail sat on a chair with an odd-looking item in his lap. He moved his hands as if conducting an orchestra, and strange yet haunting music filled the air. At first, Judith detected the sound of a tuba, but it was followed by high-pitched tones that were more like squawks. The young man's hands never touched the instrument.

"What is it?" Judith whispered to Renie.

"I'm guessing it's a theremin," Renie said. "My friend Melissa Bargroom told me about it. It's not magic, even though it looks like it. The theremin was the first electronic instrument, dating back to just after World War One."

"I've never heard of it," Judith said, "but being a music critic, Melissa ought to know."

Another flurry, not of snow, but of brilliantly colored confetti, swept across the stage. When it evaporated, drums rolled and the houselights dipped for a few moments while a murmur of anticipation welled up from the audience.

Judith, however, remained distracted. She should have called her mother from the casino floor to make sure that the old ladies were all right. She should have called Bart Bednarik to spur him on with the B&B project. She should have checked with Corinne Dooley to make sure that Sweetums wasn't causing any feline problems with the neighbor children while the Dooleys cared for him in the Flynns' absence. Judith squirmed in her chair.

"And now," the Great Mandolini announced, "for our finale, a truly death-defying performance by the lovely Salome."

Instead of stagehands, Pancho Green and the young man who'd played the theremin pushed a large cabinet out of the wings. Salome produced two lethal-looking sabers from under her silver cloak. She handed the weapons to Mandolini. Deftly, Salome swirled the cloak around her body, revealing glimpses of a sparkling silver ball gown that dazzled the eye. Then she opened the cabinet, waved her hands every which way to show that it was empty, and stepped inside, closing the door behind her.

More drum rolls. Mandolini slashed the air with the sabers, which gleamed under the stage lights. As the drums reached their crescendo, he rammed the sabers again and again into the wooden box. The audience gasped. Mandolini flung the sabers aside and stared into the farthest reaches of the cabaret. The drums rolled more softly while Mandolini strolled up to the saber-riddled box. To the clang of cymbals, he opened the door to reveal Salome, unharmed and smiling brightly in her stunning silver gown.

Applause, whistles, and cheers exploded from the onlookers. The curtain fell. A moment later, Mandolini appeared in front of the curtain and bowed. A puff of smoke suddenly filled the front of the stage. When it quickly subsided, Mandolini was gone. The houselights went up. The show was over.

"Not bad," Joe said, getting up from his chair. "I'm heading for the craps table. How about you, Bill?"

Bill was stretching his neck every which way. "I'll watch," he said.

Renie had grabbed her purse and was practically running out of the cabaret. "Quarters!" she shouted, giving her husband a quick peck on the cheek. "See you when I see you, Bill. Come on, coz. Let's kill 'em!"

Judith did her best to keep up with Renie. But her cousin was moving too fast. What was worse, Renie was short. Judith lost her somewhere beyond the dollar slots.

Earlier, Renie had been in the Summer section. Or was it Spring? Judith couldn't remember. She wandered through the maze of machines, trying to find either her cousin or a familiar sight she could recognize from her afternoon forays.

At last, she spotted the red Corvette on the platform. As luck would have it, Renie was close by, at another bank of quarter machines.

"These are good," Renie said. "The chairs are comfortable, even if we're not at a console. Try the one next to me. It's different, but it pays the same."

"Three quarters?" Judith exclaimed. "Doesn't your money go kind of fast?"

"It does, at that," Renie replied with a frown as her initial investment of twenty dollars decreased to ten. "Maybe we should move."

Judith nodded in the direction of the Corvette. "You know, I wouldn't mind trying to win that car for Joe."

"Dream on," Renie said. "Those things never pay off. You don't even get decent jackpots along the way. They're progressive machines, and I almost never play them."

"Still . . ." Judith gazed at the 'Vette's sleek rear end. "I think I'll try it anyway. At least I can tell Joe I was thinking of him when I lost our money."

"Ohhh . . ." Renie cashed out the few quarters that were left in her machine. "I'll play, too. But not for long. Those cars and trucks and boats and motorcycles they display as jackpot prizes are real sucker bait. Not to mention that if you win, you have to pay big tax bucks out of your own pocket."

The Corvette console was so busy that the cousins couldn't find two seats together. Renie spotted one toward the front of the car.

"You take that one," she said. "I'll go around to the other side and see if there's a seat open."

Judith was shaking her head in wonder. "I can't get over how intense most of these people are. Look at them, you'd think they were performing brain surgery."

Renie glanced at the line of gamblers who were hunched over their machines. "Yeah, well, it is kind of absorbing."

Judith smiled wryly at her cousin. "Yes, so I've noticed. I've never seen you concentrate so much, not even when you're working."

"This *is* working," Renie replied. "I mean, it's a way of making money. If you're lucky. See you." She scooted off to the opposite side of the console.

Judith sat down and studied the jackpots. To win the car, she would have to get three red Corvettes in a row. Cringing a bit, she removed a twenty-dollar bill from her wallet. With a grimace, she slipped the money into the slot and watched it disappear as if eaten by some voracious computer component.

Three coins were required. Judith saw her credits swiftly mount to eighty coins. Bracing herself, she pressed the button that read Play Maximum Credits.

The barrels registered a blank row. Judith pushed the button again. The numeral 7 appeared, flanked by a tire and the Corvette crossed-racing-flags symbol. On the third try, she got a mag wheel, a speedometer, and a cherry. A horn sounded, indicating that she'd won three quarters.

Encouraged, she hit the button again. And again and again and again until she was down to twenty-seven coins. Judith paused, gazing around her. No one seemed to be winning much, judging from the lack of horn honks. She sat up straight, shaking out the kinks. Her eyes wandered upward, to the car itself.

For some reason, it looked different than it had in the afternoon. Maybe it was the light. But the light didn't change inside the casino. Maybe it was the car. She stared harder, looking at the mannequin behind the wheel.

The mannequin definitely looked different. Instead of leaning back with a big smile on her face, the blonde was slumped slightly against the seat. And she definitely wasn't smiling.

That was when Judith realized that the Corvette's occupant wasn't a mannequin. It was a real person who looked like the mannequin, but who even more closely resembled the Great Mandolini's assistant, Salome.

But the most incredible thing Judith noticed was that Salome looked like she was dead.

Chapter Four

THE flashing lights and honking horns and ringing bells seemed to be going off inside Judith's head instead of around her. Was it possible to ignore the corpse in the Corvette? Maybe Salome wasn't dead. Maybe she'd passed out. Maybe Judith was overreacting.

The Lake Stillasnowamish Resort Casino was a fantastical place. Like all casinos and most resorts, it was designed to take visitors out of their drab, real lives. "Disneyland for grown-ups" was the way Renie had described her first visit to Vegas. For a few days, you could actually leave your troubles—along with your money—at the door and exist in a dream world.

Slowly, she got to her feet. Would it be crass to cash out her unused quarters? *Only,* Judith thought, *if Salome really was beyond help.* That's how she looked. *Completely still. Drained of life.* Judith had seen enough bodies to recognize death.

Before she could decide what to do next, Renie appeared at her side. "I lost the whole twenty dollars," she declared, looking vexed. "Unless you're winning, let's get out of here."

Grimacing, Judith glanced at the body and then at the people who had been sitting on either side of her. The elderly white-haired woman with glasses on a chain was riveted to her machine; the burly, middle-aged man in the plaid flannel shirt was reaching into his worn wallet to fetch another twenty. Neither of them seemed to notice that Judith or anybody else was alive.

Or dead, for that matter, thought Judith as she started to walk away from the console.

"Hey!" Renie gave Judith a small shove. "You've got over ten bucks still in the machine."

Not wanting to cause a fuss, Judith dutifully hit the Cash/Credit button and began scooping quarters into a plastic bucket.

"You dropped a couple," Renie said, bending down to pick up the stray coins. "If you do that when I'm not around, ask somebody else to pick them up for you. You don't want to bend too far and dislocate your hip. This is a vacation, you aren't looking for trouble."

"I'm not," Judith said, "but I think I've found some." Without acknowledging the puzzlement on her cousin's face, she moved away from the console, then turned to stop by the front end of the car. "Look up into the driver's seat," she whispered.

Renie, who didn't need her glasses except for close work, peered up into the 'Vette. She started to shrug, then tensed. "Good God. It's Salome."

"Yes." Judith looked around. No one was paying the slightest attention to the cousins. Except, perhaps, for the eye-in-the-sky, as the security cameras were called.

Renie grew red in the face and clenched her fists. "I don't believe it! We're supposed to be having fun!" Her voice began to rise. "Now you have to spoil it by finding another damned corpse!"

Several people turned to stare at the cousins. Judith stopped short of putting her hand over Renie's mouth. "Keep it down!" she ordered in a low, but emphatic, voice.

Still looking outraged, Renie appeared to be weighing mayhem versus propriety. Before she could make up her mind, a short but stout white-haired woman whose hands glittered with diamonds and sapphires touched Judith's arm.

"Did your friend say 'corpse'?" she asked in a quavering voice.

"Uh . . ." Judith winced. "No, no, she said 'horse.' She wants to play the ponies in the sports-book area."

The woman patted Judith's arm. "You should. I won over four hundred dollars today in the sixth race at Pimlico on a horse named Gasbag. He was a long shot, but I bet on him because that was my late husband's nickname. Good luck, dear." The woman toddled away.

Renie had simmered down. "Okay, okay, now that I haven't killed you, what do we do next?"

Judith made an effort to gather her usual logical thought processes. "I think I know where security is located. I saw the desk this afternoon when I telephoned Bart Bednarik."

To her relief, Pancho Green was chatting with one of the uniformed security men. "Ah!" the casino manager exclaimed with his toothsome grin. "Mrs. Flynn! How did you like the Great Mandolini?"

"Fine, but—"

Pancho held up a hand. "Yes, I heard about the seating incident with Inga. I must apologize for the mix-up. Inga is—"

Judith was compelled to interrupt. "Mr. Green, there's a much bigger problem at the—"

"Inga is Mandolini's sister," Pancho went on. "She and Mr. Fromm, his manager, along with whoever else might join their—"

"Mr. Green! Please! The Corvette over in the quarter section has a—"

Pancho's attention was finally captured. "The Corvette?" He frowned. "Did someone damage it during the power failure?"

"Not the car itself," Judith replied, and swallowed hard. "It's the person inside it. It looks like—"

"Person? There's no person in the car," Pancho asserted, looking relieved. "That's a dummy, a doll, a . . . you know, a mannequin."

"Not now it isn't," Judith persisted. "It looks like Salome."

Pancho chuckled. "Yes, it does a bit. We joked about that when we put the mannequin in the 'Vette. We told Salome that if she got bored between performances, she could always go sit in—"

Renie stepped forward and grabbed Pancho by his well-cut lapels. "Salome is dead. Dead, dead, dead!"

The frown returned to Pancho's swarthy face. "What do you mean, 'dead'?"

Renie let go of his lapels, closed her eyes, and let her tongue loll out of her mouth. "Like that."

"She may just be unconscious," Judith put in. "But whatever the case, she needs help. Or something," she added lamely.

At last, Pancho looked alarmed. "This isn't a joke?"

"No." If the single word didn't convince Pancho, Judith's stricken face did.

"Good God!" Pancho turned to the security man who had been going over some forms. "Amos, call your crew to SR-Five." He stopped and gave a sharp shake of his head. "No. Call in only three of them. We don't want a mob scene. And see if Doc Engelman is here tonight. I thought I saw him in the coffee shop."

Amos, who was a stocky young man of Native-American descent, stared at his boss. "What is it? What code should I give?"

"Crimson," Pancho retorted, already moving into the gaming area.

Amos's jaw dropped, but he already had a phone in his hand. His voice over the PA system was calm, however. Judith and Renie followed Pancho, but he detained them after a few steps.

"Wait here by the security desk," he said. "We're going to do whatever we have to do as discreetly as possible."

"But . . ." Judith began.

Grim faced, Pancho made a "back-off" gesture with his hands. The cousins watched him hurry away.

"This is just too gruesome," Judith declared. "What if Salome is really dead?"

Renie raked her short chestnut hair with her fingers and fidgeted with her clothes. "Of all the casinos, in all the resorts, in all the world, why did she have to die by your slot machine? Hunh," she said in surprise, "the back of my skirt feels damp. I must've gotten it wet in the rest room after the lights went out."

"That was no accidental power failure," Judith asserted.

"You may be right," Renie conceded.

Judith felt a headache coming on. "How on earth do I end up in these horrible situations? There were twenty other people playing those Corvette slots."

"Truly," Renie replied, "in a casino, you could set off a nuclear device and no one would notice. One time in Reno, I was sitting near a window at the hotel/casino where we were staying, and there was a terrible car crash just outside. Everybody looked up for about a second, then went back to playing despite the fact that all sorts of emergency vehicles showed up, sirens, flashing lights, and all. Worse yet, there was a fatality. But nobody paid any attention, including me. I read about it the next day in the newspaper."

Judith shivered. "That's awful." She hesitated, then touched Renie's arm. "Come on, we can't just stand here. Let's try to get closer to the action."

"But Pancho told us to—"

"Never mind Pancho," Judith said, already moving away. "If I've found another body, I'm entitled to see what's going on. I'm praying that Salome isn't dead, that she simply passed out, or that it's a publicity stunt or a practical joke. How can you blame me for wanting to learn the truth?"

There was no answer from Renie. Judith turned to look at her cousin, but she wasn't there.

"Damnit!" Judith swore under her breath. She gazed down the row of quarter slots. Renie's taffeta skirt stuck out a bit into the aisle. As fast as her artificial hip could carry her, Judith tromped back down the row of machines to discover her cousin pressing buttons like a maniac.

"What the hell are you doing?" Judith demanded.

Renie didn't bother to look up. "Apparently, whoever was playing this machine when the power went out left sixty credits in it and nobody noticed. This is Wild Ginger, and it's one of my favorites."

"You silly twit," Judith hissed. "Cash out or whatever, but come with me right now or I'll never speak to you again."

"Ohhh . . ." Renie pressed the Play button one more time. Two green leaves and one ginger blossom showed up on the center line. With a disgusted expression, Renie cashed out.

"The sacrifices I make," she muttered, "just because you have this obnoxious habit of finding dead bodies."

"You think I enjoy it?" Judith snapped.

"I have to wonder," Renie retorted as they approached the Corvette display where every machine had on its light to signal for a mechanic.

"What are they doing?" Judith asked. Some of the players were talking among themselves, others were looking around for assistance.

Amos, the security guard at the desk, had just reached the area. The cousins stopped in their tracks. Renie peered across the ten feet of space that separated them from the console.

"It looks as if the machines are all registering a 30033 code. That means that the hopper is empty, or that there's a mechanical failure."

A female security guard with two black braids showed up, then an older man who seemed to be the only guard wearing a gun. The players rose from their seats, most with reluctance.

As other onlookers gathered around, Judith could hear the

female guard's pleasant but firm voice: "The problem is probably due to the power failure. If you'll step well away, we'll fix it. It may take a while, so you're free to play elsewhere. Meanwhile, your money is safe. The computer has your credits recorded."

Pancho Green came around from the far side of the console. Apparently, he didn't see the cousins, who were half hidden by a life-size cutout of a showgirl. The casino manager had assumed a casual air, chatting amiably with an older goateed man. As the crowd of onlookers grew in number, Pancho held up his hands.

"Nothing to see here," he announced in his resonant voice. "Go enjoy yourselves, good luck, and get rich."

The words seemed as magical as if they were part of Mandolini's act. The gawkers began to disappear just as a quartet of workmen in white overalls unfolded a tall, plastic screen to enclose the Corvette area.

"Shoot," Judith said, "now we can't even see the car."

"That's the point," Renie replied. "I've been watching poor Salome. She hasn't moved."

Sadly, Judith shook her head. "I still can't believe it." She kept staring as the white panels were unfurled one by one, like sheets draped over a corpse. Which, she realized, was their purpose.

Pancho and the man with the goatee stepped inside the enclosure as the last piece of plastic was put into place. "He must be the doctor. What's his name? Engelstad?"

Renie shook her head. "Engelman, I think."

Judith saw the doorman, Bob Bearclaw, moving toward the panels in his stately manner. To her surprise, he, too, slipped inside.

"What's that all about?" she murmured.

"The doorman?" Renie said. "Maybe he's there to open the car door."

"Don't be callous," Judith responded, noting that her cousin was drifting backward, toward the dollar slots behind them.

Amos and the other two security guards apparently had taken their cue from Pancho. All three of them were speaking together, while Amos, with arms folded across his chest, seemed to be telling a funny story. Judith, however, didn't miss their quick, anxious glances at the enclosure.

But Judith did miss Renie. Turning around sharply, she saw her cousin at a dollar slot, deep in concentration.

"Coz!" Judith cried, then lowered her voice. "How could you?"

"I know, I know," Renie replied. "I don't usually play dollar machines, but I noticed that these seem to be hitting. Can't you hear the clatter of the coins? Dollar tokens make a very loud—and lovely—sound."

"I don't mean that," Judith said in exasperation. "I mean, how could you play anything at a time like this?"

"We don't want to get in trouble, do we?" Renie inquired in her best aging ingenue manner. "I'm covering for your extreme curiosity by playing this machine. Look, I just won ten dollars."

"I hope you get tendonitis," Judith snarled. "Nobody's paying any attention to us. Besides, what harm is there in merely watching what's going on?"

"You can't see anything," Renie pointed out, pressing the button again. "You'll hear what happened later. It's bound to get out. Not to mention that Joe knows Pancho, right? Hey! I got twenty! This thing's hot!"

Judith had never seen Renie like this. Her cousin might become absorbed in her family, her work, the baseball season, or a designer sale at Nordquist's, but she had always been able to fragment herself enough to lend Judith an ear. Maybe it was best to ignore her.

Turning back to observe the plastic panels, she noticed that the guards had fanned out beyond the area, which was cordoned off with velvet ropes attached to sturdy brass poles. More workmen were bringing in a hoist and a flatbed trailer. Once again, people began to gather near the Corvette console.

Pancho stepped out between the panels. "We seem to have an oil leak," he said with a self-deprecating grin. "We're going to have the dealership bring us a new model."

Some people groaned, others laughed. But their interest was short-lived. Judith stayed in place, once again half-hiding behind the showgirl cutout. The screens were removed to reveal the Corvette covered with a white tarp. It took less than five minutes to lift the car and place it on the trailer. The parade of guards and workers was led away by Pancho Green and the man with the goatee. Bob Bearclaw nodded at Pancho before moving toward the front of the casino in his dignified manner.

Judith felt gypped. "Are you broke yet?" she asked Renie, who was still at the dollar slot.

"Unfortunately, yes," Renie said with a disgusted expression. "But I only put in forty bucks."

"Good grief."

Renie, however, was undaunted. "Want to try roulette?"

"I don't know how to play," Judith said, a worried expression on her face.

"I'll show you," Renie replied. "It's not hard. But first, we've got to find the table with the lowest minimum."

"First," Judith said sternly, "I've got to find Joe. I have to tell him about Salome."

"He won't know anything," Renie said, leading the way to the table games.

"But he knows Pancho," Judith replied stubbornly. "Where did he say he was going? To play craps? That seems to be his favorite."

"Bill likes craps, too," Renie said. "But he has to study the tables for a long time to make sure there's a decent shooter. Otherwise, he won't play. Let's have a look. The craps tables are near the roulette wheels anyway."

Joe and Bill weren't at any of the six craps tables. While they were all crowded, the cousins observed neither whoops of joy nor high-fiving of hands. The Hot Shooter had not been found.

At the far end of the table games, they spotted Bill. He was standing a few feet back from a baccarat table, fingering his chin.

Renie approached her husband with caution. She waited until the current hand was played out before tentatively tapping him on the arm.

"Have you seen Joe lately?" she asked in a subdued voice.

Bill didn't reply immediately. Another hand was being dealt. Judith noticed that at least five of the six players were of Asian descent. All but one was using black chips. An ancient Japanese man with a scraggly gray beard put what Judith estimated was at least twenty of them on the space marked PLAYER.

"Black's a hunsky," Renie whispered, following Judith's gaze.

"You mean a hundred bucks?" Judith gasped. "He must have at least two grand out there."

"Which he just lost," Renie said softly. "Bank won." The Japanese man put out another stack. Judith saw that he had a very large pile of black chips still in front of him.

"Joe went off a couple of minutes ago with somebody I didn't recognize," Bill finally said as the new hand was dealt.

"Which way?" Judith asked.

Eyes glued to the table, Bill shrugged.

Renie started to walk away. Judith snatched at her cousin's bronze dolman sleeve. "Where are you going? Aren't you going to tell Bill about Salome?"

Renie shook her head. "Not when he's observing baccarat. He's trying to get into the rhythm of the game. Player-Player-Bank-Bank-Bank-Player-Tie-Player—"

"Shut up!" Judith cried. "I'm starting to wish I'd never come here."

"Coz." Renie eyed Judith very seriously. "You came here to relax. For once in your life, could you ignore what may be a tragedy—but has nothing to do with you—and simply enjoy yourself? That's what I'm trying to do. Honest, by the time you leave here, you'll feel refreshed."

Judith put a hand to her aching head. "Right now, I feel frazzled."

"Of course you do," Renie said, taking Judith's arm. "That's because you won't let go. Come on, let's have some fun."

Judith started to speak, but an announcement over the PA system caught her ear. "The Great Mandolini's second performance tonight has been canceled due to unforeseen circumstances. Anyone holding tickets for the show should request a refund or an exchange at the headliner desk in the front lobby. Thank you. We apologize for this inconvenience."

"'Inconvenience'!" Judith murmured. "Good grief!"

"They have to say something that isn't upsetting," Renie pointed out. "Would you prefer they tell everybody that Salome didn't defy death?"

"I need to take some aspirin," Judith replied wearily. "Where's a water fountain?"

"For some reason, they're hard to find in casinos," Renie said. "You can get a glass of water right over here at the Autumn Bar."

The cousins made their way through the drifting leaves that dissolved upon contact, like the snow in the Winter section and the blossoms in the Spring section. She hadn't noticed any special effects in the Summer portion of the casino. Maybe that was because summer was supposed to be clear skies and sunshine. In her present mood, Judith would have expected mosquitoes and wasps.

The water that she sipped to wash down the aspirin reminded her of drinking out of the rushing streams around the cabin. Facedown on a flat rock, she and Renie would slurp and gurgle in the riffles. It had been the best-tasting water in the world, and they'd been heedless of health hazards.

"I think I'll just sit here for a while," Judith declared. "Go ahead, play on. I assume you'll be at one of the roulette wheels."

Renie nodded and was off like a shot. Judith remained on the stool, studying the icicles that dripped above the liquor bottles, the small waterfall that tumbled under the glass-topped bar, and, most of all, the people.

One of them was familiar. The dishwater blonde drinking brandy at the far end was the same woman Judith had met at the elevators that afternoon. Griselda Something-or-other, nicknamed—eerily enough—Grisly. She looked upset, and Judith thought she knew why.

The place next to Grisly was occupied by a chubby beer drinker who was talking to another man on his right. Cautiously sliding off the bar stool, Judith took her unfinished water with her and sidled up to Grisly.

"I'm so sorry about what happened tonight," she said in a confidential tone. "You must be very upset."

Grisly turned sharply to stare at Judith. "What? Who are you?"

"Oh!" Judith put a hand to her breast. "I'm sorry. Of course you don't remember me. I'm nobody, really. We met this afternoon at the elevators."

Grisly's gray eyes were suspicious. "Yes," she said slowly, "I vaguely recall you now. But . . ." She turned away and stared into the brandy snifter, apparently gathering her thoughts. "Why," she finally inquired, looking again at Judith, "did you act sympathetic?"

Having gone this far, Judith had to brazen it out. "About Salome, of course. Have they had time to figure out what happened?"

Grisly choked on her brandy. Indeed, she went into a coughing fit. The chubby man next to her looked concerned; so did the silver-haired bartender. Judith proffered the rest of her water and told Grisly to raise her hands above her head.

Seconds later, the cough subsided. Grisly accepted the water glass and took a slow sip. Still gasping, she nodded at Judith as if in thanks. But as soon as she got her wind and her voice back, the wary look returned to her eyes.

"How do you know about Salome?" she demanded in a low, hoarse tone.

The chubby man finished his beer and left with his buddy. Judith sat on the vacant stool next to Grisly. "My husband's a detective," she said quietly. "He's also a friend of Pancho Green." The first part was true enough, so was the second. But the inference was misleading. As usual, when Judith stretched the truth or conveyed false information, her conscience didn't bother her one bit. The "fibs" were always for a good cause.

Grisly looked alarmed. "Pancho shouldn't allow anyone to know about this. What's wrong with him?" The question was rhetorical. Grisly wrung her thin hands in her lap.

"My husband is very discreet," Judith assured the other woman. "He's a retired police officer. He takes on a private case now and then, but naturally he knows how to keep mum."

"He told you," Grisly said accusingly.

"Not exactly," Judith admitted, since she had no idea if Joe knew anything whatsoever about Salome. "I was with Pancho when he found Salome."

Grisly's eyes widened. "You were?" She put a hand to her head. "I don't understand. You've got me all confused."

"Well, it is confusing," Judith declared. "You must have heard only in the last few minutes."

"That's so. I came straight to the bar after Pancho informed me of what had happened." Grisly shoved her brandy snifter aside. "In fact, I should go back to the greenroom right now. That's where everybody's congregating."

"Really." Judith watched Grisly get up and glance uncertainly around her. "What are they going to do?"

"I don't know," Grisly replied, then grimaced. "Whatever they do, they'd better do it right."

"What do you mean?" Judith asked, joining the other woman as she walked purposefully away from the bar.

Grisly frowned at Judith. "Why, the investigation, of course." She halted in midstep, her eyes narrowing at Judith. "What else can they do when someone's been murdered?"

Chapter Five

Frozen in place by Grisly's grisly announcement, Judith put a hand over her racing heart. Not murder. Not again. Not on vacation.

And not any of her business. Renie was right about that.

Giving herself a good shake, she looked up ahead for Griselda Vanderbehr. But Grisly had disappeared into the crowd. Judith moved on, toward the table games. She spotted Bill, observing a second baccarat table. He probably wouldn't be interested in a mere murder, Judith decided, and continued on toward the four roulette wheels.

Renie was sitting at the far end of the nearest table. As Judith approached, all she could see was her cousin's taffeta skirt as she leaned far over the table to place her bets.

"Hi," Renie said in a detached voice. "How's your headache?"

"Worse," Judith replied in a low voice as she stood behind her cousin's chair. "Salome was murdered."

The bearded croupier passed a hand over the board as the ball spun in the wheel. Renie held up a hand to hush Judith. "Hold it."

The wheel slowed down, the ball began rolling in a leisurely manner, jumped out of two numbered slots, and landed on the double zero.

"Ah!" Renie turned around to grin at Judith. "I bumped up my bet on the green—that's the single and the double zeros—which means I won a hundred and forty bucks."

Judith leaned down to whisper sharply in Renie's ear. "Salome was murdered."

Renie jerked around to look at Judith. "Good Lord!"

Judith started to explain how she'd met Griselda Vanderbehr at the Winter Bar, but Renie was thanking the croupier as he handed her a black chip, and a stack of red ones. "Hang on. I have to place my bets. Lenny here is really throwing my numbers." She put two red chips on eleven. "One for me, one for you," she told the croupier, who smiled his appreciation.

"Griselda," Judith began, "is also known as Grisly. Anyway, after she told me that Salome had been murdered, Grisly rushed off to the greenroom, where everybody was meeting. With the tribal police, I suppose. Which," Judith mused, "may explain why Salome and the car were removed so quickly. One of the men I thought was a security guard had a weapon. He may have been a cop. I'm guessing the older man with the goatee was the doctor."

"Hold it," Renie requested, zeroing in on the wheel as it began to spin.

Judith waited patiently. The ball rolled into nineteen. Renie clenched her fists in victory. "Another straight-up thirty-five to one. All right!" She glanced at Judith and held up a red chip. "This is a five-dollar minimum inside table. You can't get anything cheaper at night. Never bet the outside. That's only a two-to-one payback. You can take two numbers by putting your chip on the line, or three by putting it on the edge of the row, or four by taking the corner where they connect. Take one of my chips, try it. I insist."

Judith hesitated. Renie was collecting more red chips, two of which she handed back to the croupier.

"No eleven," she said to Lenny, "but you've been good to me."

"Thank you, miss," Lenny replied, tapping the chips on the table and putting them to one side. "Good luck."

Renie began to make more bets, leaning between the other players to reach the far end of the board. "Sorry," she apologized, bumping a short man and a tall woman. "I've had shoulder surgery. It's hard for me to bet the low numbers."

Judith stared at the black and red numbers that went up to thirty-six. The high number was the easiest to reach. With a sigh of resignation, she reached under Renie's outstretched figure to snatch at a chip and set it on thirty-six.

"Have you seen Joe?" Judith asked, gazing at the craps tables.

Renie shook her head. She was concentrating on the new roll. "Wow," she murmured, "somebody must feel lucky." She pointed to thirty-six, where a single black chip rested. "That's a hundred-dollar chip. Too bad, that number hardly ever comes up."

Judith gulped. She didn't realize the chip colors represented the same amounts for all the games.

"I wonder who put it out there?" Renie mused.

Judith clenched her fists and gritted her teeth. The ball bounced into seventeen, then four, then ricocheted into thirty-six. A wave of relief swept over her.

"I'll be darned," Renie whispered. "Let's see who placed that bet." Her brown eyes roamed the table.

"Umm . . ." Judith began, then stopped. She couldn't remember the odds that her cousin had mentioned. Inside, outside, straight up, betting the green, halves, quarters . . .

The croupier cleared away all of the other chips, but left the black chip on the table. "How come . . . ?" Judith started to ask before Lenny gave her a big smile.

"That was a bold move," he declared, deftly counting out black chips. "There you go. Good luck."

Renie gasped as the piles of black chips were placed before Judith. "You bet my hunsky? My God! You won thirty-five hundred dollars!"

Judith gaped at her cousin. "I did? No!"

"Would you like some of that in smaller chips?" Lenny inquired.

Judith turned her stare on the croupier. "Yes. No. I mean, I . . . Just give me all black. I think I'm going to pass out."

Lenny indicated the chip still on the board. "Want to try it again?"

"No! That is, I don't think so." She felt as if she were hyperventilating. "It actually belongs to my cousin."

"Tip her ten percent," Lenny laughed with a wink.

"I will," Judith said, piling the chips into her plastic bucket. She was ashamed to look at Renie. "But first, I'm going to cash in." Without another word, she raced off to find the cashiers' cages.

Stopping to ask two slot mechanics for directions, it took Judith some time to reach her destination. As it turned out, the cashiers were on the same side of the casino as security. Passing the desk, she noticed that a fair-haired young man who looked barely old enough to shave was now on duty. Judith assumed that Amos and the others were in the greenroom, involved in the investigation of Salome's murder.

Salome's murder. The phrase ate at Judith as she stood in line in front of the first of six cages. *Who could have killed her?* Judith moved up one place. *When was she killed? What was the cause of death?* Judith moved up another space. *And why was her body put into the Corvette in the middle of the casino?*

Surely the power failure hadn't been a freak of nature. It had to be deliberate, to tie in with moving the body to the car, maybe even to camouflage the murder itself. Mechanically, Judith took another half dozen steps forward. Yet Salome was still alive when the power failure had occurred. Judith was next at the window. She was so absorbed in Salome's death that the platinum-haired cashier had to rouse her.

"Hey, sweetie, you cashing in?"

"Huh?" Judith bobbled the plastic bucket. "Oh! Yes! Sorry."

The buxom cashier's name tag read "Dolly." "Wow, you did all right! Do you want a cashier's check or bills?"

"Um . . . A check, please." Judith couldn't imagine walking around the casino with thirty-six hundred-dollar bills in her purse.

"We can keep the check in the safe, if you like, sweetie," Dolly offered. "You married?"

Judith nodded.

"You want to do that?" Dolly leaned forward and spoke in confidential tones. "You never know when hubby might get the itch to play with the high rollers."

Judith felt stupid. She had money on the counter, but murder on the brain. "Okay," she agreed in a feeble voice. "A check sounds fine."

After presenting her driver's license and allowing her thumbprint to be taken, Judith watched as Dolly went to the rear and printed out the check. "Here," she said, "take a good look. When you go home, spend it on yourself. Why even bother to tell hubby about it?"

"Ah . . . Right. Thanks. Thanks very much." Judith forced a smile as Dolly handed her a receipt and slipped the check into an envelope.

"Sure, sweetie. The safe's in the back. Each drawer is filed under the guest's name." The cashier gestured with a long, manicured fingernail. "When you check out, just come here and ask for it."

"I will," Judith promised, then jerked to attention. The PA system was calling her name.

"Judith Flynn, please report to security on the main casino floor."

As ever, Judith worried that the summons was about Gertrude. Or Aunt Deb. Surely Bart Bednarik wouldn't call at this time of night.

He never worked past five. She covered the short distance to the security desk and identified herself as Judith Flynn.

"Right," the young man said, then looked down at what Judith presumed was a message. "Mr. Flynn wants you to meet him outside the greenroom. Do you know where that is?"

Judith had no idea. After complicated directions involving clearance from more security guards, an apprehensive Judith headed off to meet Joe. What could he be doing in the greenroom? Had Pancho Green consulted him about Salome's murder? Having noticed that clocks in the casino were as hard to find as water fountains, she glanced at her watch. It was going on midnight. No wonder, she thought, that she felt tired. She'd been up since before six that morning.

Her route took her close to the roulette tables, but Renie wasn't there. She scanned the immediate area, spotting her cousin next to Bill, by one of the craps tables.

Judith brushed up beside Renie. "Did you tell Bill about Salome?" she whispered as a few shouts erupted from the craps game.

Renie scowled and shook her head. "He may have found a shooter, somebody who can roll for a long time and not crap out. I think it's the guy in the maroon sweater with the wavy brown hair. We'll see how he does next time."

Rolling her eyes, Judith started to walk away, but Renie pulled on her sleeve. "Don't forget, you owe me a hunsky."

The way to the greenroom took her past the cabaret entrance and down a short hallway to a door where the security woman with the braids stood guard.

A quick glance at the guard's name tag informed Judith that she was Emily Dancingdoe. "Security on the main floor told me to meet my husband outside the greenroom," Judith explained.

Emily nodded. She was about thirty, with broad cheekbones and well-defined features. If the braids were a stereotype of her Native-American origins, she wore them with pride, like a badge. "I heard you were coming, Mrs. Flynn. Isn't it awful about Sally?"

Judith was taken aback. "Sally? Is—was that Salome's nickname?"

Emily shook her head, the braids swinging at her shoulders. "Her real name is Sally. Sally Quinn. She used to be married to Freddy, but they got a divorce."

"Freddy?"

Embarrassed, Emily put a hand to her cheek. "I'm sorry. Freddy Polson is the Great Mandolini. Anyway, Sally remarried a man named Manny Quinn."

"I see," Judith said, then added, "Manny Quinn? Is that his real name?"

"I think so," Emily replied, very seriously. "I've only spoken with him a few times."

Judith tried to file all the names and relationships inside her head, which still ached. Then she asked Emily how she could find Joe.

It turned out to be simple. On the other side of the door that Emily was guarding, there was a long corridor that led to the back-stage area, some of the dressing rooms, the technical areas, and, at the very end, the greenroom, where cast members waited for their cues. Judith couldn't miss it, Emily assured her. There was a sign on the door.

Judith couldn't have missed it if she'd tried. At the end of the corridor, Joe was pacing up and down.

"Where the hell have you been?" he demanded.

"Don't yell at me!" Judith snapped. "I have a headache, and I'm really tired."

"Okay." Joe composed himself. "Here's the deal. Salome was stabbed to death. The casino is on tribal land, but in partnership with some development outfit in Phoenix. After they moved the 'Vette and Salome—which they shouldn't have done so soon, damnit—Pancho got hold of me. Not only am I an ex-homicide cop," he went on, his voice growing louder and more intense, "but a PI. And," he all but shouted, "it seems my idiot wife found the frigging body!"

Judith flinched. Joe was very red in the face, looking as if he were about to explode. "That's not my fault," Judith said angrily. "I looked up and there she was. Besides, I was trying to win you the car. If your MG wasn't older than Mother, I would never have been there in the first place!" Judith turned her back and stomped off down the corridor. At the halfway point, she whirled around to give Joe one final blast. "Furthermore, if you hadn't gotten drunk thirty years ago and eloped with Herself, you'd never have met Pancho Green! So there!" For emphasis, she actually stomped her foot.

Even though a good thirty feet separated the Flynns, Judith heard Joe heave a sigh. "Come back here," he called in a weary, much lower voice. "There's no point in throwing blame around."

"You started it," Judith said, not budging.

Joe sighed again. "I find it unbelievable that when somebody gets murdered, you're always on the scene. Why couldn't you have taken up another hobby, like collecting small, vicious animals?"

"It's not my fault," Judith declared for what she figured was about the hundredth time.

"If I were a rational man," Joe said, still in that tired voice, "I'd agree with you. But I'm no longer rational. I may be going crazy."

"Oh, Joe . . ."

"Never mind." He waved a hand. "Here's the situation. Having anyone get murdered—let alone one of the performers—at a casino is bad business. And don't start telling me how Renie once figured that, for you, murder is a marketing tool. Pancho could call in the FBI, since the casino is on federal land because it's owned by Native Americans."

Judith nodded as Joe wiped his forehead with a handkerchief.

"But," he continued, "he doesn't want to do that yet. Like every longtime casino worker from Vegas, he's not fond of the feds. Also, the tribal elders would prefer investigating this with their own people. Since I happen to have the experience, Pancho has asked me to help out. That's what I'm doing now. I'm helping their senior detective, Jack Jackrabbit, interrogate witnesses."

"I see," Judith said. "So you want me to . . . ?"

"Not worry," Joe broke in, turning back toward the greenroom door. "I may be very late getting back to the room."

"Oh." Judith couldn't help herself. She felt disappointed. "Is there any way I can help?"

Joe was already opening the door. "Help?" He shrugged. "No. We've got it under control. See you later." He disappeared inside the greenroom.

Realizing that she shouldn't be annoyed, Judith tried to assume an indifferent air as she walked slowly down the hallway. *Under control indeed,* she thought. They were interrogating witnesses. That meant they might not have a suspect. Of course, the crime was only a couple of hours old. But Joe himself had always said that if the killer wasn't caught in the first few hours of a murder investigation, the police were usually in for the long haul.

Emily was still on the other side of the door. "Hi, Mrs. Flynn," she said. "Anything new going on back there?"

"I wouldn't know," Judith replied a bit too sharply. Seeing Emily look askance, she smiled in apology. "Sorry. I'm kind of worn out. Do you know who's in the greenroom? I was too tired to check." Another fib, another good cause.

Emily's high forehead wrinkled in concentration. "Let me think. There are a couple of other ways to get backstage, including the loading dock. I only saw the people who came off the casino floor. There was Mr. Green, Dr. Engelman, Amos Littlebird, Ronnie Roughrocks—Amos and Ronnie are security guards like me—and

Jack Jackrabbit, the tribe's detective. Everybody else came from backstage, like Freddy and Ms. Polson and Ms. Vanderbehr and . . ." Emily paused. "I suppose Mr. Fromm and maybe Ms. Mendoza and Lloyd."

"That's quite a group," Judith remarked, her head swimming. She recalled that a Mr. G. D. Fromm had been mentioned as the Great Mandolini's manager. Judith realized that she had to get used to the illusionist's real name, Freddy Polson. "Who's Ms. Mendoza? And Lloyd?"

"Micaela Mendoza is Freddy's fiancée," Emily explained. "They call her Micki. Lloyd is Lloyd Watts, who helps Freddy with some of his ideas for the act. Lloyd is the one who plays the theremin just before the last illusion." She paused again. "Mr. Quinn is probably there, too. Gosh, he must be really upset. He and Sally had been married for less than a year."

"That's a terrible shame," Judith said. "Are there children from either of Sally's marriages?"

Emily shook her head. "No. Freddy and Sally were together forever, but even after they got married a few years ago, they didn't start a family. I guess they were too busy getting the act established."

Judith wished she could take notes. "Let me get this straight. Mandolini—Freddy—used to be married to Salome—Sally. They divorced, and she remarried someone name Manny Quinn, right? But Mr. Quinn isn't involved with the act?"

"That's right," Emily said. "I don't know what Mr. Quinn does for a living. Except gamble." She put a hand to her mouth and her dark eyes grew wide. "I don't mean that in a negative way. That is, what else could he do when he has to be in the casino all the time?"

"Work?" Judith thought of Dan. Maybe Manny Quinn was a sponger like her first husband. It had required working two jobs for Judith to keep the family afloat.

"If he does, it's not around here," Emily allowed. "I'm not being critical," she added hastily. "I've heard he actually was in show business at one time. But after he and Sally got married, he preferred to stay with her when she's touring."

Judith filed away Freddy and Manny, Sally's first and second husbands. It didn't help that half the people involved had names that ended in *y*. "I gather that Inga Polson is Freddy's sister. Does she work with the act?"

"In a way," Emily said. "She's a lot older than Freddy. She's like a mother hen. She may seem gruff sometimes, but it's only because of her strong sense of family ties and her concern for her brother."

"And Griselda?" Judith inquired, thinking that Emily certainly bent over backward to say only positive things about other people.

"Grisly?" Emily giggled, revealing a single dimple. "Isn't that an unfortunate nickname? I'd hate it if I were her. But she never complains." She paused once more, no doubt grateful that she was probably known among her own intimates as nothing worse than "Emmy." "Grisly's an old family friend who sort of organizes and runs all the everyday stuff to do with the act. You know—things that Mr. Fromm doesn't have time for. She's very efficient, though Ms. Polson is a big help. In fact, sometimes it's hard to tell who's really in charge of the—"

Emily was interrupted by the opening of the door and the appearance of the man Judith recognized as Inga Polson's companion at the Flynns's usurped cabaret table. He was short and stocky, his bald head covered by an unattractive combover. He was also sweating profusely.

"This is ridiculous!" he declared, speaking to neither Judith nor Emily in particular. "I feel like I'm being grilled by the Gestapo!" He turned on Emily. "Where did that Irishman come from? I don't like him. I think he's wrong."

"Excuse me . . . ," Judith began in defense of her husband. But before she could go further, the man stomped away.

She looked at Emily "Mr. Fromm?"

"Yes." Emily sighed. "He likes to complain. Of course I'm sure he has good reasons. You know, like constructive criticism." She put a hand to her mouth a second time. "Really, I shouldn't talk about these people. You must think I'm a blabbermouth, but since you and your husband are involved in this terrible tragedy, and you're so easy to talk to, I can't seem to help myself."

"Heavens, don't apologize," Judith soothed, offering Emily her most understanding smile. "I don't know why, but I seem to be the sort of person who even strangers confide in." In truth, Judith rarely met anyone who didn't unload on her, and often without any encouragement. Her open manner and her genuine concern for other people inspired confidences whether it be in line at Falstaff's Grocery, trying on shoes at Nordquist's—or conversing with a possible murder suspect. "Besides," Judith went on, "everyone's under a strain. This is a very bad time for the casino and its employees. Tell me, have you heard why the power failed?"

Emily shrugged. "The storm, I suppose. I heard it's raining and blowing pretty hard outside."

Judith guessed that nothing short of a 7.0 earthquake would force gamblers to check on the weather. They could stay inside day after day, and the only change of seasons they'd notice would be the different parts of the Stillasnowamish casino. Before she could ask another question, Bob Bearclaw appeared, waving a gloved hand at Emily and nodding at Judith.

"Everything okay here?" he inquired.

"Oh, yes," Emily replied. "That is, all things considered."

"Right." His glance at Judith seemed benign, though for some reason she felt just a trifle uneasy. "And you, Mrs. Flynn?"

"I'm fine," Judith said rather abruptly.

"Good, good." Bob smiled at both women. "Remember, Emily, we must all be very careful." His dark eyes fixed on the young woman's face. "You understand?"

"Yes." Emily nodded in a jerky manner. "Yes, I do."

"Fine. We're in accord then." With a tip of his doorman's cap, he walked away.

A sidelong look at Emily indicated that the security guard's face had frozen. Some sort of message obviously had been passed between her and the doorman. Judith had a feeling that it meant she could learn nothing further from Emily for the present. Murmuring something about ". . . catching up with Joe later," Judith moved on to find Renie.

Her cousin was no longer in the table-games area, nor was there any sign of Bill. It was well after midnight. Bill, who was usually early to bed, had probably gone up to their room. Renie, however, was a night owl. Wearily, Judith began walking through the quarter slots in the Winter section.

Sure enough, Renie was seated in the middle of a row at a machine proclaiming "Snowballs of Bucks!"

"Hi," Judith said, sounding diffident.

"Hi," Renie replied, her eyes glued to the machine. "What's new?"

Judith sat down in the vacant chair next to Renie. "Joe's been asked to help with the homicide investigation."

"Oh." Renie checked her credits, which totaled an impressive 148. "Did Bill go to bed?"

"Yes."

"When are you going up?"

"Soon." Renie grinned at the machine as three snowmen appeared on the payoff line. "That's twenty-five bucks." She turned to Judith. "What did you just say?"

"I asked when you're going to bed."

"I always give Bill time to use the bathroom and do his neck exercises. He had his snack about an hour ago. I'll head up when this thing cools off."

"Or when you go broke."

Renie shook her head. "No. I've learned my lesson. Now that I have two hundred and forty-five coins, I'll play it down to two hundred. That way, I'll leave the floor with fifty dollars, plus whatever else I've won tonight."

Judith posed a question for Renie. "Don't you have to get up early tomorrow for the conference?"

"Yes. No." She stopped playing long enough to look at Judith. "I'm not attending."

"What?" Judith was incredulous. "How did you get out of it?"

"I didn't exactly." Renie was again concentrating on the Snowball machine. "I'm sending my mother in my place."

Chapter Six

JUDITH had no idea what time Joe returned that night. She'd reached their room shortly after midnight. A quick check next door had assured her that the mothers were already in bed and asleep. Fifteen minutes later, Judith was also under the covers and out like a light.

When she woke up the next morning shortly after nine, Judith thought at first that she was at home in the third-floor family quarters. She rolled over in bed, opened her eyes, and saw the ferns, fronds, and other lush greenery on the near wall. The events of the previous day came rushing back to her.

But Judith wasn't home, she was over an hour away, in the Lake Stillasnowamish Resort Casino. She hadn't dreamed that Salome— Sally Quinn—had been murdered. It was true. She sat up and scanned the room for Joe.

He was nowhere in sight. She called his name, in case he was in the bathroom. There was no answer. Then she noticed the note next to the phone on the nightstand.

Breakfast meeting with Pancho. Meet you at noon in the Summer Bar. Love, Joe.

"Rats!" Judith got out of bed and was starting for the bathroom when the phone rang.

"Bart here," said the voice at the other end. "We got a problem."

"Now what?" Judith snapped.

"We can't get the bigger countertop after all," the contractor explained with what Judith thought was a touch of relish. "The company you picked stopped making that size. You're going to have to choose a new one from a different source."

"Isn't a countertop a countertop as long as it fits?" Judith inquired in annoyance.

"Heck, no." Bart chuckled, a sinister sound to Judith's ears. "You got the kind that has a big burner in the middle, you got the kind that has a vertical burner to one side, you got the kind that—"

"You choose," Judith broke in. "I can't drive all the way into town to select another countertop stove."

"I can't take that responsibility," Bart said, aghast. "I might pick out one you'd hate or one that was faulty, and then you'd sue the pants off me. It happens. I know, I've been there. Contractors should have malpractice insurance, like doctors. I know a contractor over in Boise who lost his business because he got sued when the wife let him pick out her switch plates."

"Can't the countertop wait until we get back from vacation?" Judith asked, rubbing her forehead. She hadn't been awake for more than five minutes, and already her headache was returning.

"Heck, no," Bart replied, sounding as if Judith had asked him to fly to Tokyo without a plane. "All the electrical stuff has to be done at the same time. The fridge is coming today, the dishwasher's already here. If the electrician has to come back next week, it'll cost a bundle. You're the one who left town. This countertop deal has to be taken care of ASAP."

For a few seconds, Judith held the phone away from her ear. If there was still freeway construction, it'd take half of the day to drive into the city and back, confer with Bart, shop for a new countertop, and then listen to him complain about why the one she'd picked wasn't going to work.

But she had no choice. "Okay," she agreed with a big sigh. "I'll grab some breakfast and hit the road. I should be at the house around ten-thirty, quarter to eleven. Or should I meet you at one of the appliance stores?"

"Better meet me here at your place," Bart said. "I'll call around, see if I can get a good deal somewhere. See you."

Resignedly, Judith tapped on Gertrude's door. The old lady didn't answer. No doubt she was either feigning deafness—or too deaf to hear the knock. Judith was never sure which was the case. She yanked open the door to find the old lady watching TV and eating what looked like an immense breakfast.

"Where's Aunt Deb?" Judith asked.

"What?" Gertrude cupped a hand over her left ear. "Sorry, I don't need any brushes today, Mr. Fuller."

"Mother . . . " Judith was in no mood for games with Gertrude. "Where's Aunt Deb?"

"Wouldn't you like to know," Gertrude replied, wagging a finger at her daughter. "Maybe I done her in."

Exasperated, Judith looked in the bathroom. The spacious, handicapped-access facility was vacant. "Did Aunt Deb actually go to the graphic-design conference?"

"Sure," Gertrude replied, pushing aside the finished grapefruit half on her breakfast tray. "You know Deb—if she gets a chance to meet a bunch of people, she's off and running. So to speak."

Judith had thought Renie was kidding. "Good grief." She paused. "How long has she been gone?"

Gertrude shrugged. "An hour? I don't keep track of time when I'm alone with my favorite company—me. Even when I start talking to myself, I know when to shut up. Deb doesn't."

How long would it take before the conference officials found out that Deborah Grover wasn't Serena Jones? Judith thought back to the conferences she'd attended as a city librarian. Some of the attendees had been as old as Aunt Deb and some had been equally infirm and some had been both. Maybe the old girl could pull it off. She certainly possessed the charm and social skills for the job. Renie might have the artistic talent, but, as her cousin had once quoted a fellow conferencegoer, "Serena Jones takes no prisoners."

"I have to go into town to choose another stove," Judith said. "I'll be back sometime this afternoon."

Gertrude, who was eating a fried egg and watching a morning talk show, didn't miss a beat. "Be here by four. The bingo parlor opens then. I'll need a push to get there."

"Your wheelchair's motorized, remember?" Judith pointed out. "You can push yourself."

"Oh." Gertrude glanced down at the conveyance in which she was sitting. "So I can. I forgot. G'bye."

On her way out of the casino, Judith remembered to leave a note for Joe at the Summer Bar. She saw no hint that a murder investigation was under way. On the platform by the quarter progressive machines, the red Corvette had been replaced by a yellow model.

It took exactly ninety minutes to get to Hillside Manor. Judith had decided to skip breakfast except for a doughnut and coffee that she picked up from a barista in the casino. Getting out of the car, she paused to bestow a fond look on her house. The Edwardian-era prairie craftsman already showed off its improvements. The newly shingled roof was a grayish blue; the exterior was a pristine white. Judith had wanted a blue-and-black roof; she'd chosen navy with white and red trim for the exterior. And she still didn't know if she liked the dark shutters that had been installed. Shutters weren't a popular—or useful—Pacific Northwest addition, except on Dutch colonials like Renie's. But Judith had lost the argument with the architect. The shutters would remain until she got sick of them and then Skjoval Tolvang could tear them off.

Still, the house looked better, and not just because the fire damage had been fixed. There had been structural improvements as well, though they could not be seen by the naked eye. All in all, Judith felt a sense of pride as she approached the porch.

It was only then that she realized Bart Bednarik's red-and-green van wasn't parked in the driveway or the cul-de-sac. Judith glanced at her watch. It was 10:32. When she looked up again, she saw a truck turning the corner and coming toward her. The truck slowed to a crawl. A blond, curly-haired man poked his head out of the cab's passenger side.

"You Mrs. Lynn?" he asked.

"Flynn," Judith called back. The truck's lettering read "Cool & Cold Refrigeration." "Have you got my new fridge?"

The man had ducked back inside and didn't respond. Judith watched as the truck pulled up behind her in the driveway. The curly-haired man got out on one side and a dark-haired, broad-shouldered man got out on the other.

"Which entrance?" the dark-haired driver asked.

"The back," Judith replied, noting that the man looked as if he could be Native American. "Do you know where Mr. Bednarik is?"

"Sorry, no. He must have been held up somewhere," the dark-haired man said, then held out a hand. "I'm Jim Twomoons." He nodded at his coworker, who was opening the back of the truck. "That's Curly Slowe. It looks like you bought top of the line."

"I did?" Judith gulped. She knew that because she needed a large refrigerator it would cost more. But she didn't know how much. "What's the bottom line?"

Jim Twomoons reached into the truck's cab and brought out a clipboard. "With delivery and installation, it's three thousand, four hundred ninety-five dollars and twelve cents."

Judith blanched. "Goodness. I didn't think the total would come to more than two thousand." Suddenly, she remembered the cashier's check for thirty-five hundred dollars back at the casino. "Oh, well. It's a nice one, right?"

"The best," Jim assured her. "You want to open up for us?"

Judith obliged. As she entered the kitchen, it seemed like days, rather than a little more than twenty-four hours, since she'd been inside the house. In truth, nothing much had changed, which annoyed Judith. Except for the new backsplashes, she couldn't see that Bart Bednarik had made much progress during the Flynns' absence.

Jim and Curly pushed the big fridge down the back hallway and into the kitchen.

"We'll pull the old one," Jim said. "We'll also take it away."

"Good," Judith said. "Not all appliance companies do that."

"We aim to please," Jim declared.

Judith left the men to their task. The long living room felt more spacious than ever with several pieces of furniture at the upholsterer's. The matching white sofas in front of the fireplace had been soiled beyond redemption by the firefighters. Judith didn't mind. They were worn in numerous places, as were the three side chairs. She'd chosen navy—the same shade she'd originally picked out for the house—to re-cover the sofas, blue florals for two of the side chairs, and Chinese red for the third.

She was about to dial Bart Bednarik's cell phone when Jim entered the living room. "We've got a problem," he said, actually looking as if it mattered to him as well as to Judith. "The electrician hasn't completed his work with the refrigerator outlet."

Judith grimaced. "He was supposed to be here today. That's why I came back to town from the Lake Stillasnowamish Resort Casino."

Jim grinned. "Is that where you folks are staying? I'm a Stillasnowamish myself."

"Really?" Judith's annoyance faded momentarily. "You probably know some of the people who work at the casino."

"Sure," Jim replied. "We're a small tribe. And Cold & Cool put in all their refrigeration units. I spent two weeks working there before they opened. The folks who run the resort are nice people, good people."

"Yes, they're very nice. Do you live near the resort, by any chance?"

Jim shook his head. "I never did. My folks moved to the city before I was born."

Judith figured that Jim Twomoons hadn't heard about the tragedy yet. Apparently, Salome's murder hadn't made the news, no doubt because Pancho Green and the tribal elders were still keeping the lid on the story. "I'm going to call Bart to see where on earth he is," Judith said. "I'd also like to know what's happened to the electrician. Frankly, I'm not happy with either of them."

"Oh, Mrs. Flynn," Jim said with a small smile, "I'm sure they have their reasons for not being here yet. Trouble of some sort, I'd guess. Freeway tie-ups, family crises, maybe even an illness. You can't be too hard on folks."

"You're more understanding than I am," Judith retorted.

"It's part of our culture. We know it drives people crazy some-times," Jim went on with a disarming smile, "but we always think the best of other people. It's one of the ways we keep in tune with nature and the earth. And you know, most of the time we're right. Very few folks are out to deliberately upset other folks. Things happen, things we can't foresee. We have a saying, 'Only the flicker knows.' It usu-ally means something bad will—"

The phone on the cherrywood table rang. Judith gave Jim an apologetic look and picked up the receiver.

"Mrs. Flynn?" It was Bart Bednarik, with a bad connection. "I'm stuck on the other side of the lake. There's an overturned van on the floating bridge. Has Artie Chow shown up yet?"

"Is Artie the electrician?" Judith thought Bart had said he was, but the crackling in her ear made it difficult to understand. "Just get here as soon as you can. And find Artie." Frustrated, she clicked off.

"Trouble?" Jim asked in his usual mild tone.

"Yes." Judith sighed. "You were right—there's a wreck on the floating bridge. Bart's stuck in traffic."

"There you go," Jim said. "It's not poor Bart's fault."

"So where's Artie?" Judith inquired with a glum expression.

"Maybe he's stuck, too," Jim suggested. "Curly and I'll load up the old fridge while we're waiting."

Judith stayed in the living room. Of course, the workmen would be charging by the hour. And sometimes it took hours to clear up a wreck on the bridge. She paced the living room, taking an occasional side trip to the front door to see if Artie Chow had shown up. Finally, she went upstairs to check the guest rooms.

All was well. Room 1, which had borne the brunt of the fire, had been re-wallpapered with a whimsy of butterflies and blossoms. The new lace curtains and bed linens carried out the theme with more butterflies. Judith was pleased with the result.

The five other guest rooms also had fresh paint and wallpaper, ranging in patterns from Japanese peonies to the French countryside. Judith had just closed the door on room 6 when she heard Jim Twomoons calling to her. Taking the back stairs, she found Jim in the hallway, by the pantry.

"I feel terrible about this," he said, "but we're going to have to go now. We have a delivery to make across the ship canal at eleven forty-five. We'll come back after that."

"Oh, please do!" Judith exclaimed, all but groveling. "I'm sure the electrician will be here by then."

Ruefully, Judith watched the refrigerator truck drive out of the cul-de-sac. She was on her way back to the kitchen when the phone rang. This time she answered it on its base by the sink.

"Me again," said Bart Bednarik, who had managed to lose the static of the previous call. "I hadn't gotten onto the bridge yet when I phoned you earlier, so I decided to drive around the lake. I'm making much better time."

"Good," Judith said in relief. "How soon will you be here?"

"Well . . . that's the thing. I won't be at your place today after all."

"What?"

"Hey, don't blame me," he retorted as Judith heard the hum of traffic in the background. "Here's the deal. You know the van that overturned on the bridge?"

"No, I don't," Judith replied coldly. "What about it?"

"Artie Chow was driving it. He's on his way to the hospital with a possible broken collarbone. I got a call from his office just a couple of minutes ago. It looks like I'll have to find another electrician."

"Will he be okay?" Judith asked, feeling slightly more pity for Artie than for herself.

"Sure, sure, Artie's tough," Bart asserted. "But he won't be able to work for a while, and he runs a one-man show when it comes to older houses like yours. It won't be easy, but I'll see what I can do."

Judith held her head with the hand that wasn't holding the phone. "Can you get one by the time Jim and Curly get back to install the fridge?"

"Screw you, moron!" Bart yelled.

"I beg your pardon?" Judith's temper was about to explode.

"Sorry, some guy in an SUV cut me off. What time are the guys due back?"

Judith glanced at the old schoolhouse clock that was lying on the kitchen counter. It was just after eleven-thirty. "One o'clock?" she ventured.

"Oh, boy . . . I doubt it. Anybody who's any good is all sewed up for the day. Maybe for two or three days. I'll have to get back to you on that. Got to go, I'm pulling in for my lunch break." Bart rang off.

Judith was fit to be tied, in a quandary and wishing she'd gone to Antarctica where she'd be cold but at least she'd be incommunicado. Sitting in the chair by her computer, she tried to figure out her next move. Worse yet, she was hungry and there was no food in the house.

She was still calculating her options when the attack came. Her assailant jumped on her back, sank his claws into her flesh, and let out a fierce battle cry.

"Sweetums, you beast!" Judith cried, frantically trying to get the cat to loosen his hold.

"Mee-ooww-rr!" Sweetums growled as Judith finally freed herself and held the animal in front of her.

"Hey, I'm sorry we had to go away," she said, gasping for breath. "You're supposed to be having fun with the Dooley kids."

Sweetums spat in Judith's face, wriggled free, and landed on the kitchen floor where he sat with his tail curled around him and scornfully stared at Judith with his beady eyes.

Judith stared back. The contest went on for almost a full minute before Judith surrendered and looked away. With a triumphant swish of his plumelike tail, Sweetums sashayed out to the pantry.

"Why not?" Judith murmured. She followed the cat, retrieved a can of his favorite food, and took it over to the electric can opener on the far counter. Nothing happened. Judith had forgotten that the electricity in the kitchen was turned off. Rummaging in a drawer, she found her old-fashioned manual can opener.

"I feel like joining you," she said, filling a bowl with cat food.

The phone rang again. "Bart here," he said, sounding as if his mouth was full. "We got lucky. Hardy Mills can come out tomorrow morning."

Judith hesitated. "That's the best you can do?"

"Yep. Hardy's a good one, as good as Artie."

Hardy and Artie, Artie and Hardy. Judith's headache had returned at full strength. "I guess that's what we'll have to do," she said with a sigh.

"One little problem, though," Bart said. "I got hold of Jim and Curly. They can't make it tomorrow, they're booked solid with some condos in the north end. They'll try to be at your place first thing Thursday morning."

"Okay." There seemed no room for argument. "Let me know of any more changes. What's happening with the countertop? That's why I came back to the city, remember?"

"The countertop?" Bart sounded baffled. "Oh—*that* countertop. I'm waiting for a jingle from Ansonia Appliance. They're the only ones in town who might have the size you want in their warehouse. I should hear back by two. If they've got it, we can drive out to the south end and have a look-see."

"What's the point in me looking at it if that's the only one available?" Judith demanded.

Bart didn't respond right away. "You got a point. None, I guess. But what if you don't like it? We're back to square one. If it's wrong, you still might sue me."

"No," Judith said in a dead-calm voice. "I won't sue you. But if that countertop isn't in by tomorrow, I will kill you."

"Can you put that in writing?" Bart responded. "The part about not suing me, I mean."

"If you have a countertop installed in twenty-four hours, I will. Meanwhile," Judith went on, eyeing the aspirin bottle on the window-sill above the sink, "what else should be done around here today?"

"Oh, boy—I don't know. We've got everything pretty well in hand. Except for the plumbing, of course. I'll have to get back to you on that."

"Do that," Judith snapped. "We want everything completed by the weekend, when we return from the resort."

"We'll see what we can do," Bart said. "Decisions, decisions. Life's rough."

"What decisions now?"

"My pie. It's apple. Ice cream or cheese? What to do, what to do?"

"Just do something, and do it as soon as you finish your damned pie," Judith all but shouted and slammed the phone back into the cradle.

Reaching for the aspirin bottle, she cursed Bart for having sent her on a fool's errand. She'd driven all the way into the city for nothing. Judith got a glass out of the cupboard and turned on the tap.

No water flowed. She'd forgotten that the plumbing had also been shut off.

Judith arrived back at the Lake Stillasnowamish Resort Casino shortly after two. She hadn't seen Bob Bearclaw when she'd left that morning, but he was on duty now, and greeted her with a big smile and a tip of his doorman's cap.

"Mrs. Flynn," he said as she handed her keys to one of the valets. "I heard you had to go back to the city. Is everything all right?"

Judith grimaced. "Not really." Noting a look of concern on Bob's face, she tried to smile. "I mean, it's nothing tragic. We're renovating our house, and there are so many complications. It's very frustrating."

"Oh, yes. But," Bob continued, "a true test of patience and perseverance. Like all troubling experiences, it will strengthen you."

"I suppose," Judith said dubiously. Since she was about to pass out from hunger, she felt anything but strong. "Would you know where I might find my husband?"

Bob wore a slight frown. "No, I'm sorry to say I don't know where Mr. Flynn is. The last I saw of him was around noon, eating lunch in the coffee shop with Mr. Green, Mr. Fromm, and Jack Jackrabbit. Would you like me to have him paged?"

"No, I'm going to have some lunch myself first. Thank you, Bob." Judith started up the stone steps, then turned as if an afterthought had struck her. "Do you know if there are any new developments in the homicide case?"

Bob smiled in a deferential manner. "I couldn't really say, Mrs. Flynn. I'm sorry."

Couldn't or wouldn't? Judith wondered as she entered the casino. Bob Bearclaw seemed to know more than he was letting on. But as a resort employee, discretion would be his byword.

Judith decided it would be faster to eat from the twenty-four-hour buffet than to go to the coffee shop. She followed the arrows on the sign above her head and started in the direction that took her past the conference rooms just beyond the lobby. Apparently, the graphic designers were on a break. The corridor was crowded with people sipping beverages in paper and plastic cups. Moving slowly through the congestion, she spotted Aunt Deb in her wheelchair, chatting with a half dozen people. Not knowing how to address her aunt under the circumstances, Judith made her way around the edge of the gathering in order not to be seen.

She wasn't quick enough.

"Yoo-hoo, Judith," Aunt Deb called. "Come meet some very dear people."

Obediently, Judith hoofed it over to her aunt. A quick glance informed her that Deb was indeed passing herself off as her daughter. The name tag on her green dress read "Serena Jones, Ca-Jones Designs."

Adroitly, Aunt Deb made the introductions. All but one of the group—a gray-haired man in tweeds—was at least forty years younger than Judith's aunt.

"Isn't this nice?" Aunt Deb enthused. "I've met such lovely people."

"That's wonderful, Aunt . . . Serena," Judith said. Judging from the smiles on the designers' faces, they thought it was wonderful, too.

"They're all very clever," Aunt Deb declared. "I hope I can hold my own on the panel this afternoon."

Judith tried to hide her surprise. "You're on a panel?"

"Yes," Aunt Deb responded with a little laugh. "We're discussing innovation. And," she added with a sharp look at Judith, "concepts."

"That sounds right up your alley," Judith said, giving her aunt's shoulder a squeeze.

"Oh, yes," put in a young man with a shaved head, "Ms. Jones pointed out to us that we overuse the word 'concept,' and that it doesn't always mean what we think it does."

"Not to mention," added a plump black woman who was young enough to be Aunt Deb's great-granddaughter, "she keeps us in high spirits. Ms. Jones is s-o-o-o good natured."

"Yes, she is," Judith agreed, wondering what might have happened if Gertrude had attended the conference instead of Aunt Deb. "I'm pleased to meet you all. Enjoy the conference," she said, starting to walk away.

"Judith," Aunt Deb called out. "If you see . . . Debbie, tell her to put on an extra sweater. It seems a bit cool this afternoon."

"I'll tell her," Judith promised, nodding and smiling as she left her aunt's coterie.

The buffet line was mercifully short. Within five minutes, Judith had her plate filled and was looking for an empty table. Out of the corner of her eye, she spotted Griselda Vanderbehr eating alone on the other side of the dining room.

Judith made a beeline for Freddy Polson's assistant. "Hi," she said, sitting down across from the other woman. "I had to go back into the city, so I don't know the latest with the investigation. Can you fill me in?"

Grisly looked suspicious. "Why?"

Judith assumed her most helpless expression. "I haven't had time since I got back to see Joe." She pointed at her plate. "I missed lunch."

Grisly remained skeptical. "What were you doing in the city?"

"I had to see about a counter—" Judith feigned a cough. "Well, not exactly a counterculture. That's the wrong choice of words. I was looking into Stillasnowamish customs with one of the tribal members who met me at my house." As fibs went, Judith thought, it wasn't the worst one she'd ever told.

"Oh." The suspicion began to ebb from Grisly's face. "What has that got to do with Sally's murder?"

Judith swallowed a bite of ham. "It helps Joe to better understand the Native-American witnesses. I often do research for him when he's working a case." True enough, even if Joe rarely requested his wife's aid.

"I suppose that makes sense," Grisly remarked, though she still didn't look entirely convinced.

"Do you know where Joe is?" Judith inquired. "I should meet up with him as soon as I finish lunch."

Grisly put aside her half-eaten slice of lemon meringue pie. "Try Pancho Green's office on the second floor. That's where they moved the investigation. The greenroom is needed for the replacement act."

Judith was surprised. "They already booked another act?"

Grisly nodded before lighting a cigarette. "There's always somebody on standby. This time it's a Country & Western band. The cabaret's dark tonight anyway since we get Tuesdays off."

"I must admit," Judith said in a musing tone, "this case has me stumped."

"Really?" Grisly didn't sound very interested in Judith's reaction.

"It's the timing," Judith continued, ignoring the look of indifference on her companion's face. "The lights went out before Salome—

Sally—was killed. She was there for her turn with the cabinet and the sabers after the power came back on. So how did her body get into the Corvette on the casino floor?"

Grisly shrugged. "That's what everybody'd like to know."

"It seems to me," Judith said in a humble voice, "there's only one answer to that."

"Really?" Grisly repeated, still not exhibiting much curiosity.

"Of course." Judith's dark eyes fixed on the other woman's thin face. "That wasn't Salome who appeared in the second part of the act. It must have been an impostor."

Chapter Seven

"THAT'S impossible," Grisly scoffed. "Freddy would've known if someone had impersonated Sally."

Judith sipped from her diet 7-UP. "It's the logical explanation. I firmly believe in logic."

Grisly frowned into space. When she spoke, she seemed to be talking to herself. "It can't be. Freddy and Sally worked together for years, they'd been married, they'd known each other forever. He could never make such a mistake. Unless . . ." Grisly clapped her hands to her face.

"Yes?" Judith coaxed.

But the other woman defiantly shook her head. "No. It's not possible."

"What's not possible?"

What little color Grisly had in her cheeks drained away as she stood up. "It doesn't matter. It was an insane idea." None too steadily, she walked away from Judith.

Pancho Green's office was at the end of the corridor. The stained-cedar door was surrounded by frosted glass with etchings of trees, birds, and mountains. Upon entering, Judith saw Emily, the security guard, behind the receptionist's desk.

"Hi, Mrs. Flynn," Emily said with a smile that showed off her dimple. "Are you looking for Mr. Flynn?"

"I am," Judith replied. She gestured at a door on her right. "Is he in there?"

Emily nodded. "He's with Mr. Green and Mr. Fromm and Jack Jackrabbit. Oh, Freddy Polson is there, too. Have you met him yet?"

"No," Judith said. "Maybe I should do that now." She started for the door, then turned back. "Are you the regular receptionist?"

Emily shook her head. "They—Mr. Green and Mr. Jackrabbit— felt that someone from security should be up here during the investigation. The regular receptionist has been put in charge of making sure there are no leaks to the press. The publicity would be terrible."

Judith thought of her own bouts of bad publicity. "It could," she hedged, though Hillside Manor's reputation hadn't yet suffered irreparable damage.

"Mr. Green knows he can't stall forever," Emily explained, "but he's trying to buy just a few days in the hope of solving the case."

"That's understandable." Anxious to enter the inner office, Judith made no further comment. She was turning the doorknob when Emily spoke up in an uncertain voice:

"Are you sure it's okay for you to join them?"

"Oh, sure," Judith declared, and breezed through the door.

Through a cloud of cigarette and cigar smoke, the five men at the long oval table stared at Judith.

"Hi." She smiled at the ten curious eyes. She recognized Freddy Polson, though he looked sallow without his stage makeup. His mustache was also missing, and his brown hair looked much thinner. Judith assumed the other man was Jack Jackrabbit. He was about Freddy's age, also dark, but with more hair and slightly broader facial features.

"What are you doing here?" Joe asked in a deceptively mild tone.

"Trying to find you," Judith replied, equally benign. She sat down in one of the empty chairs. "How's everything going?"

Joe stood up. "We were just about to take a break. Come on, we'll go down to the coffee shop. I skimped on lunch. You can tell me all about what's going on back at the house."

Judith didn't budge. "Oh, Joe, please introduce me to these people I don't know. They'll think I'm standoffish if you don't."

Reluctantly, Joe gestured at the sallow-faced young man first. "This is Freddy Polson, the Great Mandolini."

Freddy half-rose and extended his hand. "I don't feel so great right now. I'm really upset."

Pancho put a hand on the illusionist's back. "You have a right to be, Freddy. Even if your marriage to Sally didn't work out, you still made a terrific team onstage."

Freddy seemed to be looking past Judith. "I don't know what I'll do without her."

"You have my greatest sympathy," Judith responded, feeling Freddy's cold, limp hand in hers. She turned to the fourth man. "You must be Mr. Jackrabbit."

"That's right," Jack said, also shaking Judith's hand. Unlike Freddy, Jack possessed a firm grip. His expression was polite, but his eyes were slightly hooded. *Maybe,* Judith thought, *the shielded eyes helped Jack deflect the bad things that people did.* A detective, no matter what his ethnic origins or his tribal beliefs, couldn't always think the best of others.

"I can't wait to hear how the investigation is progressing," Judith said, exercising her most engaging smile for Jack. "Unless . . ." She darted a quick glance at her glowering husband. "Unless you'd rather tell me yourself. I mean, you're in charge here, right?"

"At this point," Jack replied modestly. "The FBI will have to come in soon, I'm afraid."

"Does that mean you already have a suspect?" Judith inquired, her dark eyes round with feigned surprise.

Jack hesitated as Joe gave him a warning look and Pancho shifted uneasily in his chair. "I'll let Mr. Flynn fill you in," Jack finally said.

Joe clamped a hand on Judith's arm, but his voice was light. "Will do. Come along, my darling, I yearn for a cheeseburger and fries."

"Okay, okay," Judith said when they were in the corridor. "Let go." She yanked her arm out of her husband's grasp. "I don't see why you're being such a pill about this murder case. It isn't as if we haven't worked together before. What about the homicide that ruined the B&B and put us in this mess to begin with? Didn't I figure out who the killer was before you did?"

"A lucky break," Joe retorted, punching the elevator button with unusual force. "You're a killer magnet. If I hadn't gone to the hardware store that morning to get a new hinge for the kitchen cupboard . . ."

The elevator doors slid open, revealing the stout figure of Inga Polson. "Where's my brother?" she demanded, charging at Joe like a bulldozer.

"In Pancho's office," Joe said, trying in vain to reach around Inga to hold the door.

"What are you doing to him?" Inga growled in her deep voice. Frantically, she rubbed at her hands. "Freddy's very sensitive. He's an *artiste*."

"Jack Jackrabbit is merely asking some questions," Joe said as the elevator doors closed. "Freddy's fine. Go see for yourself."

Inga's small eyes narrowed. She shook a finger in Joe's face. "Don't think I don't know what's going on around here. It's a conspiracy, that's what it is. I've already called our attorney."

"You're jumping the gun," Joe said calmly. "Freddy's a witness, that's all. His ex-wife, his partner in the act, has been killed. I'm told they were still friends. Who'd know better than Freddy why someone might have wanted her dead?"

"It's obvious who killed Sally," Inga declared, raking her nails over her hands in agitation. "I know; Mr. Fromm knows. But Freddy's naive. It's because he's an *artiste*. He's sensitive."

"I believe you mentioned that," Joe murmured, nimbly stepping around Inga to poke the elevator button again.

"Freddy should never have let them question him without me," Inga huffed, finally moving away. "I wouldn't have left him alone this afternoon, but I was exhausted after last night. I had to rest. I'm not as strong as I look."

"I hope not," Joe said under his breath as Inga stomped off toward Pancho's office. "That woman is driving us nuts."

"How come?" Judith asked as another elevator arrived.

"She's too damned protective of her kid brother," Joe responded, poking the button for the main floor. "I get the impression she practically raised Freddy herself."

As Joe seemed to open up a bit, Judith's annoyance faded. "What happened to their parents?"

Joe shrugged as they got out of the elevator and headed for the coffee shop. "I gather they died young. Freddy and Inga are from Shoshone, Idaho, originally. So's Sally, who was a neighbor. And Griselda Vanderbehr. Their acquaintanceship dates back to grade school, I think."

"They all go back a long way," Judith remarked.

"Right." Joe stopped short of the hostess desk where an auburn-haired young woman offered the Flynns a welcoming smile before leading them to a window table.

Judith decided to keep her questions people oriented. "Have you met Sally's second husband, Manny Quinn?"

Behind the big plastic menu, Joe nodded.

"What's he like?"

Joe seemed absorbed in the menu's selections. He didn't speak until a pink-cheeked waitress appeared. "I'll have the bacon burger with fries, and a green salad. Bleu cheese dressing, coffee, and whatever my lovely bride here would like."

"I just ate," Judith said, "but I'll have some coffee, please."

The waitress, who could smile as well as the rest of the hired help, darted away. Judith persevered. "What did you think of Manny Quinn?"

"Manny?" Joe removed his reading glasses. "He strikes me as a bit of a hustler, but he seemed pretty shaken by his wife's death. They'd only been married a year or so."

"I had lunch at the buffet, with Grisly," Judith remarked. "She was shocked by my idea."

"What idea?"

Judith shrugged. "That Sally was killed during the power failure."

"Oh." Joe yawned.

"Don't you agree?"

"It could play out that way," Joe allowed.

"So whoever the blonde was in the second half of the performance, she was an impostor, right?"

"Maybe so," Joe said without much enthusiasm.

Judith tried to hide her exasperation. "What do you think?"

"Time of death is hard to establish within, say, thirty minutes to an hour. According to Doc Engelman, Sally could have been killed anytime between nine and ten."

"Is this Engelman reliable?" Judith queried.

"Jack and Pancho think so," Joe replied as their beverages arrived. "He's not a tribal member, but he lives around here, near the family cabin. Engelman's retired, but he served as county coroner a few years ago. He keeps his hand in by caring for the Stillasnowamish people."

"It can't be that hard to fix the time of death," Judith asserted. "We saw Sally with our own eyes, at least until . . ." She thought back to the last moment she'd gotten a really good look at the whirling, twirling Salome. "Maybe we really didn't see her after the power failure."

Joe evinced mild interest. "You're saying the woman who got in the cabinet and who reappeared was an impostor?"

"Exactly. It had to be that way." Judith's voice was gaining momentum. "It's the only explanation for how Sally's corpse got into the 'Vette."

Joe frowned. "Freddy would have noticed if Salome wasn't Sally."

"Unless he was in on the plot to kill her. Or had already killed her himself while he was offstage. In fact," Judith went on, "what if Freddy's spiel in the dark was a recording? He could have been murdering Sally and getting rid of her body."

Joe considered the idea. "Not impossible. But who impersonated Sally then? Griselda Vanderbehr's too thin. Micki Mendoza's too short. Inga Polson's too heavy. Besides, she was seated in the audience."

"Did you watch her the whole time? I didn't," Judith pointed out. "Oh, I know she couldn't have impersonated Sally because of her size. But with all that cape twirling, the audience didn't get a really good look at her."

"Something's not right," Joe said with a shake of his head. "After the saber thrusts and the cabinet was open again, we all saw Sally standing there in her silver dress without the cape."

"I know." Judith sighed. "It's really a puzzle. And why did Pancho and Lloyd roll out the cabinet in the first place? The stagehands did all the other grunt work before that."

"The stagehands had been called out to help on the casino floor during the power failure," Joe replied. "They hadn't come back yet. Pancho and Lloyd filled in for them."

"Did they take the cabinet away after the curtain fell?"

"No," Joe said. "There's some confusion about who did. Pancho got paged to check out a possible cheater at the blackjack tables. Lloyd was working on that weird musical instrument of his."

"The theremin," Judith remarked absently. "Where were Grisly and Micki at the end of the performance?"

"They met Freddy when he came offstage. They always do that, at least since Freddy got engaged to Micki." Joe gazed through the window at the cedar trees. The March rain was still fitful. A stiff breeze made the evergreen branches sway like a hula skirt. "At this point," Joe finally said, looking back at his wife, "I feel stumped."

Judith's expression softened at the unexpected admission. "You're never stumped," she declared. "Or do you mean stymied?"

"Either. Both." Joe accepted his bacon burger, fries, and salad from the waitress. "Jack Jackrabbit's frustrated, too. I guess it's time to call in the feds."

"Have you found the weapon?" Judith asked, filching a fry from Joe's plate.

Joe nodded. "It was one of those sabers that Freddy uses in his act. It was hidden downstairs behind some scenery. Unfortunately, Freddy has six of those things as backup. His prints are all over them; so are those belonging to other members of the company. For all we know, the killer could have worn . . ." Joe stopped speaking as a fair-haired young man with a scraggly goatee came up to the table. "Hi, Lloyd," Joe said in greeting. "What's up?"

"Not much," the young man replied, a doleful look on his faintly pockmarked face. "Bummer, eh?"

"It is at that," Joe allowed. "Want to sit down? I don't believe you've met my wife, Judith."

Lloyd sat down next to Joe and reached across the table to shake Judith's hand. She recognized him from his number with the theremin. "You must be Freddy's assistant," she said with a smile. "I'm pleased to meet you. Where do you get your ideas?"

"Ohh . . ." Lloyd ran a hand through his longish, unkempt hair, which was no longer tied back in a ponytail. "Everywhere. Anywhere. You look." He held up his empty hand. "You see." He closed the hand and waved it around his head. "You look again." Lloyd's hand opened to reveal a deck of cards. He held them out, then put them in the front pocket of his denim jacket. "Like that."

Judith was bemused. "How did you do that?"

Lloyd wore an "aw-shucks" expression. "Easy. Think about it."

"It's fascinating," Judith asserted. "How long have you been creating illusions?"

Lloyd offered Judith a diffident smile. "Forever. Long, cold winters in Medicine Hat, Alberta. Imagination. That's how I amused myself. Then I'd try the tricks on family, chums."

"I think that's great," Judith enthused. "How did you get together with Freddy?"

"Sun Valley, three years ago." Lloyd ducked his head, as if embarrassed. "Freddy and Sally were there. Performing. I met them. Freddy was on his way up. He needed help with the creative part. He hired me. Here I am." Lloyd suddenly looked bleak. "But Sally isn't. I can't believe she's dead."

The waitress reappeared to ask for Lloyd's order, but it turned out that he hadn't come to eat. "I was looking for Manny," he explained to the Flynns. "Poor guy's all broken up. He and Sally were really in love."

"I haven't seen Manny since earlier today," Joe put in. "I take it he's making the funeral arrangements?"

Lloyd nodded once. "I guess. But Manny's from back east. I hope he doesn't have Sally buried there. Doesn't seem right, eh? She was a western girl."

"I'm sure her husband will do what he thinks is right," Judith remarked. "Are her parents still living?"

Lloyd shook his head. "Died in a tractor accident."

Judith frowned. "What happened?"

Lloyd screwed up his face, apparently in an attempt to remember. "Sally's dad was into tractor pull. Tractor got loose. Crushed him and his missus. Show business runs in the family."

And the tractor runs amok, Judith thought. Tractor pulls weren't her idea of show business, but she didn't comment except to murmur that it was a shame.

"Got to go," Lloyd said, standing up. "Manny may be in the casino. Nice meeting you, eh?"

"Witness or suspect?" Judith said after Lloyd was out of hearing range.

"Both." Joe wiped his mouth with a paper napkin. "Anybody connected to the act is a suspect."

"That's not such a long list," Judith remarked, counting off the people involved. "Lloyd, Grisly, Inga, Mr. Fromm—who did I leave out?"

"Micki Mendoza, for one. Freddy's girlfriend is also an aspiring performer." Joe looked at his place setting and scowled. "Where's my coffee?" He signaled for the waitress who was at the end of the aisle. "Coffee," he mouthed, pantomiming cup to lips.

"I forgot about Micki," Judith said as the waitress brought Joe his coffee, refilled Judith's cup, and presented the bill. "Is she another blonde?"

"No, she's got terrific long red hair. Of course," Joe added, "it might not be natural."

"True."

"And don't forget Manny Quinn," Joe reminded Judith. "A spouse is always suspect number one."

"I suppose," Judith mused after a pause, "alibis aren't worth much, since you don't know when the murder occurred."

Joe didn't bother to respond. "Really," Judith said after a lengthy silence, "I'd like to help. You know, talk to these people. It's my way."

"Uh-huh." Joe's response seemed ambiguous. He studied the bill, then put two silver dollars on the table for the tip. "Let's go. I should get back to the meeting."

The reservoir of goodwill that Joe had built up in the past half hour sprung a leak. "To what purpose?" Judith snapped, trailing her husband out to the cashier. "It sounds like you're getting nowhere. Why can't I at least talk to people?"

"Go ahead," Joe said as he waited for change. "I can't stop you, God knows. Besides, I'm going to suggest that we call in the feds. We should have done that right away."

"Then do it," Judith barked. "I'm going to do . . ." She wasn't sure what she would do. ". . . something," she finished on a lame note.

"Okay. See you." He brushed Judith's forehead with his lips.

"When?"

"Oh . . ." Joe glanced over his shoulder. "Six, six-thirty, in the room?"

"Fine." Judith purposely moved in the opposite direction, finding herself in the winter wonderland of dollar slot machines. She would have moved on if she hadn't spotted a young woman with flaming-red hair at a machine in the middle of the row. On a hunch, Judith sat down at the machine next to the redhead.

The machine featured different types of snowflakes and required three coins. Judith winced as she took a twenty out of her wallet. Then she glanced at the redhead's stash. Two grooved red containers must have held at least a hundred dollars apiece. They were almost full, and the redhead's tray was covered with coins. Judith got out another twenty. It was obvious that her neighbor wasn't going anywhere for a while. An investment would have to be made. Assuming, of course, the woman was Micki Mendoza.

Whoever the redhead was, she was stunning in an artificial sort of way. Her well-defined features were carefully, even lavishly made up, and the flaming-red hair was pulled back from her face to hang long and curly over her shoulders. She wore a short off-the-shoulder black dress with a wide ruffle at the top and another at the hem. Her black ankle-strap pumps had four-inch heels. They made Judith dizzy just to look at them.

"You're doing well," Judith remarked as more silver dollars rattled and clattered into the young woman's tray.

"It's okay," the redhead said with a shrug of her bare shoulders.

With a sense of recklessness, Judith pushed the Credit button. *Three dollars,* she thought. *Enough for two pounds of hamburger on sale at Falstaff's Grocery.* As she feared, no winning combination showed up on the center line. At least the different snowflakes were pretty.

She tried again. No luck. Six dollars gone. She could buy a flat of primroses for the planter on the front porch with that money.

"Have you been playing your machine long?" Judith inquired of the redhead.

"What?" The woman turned to Judith. "Oh. Half an hour, maybe. I don't keep track of time." The redhead struck more gold.

Judith struck out. Nine dollars wasted. She could have bought a big pot roast for that price.

"Maybe I should try the machine on your other side," Judith remarked. "I'm told that slots next to each other can both be hot."

The redhead didn't look up. "Yeah, that's what they say. It's bull."

"Really? I'm new at this, so I'll take your word for it. I might as well stay put."

No response. No luck, either. For twelve dollars, Judith could have bought an azalea tree for the backyard.

"Have you won the big jackpot?" Judith inquired.

"Are you kidding? The most I've gotten is the three grand firs. You have to get the evergreen symbols to win the ten grand."

"The grand firs must pay well," Judith said, craning her neck to look at the redhead's machines. "Oh, I see. It's all trees except for the symbol that says 'Evergreen Giant Jackpot.' Goodness," she went on, her eyes widening, "the grand firs are a grand."

"Right." The redhead didn't sound very enthusiastic. "Maybe I should have gone with Manny to play the Vernal Equinox high-roller machines. He swears they pay off. But fifteen bucks at once is a bit much. The last time I tried it, I lost three bills in five minutes."

Judith was puzzled. "Three bills?"

"A bill is a hundred dollars." Briefly, the redhead studied Judith. "You *must* be new to all this."

"I wasn't kidding," Judith admitted, then added with a humble expression, "I'm lucky I sat down next to somebody who knows what she's doing. My name's Judith."

"Hi. I'm Micki." She held out a hand that sported a large green emerald. The left hand displayed a brilliant marquis-cut diamond.

Judith hesitated. She wasn't sure how long she could play dumb about Micki's connection to the Mandolini ménage. The decision was made for her when she was almost pushed to the floor from behind.

"Ooops!" Two bright green–clad arms grasped wildly at Judith's chair. "Sorry!" cried Renie, struggling to regain her equilibrium. "Ooof!" Catching her breath, she bent down to pick up the quarters that had fallen out of her bucket. "Are you okay?"

"I'm fine, if startled," Judith replied. "What on earth are you doing?"

"Being startled by seeing you in the dollar section," Renie answered, now on her hands and knees to gather in the fallen coins. "What are you doing here? Sleuthing?"

Judith winced as Micki frowned at both cousins.

"I mean," Renie explained, finally standing up, "I couldn't imagine it was you being reckless with money. What's going on?"

Micki leaned forward in her chair to face Renie. "What did you say?"

Renie turned to look at the other woman. "Wow! That's some red hair you've got there. It looks like your head's on fire. Butt out, I'm talking to my cousin."

"Um," Judith intervened, "coz, this is Micki Mendoza."

Micki swung her head in Judith's direction. "How did you know my last name?"

"Ahh . . ." It was no good. A fib was useless at this point, especially since Renie looked blank. Judith had to confess. "My last name's Flynn. My husband, Joe, is helping with Sally's murder investigation."

"I knew it," Renie said under her breath.

Micki shot Judith an angry look. "So why didn't you say so in the first place?" She began scooping up silver dollars and dumping them in a bucket. "How did you know who I was? You did know, didn't you?"

"I guessed," Judith said, looking apologetic. "Because of your gorgeous hair."

Micki gestured at Renie, who still seemed puzzled. "Bucky here doesn't think it's so gorgeous."

"Hey," Renie said sharply, annoyed by the reference to her overbite, "so I'm sorry, okay? I thought you were some pushy intruder."

With an effort, Micki picked up all her coins. It was obvious that they were heavy. "I'm out of here," she announced.

The cousins watched her flounce away, the ruffles on her dress almost creating a breeze.

Renie turned to Judith. "Who the heck is Micki Mendoza and why do you care?"

"She's Freddy Polson's girlfriend. Or fiancée, I think."

Renie still looked mystified. "Who's Freddy Polson?"

Judith sighed. Obviously, Renie hadn't paid attention to anything that Judith had said about the murder case. "He's the Great Mandolini."

"Oh." Renie was a trifle shamefaced. "I guess I haven't taken in much of this murder thing."

"I guess not." Judith slammed the Credit button to retrieve her twenty-eight coins.

"I haven't seen you all day," Renie said, looking chagrined. "Or Joe. I called your mother around eleven. She told me you'd gone skiing."

"You knew that wasn't true," Judith said in a vexed voice. "I can't ski with these hips, and Joe never learned."

"I know, I know," Renie said, trotting along the aisle, behind Judith. "Where were you?"

Up ahead, Judith spotted the end of a horseshoe of high-stakes blackjack tables that didn't open until evening. "Let's sit," she said, though it took some effort for her to get onto the taller chair. "Let me start at the beginning." As succinctly as possible, she recounted her adventures back at the B&B. Renie looked suitably dismayed, surprised, and sympathetic in turn.

"That's awful," she finally declared. "What's worse, it's not all."

Judith was taken aback. "What do you mean?"

Renie took a deep breath. "We got a call this morning from the idiot who's working on the cabin. Armbuster has all sorts of questions and problems about that project. Bill drove down there around noon. He's not back yet, as far as I know."

"Did they pour the foundation yesterday?" Judith asked.

Renie shook her head. "It was too wet. But that's not the main problem. The ground's too soft, according to Armbuster. Apparently, he thinks the new building should be built about twenty yards farther from the river. That means it'll be closer to the highway. I wanted to consult with you before Bill took off, but neither you nor Joe was around. Bill had to get going so he wouldn't get back too late for his afternoon walk."

Judith checked her watch. "It's almost four-thirty. Where do you suppose he is?"

"I don't know. Maybe I should go up to the room to see if he's called. Now it's past his usual nap time."

As ever, Judith was impressed—and somewhat daunted—by Bill's disciplined schedule, especially in retirement. However, she was also concerned about the project at the cabin site.

"I suppose I ought to drive down there tomorrow," Judith said, more to herself than to her cousin. "If they go back too far, they could end up in that quicksand bog."

"True," Renie noted. "But that's really close to the highway."

Judith reflected—and remembered. When she and Renie were kids, they had ventured too far into the bog, which technically wasn't quicksand but mud from a pond that had all but evaporated. Judith had started to sink. At that time, the four cabins were intact, and much farther from the highway—and the bog—than after the flood swept away a goodly portion of family property. No one could hear them scream from the bog. It had been up to Renie—who'd been a small, skinny child—to haul Judith out of the quicksand. Somehow, she'd managed, but Judith had lost her new summer sandals, sucked into the muck. Since one of the few things that Gertrude and Deb agreed on was how to clothe their daughters—and which sales to frequent—Renie had the same pair. The surviving sandals had been a reminder of how close the cousins had come to disaster.

"What do you think?" Judith finally asked.

Renie was watching a middle-aged couple engaged in an argument. Gambling often brought out the worst in people, especially married couples. "About what?"

"About me driving down there tomorrow?"

Renie shrugged. "It's your project."

"Maybe I should just call Armbuster—I mean, Armstrong—to-night."

"That should work." Renie grinned as the wife slugged the hus-band with her heavy drawstring handbag. "Caught any killers lately?"

"No. And," Judith went on, distracted as she was by the husband who was trying to yank the handbag out of his wife's hands, "nobody else has, either."

"That's a shame," Renie said as a pit boss arrived to referee.

"You begged me not to give you any more money," the wife yelled at her husband. "You're not getting it now!"

"That was then, this is now!" the husband shouted back as the pit boss tried to restrain him.

Renie was trying to ignore the feuding couple. "Did you say Joe had gotten involved?"

Security had arrived, attempting to hustle husband and wife off in different directions.

"Never mind what I said!" the man called over his shoulder. "I've got a sure thing!"

"So do I," retorted his better half, "and it's in my purse!"

Before answering Renie, Judith watched the couple being escorted off the floor. Relative peace returned to the casino. "Yes," she finally said, "but he and the tribal detective aren't getting very far."

"Early days." Renie slipped off her chair. "I'd better check on Bill. Do you want to meet for dinner? I'm thinking coffee shop."

"How come? Aren't you winning?"

Renie held out her bucket, which didn't contain many more quarters than the ones she'd spilled on the floor. "That's it. It's been a bad day."

"That doesn't look good," Judith remarked. "What have you got in there? About six bucks?"

"That sounds right." Renie started to walk away, then stopped to speak over her shoulder. "Six-thirty, seven, if you want to meet us. Assuming I find Bill."

Renie seemed downcast, but Judith didn't feel sorry for her. Her cousin would have been much better off helping to solve the murder case than frittering her money away on the slots. As Judith stood up, a pang of guilt struck her. Without even trying—and using Renie's chip to boot—Judith had struck it rich. Maybe she should take it easy on her cousin.

On the other hand, Judith wasn't having much of a vacation, either. Now she had the cabin project to add to her list of worries. She found herself wandering toward the front of the casino. Through the glass doors, she saw that it had stopped raining. A breath of fresh air might give her an energy boost.

Stepping outside, she noticed Pancho Green talking to a man with slicked-back silver hair and long sideburns. Like Pancho, he was wearing an expensive suit, but Judith didn't recognize him as one of the pit bosses. The men were a few feet in front of her. Quietly, she crept closer to hear what they were saying.

". . . jump the gun," Pancho said with a scowl. "Besides, you'll only piss off the feds. You know what that could mean."

The other man seemed to recoil. He was taller and younger than Pancho, but not as broad. Judith guessed him to be in his late thirties, perhaps older. It was hard to tell with that silver hair.

"Are you threatening me?" the man shot back.

Pancho put out a hand, but didn't touch the other man. "Hell, no, Manny. Why would I do that?"

Bob Bearclaw appeared from the parking-valet kiosk. He paused, looking up from the drive to Pancho and his companion, who Judith figured must be Manny Quinn.

Manny's belligerent expression faded. "You wouldn't, I guess." He shot a wary glance at Judith. "What would you expect that old bag of a sister to say?"

"Come on, Manny . . ." Pancho began.

Bob Bearclaw had noiselessly approached the two men. "Your car will be right out," he said to Manny. Bob spoke as softly as he walked. Manny suddenly looked cowed. With his usual dignity, the doorman walked away.

"Thanks," Manny murmured, starting down the stairs. After two steps, he turned around and came back to Pancho. Leaning toward the casino manager, Manny Quinn's voice was low and harsh. "I don't care what anybody else says. I know damned well that Freddy killed my Sally, and by God, he'll pay—one way or another."

Chapter Eight

Tʜᴇ glass door swung out, almost knocking Judith down. Inga Polson's stout figure hurtled out of the casino, her harsh voice screaming at Manny Quinn.

"Get back here, you wretched man! Don't you dare leave!" Inga stood on the top step, bosom heaving, arms waving.

Manny looked up from the black Lexus the valet had brought out for him. "Stop it, Inga," he said in a hostile voice. "You're making a fool of yourself."

Pancho put a restraining hand on Inga's shoulder. "Let him go," he said softly.

Manny took the opportunity to duck inside his car. A moment later, he roared out of the drive and headed for the highway. Inga stood rooted to the spot, bristling with outrage.

"Go inside, have a drink," Pancho urged. "In fact, I'll go with you. I could use a drink myself."

He tried to steer Inga into the casino, but she refused to budge. "I want my car," she announced, wringing her hands. "I want it now!"

Pancho tightened his grip on Inga's shoulder. "Don't. You're in no state to drive, especially on these winding roads. It's going to rain again, and it might be mixed with some snow."

Inga tried to yank herself away, but Pancho's grasp was firm. "What are you, the weatherman? I want to know what that loser is up to! I don't trust Manny Quinn an inch!"

Judith noticed that Bob Bearclaw had kept his back turned to the embattled pair. But when Inga kicked Pancho in the shins, forcing him to loosen his hold, Bob turned just in time to block the angry woman's path down the stairs.

"Now, Ms. Polson," he said gently, "you need to take a deep breath. Smell the evergreens, listen to the wind, look up at the passing clouds. Become one with nature. You'll feel much better."

Waving her fist, Inga started to speak, but stopped. To Judith's surprise, she did exactly as Bob had suggested: a deep breath, a tilt of her head, a glance at the sky. The gaze she settled on the doorman was far from serene, however.

"So I've done it," she said sharply. "Now what?"

Bob merely smiled.

"Well?" Inga pressed.

Bob turned away to assist an SUV filled with new arrivals. Inga stared at him for a moment, then stomped back up the stairs. Pancho had disappeared. Intent upon the scene between Freddy's sister and the casino doorman, Judith hadn't noticed Pancho leave.

"Well?" Inga demanded as she reached the top step. "What are you looking at?"

"Nothing," Judith replied innocently. "I came outside for some air."

"I can't say that I think much of your husband as a detective," Inga declared, scratching at her hands. "He won't listen to a word I say."

"That doesn't sound like Joe," Judith responded. Joe was an excellent listener, trained to hear each syllable, every nuance. "Why do you say that?"

"Because I know who killed Sally," Inga said so loudly that the new-comers from the SUV turned to stare as they came up the steps.

Judith maintained her innocent expression. "Who?"

Inga narrowed her eyes at Judith. "Why should I tell you? I've already told your husband at least six times. He ignores me."

"Do you have any proof?" Judith inquired. "Joe's a professional, he believes in hard evidence."

"Evidence!" Inga threw both hands up in the air. Judith noticed that they were red and raw. The woman must be a nervous wreck. "Why do you have to have evidence when the truth is plain as the nose on your face?"

"Then tell me who killed Sally," Judith said simply.

Inga's shrewd eyes studied Judith closely. "Why should I trust you? You're not involved in the investigation."

"That's not precisely true," Judith replied. "Joe always discusses his cases with me." Most of the time. Occasionally. The truth was in there somewhere. "As a matter of fact, we talked about the investigation shortly before I came outside." That was definitely true. Judith felt very virtuous.

Inga, however, shook her head. "I can't. I don't know you. I can't trust you. I'm not even sure I should trust your husband. He seems to be a friend of Pancho."

Judith shivered as the wind picked up. "What's wrong with Pancho?"

"Never mind," Inga said, starting for the entrance. "You ask too many questions." She bustled on inside.

Judith remained near the door. She didn't want Inga to think she was following her. The wind in the evergreens blew harder. Judith heard the cry of a flicker in one of the nearby cedars. She looked up but couldn't spot the bird.

Bob Bearclaw was looking up, too. He stood very still for several seconds, then shook his head and walked on.

Judith shivered again.

"Bill went straight to bed," Renie announced, meeting Judith just inside the casino. "I haven't talked to him yet. He was out for the count. I'll wake him around six if he isn't up by then."

"Coz," Judith said in a humble tone, "as long as you're losing, why not take a break and brainstorm with me? I think I'm making some progress."

Renie looked puzzled. "With . . . ?"

"The homicide case," Judith replied, now no longer humble, but irritated. "Let's have a drink and talk."

Renie looked at her watch. "Okay, but I have to collect Mom from the conference at five-thirty. That gives us half an hour."

The cousins proceeded to the Autumn Bar, where realistic maple, cottonwood, alder, and mountain-ash leaves formed a canopy of every imaginable fall color. They sat down at a small round table set on a pedestal that looked like a real tree stump.

"What do you remember about the magic act?" Judith asked.

Renie looked intentionally vague. "That it was long? That I was bored? That the lights went out? That the live Salome turned into a dead salami?"

"That's crass," Judith remarked.

"It's also true, or we wouldn't be sitting here like a couple of dopes trying to figure out how Salome got that way." Renie paused to give her order as a young man placed two coasters on the table. "You're trying to sucker me into this thing, coz," Renie went on after the waiter had left with both beverage requests. "Which means, I surmise, that you're stuck. Joe's not sharing."

"He is and he isn't," Judith replied as a middle-aged blonde sat down with her poodle at an adjacent table. "The problem is, Joe and the other detective, Jack Jackrabbit, are feeling frustrated. Joe wants to call in the FBI."

"Isn't that the usual way since the reservation's on federal land?"

"I guess so." Judith watched the blonde insist on a coaster for her poodle. The large dog wore a rhinestone-studded collar and looked as if he—or she—had been clipped recently.

"Fou-Fou drinks only French wines," the woman declared. "She prefers a Pinot Gris from the Loire Valley."

Renie turned to see what had captured Judith's attention. Apparently, the waiter, whose back was turned to the cousins, had demurred about serving alcoholic beverages to a dog.

"Nonsense!" the woman retorted with a snap of her fingers. "I've never once known Fou-Fou to overindulge! Her behavior is impeccable. And in human years, she's over twenty-one."

"Does she have a driver's license?" the waiter inquired with a straight face.

"Of course not! She can't pass the written exam. Now be a good lad and see that Fou-Fou is served."

The waiter said something that seemed to temporarily appease the woman. With a faint shake of his head, he went back to the bar.

"She prefers a bowl, of course," the woman called after him. "Leaded crystal."

"Hoo, boy," Renie murmured, turning around to face Judith. "And you think we're nuts because Clarence wears swimming trunks."

"He's a rabbit," Judith pointed out.

"So?"

Judith's Scotch and Renie's bourbon arrived before the cousins could launch into a discussion of the Joneses' weird menagerie, which included a dwarf Holland lop, a stuffed ape named Oscar, and a small, cheerful doll who always accompanied any family member headed for the hospital. There was also another doll named Cleo who was said to be a rabid Oakland Raider fan and swore like a sailor. Or a Raider fan, which was much worse.

"Let's get focused," Judith said with a serious expression. "Think back to the performance, and don't make any smart cracks. Tell me what you saw."

"Oh, jeez," Renie cried, "all of it?"

"No," Judith replied, "just from after the power failure."

"Okay." Renie took a sip from her drink, then gazed up into the autumn foliage as if it were a cluster of tea leaves she could read. "Mandolini was still blabbing about the history of illusion."

"Was he in the same place he'd been when we left to go to the rest room?"

"You mean onstage? Yes, toward the front. Why?"

"Just asking."

The waiter returned to the adjacent table with a glass of wine and a glass bowl, possibly not made of leaded crystal. The blonde, however, seemed content. So did Fou-Fou, who immediately began slurping up the bowl's contents.

"I'll bet that's not really wine," Renie said.

"You may be right. Come on," Judith urged, "concentrate."

"Mandolini went offstage," Renie resumed. "The guy with the theremin came on, downstage. Then we had snow or something and Mandolini reappeared to announce the"—Renie grimaced—"death-defying finale."

"Very good." Judith nodded.

Renie shot her cousin an acerbic look. "Okay, okay." Renie closed her eyes and screwed up her face in an exaggerated manner. "The cabinet comes out. Or does Salome show up first? I forget."

"Think."

"Salome shows up, announced by Mandolini. Then comes the cabinet, pushed by the theremin guy and Joe's buddy, right?"

"That would be Pancho Green, the casino manager," Judith said. "The 'theremin guy,' as you call him, is Lloyd Watts, the other creative force behind the illusions."

"Oh." Renie paused to take another sip. "I thought they were part of the segment at first, but they didn't show up again. What happened to the stagehands we saw in the first part of the performance?"

Judith explained about how the stagehands had been called in to help during the power failure. "Then what?" she urged Renie.

"Salome hops around and swings her cape like a matador, then she shows that the cabinet is empty," Renie recalled. "She steps inside, Mandolini closes the doors, and then there's a lot of suspense and drums and whatnot before he begins slashing the thing with his sabers. When he's done, he opens the cabinet, and there's Salome, sans cape but allegedly intact. Tumultuous applause. Curtain. I rush off to gamble. How's that?"

"Good," Judith said. "That's how I remember it, too. So when was Salome—her real name is Sally, by the way—killed?"

Renie tapped her nails on the tabletop. "You're talking illusion here," she finally said. "Or impersonation. Thus, Salome—Sally— was killed while the lights were out. It's the only way her body could have been transported to the Corvette without anybody noticing."

"Where do you think she was murdered?" Judith asked.

"Where?" Renie echoed. "Backstage, I suppose. Her dressing room, maybe. Of course it was dark . . ."

"Exactly." Judith stopped as the poodle's owner signaled to the waiter.

"Another round, please," the blonde called out. "For both of us."

"Since it was dark," Judith continued, fighting to obliterate a mental image of Sweetums seated in a bar and wearing a dead mouse as a pendant on a diamond chain, "the killer had to work fast. Stab Sally, remove body, go from the cabaret area to the casino floor, remove the mannequin, and put Sally in the driver's seat. So to speak."

Renie nodded. "How long were the lights out? Ten minutes?"

"It could have been longer," Judith allowed. "We couldn't see our watches in the dark. It seems to me that we spent several minutes on the casino floor after we came out of the rest room."

Fou-Fou and her owner were both lapping up their second servings. Judith forced herself not to stare.

"Are you thinking what I'm thinking?" Renie asked with a conspiratorial expression.

"That one person couldn't have done all that?" Judith nodded. "Yes. Unfortunately, I'm afraid we're talking about not one, but two killers. Somehow, that's worse."

Renie gave a slight shake of her head. "It could be worse than that. What if there were more than two?"

The cousins left the bar just as the blonde and her poodle were on their third round. The woman was looking bleary-eyed; the dog seemed alert and was eyeing a bowl of mixed nuts on the bar. Since Judith didn't have to meet Joe until between six and six-thirty, she offered to accompany Renie to fetch her mother from the conference.

The sign on the meeting room door read, "INNOVATIONS FOR THE TWENTY-FIRST CENTURY, Drawing on the Past to Create the Future, 4 to 5:30." Just as Judith and Renie arrived, the double doors swung open and a happy and energized group of attendees began pouring out into the hallway.

"Amazing," somebody remarked. "Provocative," another said. "The best conference yet," enthused someone else.

"Don't tell me I actually missed something good," Renie whispered to Judith as the cousins went against the flow to find Aunt Deb. "These things are usually a big bore where I have to stick pins in my palms to stay awake."

"I used to enjoy the library meetings I attended," Judith said. "There were so many nice people. Of course, I really think librarians are special."

The crowd, which had probably numbered over a hundred people, was dispersing except for about twenty people who remained clustered near the speakers' dais.

"Where's Mom?" Renie asked. "Do you suppose she left early? She might have gotten tired. Or maybe they took her out ahead of everybody else because she's in a wheelchair." Renie pigeonholed a short woman with long hair who was collecting brochures and other leftovers from the folding chairs. "Have you seen Mrs. Gro—" She stopped and feigned a cough. "Sorry. Ms. Jones?"

The woman, who wore her glasses on a silver chain around her neck, smiled broadly. "I certainly have, and am I glad." She gestured toward the dais. "She's still here, holding court. What an amazing woman!"

"Good grief," Renie murmured just as the hangers-on seemed to part like the Red Sea to reveal Aunt Deb in all her amiable glory. "Thank God this is a western regional conference, with hardly anybody here from town," Renie whispered to Judith. "I don't recognize a single person. Thus, they don't know that my mother is a big fraud."

"Renie, dear," Aunt Deb called, propelling herself away from her admirers, "are you warm enough?"

"Thank God," Renie also murmured, "none of them would know me as Renie anyway."

Aunt Deb gave a final wave to her coterie. "Such lovely people," she said with a pleasurable sigh. "I can't wait for tomorrow's session. It's about the Internet."

"But," Renie objected as they moved out into the hallway, "you don't know anything about computers."

"That's so," Aunt Deb admitted, "but I type rather well. I had to, when I was a legal secretary to Mr. Whiffel. And if I do say so myself, they liked my contribution on the panel. In fact, they were agog."

"Your contribution?" Renie shot Judith a quick glance as they waited for the elevator. "What was it?"

"Stick figures," Aunt Deb replied, wheeling herself into the elevator. "The panel was past and future, you know. They referred to something as 'retro.' Well, it seemed to me that nothing was more 'retro' than old-fashioned stick figures. No one seems to draw them anymore. The other people just loved it. They're calling stick figures . . . let me see, what was it now? Oh, yes, 'stick figures are the comfort food of graphic design.' Isn't that sweet?"

Fortunately, Aunt Deb couldn't see her daughter's reaction, which was to run a finger across her throat in a slashing motion. Judith, however, felt compelled to say something kind.

"I can see that," she declared. "It seems these days people are try-ing to find ties to the past. Nostalgia is reassuring because it's so safe. We lived through it and know how everything turned out."

Aunt Deb nodded. "That's what I said. Stick figures take people back to their childhoods, where everything was clear and simple. As someone remarked, a stick figure can represent any race or religion or either sex. I think it's good that these nice folks consider stick fig-ures the wave of the future."

Renie was still shaking her head when they arrived at their floor. Upon entering the old ladies' room, they found Gertrude in front of the TV, playing keno and smoking a cigarette.

"Back already?" she said to Deb. "Seems like you just left. Now shut up all of you and don't break my concentration. The numbers for this game are coming up in about ten seconds."

Judith had to bite her tongue. But except for a couple of gentle coughs and a martyred sigh, even Deb kept quiet while Gertrude waited for the game to end.

"Aha!" she exclaimed as the last number lighted up. "I got three out of twenty. That means I get another free game."

"Mother," Judith inquired, "how many games have you played?"

Through a gray haze of smoke, Gertrude scowled at her daughter. "How should I know? They number the blasted things, but some-times they're red, sometimes they're green. Look, here comes number two hundred and six green. Next time it might be four hundred and eight red. The only numbers I care about are the ones I pick and the ones that come up. When's supper?"

"Whenever you want it," Judith said, handing Gertrude the room service menu.

"I'm practically sticks up from starvation," Gertrude said. "I like my supper at five. Do you know what time it is?"

"Yes, Mother." Judith deliberately stood in front of the TV screen. "You can order whenever you like. I'm not serving you here. And I don't want you playing keno the whole time. You're bound to lose."

"It costs a dollar," Gertrude declared. "I've won at least ten dollars so far and a half dozen free games. I played bingo yesterday in the parlor downstairs and won fifty bucks. Go away. I have to pick my keno numbers right now."

"But, Mother—" Judith began.

"Beat it." Gertrude waved an arm in a shooing gesture. "Don't pull a fast one and stand there so I can't see the TV." She turned a hard stare on Deb. "And don't start gabbing your head off. I don't want to hear about all the nice people you met and how nice the food was and wasn't it nice that you didn't fall out of the wheelchair and break your neck. I'm busy."

"I wonder," Judith said as they left their mothers, "if I could disconnect her."

Renie brightened. "Permanently?"

"No." Judith looked askance at her cousin. "I mean, from playing those TV keno games. I'm afraid she's going to run up a terrible bill."

"It sounds like she's won a little," Renie pointed out. "Besides, what else has she got to do all day?"

"What she does at home," Judith responded. "Watch TV shows. Play solitaire. Do the jumble puzzles in the newspaper."

"My mom talks on the phone and entertains her parade of

callers," Renie mused. "It's like holding court. Oh, she reads and does the crossword puzzle and sometimes she watches TV, but unlike Aunt Gert, Mom's a social animal. Like you, coz."

"Right." But Judith's mind wasn't on family traits. "When are you going to wake Bill up?"

Renie looked at her watch. "Now. It's going on six. Why?"

"I'd like to find out what's going on at the cabin," Judith replied. "Do you mind?"

"No, come on in."

Bill didn't need rousing. He was doing his exercises when the cousins entered the Joneses' quarters. Renie signaled for Judith to be quiet. Bill sat up straight on a chair in the middle of the room, performing a ritual that involved arm, back, and neck work. He didn't seem aware that his wife and her cousin were standing five feet away from him.

Two or three minutes passed before Bill stopped, panting slightly. "Ah!" he exclaimed, startled. "What now?"

"The cabin," Renie said. "Judith—and I—want to know."

With a heavy sigh, Bill got up from the chair and put it back in its place by the desk. "Something's off," he said, his face stern. "Where did you two get this contractor?"

"I didn't—" Renie began before Judith interrupted her.

"He's related to Bart Bednarik, the contractor who's working on the B&B. What's wrong? Is he crooked?"

As always, Bill took the time to think before he answered. "Not exactly crooked. Shifty, maybe. What's his name? Dale Armstrong?" He saw Judith nod. "He seemed too damned anxious to get rid of me. He said they were all tied up trying to figure out where to lay the foundation for the new building. But it looked to me as if they were concentrating on that swampy area at the back of the lot, near the highway."

"The quicksand," Renie said in surprise. "I don't get it."

Bill gave his wife a dubious look. "It can't be quicksand. Not near a river."

"It felt like quicksand to us when we were kids," Renie retorted. "Did I ever tell you about the time—"

"Yes, I'm sure you did," Bill broke in. "The point is, I think Armstrong's stalling. I also think he has something to hide."

"Like what?" Renie demanded. "A very large bill for sitting on his dead butt?"

Bill shrugged. "I don't know. It's not up to me, but if I were you, Judith, I'd take Joe along and go see him tomorrow."

Judith winced. Not only was Joe involved in a homicide investigation, but he was less than enthusiastic about his wife taking on another business venture. Indeed, if the fire hadn't already put a hole in Hillside Manor's roof, Joe would have made one of his own when he exploded over Judith's announcement that she wanted to build another B&B. It was only after Judith had promised she'd hire someone to run the riverfront operation that Joe's boiling point had gone down to simmer.

"I'll see if Joe can get away," she finally said, then gave Renie an appealing look. "Coz . . . ?"

Renie slapped a hand to her head. "Oh, jeez! I thought I was on vacation!"

"You're supposed to be at a conference," Judith reminded her cousin.

Bill was putting a money clip, a handkerchief, a tiny notebook, and other assorted items into the various compartments of his tan corduroy vest. The vest was lucky, Renie had informed Judith, and Bill wore it only when he gambled. "I don't think you two should go by yourselves," he said. "I don't like the feel of the place. But somebody should check things out."

"I'll talk to Joe," Judith said. "It's weird. I can't think why anything strange would be going on at the cabin site."

"Maybe I imagined it," Bill said.

"No, you didn't," Renie put in. "Say, if you didn't stick around, how come you were gone so long?"

Bill adjusted his glasses. "I had lunch in Glacier Falls," he said, referring to the old logging town some nine miles west of the family retreat. "Then I decided to double back over the bridge a mile or so east of the cabin. Nobody was around at the summer place across the river, so I did a bit of spying. Unfortunately, there wasn't much to see. Armstrong and his workmen must have stayed back near the highway. Then I took my daily walk along the river. It was interesting, especially where you could see the old railroad bed and a couple of trestles and even a boarded-up tunnel. The river gets narrow in that gorge a mile or so from the cabin. There's some beautiful scenery along the way."

"I know," Renie said. "We used to go on hikes through there with my dad. But of course it's probably different now. The river changes channels in so many places over the course of time."

"Speaking of change," Judith put in, "I'd better do that before dinner. You still on for the coffee shop?"

Bill grunted his agreement; Renie said that was fine. Judith went to the Flynns' room, but Joe hadn't yet arrived. The room wasn't vacant, however. Micki Mendoza sat in a turquoise armchair, chewing on a fingernail.

"Excuse me?" Judith said, both surprised and indignant. "How did you get in?"

"I talked Pancho Green into giving me a pass key," Micki replied without apology. "I heard you were a famous detective. Is it true?"

Judith closed the door behind her. "Who told you that?"

"Emily, the security guard. She says you even have an Internet site."

"What?" Judith sat down on the bed. "What are you talking about?"

Micki nodded. "I guess you impressed her this morning. Then she remembered you from something she saw on TV a couple of years ago. You were on the news, telling about how you managed to solve all kinds of murder cases. Emily looked you up on the Internet, and there you were. 'Female Amateur Sleuth Tracking Offenders.' Your code name is 'Fatso.'"

Judith frowned at the acronym. "Don't you mean Fasto?"

Micki shrugged. "Whatever. I thought it said Fatso."

"Swell." Judith held her head. After having spent her adolescence as an overweight teenager, she had struggled most of her life to keep her statuesque figure trim, if not slim. It seemed too cruel that if indeed she had attained a certain amount of notoriety, she'd end up being called Fatso. "You're not kidding me, are you?" she finally asked in an attempt to salvage a shred of dignity.

"No," Micki insisted. "That isn't why I'm here, but I had to check you out before I came. You see, I need your help."

Judith held up her hands. "Stop right there. My husband is already involved. Besides, the FBI is stepping in."

The rings on Micki's hands flashed as she waved away Judith's statement. "No, they're not. These days, the feds have more to do than poke their noses in a murder on an Indian reservation way up in the northwest corner of the country. Besides, the tribal guys figure that if things get tough, they can call in the local sheriff for technical support and lab stuff."

A light went on inside Judith's head. Or maybe it was the glare of Micki's gems. "Who's the sheriff these days?"

Micki laughed, but it wasn't a mirthful sound. "I heard he was elected a few years ago after he solved a big case involving a prominent artist who lived around here. It's a funny name—Abbott N. Costello."

The light was accompanied by warning whistles, buzzers, and beeps. Judith remembered the former undersheriff all too well and none too fondly.

Only his name was funny. The last person she wanted to meet at the Lake Stillasnowamish Resort Casino was Abbott N. Costello.

Chapter Nine

JUDITH didn't comment on the possibility of Sheriff Costello taking part in the murder investigation. But the mere mention of his name made her hackles rise, especially if he'd won over the voters by claiming to have fingered Riley Tobias's killer. Riley had lived next door to the family's cabin on the river, and was an old acquaintance. By chance, he'd been murdered while Judith and Renie had been spending a few days rusticating on the river property. It was Judith who had nailed the culprit and had almost lost her life in the process.

"If," Judith began, after collecting her wits, "the FBI trusts the tribal police to solve the case, why don't you?"

Micki shrugged. She was wearing a low-cut white satin blouse with a purple velour skirt. Her red hair was done up in masses of curls on top of her head. Judith could see why Freddy Polson had been smitten, perhaps even why his first marriage had broken up.

"It's not that I'm prejudiced," Micki said, "it's the small-time part I don't like. I'm not from around here. I grew up in L.A. Besides, I don't like cops in general."

Judith wondered if that was because Micki had had some run-ins with the police. "So why me?"

"You're a woman," Micki replied. "Women have intuition when it comes to people. They don't ask 'how' so much as they want to know 'why.' Besides, you're Fatso."

"Thanks." Judith tried not to show her displeasure. "Frankly, I'm not sure how—to borrow the word—you want me to help."

"According to your FATSO site," Micki explained, "you have this terrific knack for talking to people. They trust you, they confide in you. That's all I want you to do—talk to the people in Freddy's entourage. I can make sure that happens."

Judith considered Micki's request. "Why do you want me to do this? Since you know all these people, why can't you engage them in conversation?"

"First," Micki said, holding up an index finger, "I don't have your knack." She held up another finger. "Second, I come off as abrasive. Third," she continued, holding up her ring finger with its sparkling stone, "I don't always get along with everybody. And fourth and most important," she went on, wiggling her pinky, "I don't want to see Freddy framed for this murder, which is how things seem to be going."

"Really?" Judith studied the young woman's face, but it was hard to discern her true emotions. "You must love him very much," Judith finally said.

"I sure do," Micki retorted. "Sally never appreciated him. He's very sensitive. He's an *artiste*."

"Yes," Judith murmured, recalling Inga Polson's assertions about her brother, "so I've been told."

"Well?" Micki's tone was a challenge.

Still, Judith hesitated. She could hear the rain spattering the windows and the cawing of a crow. The forest, the mountains, the river—even the rain—were balm to her soul. Yet a sense of misgiving crept over her.

Micki was giving her the opportunity to get involved in the case.

Joe's ambivalent attitude rankled. "I believe in justice. But first, you have to tell me why you think your fiancé is being framed for his ex-wife's murder."

Micki's violet-eyed gaze traveled from the desk to the dresser to the nightstand. "I don't suppose you've got anything to drink around here."

"I'm sorry, I don't." Judith was about to offer her uninvited guest room service, but Joe would probably be showing up momentarily. She didn't want Micki Mendoza to settle in for the evening.

"Oh." Micki's disappointment seemed genuine. "Okay. Never mind. You asked why I think Freddy is being framed. It's simple. Because he's an illusionist, people think he can do all kinds of tricks. I mean, they figure that if he can make a cougar disappear into thin air or produce a bunch of bunnies out of his sleeve, he knows how to fool the cops. It's stupid, really, but I get that impression."

"From the cops?" Judith asked.

"Well . . ." Micki raked a hand through her red curls. "Maybe not exactly. With them, it's like he's the obvious suspect because he's Sally's ex. That's really dumb, because Freddy and Sally parted on good terms. Otherwise, they wouldn't have kept the act together. Illusionists' assistants aren't exactly a dime a dozen. They have to be on the same page every second that they're working with the star. They practically have to be able to read each other's minds."

"I can see that," Judith agreed. "How long had Freddy and Sally known each other? I gather they went way back."

"They did." Micki nodded emphatically. "They grew up about three blocks from each other, in Idaho. They met, like, in kindergarten. They were still in their teens when they got married. Neither of them had much experience out in the real world." She shot Judith a glance that said the same could not be said of Micaela Mendoza.

"They must have stayed married for several years," Judith noted. "How old is Freddy? He looks about thirty or so."

"You're close," Micki replied with an impish smile. "It's that boy-ish quality he has when he's not performing. I mean, it's, like, real. I think performers are often shy. That's why they go on the stage or whatever. They can hide behind a make-believe personality."

"That's so," Judith agreed.

Briefly, Micki seemed lost in thought. "What did you say? That Freddy and Sally must have been married for several years?" Judith nodded. "Over twelve years," Micki said. "They split about three years ago. A year or so later, after the divorce was final, Sally married Manny Quinn."

"Do you have any concrete evidence that someone's trying to frame Freddy?" Judith inquired, a quick glance at the digital clock on the nightstand telling her that it was almost six-thirty. Joe should be back in the room any minute. "Who do you think it is? The real killer?"

Micki shot Judith a patronizing look. "Who else? It has to be Sally's murderer." She gave the room another once-over. "You sure you don't have any booze?"

"Yes." Judith was growing impatient and a trifle edgy. "Go on, tell me who you think is trying to pin the homicide on Freddy."

"It's those damned sabers," Micki replied, looking surly. "The cops say one of them killed Sally, which points to Freddy because he never allowed anybody to touch them. He's really superstitious about some of his props."

Judith frowned. "So you're saying that someone else used one of the sabers to commit murder?"

"Right. To throw suspicion onto Freddy."

The rationale seemed overly simplistic to Judith. "How many sabers does Freddy have?" she asked, noting that the digital clock read 6:31.

"Four," Micki replied. "The pair he uses in the act and a backup pair."

"Where does he keep them?"

"In a case downstairs."

"Downstairs?" Judith was puzzled.

"Yes," Micki explained, "there's a big area down there for all sorts of props."

Judith looked at Micki earnestly. "Are the sabers that aren't being used locked up?"

"No. I mean, everybody knows how Freddy feels about them," Micki replied. "They wouldn't dare touch them, not even Sally."

But one of the sabers had touched Sally, Judith thought to herself, *and in a most lethal kind of way.* "Who do you think did it?"

Micki leaned forward in the chair. "If I tell you, will you keep it to yourself?"

"Of course."

For several seconds, Judith felt she was under intense scrutiny.

"Okay," Micki said at last, "it's pretty obvious to me who wanted Sally dead. The killer has to be—"

Like a bad movie, the door opened and Joe breezed in. "Hey, Jude-girl, I got held up by—" He stopped halfway into the room, his eyes fixed on Micki. "What's going on?"

Micki got out of the chair and started for the door. "I just stopped by to talk," she said to Joe. "I'll catch you later, Mrs. F."

Joe watched Micki depart. "What was that all about?"

Judith swiftly considered her options. Discretion, she decided, would be best. "Micki's upset about the murder. She wanted to talk to someone. Someone outside the act, that is. What's going on with the investigation?"

"They're going to get the lab work done by the county," Joe replied, pulling his lambs wool sweater over his head. "Does the name Abbott N. Costello mean anything to you? It sounds familiar to me. Other than for the obvious reason, of course."

Joe's back was turned, which was a good thing since Judith goggled at the mention of her old nemesis's name. "Sort of," she hedged. There was no point in reminding Joe that TV cameras had captured the conclusion of the drama at the cabin. Joe had seen it on the news and had not been pleased to discover that his wife had gotten herself involved in another dangerous homicide investigation. "We're supposed to meet Bill and Renie in the coffee shop about now."

"I won't be long," Joe called over his shoulder as he headed into the bathroom. "I'm going to shower and change. It's been a long day. Go ahead, I'll see you down there."

Judith decided she should change, too, so she waited for Joe. Twenty minutes later, they were seated with Bill and Renie in the busy coffee shop. Having had to wait in line, the Joneses had sat down only a few minutes before the Flynns' arrival. Consequently, Renie was both hungry and crabby.

"I thought they had trout," Renie snarled, closing the menu with a loud slap. "Maybe most of us can't catch any fish around here anymore, but couldn't the Stillasnowamish use a gill net like the rest of the Native Americans?"

"Maybe there aren't any trout left even for them," Joe remarked.

"Phooey," Renie retorted. "They know these streams. They could find a trout if they wanted to. All I want is one."

"Can it," Bill said under his breath.

Renie made a face at her husband. "You don't know how good a rainbow trout can be. You're from Wisconsin. You people eat awful things, like sunfish and Midwestern pike."

"That's Northern pike," Bill corrected.

"So what?" Renie said with a sneer. "They swim in all those mosquito-infested lakes in the upper Midwest. That can't make them tasty or healthy."

"I've never seen a fish with mosquito bites," Bill countered. "Shut up and order the crab. It suits you."

Judith decided it was time to intervene. "Bill, tell Joe about the reaction you got at the cabin today."

While Bill related his visit to the cabin and the waitress took the foursome's orders, Judith's mind drifted. So did her eyes, which scanned the coffee shop, trying to locate any members of the Mandolini troupe. It was only when she was finishing her entrée of halibut cheeks that she spotted Lloyd Watts, by himself, being seated across the room.

"I have to go to the bathroom," Judith announced, gobbling up the last two bites of halibut. "Excuse me."

She dashed away before anyone could say anything. Making an end run at the front of the coffee shop, Judith came back to approach Freddy Polson's associate.

Lloyd was absorbed in reading the menu. Cautiously, Judith pulled out the empty chair from the table for two. "May I?"

The young man gave a start, then frowned before recognition dawned. "Mrs. Flynn? Sure, go ahead."

Judith explained that she and Joe and their relatives were seated at another table. "I just happened to notice you when I came back from the rest room," she fibbed. "I thought I'd stop by to ask how everyone in the troupe is doing."

Shrugging, Lloyd set the menu down. "How you would expect. Everybody—well, almost everybody—liked Sally. Had a way about her, she did."

"I met her shortly before she was killed," Judith said. "Sally seemed very pleasant."

"Pleasant. Yes, she was that. And more." Lloyd looked wistful.

Judith spoke softly. "You were fond of her, I take it?"

"Yes."

Judith tried to remember what little she knew so far about Lloyd

Watts. "You must have met Sally and Freddy about the time their marriage was breaking up."

Lloyd gave a single nod.

"In Sun Valley, right?"

He nodded again.

"That must have been a difficult time for them both," Judith remarked.

He opened his mouth to answer, but the waiter interrupted. After ordering chicken-fried steak and a green salad, Lloyd resumed answering Judith's question. "In a way." He paused. "It was . . . how do you say it? Amicable, eh?"

"Yes," Judith agreed. "That's the term. Sally and Freddy were fortunate. So many marriages end in rancor and hostility."

Lloyd said nothing. Instead, he picked up the plastic salt and pepper shakers and covered them with a paper napkin. With a quick glance at Judith, he removed the napkin to reveal a deck of cards split into four piles divided by suit. As Judith gasped, Lloyd hid the cards with the napkin, waited a couple of seconds, and then removed it again. The salt and pepper shakers reappeared; the cards were gone.

"Look under the menu," he said.

Carefully, Judith lifted the menu that Lloyd had earlier placed to his right. Sure enough, the cards were there.

Judith grinned at Lloyd. "I won't ask how you did that. You wouldn't tell me."

"Can't," Lloyd said with a helpless gesture. "Trick of the trade."

"And a fairly easy one, I'll bet," Judith remarked. "If you know how."

Lloyd nodded in an offhand manner. "Parlor tricks. I could teach—"

The coffee shop was plunged into darkness. Judith was so shocked that she couldn't utter a sound. Others, however, cried out in surprise and fear. A clatter of plates and the breaking of glassware sounded nearby. Someone—a man with an accent—uttered obscenities.

Judith finally found her voice. "How can this happen twice?" She stopped speaking as a sense of dread overwhelmed her. She was certain that the first outage had been caused deliberately to mask the dreadful deeds surrounding Sally's murder. Was this an encore? Perhaps the restoration after the original failure had gone awry. A plain old-fashioned short circuit would be reassuring.

The familiar shouts and sounds of scurrying feet could be heard in the darkness. So could a strident female voice issuing a threat: "Touch that last Dungeness crab leg and prepare to die!"

Renie, Judith thought with a small sense of relief. At least something was still normal out there in the midnight gloom.

Judith felt someone jostle her arm and grunt in what sounded like an apology. She said nothing for a few moments, until lighted candles began appearing like so many fireflies around the room. As a waiter placed one of the candles on the table across the aisle, Judith adjusted her eyes to the flame's amber glow.

"Weird, eh?" Lloyd wore a wry expression, his fists propping up his chin.

"Very weird," Judith replied. "Scary, too." She turned to look behind her, toward the front of the coffee shop. Near one of the bussing stations, broken glass caught the flickering candlelight like diamonds in a tiara. *Or rhinestones on a poodle*, Judith thought.

Beyond the scattered glass and china shards, the blonde from the bar stood frozen. Fou-Fou the poodle panted at her owner's side, then let out a high-pitched, haunting howl.

The blonde turned slowly toward the dog, and as she did, the candlelight bounced off the object she held in her hand.

Judith gasped. It was a saber, and it dripped with blood.

. . .

Two seconds later, the lights came back on. Judith stood up to look across the room. Joe was also on his feet, his eyes fixed on the blonde who was holding the bloody saber.

"Stay in your places, please," Joe ordered as he moved swiftly toward the woman, who appeared to be dazed. His voice was calm but carried to the farthest reaches of the coffee shop. Even the chef and his cooks stood at attention behind the service counter. The hostess, however, had taken a few hesitant steps in the blonde's direction.

Joe raised a hand to forestall her. "I'm Detective Joe Flynn. Let me handle this."

The poodle was pawing the tiled floor even as his mistress stared blankly into the coffee shop. Judith strained across the distance of thirty feet to see what was happening. Joe didn't touch the woman, but spoke so softly that Judith couldn't hear. The woman was unresponsive; the poodle was still agitated.

Joe turned, his gaze traveling around the big room as if he were trying to memorize each face and reaction. "We have to make sure the restaurant is secure, so please be patient," he requested as his discerning eye stopped at the rear exit. Jack Jackrabbit had just come through the door. "Here's the tribal detective now," Joe announced. "He'll be able to make sure everything is all right. Meanwhile, enjoy your meal."

Excited, even frenzied voices erupted at table after table. Jack joined Joe just as a woman's piercing scream could be heard in the distance.

Judith couldn't stand it. She jumped to her feet, heedless of Joe's warning, careless of the crumbs on her black slacks, oblivious to the frightened diners who gaped at her temerity.

"Hey," Lloyd said in a worried tone, "shouldn't you . . . sit?"

"I've sat long enough," Judith said grimly. "This place is out of control."

But even as she advanced, Pancho Green and Dr. Engelman were hurrying toward the coffee shop. Jack Jackrabbit indicated the immobile blonde, then raced after Joe in the direction of the rest rooms just beyond the cashier's counter.

Pancho was seething. "What the hell is going on around here?" he demanded under his breath as he pointed to the woman, who still clutched the saber. "What is this?"

Judith opened her mouth to answer, but gave a start when Bill moved quietly to intervene. "This person appears to be in a catatonic state."

Pancho stared at Bill, then looked at Judith. "She is?"

"No," Bill answered patiently, "not her. The blonde."

"Who are you?" Pancho asked, his chin thrust out at Bill.

"I'm a doctor," he replied, "of psychology. Let me be more specific. I believe she's suffering from organic psychosis, which often produces the same symptoms as schizophrenia."

"That's true," Dr. Engelman put in.

Renie had come up behind Bill. "Can you help her?"

"Not at this point." Bill turned to Dr. Engelman. "Have you got gloves with you?"

"No," Engelman replied, "but I can get some from the chef's crew." A tall, lean man of about seventy, the physician strode off to the kitchen.

For lack of anything better to do, Judith tried to comfort the poodle. "There, there, Fou-Fou," she whispered, "it's going to be fine. Dr. Bill is here."

"Ah!" Pancho exclaimed, wagging a finger at Bill. "I remember! You're somehow related to Joe Flynn."

Bill acknowledged that that was so. Two of the security guards appeared with a gurney, apparently having been summoned by the restaurant hostess. Dr. Engelman returned, holding several pairs of sanitary gloves in his hand.

"Two for you, two for me," the doctor said, handing a pair to Bill.

After slipping on the gloves, Bill slowly began prying the blonde's fingers from around the saber's hilt. Thumb, forefinger, middle finger, ring finger, pinky. Judith held her breath. One of the guards produced a large plastic bag. Bill now held the saber, and was frowning at the blood. With a careful, deliberate motion, he slipped the weapon into the bag.

The blonde collapsed onto the tiles like a rag doll.

Judith and the others stared at the motionless body on the floor. Bill told the guards to put her on the gurney. Pancho asked if an ambulance had been called. One of the guards said that it had.

Bill, however, shook his head, then glanced at Dr. Engelman. "Do you think she needs to be hospitalized?"

Engelman stroked his goatee as he studied the blonde's inert form. "Not really," he replied as he turned to Pancho. "Except for liability reasons, she could probably stay here."

"But obviously something's wrong with her," Pancho declared. "I'll make the call. She goes to the hospital in Glacier Falls. It's small, but they can handle it. If not, down the line, they'll send her on to a bigger hospital."

Engelman shrugged his sloping shoulders. "That's up to you. Better safe than sorry, of course." He looked at Bill again. So did the others.

"How do you know there's nothing seriously wrong with her?" Renie asked. "You said yourself she's suffering from . . . what was it? Organic psychosis?"

"That's right," Bill agreed, removing the gloves. "Which is another way of saying she's dead drunk."

Dr. Engelman opted to accompany the woman to the hospital. Feeling bewildered as well as worried about what had happened to Joe and Jack in the rest room area, Judith idly brushed the crumbs from her slacks. They felt gritty, like sand.

"Drat," she murmured to Renie, "I can't get this stuff off my . . ." It suddenly dawned on Judith that she hadn't eaten anything while she was seated with Lloyd Watts.

"You're all sparkly," Renie said. "What have you've got all over yourself? It looks like that glitter stuff women wear for festive occasions."

Judith studied both her hands and her slacks. "It *is* glitter stuff. Where'd it come from?" She looked around the coffee shop, where the guests were still abuzz. "There aren't any decorations with gold glitter. Hunh. I don't get it."

She was still puzzling over the glitter and trying to wipe it off with a damp napkin from the bussing station when Joe came out of the rest room area. Judith saw at once that he was wearing his professional expression. But instead of joining his wife, he went straight to Pancho Green. With Renie at her side, Judith moved forward a few steps to hear.

Neither of the cousins could make out what Joe said. But Pancho's voice rang out clear and horrified.

"No! How can that be? Not another murder!"

Chapter Ten

JUDITH was almost crushed by the panicky guests, who started a stampede out of the coffee shop. Chairs and tables were overturned, glassware crashed, silver rattled, and china shattered as at least three dozen diners made their way toward the exit.

They didn't get very far. Someone had already roped off the entrance from the casino floor to the coffee shop. Emily and her fellow security guard, Amos, maintained an implacable stance, arms folded across their chests and feet planted firmly apart.

Nudging and shoving, Judith managed to worm her way out of the crowd. Finally reaching the upholstered bench where guests waited to be called to a table, she collapsed. Her hip seemed intact, but her nerves were frazzled. There was no sign of Joe, who was undoubtedly surrounded by the crowd that scrambled around the restaurant entrance.

But Judith did see her cousin weaving her way toward the bench. Being small, Renie was able to wind between tall legs and slip through minute gaps between people. A pinch here, a poke there, and an occasional "Lady-with-a-baby-coming-through" abetted her progress. She was also prone to swear, which she was now doing, an ear-jarring stream of obscenities that caused human obstacles to give way.

"I thought you were being trampled," Renie panted as she flopped down on the bench next to Judith. "Are you okay?"

"No," Judith retorted. "How could I be okay? This is the worst vacation I've ever taken."

"I know," Renie agreed. "But this little mob isn't anything like our audience with the pope in Rome almost forty years ago. At the time, I was sure we'd be killed by devout Christians of every color and country."

"You hid in a confessional, as I recall."

"With an African-American schoolteacher from Tennessee who was a Methodist." Renie took a deep breath. "We bonded."

"So who's dead now?" Judith asked as the crowd began to quiet.

"I don't know," Renie replied. "When I saw you getting swept away, I took the low road to your battered side."

"Whoever it was," Judith said, "must have been killed in one of the rest rooms. I'd like to find out who has the savvy to turn off the power in this place."

"Maybe you just throw a switch," Renie suggested. "You know, like at home, when you hit the one marked Main on your fuse box."

"I wonder," Judith murmured. For a moment she regarded the milling crowd with an eye of detachment. "Are we the only ones here who aren't freaking out?"

"We," Renie reminded Judith, "are probably the only ones who have had encounters with multiple corpses. We're numb."

"I don't want to be that way," Judith countered. "I want to care. I want to feel the senselessness of it, the tragedy."

"Right." Renie looked up at the ceiling.

Judith poked her cousin in the arm. "I mean it. Let's face it, you're kind of hard-hearted. That is, you're more like my mother and I'm more like yours. Aunt Deb and I can empathize with the pain of others. You and Mother—well, you're both tougher."

"It's armor," Renie said. "Aunt Gert and I shield ourselves from life's horrors. It's the only way we can survive. Who knows? Maybe deep down, we're more sympathetic, but we have to act tough to keep from going under."

Judith studied Renie's profile, pug nose, short chin, and all. "Maybe."

It appeared that Emily and Amos were allowing diners to leave after giving names and room numbers or local addresses. The crowd thinned out. But Judith still couldn't see Joe. The two security guards remained in charge of the area outside the rest rooms, conducting their duties in a professional manner.

"Joe and the others must be in one of the rest rooms with the body. Let's go look," Judith said, standing up. She had taken only a step when she espied G. D. Fromm, Freddy's manager, coming out of the coffee shop. "Odd," Judith whispered, "I don't recall seeing him before the lights went out."

"Were you looking for him?" Renie asked, then answered her own question. "Of course you were. Or for any of the other Mandolini act hangers-on. I saw you come from Lloyd's table."

Judith spotted Lloyd, still at his table, calmly eating chicken-fried steak. Of all the customers in the coffee shop, he looked the least affected by the shocking events of the past quarter hour. His demeanor struck Judith as odd. Or maybe not. Lloyd was a bit different, no doubt because of his creative nature. Judith figured he must have the ability to become totally focused in order to develop and carry out his illusions.

She watched Fromm pass muster with the security guards and bustle out of the coffee shop area. Just as she and Renie crossed over to the rest rooms, Bill emerged, looking grim.

"You don't want to go in there," he said to the cousins. "It's not a pretty sight. Joe's still with the victim."

"Who is it?" Judith asked, her voice strident.

Bill removed a small notebook from his pocket. A deliberate man who gave life to the cliché "absent-minded professor," he tended to write everything down, including the names of his children.

"Micaela Consuela Mendoza."

"Micki!" Judith cried. "But I spoke with her just a few minutes before we came down to dinner!"

"Apparently," Bill noted dryly, "whatever you said didn't prevent her from being stabbed to death."

Judith waved her hand in a frustrated manner. "You know what I mean. She was alive. She certainly didn't act as if she was afraid of anything or anyone."

Bill frowned. "Irrelevant."

"No," Judith said sharply. "Maybe not." She lowered her voice so that only Bill and Renie could hear. "Micki was in our room when I got back before dinner. She was about to tell me who killed Sally when Joe interrupted her. At that point, she left."

"That's odd," Renie remarked. "Why not tell both of you?"

"Micki didn't like cops," Judith said. "That's why she came to me. She'd heard about my knack for listening to people." Skipping the part about Emily and the Internet site, Judith looked at Bill. "You say she was stabbed?"

Bill nodded. "Apparently with the saber the blonde was holding. Who is she?"

Judith looked around the foyer. Only a handful of guests were still waiting to exit. Bob Bearclaw was holding the poodle, which seemed to have calmed down. With his keen eyes studying every individual in his line of sight, the doorman seemed to have assumed authority.

Bill put a hand on each of the cousins' backs. "Come on, let's get out of here. We're in the way."

Judith saw what Bill meant as medics rolled a gurney toward them on their way to the rest room. The threesome edged over to the velvet ropes, then got into the short line of people who were leaving the coffee shop area.

"Let's move to the Autumn Bar," Judith suggested as Amos waved them through. "It's the closest, so probably it'd be the first place Joe would look for us when he's finished. If he ever finishes," she added.

The bar was almost full, mainly, it seemed, with customers abuzz about the most recent tragedy. Bill managed to secure a table in the farthest corner, under a sinewy branch of artificial gold-and-orange maple.

"Say," Judith said, recognizing the young waiter serving the next table, "he's the one who waited on the blonde and her dog, Fou-Fou. Maybe he knows who she is."

"You've seen her before?" Bill asked in surprise.

"Not more than a couple of hours ago," Renie said. "She and the poodle were well on their way to getting wasted."

"The woman certainly was that," Bill noted. "The dog seemed fairly sober, though."

"Maybe the dog knew when to quit," Judith said. "Ah—here's the waiter."

"You're back, ladies," the young man said, looking suitably somber. "Have you come from the coffee shop, by any chance? Everybody else here seems to have been on hand for . . . well, for what happened."

Judith noted that the waiter's name tag identified him as Cyril. "Do you know the blonde woman who was with the poodle?"

The question seemed to startle the young man. "The one with the dog that drinks?" He shook his head. "I'd never seen her before this afternoon. Why?"

Judith explained that the blonde was the woman who had been found holding the bloody saber.

"No kidding!" Cyril's eyes got very big. "I didn't know that. Every-body I've talked to in the bar has sort of babbled."

"But you'd never seen her until this afternoon?" Judith said.

Cyril shook his head. "I've had customers with dogs and cats before, even snakes and ferrets and monkeys, but none of the ani-mals drank liquor."

Which, Judith figured, was just as well. Cyril took the group's orders and returned to the bar.

"Where's the best place to stab someone?" Judith asked.

Renie wrinkled her pug nose. "In the heart?"

Judith looked askance at her cousin. "I'm talking geography, not anatomy."

"I think Judith's referring to the bathroom," Bill put in, "or in this case, the rest room. You can clean up fast."

"Exactly," Judith said.

"Sally wasn't stabbed in the rest room," Renie noted. "In fact, do we know where she was stabbed? And I don't mean the heart this time."

Judith scowled at Renie. "Joe hasn't told me. But I'm betting on the area under the stage. Don't you think that Sally must have dropped through a trapdoor before Freddy did his thing with the sabers?"

"You're assuming that was Sally," Renie countered. "I thought we figured that because of the time factor with the power failure, some-one must have impersonated Sally. The question is, who? Inga's too stout. I don't know where Micki would have put all that red hair, not to mention the fact that she's too petite. Who am I leaving out?"

"Grisly," Judith responded. "She's fair haired and tall. The prob-lem is, she doesn't have Sally's figure for the grand finale."

"Whoever it was," Renie said, "swirled around in that big cape before she got in the cabinet. You really couldn't see much of her shape."

"But she'd shed the cape when Freddy opened it at the end," Bill pointed out. "The evening gown revealed a knockout figure."

"You would notice that," Renie murmured.

"The part about the curves bothers me," Judith said in a musing tone.

Cyril returned with their drinks. Judith knew how busy he was with the crush of customers, but she had another question to ask him.

"How long did the blond woman stay in the bar after my cousin and I left?"

Cyril thought for a moment. "Twenty, thirty minutes? The lady and the poodle had a total of five drinks apiece."

Judith was puzzled. In those hardscrabble years when she worked days at the local library and nights behind the bar at the Meat & Mingle, five drinks usually didn't put a customer into a catatonic state. Unless they'd had a head start, of course. "Did the blonde stick to wine?"

"No," Cyril replied. "She ordered tequila shots when that older guy joined her."

Judith's eyes bugged. "Older guy? Do you know who it was?"

"Oh, sure," Cyril answered, turning to look toward the far end of the bar. "I've waited on him several times in the last few days. It was him." He pointed a finger at the bulky form of G. D. Fromm, who was straddling his bar stool as if it were a pony to oblivion.

Judith tried to keep the excitement out of her voice. "Did that man and the blonde seem to know each other or was he hitting on her?"

Nodding to a thirsty couple at a nearby table, Cyril considered the question. "Gosh—I'm not sure. It got really busy about then, with all the predinner trade. Hey, I'm sorry, but I've got to wait on these other customers. I'll be back if you want another round."

"I didn't come here to get smashed," Renie declared. "I came here to lose my money. Suddenly, I feel lucky again."

"Go for it," Bill said amiably. "I'll look out back for a cardboard box we can live in after we leave."

Renie, however, sipped daintily at her Drambuie. "I intend to enjoy my drink before I impoverish us. Besides, if I lose all our money, we won't have to help pay for our children's weddings."

"A point well taken," Bill said.

Judith barely heard the banter between Renie and Bill. She was watching G. D. Fromm drink what looked like brandy. She was also wishing that the people who sat on the bar stools to each side of Fromm would make their departure.

Inspiration struck. "I need a glass of water to take my pain pills," Judith said suddenly. "I don't want to bother Cyril, so I'll go up to the bar and get it myself."

Bill and Renie made no comment. Judith angled her way between the tables. Freddy Polson's manager was sitting on the next-to-the-last bar stool, by the serving counter. Judith noted that G. D. Fromm was indeed drinking brandy, savoring every sniff and swallow.

The bartender, a stocky black-haired woman with a dour expression, was busy mixing drinks. Judith was in no hurry. She assumed a nonchalant air, studying the bottles behind the bar, the glassware, and the leaf-shaped etchings on the counter's glass top.

Judith's seemingly blasé manner was jarred when Grisly Vanderbehr hurtled toward G. D. Fromm.

"G.D.," she practically shouted, "you've got to come to Freddy's suite at once. He's a mess. Even Inga can't do anything with him."

G.D. barely looked up from his brandy. "So what makes you think I can?"

Grisly pinched G.D.'s ear. "If Inga says you can help, then you can. Inga knows what's good for Freddy. So do I. Get off your fat butt and come upstairs."

G.D. angrily shook off Grisly's hold on his ear. "I'll come when I damned well feel like it," he said in a rumbling basso. "I'm going to finish my drink first."

Grisly stood back a few inches, thin arms crossed over her flat bosom. "Fine. Freddy's lost an ex-wife and a fiancée in the last twenty-four hours. Just sit there like a big toad and see the whole act go down the toilet. It's your livelihood, not mine." She swung around and stomped out of the bar.

"Livelihood, my ass," G.D. snarled to nobody in particular. "As if she's ever worked a day in her worthless life." He sniffed and sipped.

The young man who'd been sitting on the bar stool at the end of the counter guzzled down the rest of his beer, tossed a ten-dollar bill next to his tab, and walked off. Judith slid into his place.

"I'm so sorry for what's happened with the Great Mandolini," she said softly. "My husband's kept me informed."

Rubbing at the ear that Grisly had pinched, G.D.'s beady, dark eyes glared at Judith. "And who the hell are you?"

"Mrs. Flynn," Judith replied in the same soft voice. "Mrs. Joe Flynn."

G.D. raised his bushy eyebrows, but his attitude thawed a bit. "The private dick? Hunh. I thought I'd seen you around. You're Fatso, right?"

Judith flinched. "Uh . . . yes, I am. Who told you that?"

G.D. frowned. "I don't remember. Inga, maybe."

The bartender came up to Judith. "What'll it be, hon?" she asked in a whiskey soprano.

"Just a glass of water, please," Judith said humbly. "My Galliano-rocks is back at the table," she added, pointing over her shoulder. "I have to take my pain pills."

"Right." The bartender moved down to the water-dispensing area, filled a glass, and plunked it down in front of Judith. "Cheers."

"Thank you." Judith realized that she hadn't brought her purse with her. She also realized that she was over an hour away from her next dose of pain pills. "Freddy must be overcome," she said. "How can he bear it?"

"So he's got a choice?" G.D. growled. "Hell, if I were him, and had all those meddlesome women hanging around my neck, I'd be damned glad to get rid of a couple of 'em." The manager took another sniff and another swig.

"'Meddlesome'?" Judith repeated.

G.D. shot her a dark look. "Never mind. Forget what I said." His small eyes darted to the counter. "I don't see any pills, Fatso."

Judith knew dismissal when she heard it. But that didn't mean she was going to walk away meekly. "How long have you been Freddy's manager?"

G.D. shrugged. "Almost four years. How come you're so snoopy?"

"Because," she replied, trying not to grit her teeth, "I'm Fatso."

"Oh." G.D. chuckled unpleasantly. "I almost forgot. So you go around quizzing people, huh? Well, I don't feel like being quizzed."

Out of the corner of her eye, Judith saw Bill and Renie get up and move out of the bar. "Damn!" Judith swore under her breath. "My purse! My drink!" Heedless of her artificial hip, she slid off the bar stool and headed for the now-vacant table.

Her purse was still under her chair; the Galliano-rocks remained on the table. Judith scooped up both, then started back to the bar.

G.D. Fromm was gone. She watched him disappear beyond a half dozen people waiting for a table. About twenty yards away, she saw Bill and Renie part company. He was headed for the table games. Renie was marching off to the quarter slots in the Autumn section. Judith followed, in pursuit.

"You left my purse unattended," Judith cried when she caught up with Renie, who was sitting down at a Fall into Riches machine. "I could have been robbed!"

"Try a one-armed bandit instead," Renie replied in a voice that was aggravatingly calm. "Take a seat."

Judith was still annoyed with Renie. "How could you and Bill walk off and leave my purse like that? Why didn't you bring it up to me at the bar? Not to mention my drink."

"Why don't you take responsibility for going off and leaving us while you play detective?" Renie shot back, slinging quarters into her machine. "We'd already left once to go to the rest room. Nobody stole your damned purse then."

"I can't believe you two," Judith grumbled as she sat down next to her cousin. "I'm checking to make sure nobody stole my wallet." Rummaging in her capacious black bag, Judith felt the wallet, safe and sound. She also felt something else that she couldn't identify by touch. Taking it out, she saw that it was a cocktail napkin from the bar. Someone had written on it in a hasty scrawl.

"Good Lord!" Judith gasped. "Look at this!" With an unsteady hand, Judith shoved the note in front of Renie.

"Butt Out Or You'll Be Next."

A disinterested Renie leaned over to read the napkin's message. She gave a start and her expression showed alarm. "Could it be a joke?"

"If it is," Judith replied on a steely note, "I'm not laughing."

Chapter Eleven

R ENIE was still looking at the note. "Who do you think wrote that?"

"I don't know." Judith reexamined the napkin. "Whoever it was must have come along while you and your equally careless husband left my purse unguarded."

"Stick it," Renie said. "You get so caught up in playing detective that you forget your real life. As in being responsible for your own possessions."

Judith shot Renie a reproachful look. "You've turned into someone I hardly recognize since you got to the casino. You're all about greed."

"That's why I go to casinos, dopey," Renie said in a sour voice.

Judith, who didn't like to argue nearly as much as her cousin did, and rarely convinced Renie that she was wrong, dropped the subject. "I'm taking this note to Joe."

"Do you know where he is?" Renie inquired, rolling the barrels on her three-quarter slot.

"Probably still with Micki's body," Judith replied. "They haven't had very long to take pictures and do the rest of the crime-scene stuff. Say, where did you go to the rest room? The one by the coffee shop is closed."

"Right." Renie jerked her arm in the opposite direction. "There are rest rooms between the bar and the Autumn section."

"I'm surprised you take time out to use the bathroom," Judith retorted, still clutching the note. "I thought maybe you used those plastic buckets." She stood up again. "I'm leaving now."

Renie stayed focused on the slot machine. "'Bye. Good luck."

"Impossible," Judith declared as she walked away. "If I didn't love her, I'd hate her."

The mood in the casino struck Judith as subdued. Or maybe she was imbuing gamblers with too much sensitivity. If Renie was typical, then a wholesale massacre could take place and the gamblers would scarcely bat an eye.

The entrance to the coffee shop was still guarded by Emily and Amos. The crowd had thinned out considerably, though a few gawkers wandered by outside the roped-off area. *Not gamblers,* Judith thought, *or they wouldn't be interested.*

"Hi, Emily, Amos," Judith said in greeting. "Is my husband still with the victim?"

Emily offered Judith a warm smile. "I was wondering when you'd be here to help. I saw you leave with Mr. and Mrs. Jones. Are they suspects?"

"Yes," Judith said, her face serious as virtue lost out to mischief. "Yes, they are. Keep an eye on them, especially her. Mrs. Jones may be dangerous."

Emily's eyes widened. "Really? She looks so . . ."

"Small and weak?" Judith shook her head. "Don't buy into it. It's a facade. She knows more martial arts than Jackie Chan."

"Wow!" Emily looked impressed.

Amos's expression, however, was slightly skeptical. "Were you interrogating them?" he inquired politely.

"Certainly," Judith responded. "Now what about Joe?"

"He went upstairs to Mr. Green's office just a couple of minutes ago," Emily said. "I think they're going to remove the body soon. Oh—here comes the sheriff now."

Judith's head swiveled in the direction of the rest rooms. To her dismay, Abbott N. Costello strode out into the foyer. So did another man in a similar gray uniform who also looked all too familiar. Dabney Plummer, Judith recalled. Seven years earlier, Dabney had been more boy than man. Now his tall, lean figure had fleshed out and his youthful features had sharpened. He had been more like Costello's lackey than his associate. As the duo came closer, Judith ducked her head.

"I'm going to find Joe," she murmured and somehow managed to escape undetected by the sheriff and his deputy.

To Judith's surprise, the receptionist's desk that Emily had manned earlier was now occupied by Grisly Vanderbehr. She gave Judith a hostile look.

"What do you want?" Grisly demanded.

"I want to speak to my husband." Judith nodded toward the closed door that led into Pancho's inner sanctum. "He's in there, isn't he?"

"He's busy in there," Grisly snapped. "Do you want to leave a message?"

"No, I do not," Judith said emphatically. "What I have to say to Mr. Flynn is urgent."

"Oooh . . ." Grisly slapped a hand on the desk. "Okay, okay, but make it quick."

Judith was sufficiently surprised by the number of people who had crowded into Pancho's office: There was Pancho himself, G. D. Fromm, Lloyd Watts, Manny Quinn, Jack Jackrabbit, and, of course, Joe. But what startled Judith most was the sight of Freddy Polson, propped up in a chair and being ministered to by his sister, Inga. Freddy's skin was very pale, his cheeks looked sunken, and his eyes were red. His sister appeared to be proffering some kind of hot drink in a mug.

Everyone except the Polson duo stared when Judith entered the room. She pointed to Joe. "May I? It'll take only a minute."

Joe looked more annoyed than curious, but he stood up and walked over to Judith.

"Look," she said, showing him the cocktail napkin with its dire warning.

Joe excused himself and propelled Judith not only out of the room, but through the reception area and into the hallway. "Where the hell did that come from?" he asked in an irritable tone.

Judith explained how Renie and Bill had left her purse unattended in the Autumn Bar. "They were probably gone for five minutes or so. The bar was crowded. Anyone could have slipped the note in my purse."

Joe sighed deeply. "Not quite anyone. You said you left your purse under the chair? This person might have seen you put it there. What it comes down to is who, if anybody, among our potential suspects did you see in the bar?"

"Umm . . ." In her explanation about the purse, Judith had omitted the part about accosting G. D. Fromm, merely saying that she'd gone up to get a glass of water from the bartender. "Mr. Fromm was there," she said in a casual voice. "So was Grisly, but only briefly, as far as I know. She came to fetch Mr. Fromm."

"That makes two," Joe said.

"I kind of doubt it was Mr. Fromm. I saw him leave and he wasn't near my purse."

"One, then," Joe amended. "I suppose someone else could have done it while you were taking your pills."

"Ah . . . yes, my pills."

Joe was regarding his wife with professional skepticism. "Did you notice Bill and Renie leave for the cans?"

"No," Judith admitted. "I was admiring the bar."

"Sheesh." Joe held out his hand. "Give me that napkin. I'll turn it over to the lab, just in case."

Judith obeyed. "The lab? What lab?"

"The county sheriff's lab," Joe said, holding the napkin's corner between his thumb and forefinger. "The FBI has bailed on us for the time being. They're chasing terrorists, or some other bunch of damned fools. We're going to use the county lab, since Sheriff Costello has been good enough to offer it."

Good wasn't a word that Judith associated with Abbott N. Costello. *Pigheaded, Inflexible,* and *Egotistical* came more readily to mind. But all Judith said was, "Okay."

"I've got to go back in there," Joe said, indicating the door to Pancho's outer office. "Inga Polson is considering sending her brother to the hospital. She thinks he's having a breakdown."

"Oh, dear. I suppose you can't blame him after losing two of the women he loved most," Judith said.

"True," Joe responded, his hand on the doorknob. "Even if he might have caused the loss."

Judith was surprised. "Do you really think he killed Sally and Micki?"

"Anything's possible," Joe said with a shrug. "As for Freddy being overcome—some killers can actually make themselves believe they didn't do it. And others are so overwhelmed with guilt and grief that they fall apart. The mind plays strange tricks when terrible, irreversible wrongs occur."

"Yes," Judith agreed, "that's true." She hesitated as Joe started to open the door. "May I come with you?"

Joe looked pained. "You shouldn't. This is an official double-homicide investigation."

"Where's Sheriff Costello?"

"Still at the crime scene," Joe replied, looking antsy. "For now, he's technical support only."

Judith didn't express her relief aloud. She pointed to the partially open door. "Can I?"

Joe was obviously debating with himself. "Not right now," he finally said. "Wait until we see what happens to Freddy. It's pretty awkward in there at the moment."

Since Joe hadn't given her a flat-out no, Judith's spirits picked up. "That's okay. You don't mind if I speak with Grisly, do you?"

Joe paused. "No, go ahead. We're short of manpower. Grisly's acting as security in the reception area."

"A suspect—I mean, a witness—as security?" Judith asked, puzzled.

"She's used to keeping the groupies away from Freddy," Joe said. "Besides, she's all we've got." His green eyes lit up. "Unless you want to sit in for her."

"Sure," Judith said, trying not to sound too eager. "I'd be glad to do it. Shall I?" She took a step toward the threshold.

"You're on," Joe said. "You tell her. And send her into the inner office, okay?" He breezed through the reception area and was gone.

Judith wasn't going to waste her opportunity, however. She went through the outer door, leaned against the desk, and offered Grisly a sympathetic smile. "You must be worn out."

"What?" Grisly spoke sharply. "Oh. Yes, I am. It's been a grueling twenty-four hours."

Judith cleared a space and perched on the desk. "I understand you've known Freddy and Sally since you were all kids in Shoshone, Idaho."

"Right." Grisly, who was doodling on a notepad, only glanced at Judith.

"You all went to grade school together, didn't you?"

"Right." Grisly was making slashing notations with a ballpoint pen. They looked like rainfall to Judith. Or maybe tears.

"Wasn't Sally the girl next door?"

"Not to me." Grisly kept doodling.

"I meant to Freddy," Judith said, trying to be patient.

"Oh. Well, almost. They lived on the same street."

"But you all went through school together," Judith pointed out.

"Through grade school. Right." Abruptly, Grisly stopped doodling and scrunched up the piece of paper. "Lay off, will you? I don't feel like talking about this stuff. It's a really bad time for me."

"And everybody else," Judith reminded Grisly. "You're done here. I'm taking over. They want you in the inner office."

"My, my," Grisly said in a sarcastic tone, "since when did they put you in charge?"

"Since my husband told me to take over here," Judith replied crossly as the door opened to reveal G. D. Fromm and Lloyd Watts carrying Freddy Polson out of the inner office. Inga Polson and Pancho Green followed the trio into the reception area.

"We're putting Freddy to bed," Pancho announced. "Doc Engelman should be back soon. He can give Freddy a sedative. Inga will sit with him in the meantime."

Freddy was twitching all over the place, as if he was having a seizure. G.D. and Lloyd were having trouble getting him out into the hallway.

"Be careful!" Inga bellowed. "Freddy's delicate, he's sensitive! He's not a bag of barley!"

"Yeah, yeah, yeah," G.D. shot back as he edged past Judith and into the corridor. "We know who the bag is around here."

Judith caught Inga's hostile glare as she trooped behind the men. But something else caught her eye as well: There was a flash or two of glitter on the back of G.D.'s suit jacket. It looked very much like the flecks that Judith had brushed off her own clothing earlier in the evening. She wondered if Fromm had been the man who'd bumped into her in the darkened coffee shop.

Grisly banged on the door behind the little group. "Even though he's Freddy's manager, G.D. doesn't act like it sometimes. Poor Freddy." With a worried expression, she stalked off into the inner office.

Judith sat down at the desk. To her disappointment, Grisly hadn't left any telltale items behind. The drawers revealed nothing of interest except for materials and supplies that Pancho's regular receptionist used. Even the daybook didn't contain anything that might be regarded as suspicious. The receptionist—whose name was Alberta Saenz, according to her individualized memo pad—was terse in her notations for Pancho's business day:

Monday, March 5—L.R. re St. Patrick's Day promos, 9 A.M.

           D.A. re land survey, 10 A.M.

           P.J. re St. Patrick's Day menu, 11:15 A.M.

           Lunch—county commissioners, noon

           R.B. re investment portfolio, 2 P.M.

           N.G., USDI, 3:30 P.M.

           G.D.F. re main stage, 4:45 P.M.

All entries had been canceled for Tuesday, March sixth, and Wednesday, March seventh. No doubt, Judith thought, because of the tragedy. In any event, the half dozen that had been scheduled seemed mainly to deal with the upcoming St. Patrick's Day festivities and a look ahead to Easter.

The only thing on Monday's agenda that caught Judith's eye was the last afternoon appointment with G.D.F., who, she assumed, was G. D. Fromm. But that wasn't surprising. Freddy's act was playing in the cabaret. Looking at the casino's entertainment schedule, she noted that the Great Mandolini had opened Friday, March second, and was slated to run through the nineteenth. The replacement act, which had been penciled in by someone, was a Country & Western band called the Kitshickers. The grunge group that had opened for Freddy's act would do the same for the new troupe.

Judith drummed her nails on the desk. Who was still in Pancho's office? The exodus had been fairly large. Joe was still in there, so were Pancho, Grisly, Jack Jackrabbit, and Manny Quinn. That was about it.

Or was, until Lloyd Watts and G. D. Fromm returned from taking Freddy to his room. Lloyd paused to nod at Judith, but G.D. bustled toward the second door.

Judith couldn't resist. "Mr. Fromm," she called out, "could you come here for a moment?"

Fromm gave Judith a puzzled look. "What now?"

"Nothing important," Judith simpered as G.D. took a couple of backward steps. "I didn't notice when we were in the bar because it was so dark, but," she went on, rising from the chair and coming around the desk, "you have something on your suit coat."

"Huh?" G.D. shot Judith a doubtful glance, then wiggled a bit as Judith brushed him off. "What is it? Bugs?"

"No," Judith replied, examining the four tiny specks on her palm, "not unless they're gold bugs. What is this stuff?"

G.D. stared at the hand that Judith held out to him. She thought he gave a little start, but he shook his head so emphatically that his combover slipped a notch. "Who knows? Something off the stage sets or the costumes, maybe. I'm outta here." He tromped into Pancho's office.

Lloyd, however, lingered. "Let me have a look, eh?"

"Sure." Judith showed him the specks. "They shine."

"They do." Lloyd pressed one onto his middle finger to examine it more closely. "Some kind of glitter. I think one of Sally's costumes has this on it. But she didn't wear it Monday night."

"This is Tuesday," Judith pointed out. "Was G.D. wearing the same suit yesterday?"

Lloyd looked uneasy. "Gosh . . . I don't know. He always wears a dark suit. Could be the same one, for all I know."

Something was niggling at Judith's brain. It was more gold glitter, but she couldn't remember where she'd seen it. "Who's in charge of the costumes?"

"Grisly," Lloyd replied. "She takes care of all the gear. Props, too. Everything."

"I see," Judith said. But she didn't see much except the glittery specks that still adhered to her palm. With a shrug, she wiped them off with a Kleenex from a box on the desk. "It probably doesn't mean a thing."

"Better go inside," Lloyd murmured and hurried into the office.

"Rats!" Judith said aloud when the door closed behind Lloyd. She didn't seem to be getting anywhere with the murder case. She couldn't even get into Pancho's office. Frustrated, she plopped back down in the chair. The phone rang as soon as she was seated.

"Pancho Green's office," she said in her best telephone voice. "May I help you?"

"Who's this?" the man at the other end asked, sounding puzzled.

Judith recognized Doc Engelman's voice. "It's Judith Flynn, Joe's wife, Doctor. I'm manning the reception desk in Pancho's office."

"Good for you," Doc Engelman said. "Can you deliver a message to your husband and Jack Jackrabbit?"

"Certainly," Judith replied. "Are you still at the hospital?"

"Yes, the one here in Glacier Falls," Doc said. "I'm sticking around for a bit to make sure Mrs. Flax can be released."

"Mrs. Flax?" Judith repeated.

"Yes, she's the woman who was holding the saber. We managed to ID her through the hotel's front desk," Doc explained. "She checked in last night. Her name is Marta Ormond Flax, age forty-six, from Salt Lake City, Utah. The poodle is Fou-Fou Eugenie des

Plaines, age five, also from Salt Lake. The dog, I believe, is still at the hotel."

Judith had jotted down all the information. "I gather Mrs. Flax is going to be okay?"

"She'd be better if she went straight to rehab," Doc asserted. "But that's not up to me."

Judith cleared her throat. "Don't be put off by the question, but is there a policeman with her at the hospital?"

"Why do you ask?"

"Since she was holding what might be a murder weapon," Judith explained, "she could be a suspect. My husband would want to know if someone is stationed there."

"He already knows," Engelman replied a bit gruffly. "It's that county deputy, Plummer. Just pass on the information about Mrs. Flax's condition, okay?"

Judith said she would. After hanging up, she realized that she could ring Pancho's inner office. But she preferred delivering the message in person. A rap on the door brought her face-to-face with Jack Jackrabbit.

"What is it?" he asked, his thin face serious.

"May I come in?"

Jack glanced over his shoulder, into the smoky room. "Why?" he inquired when there was no response from the others, including Joe.

"I have a message from Dr. Engelman." Judith tried to edge into the room.

Jack stood his ground. "What is it?"

"It's confidential."

Jack looked puzzled. "There's nobody here but us."

Judith looked past Jack to Joe, who was unwrapping a cigar and ignoring his wife. "Oooh . . ." With an angry gesture, Judith handed over the note she'd written. "Here. Read it for yourself. By the way," she said over her shoulder as she headed back into the reception area, "I quit."

"Quit what?" Jack asked as Judith slammed the door in his face.

She snatched up her purse and marched out of the office and into the hall, telling herself there was absolutely no reason why she had to spend the evening stuck behind a desk. It appeared there was no way she was going to be allowed into the inner sanctum. She got in the elevator and got off on the casino floor. Renie could darn well stop shoveling quarters into those blasted machines and do something worthwhile.

It took Judith almost ten minutes to find her cousin, who had moved on to the Summer section.

"Have you won anything yet?" Judith asked in a crabby voice.

Renie looked up from her Super Sunshine slot. "Dribs and drabs. What's with you?"

"I'm mad. Frustrated, too," Judith replied, sitting down next to Renie. "I don't understand Joe."

"What's to understand? He's a man." Renie shoved a twenty-dollar bill into the machine. "Play that next one. Some old coot won a hundred bucks on it a few minutes ago."

"You play it," Judith snapped.

"I would except somebody won four hundred dollars off this one just before I showed up," Renie replied. "I figure it might still be hot. Go on, take a chance."

Judith figured it might be best to humor her cousin for a few minutes. "Okay," she said with a sigh of resignation. "I'll put a ten into it. No more."

"Aha!" Renie was smiling at the machine. "I got twenty bucks! This one's okay!"

Judith pushed the button and saw two suns and a rain cloud show up. "This one's not."

"Give it time," Renie said. "What's your problem with Joe?"

"One minute, he seems to think I could be of help just talking to people involved in the case," Judith explained as a sun, a moon, and a jackpot symbol showed across the line. "Then the next, he won't let me near the suspects. I don't get it."

"I suppose he has to present a professional facade to the casino folks," Renie said. "Hey—another twenty!"

"Good for you," Judith said without enthusiasm. "I've been sitting in Pancho's office like a big twerp for the past half hour, doing absolutely nothing. It makes me antsy." She paused, gazing at the screen. "What's with these three symbols?"

Renie leaned over to take a look. "Holy cats! That's the jackpot! You just won a thousand bucks!"

Judith frowned. "Is that why those bells are going off and the light is flashing?"

"That's right!" Renie had gotten out of her chair and was jumping up and down behind Judith. "Coz, you're amazing! Didn't I tell you that thing was hot? High fives!"

Judith held up a limp hand. Renie slapped it so hard that Judith marveled her cousin didn't dislocate her shoulder.

But Renie wasn't done celebrating. She leaned past Judith to kiss the slot machine, then did a little dance in the aisle. "Wahoo!" she cried. "Yippee! Hooray for coz!"

"Cut it out," Judith said sharply as a crowd began to gather. "You're embarrassing me."

Renie stopped in midstep. "Huh?" She looked around at the spectators. "Oh. Nothing to see here, nothing to see here."

The small crowd didn't agree. They saw the three symbols lined up on the screen and began to applaud.

Judith flinched. "Goodness," she breathed. "What do I do now?"

"Cash out," Renie said. "It's set on credit now. Here." She pressed the appropriate button. A cascade of coins began crashing into the metal tray.

"Good Lord," Judith exclaimed, "how am I going to carry all these quarters to the coin booth?"

"You aren't," Renie replied. "Look." She pointed to the instructions at the top of the machine. "This thing only pays the first four hundred quarters. They'll bring you the rest of it in bills." Renie's head jerked up. "Here comes a mechanic now."

The mechanic was followed by a cocktail waitress who was followed by two men who looked like floor bosses, all of whom showered profuse congratulations on Judith. Players passing by stopped in admiration. The machine, which had finally dumped all of its treasure, was opened with a key. Another mechanic showed up with a fresh bag of quarters. Meanwhile, one of the floor bosses made some notations, then opened his wallet and handed Judith nine one-hundred-dollar bills. The hopper was refilled. Judith was asked to pull off the winning jackpot so no one else could claim to have won it. The new spin netted her another twenty-five dollars.

"I don't believe this," Judith gasped as the casino employees practically bowed and scraped their way back down the aisle. The onlookers were talking among themselves, their words running the gamut from pleasure to envy.

"Believe it," Renie said with a grin. "I'll help you scoop up the coins. You'll need three buckets for all of this."

The cousins dug and delved for several minutes. Finally, Judith cashed out her latest winnings while Renie emptied about two hundred quarters of her own into a separate bucket.

The coins were heavy. The cousins slowly made their way to the nearest change booth where Judith was given another hunsky, plus an additional thirty-three dollars.

"I'm taking the hundreds to the safe," she declared with an ominous glance at her cousin. "I wouldn't want to leave my purse full of hundred-dollar bills with my loved ones and have it stolen. Want to come with me?"

Unfazed by the barb, Renie demurred. "I'm going back to those same machines if the vultures haven't already taken over. I'll see you when you get done."

Dolly was on duty again at the cashier's window. "Aha!" she exclaimed with a toothy smile. "You must be reeling 'em in. Whatcha got now, sweetie?"

Carefully, Judith counted out the ten bills, but held on to the last one. "I just remembered—I owe my cousin a hundred dollars. I'll keep one bill for her."

Dolly laughed, a rich, throaty sound. "Keep it in the family, that's the way. Do you want a cashier's check or shall I put the bills in the safe with your other winnings?"

"I'll have you make out a cashier's check and put it in the safe like you did the other time," Judith said.

"You're the boss," Dolly said, taking the money. "I'll be back in a jiffy with your receipt."

Judith glanced over her shoulder. Five people stood in line behind her. She smiled apologetically. A dark-haired woman whose skin was weathered by the sun and whose glasses had frames shaped like butterfly wings came out from the back to open a second cashier's window. Two of the people behind Judith stepped out of the line and moved toward the counter.

It seemed to be taking Dolly a long time to type up a check, write a receipt, and put the money in the safe. Could the bills be counterfeit? There'd been an article in the newspaper recently about phony twenties and even some bogus hundreds being passed in the area. Judith began to fret.

But a moment later, Dolly reappeared, receipt in hand. Her usual cheerful expression was gone, however, replaced by a worried look.

Behind the window's gilded bars, she leaned as close as she could to Judith.

"I'm so sorry, Mrs. Flynn," she whispered. "I think a mistake has been made."

Judith's worst fears were confirmed. "The money's no good?"

Dolly looked shocked. "Oh, no! It's not that." Her voice had risen, but she lowered it once more. "I believe one of the new hires got confused and put something into your safe by mistake." She glanced around nervously, then spoke so softly that Judith could hardly hear her. "You didn't have us put a bag of gold nuggets in the safe, did you?"

Chapter Twelve

Judith caught herself before speaking too loudly. "No," she said softly but firmly. "No gold nuggets. Definitely not."

Dolly's shoulders slumped in relief. "That's what I thought. Really, you'd think young people these days would know the alphabet. I'll take care of the matter right away. Meanwhile, here's your receipt and four comps for dinner tomorrow night in our premier restaurant, the Johnny-Jump-Up Room. It's our way of apologizing for the mix-up. Now," she went on, her voice back to normal, "you run along and knock 'em dead."

Judith was so lost in thought as she made her way back to the Summer section that she almost collided with Joe.

"Hey!" he exclaimed, catching her by the arm. "What's up? You're in a daze."

"Oh!" She smiled halfheartedly at her husband. "Are you finished with the interviews?"

Joe nodded. "For now. Not that they've done us much good."

Judith refrained from saying that if she had more opportunity to converse with the suspects, she might be able to learn some helpful information. Instead, she merely offered Joe commiseration.

"The evening's still young," he remarked, gazing at the baccarat tables where Bill was studying one of the games. "It's not quite ten o'clock. I think I'll get Bill to further my baccarat education."

"Okay." As with her earlier winnings, Judith decided not to tell Joe about her most recent windfall. She couldn't mention the mistake about the gold nuggets, either. If she did, she'd have to explain why she was at the cashier's window. Her silence would serve him right for keeping her out of the interview room. "I'll be with Renie. Wherever she might be."

"Okay," Joe said, starting toward Bill. "If I don't see you around in the casino, I'll go to the room about midnight."

"Fine," Judith said before continuing on her quest to find Renie.

It wasn't difficult. Renie was still in the Summer section, but she had taken off a shoe and was pounding the slot machine in front of her and swearing at the top of her lungs. A half dozen onlookers stood well back, cringing at each cuss word and wincing at every whack.

"Coz!" Judith cried, hurrying up to her irate cousin. "Stop that! You're making a spectacle of yourself!"

Renie let out one more shriek and gave the slot machine a swift kick with her stockinged foot. "Ow!" She scowled, rubbed her foot, and shot the gawkers a menacing look. "Beat it, or I'll charge admission. That's the only way I'm going to make any money in this stupid place."

The spectators moved away, some of them shaking their heads, others chuckling. Renie put her shoe back on and turned to Judith. "Well?"

"I take it you're losing," Judith said in a calm voice.

"Yes, I'm losing," Renie retorted. "How can you possibly tell?"

Judith reached into her purse and took out her wallet. "Never mind. Though I do wonder why you still throw temper tantrums and beat up inanimate objects when you're almost old enough for Medicare."

"So what? If I hurt myself when I hit sixty-five, I'll get better medical coverage." Renie fingered her chin. "Or will I? I've never understood Medicare."

"Never mind," Judith said with a sigh, handing over the hundred-dollar bill she owed her cousin from the roulette winnings. "As long as you're losing, why don't you come with me?"

Renie, who was eyeing the slot machines with loathing, accepted the money with mumbled thanks. "Come where?" she asked.

"Backstage."

"We can't go there. It's performance time."

"Not on a Tuesday," Judith said, marching in the direction of the cabaret. "The guests will be attending the French revue and the would-be Elvis shows on the second stage."

The first thing that the cousins noticed when they got to the door that led backstage was that the crime-scene tape was gone. So was any sign of a security guard. The only deterrent to their passage was a large sign that read "Keep Out." Judith and Renie ignored it.

But the door was locked.

"You can pick a lock," Renie said. "Go for it."

Judith grimaced. It was true that she had the expertise. During her marriage to Dan, it had been necessary to open desk drawers and strongboxes simply to learn if there was a lien on the McMonigle house or if they'd been charged with income-tax evasion and were headed for the federal penitentiary.

"People are going by," Judith protested. "I don't dare. We'll get in trouble."

"So?"

"Don't be stupid." Judith fixed Renie with a warning stare. "Do you want to get thrown out of the resort?"

Renie looked as if she were weighing the consequences. "You're right," she finally said with a shrug. "It was a dumb idea anyway. Maybe I should try roulette or blackjack."

"Maybe not," Judith murmured, looking beyond Renie to the approaching figure of Manny Quinn. "Hold it, here comes Mr. Quinn."

"What's up?" he asked.

"No one told us this door was locked," Judith said with a perturbed expression. "You're Manny Quinn, aren't you? Have you got a key?"

"Yeah," Manny replied, a wary glint in his gray eyes. "So what?"

"So you can let us in," Judith said. "Really, this is too frustrating. How can I get my husband's glasses if the door's locked? I'm Mrs. Joe Flynn."

"Men," Renie said, rolling her eyes.

Manny studied Judith for a moment, perhaps trying to place her. "Flynn left his glasses in there?"

"Yes," Judith responded. "He doesn't wear them all the time, but he needs them for reading."

"What the hell," Manny muttered. "Here, follow me." He palmed a key from the pocket of his tailored slacks and slipped it into the lock. "Ladies first," he said, making an expansive gesture.

"Thanks, Mr. Quinn," Judith said. "Will we be able to get out or should we wait for you?"

Manny didn't need a key to open the second door. "I may be a while. I think it's unlocked from this side anyway. If not, get one of the techs to let you out." He allowed the cousins to go first, then paused at a mirror to smooth his silver hair. "Do you know where your old man left his glasses?"

"Umm . . . Somewhere near the Mandolini costumes, I think."

"Then you go downstairs," Manny said. "There's a spiral staircase over there by that red piano."

Judith found the steel steps and led the way to the basement. "It's kind of dark down here," she said, descending the staircase with caution.

"By the way, why are we here?" Renie asked as they reached the bottom.

"Aside from the fact that we're trying to help Joe solve a double homicide," Judith said, feeling along the wall for a light switch, "I'm curious. I've never been behind the scenes in a theater before."

"I have," Renie replied. "It's not that big a thrill. Why don't we try the lamp over in the corner? Maybe it turns on higher than dim."

The lamp, of the gooseneck variety, had only one wattage, but there was a switch next to the plug in. Judith clicked it. Two overhead bulbs came on, giving sufficient light for exploration.

"I don't suppose they keep the animals down here," Judith said, taking in the area that was about the size of a baseball diamond.

"Hardly," Renie replied. "They're outside somewhere, probably in trailers."

"Good." Judith's gaze roamed around the cluttered basement. There were wardrobes marked "Costumes," piles of scenery, musical instruments, and every imaginable prop, from a church altar to twelve-foot-high flamingos on stilts. "This is a maze," she said. "Look, here's an old wind-up Victrola like the one we had at the cabin. And there's a washstand just like mine that I use for the minibar in the dining room."

"This wardrobe is marked 'Vintage,'" Renie noted. "I'll bet it's full of clothes that we wore in our younger years. You've probably still got some of them since you never throw anything out."

Judith didn't respond to her cousin's dig. Instead, she was studying another wardrobe that had "Mandolini" stenciled on its side. "Let's have a peek," she said, carefully trying to pry open the front of the wooden box.

A shimmering array of costumes was revealed to the cousins.

There were long gowns, bathing suits, cloaks, capes, and even a couple of cat costumes.

"Sally's," Judith remarked. "The rest of it looks like Freddy's outfits. Dark suits, capes, white shirts. Of course, the costume Sally wore when she was killed isn't here."

Renie's trained eye had zeroed in on a strapless copper gown that looked smaller and shorter than the others. Underneath it was a purple satin number about the same size.

"What do you make of these two?" Renie asked, fingering the satin material.

It took Judith a few seconds to understand what her cousin meant. "Ah. Those two outfits wouldn't fit Sally." She studied the gowns for a moment or two. "Micki?"

"Backup?" Renie said.

"Maybe." Carefully, Judith lifted the gowns just enough to check the labels for sizing. "These are both a six. The others are a ten."

"So Micki was the understudy?"

"I suppose there'd have to be one," Judith said. "But that wasn't Micki we saw at the end of the act. So how—" She stopped abruptly, espying the silver gown underneath the two size sixes. "Good Lord," she gasped. "This *is* the dress that Sally wore in the saber scene!"

"It can't be," Renie declared. "That dress would be evidence."

"Yes, it would," Judith agreed, removing the sparkling silver gown. "But it's unharmed." She locked gazes with her cousin. "Which can mean only one thing—this is a duplicate. So who wore it?"

"We've been through that," Renie replied. "Grisly is the only one who might fit into one of Sally's costumes."

"No, she isn't," Judith said, staring at the silver gown. "How about Marta Flax of Salt Lake City?"

Renie was mystified. "Huh?"

"The blonde with the poodle," Judith said. "Doc Engelman told me who she is. Marta checked into the resort yesterday."

"She almost checked out today," Renie noted, "permanently. So who is she now that she's not catatonic?"

Judith was still gazing at the ball gown and didn't answer right away. "What? Oh—all I know is her name and where she's from. But she's the right size and has blond hair. You know, we ought to take this dress to Joe so he can send it to the county lab for DNA testing."

"You'd better not touch it," Renie said. "Get Joe or Jack Jackrabbit to do it. We might screw it up."

"You're right," Judith agreed, making sure everything in the wardrobe was arranged in its proper order. "I'll tell Joe right away."

The cousins were closing the door when they heard a voice from somewhere above them.

"Who's there?"

Judith turned quickly, gazing up at the spiral staircase. All she could see were feet. Sneakers and pants cuffs. The voice belonged to a man. Before Judith could respond, Renie spoke up.

"We're burglars. Who wants to know?"

"What?" The man moved slowly down the stairs.

Judith recognized Lloyd Watts. "Lloyd! You scared us. Have you met my cousin, Serena?"

Lloyd looked relieved. "Not burglars, eh?"

"Hardly," Judith said as Lloyd joined them. "We just wanted to look around. I've never been backstage before. It's fascinating."

Lloyd waved a hand. "All this junk?"

"It's interesting junk," Judith said. "How can you tell where everything is?"

Lloyd shrugged. "Easy. I know what's ours and what isn't. I came down to get my theremin. Somebody put it down here after . . . the tragedy. I like to keep it with me. They're kind of rare."

"I enjoyed your performance," Renie said. "I'd heard about the theremin, but I'd never seen it played before. It certainly suits a magic act. Illusion, I mean."

"It's a different kind of soul music," Lloyd said. "You don't touch it. So it's like playing with your soul. You know—a communion, a spiritual thing." He stopped speaking as he scanned the section where several instruments were stored. "Ah. There it is. Doesn't seem right. Not with drums and oboes and banjos."

Lloyd retrieved his precious theremin, gave the cousins a diffident smile, and headed back up the staircase.

"Shall we?" Renie asked of Judith as Lloyd's sneakers disappeared from view.

"We might as well," Judith said. "Let me turn off the overhead lights."

She flicked the switch on the wall, leaving only the gooseneck lamp for illumination. Despite the dim light, Judith was still gazing around the basement. She didn't see the cord from the lamp, and tripped over it.

"Oops!" she cried, catching herself on an item that was encased in heavy plastic.

"Are you okay?" Renie asked, alarmed.

"Yes, I'm fine." Judith turned around. "The lamp's fine, too. I was afraid I might have knocked it over."

"Give yourself a minute," Renie cautioned as she moved closer to Judith. "Make sure your hip's all right."

The cousins both jumped and screamed as a hurtling object fell from above and crashed on the exact spot where Renie had just been standing.

"My God!" Judith cried. "What is it? You could have been killed!"

"So could you," Renie said, her eyes huge and her face pale. "Whatever it is landed only a couple of feet away from both of us." Tentatively, she took a step closer to the bulky object. "It's one of those sandbag things they use for theater curtains." She stared up into the far reaches of the basement ceiling. "There's a catwalk up there. But I don't see anything now."

"It must have been an accident," Judith said, but she felt uneasy as well as shaken. It had probably been foolish to insist upon snooping in the basement. Maybe fate was telling Judith to mind her own business for once.

Given her nature, that was impossible. Still clinging to the large plastic wrapping, she tried to settle her nerves. And the longer she held on to the plastic, the more her curiosity grew. "What is this thing? They're two of them, in fact."

"Two whats?" Renie asked, taking one last look up into the shadowy area above them.

Judith grimaced. "This is weird. They feel like statues."

"That's not weird," Renie replied. "This place is jammed with props."

Acknowledging that Renie was right, Judith started to walk away. But something stopped her in her tracks. "I have to peek," she declared. "Let me see if I can open this plastic just enough to see whether it's the *Venus de Milo* or Minnie Pearl."

What Judith felt was smooth, probably vinyl, and very shapely. She tugged at the Velcro that held the plastic together. The wrap slowly parted, revealing what looked like a life-size Barbie doll. Or Sally Quinn.

"Yikes!" Renie exclaimed. "She's in the altogether!"

"But not anatomically correct," Judith pointed out. "This looks more like it was made by Mattel than Michelangelo."

"It certainly looks like Sally—or would, from a distance," Renie pointed out.

"Let's see the other one," Judith said, and went through the same process again. "Bigger, taller, less curvy." She held the plastic apart so Renie could see. "Behold—a Ken doll, only with dark hair like Freddy's."

Renie rubbed at her short chin. "So I see. But why?"

"Obviously part of their illusions," Judith reasoned. "You know—

Freddy or Sally would appear someplace where they couldn't possibly be. The audience sees the mannequin onstage for just a split second, then the curtain falls."

"Mannequin?" Renie echoed.

Judith gave Renie a quirky smile. "Yes. Mannequin. Like the one in the Corvette. Do you remember somebody saying that Sally actually looked like a Barbie doll?"

"Not really," Renie admitted. "Maybe I wasn't around at the time."

"Highly likely," Judith remarked with a touch of asperity. "You seldom are."

"Okay, okay," Renie shot back, "so I came here to enjoy myself. I could use a break. I spend six, seven hours a day in the basement, working my tail off. It's so cold down there in the winter that I have to wear three sweaters. The office is underground, the windows are tiny. I'm turning into a mole. Look. I think I'm growing whiskers. And I definitely have mole eyes. If I see the sun, I have to cover my face with a dishrag."

"Do moles have whiskers?" Judith inquired in an irritatingly calm voice.

"How would I know? I can't see them." Renie turned her back and started for the staircase.

"Hey!" Judith shouted. "How about helping me rewrap these dummies?"

"You do it," Renie retorted. "They're your kind of people."

"Coz!" Judith's temper snapped. "I work hard, too. Get your butt over here and give me a hand."

"Ohhh . . ." Renie took a deep breath and complied. "Sorry. I feel overwhelmed these days, what with all three weddings on the horizon, my regular workload, trying to be a good wife to Bill, taking care of Mom, keeping up the house and garden—it'd be nice to go somewhere with you and not find a corpse. Or two."

"You think I wouldn't like that?" Judith responded as they fastened the plastic covers on the mannequins. "Not only do I have to do most of the things you mentioned, but I'm in the middle of two huge renovation projects. Still, when I happen to be an innocent bystander in a homicide—or two—I have this obsession with finding out who did it. I want to know the truth. I have to do my part to see that justice is done."

Renie smiled and shook her head. "You're too damned noble for your own good."

"Nonsense." Judith pressed the last of the Velcro strips together. "It's why I became a librarian. I wanted to help people. They'd come into the library and request some obscure book nobody had ever heard of. I had to find it. I couldn't bear the disappointment in their eyes. So I'd dig and dig and dig until I found a copy. It took months sometimes, but the pleasure on those patrons' faces gave me great satisfaction. I guess it's the same thing with finding out who did it." She shrugged. "It's just the way I am."

Renie patted Judith's shoulder. "Despite all the awful things I say, I admire you for it. You know that."

Judith hugged Renie. There was no reason to say anything. Judith was close to tears; Renie was dry-eyed, and wearing an ironic expression.

"Let's find the husbands," she said.

"That shouldn't be hard," Judith replied with a sniffle or two. "Less than half an hour ago, they were at the baccarat tables."

Sure enough, Joe and Bill were still there, both so absorbed that their wives had to poke them to get their attention.

Bill waved a hand for silence. Joe ignored Judith. The cards were dealt out of the shoe. There were two hands, one for Player, one for Bank. It seemed to Judith that face cards didn't count. It also appeared that a total of eight or nine were the desirable numbers.

Judith tugged at Joe's sleeve. "Please, this is important," she whispered.

"Not now." Joe looked very serious.

Judith gritted her teeth. Player won the next hand. And the next and the next.

"Let's see if this is a run," Bill said to Joe.

Joe nodded. Player won again. The eight people seated at the table seemed to be winning.

Another half dozen hands were played before the dealer announced a new shoe. The players stood up, except for an elderly Chinese man who was consulting some notes he'd made. He was frail and his clothes were shabby. Judith watched him hold up a hand to the dealer.

"Twenty-five," the old man said.

Judith frowned. "He shouldn't bet twenty-five dollars. He looks so poor."

"That's not a request for dollars," Bill said, stretching his neck muscles. "It's for twenty-five grand on his line of credit."

Judith gaped. "But he's practically wearing rags!"

Bill nodded. "It's his lucky outfit. He wouldn't change it for the world. I've seen him lose ten grand on one hand. He probably came over to this country from Hong Kong, bringing all his wealth with him."

Judith shook her head. "That's incredible."

Joe had turned to face Judith. "What do you want now?" he asked in an impatient tone.

Trying to be concise, as well as even tempered, Judith explained about the silver gown in the basement wardrobe. At first, Joe didn't look pleased with his wife's account of prowling around in the bowels of the casino. But though his expression remained unmoved, a glint of interest surfaced in his green eyes.

"What are you suggesting?"

"That someone impersonated Sally at the end of the act," Judith said doggedly. "I thought that was established."

"It's conjecture," Joe said, though he had grown thoughtful. "I'll page Jack Jackrabbit. We'll take a look."

Renie and Bill had moved away from the table during the lengthy task of shuffling the several decks used for baccarat. Renie was scanning the blackjack tables as Bill strolled behind her. Judith stayed put while Joe went to a house phone. He was back in less than two minutes.

"I'll meet him in the basement," Joe said, on the move. "See you."

"Hey!" Judith cried. "I'm coming, too. You won't know where to find the dress."

Joe stopped and looked at Judith. "What? Oh. I suppose you're right."

Her husband's lack of enthusiasm irked Judith, but she said nothing. When they reached the locked door to the backstage area, Joe produced a key, but suddenly stopped and gave Judith a sheepish look. "How do we get downstairs? I haven't been there. Jack and his guys checked it out."

Judith, trying not to seem smug, pointed to the red piano. "That way," she said.

Down the spiral staircase they went, into the dimly lighted basement. Judith walked directly to the wall switch, then pointed out the wardrobes marked "Mandolini."

"It's the one on the right," Judith said.

"Hey!" a voice called from behind what looked like Egyptian mummy cases. "Is that you, Flynn?"

"Jack?" Joe called back. "Over here, with the wardrobes."

Jack Jackrabbit appeared, brushing dust from his clothes. "I must have gotten here about a minute before you did," he said, looking somewhat surprised to see Judith with Joe. "I was already near the backstage entrance." He made a little bow to Judith. "Nice to see you, Mrs. Flynn."

"My wife and her cousin made a discovery about an hour ago,"

Joe explained. "My lovely bride had never been backstage and she wanted to see what it was like." He flashed Judith a warning glance. "You know how it is with women—they love to look at costumes, especially the women's clothes."

Jack nodded. "My wife wishes we lived closer to a big mall. If we did, I'd have to take on two jobs. But she always looks beautiful no matter what she wears."

"What a wonderful thing to say," Judith said with a sharp glance at Joe.

"Very nice, very nice," Joe murmured, his rubicund face growing darker. "Let's see what you've got in there, *darling*."

The wardrobe opened at a touch this time. Judith showed Joe and Jack the two costumes that obviously didn't belong to Sally. "But underneath this purple satin is a . . ." She stopped and stared.

The sparkling silver ball gown was gone.

Chapter Thirteen

IT'S got to be here somewhere," Judith said, frantically searching through the costumes.

"Maybe it's in this other one," Joe said.

"No." Judith shook her head emphatically. "That's for the grunge band, Craven Raven."

Joe gazed at the items in the wardrobe. "We've got the original gown taken from the body. Are you sure this one was a duplicate? There are some other shiny things in that box."

"I saw it, Renie saw it," Judith asserted. "In fact, Renie was the one who noticed it first."

Joe nodded. He wouldn't argue with his wife's powers of observation nor, for that matter, with any woman's recognition of unusual apparel. "Okay. But it's not there now." He turned to Jack. "What's your take?"

Jack didn't answer directly. He stood very still, staring into the wardrobe. "Someone has removed the dress. The question is, why?"

"Because it's evidence," Judith blurted out.

Joe looked startled. "We know that. We're cops, remember?"

Embarrassed, Judith turned to Jack. "I'm sorry, I didn't mean to imply . . ."

He smiled and waved a hand. "As members of the tribal police, we work a little differently, Mrs. Flynn. In our culture, we don't jump to conclusions or take things at face value. We may seem slower to act than other Americans." He paused just long enough to let his meaning sink in.

Judith kept her mouth shut. "Other Americans" were a mongrel bunch, with backgrounds from all over the globe. There was more purity in the Stillasnowamish tribe. Their culture seemed more complex, more in tune with the elements.

Jack continued speaking. "We should examine the entire wardrobe. I'll get a couple of my people to take it out of here."

"Sounds good," Joe said with a nod. "Do you want me to wait around with you?"

Jack already had his cell phone in hand. "No, that's okay. You go enjoy the rest of the evening with your charming wife." He smiled warmly at Judith.

Neither of the Flynns spoke until they were back in the corridor on the main floor. Judith stopped trying to keep up with Joe's brisk pace.

"Whoa," she called out. "I want a word with you. Now."

Frowning, Joe turned around and took a couple of steps closer to Judith. "Why?"

"I don't get you," Judith said. "You tell me it's fine to hold a conversation with your suspects or witnesses or whatever, and then you do everything you can to keep me from having access to them except by accidental encounters."

"Look, Jude-girl, there's a ruthless killer loose and I don't want you to—"

Judith put her fingers in her ears. "I'm not listening. I'm not finished, either." Seeing that Joe had closed his mouth, she took her fingers out of her ears. "There's always a ruthless killer loose. And sometimes you've been very good at letting me help find that killer. But with this case, you're skating all over the place. What's going on with you?"

Joe had grown somber. "There are some things I can't tell you right now. Do you trust me?"

"What are you talking about?"

Joe put his hands on Judith's shoulders. "When I say 'trust,' I mean total trust, what a husband and wife should have between them."

Perplexed, Judith studied Joe's face. He seemed open, candid, direct. "Yes. Yes, of course I trust you. But I still don't understand."

"Okay." He squeezed her shoulders. "For now, let's leave it at that. Later, I hope, I'll be able to explain."

There was something unusual in Joe's expression. It made Judith uneasy. It suddenly dawned on her that what she saw on her husband's face was fear. That wasn't like him. During his entire career, he had put his life on the line.

"Are you in danger?" she asked with alarm.

Joe's laugh was hollow. "Me? Hell, no." He put his arm around Judith. "Let's go try that baccarat. I like it. The player seems to have a fighting chance."

"I don't understand it," Judith admitted as they moved onto the casino floor. "I'll see if Renie's playing blackjack. I know how to do that."

"Okay," Joe said, then gently kissed Judith's forehead. "Have fun. Don't worry."

Judith watched her husband stroll toward the baccarat tables. *He says he's not in danger,* she thought. *Maybe he's not. But somebody is.*

She had just spotted Renie at a five-dollar blackjack game when it dawned on her that Joe was telling the truth. A little shiver ran up Judith's spine as she realized *she* could be at risk.

. . .

"Cocktails?" inquired the chipper strawberry-blond waitress as Judith sat down at the table's only empty chair, which was, fortuitously, next to Renie.

"Yes," Judith replied eagerly. "Scotch-rocks. Please."

Renie was drinking Pepsi. "What's new?"

"The dress is gone," Judith whispered.

Renie passed a hand over her cards, indicating to the dealer that she was satisfied with her hand. "Really?"

"Yes. Joe and Jack Jackrabbit were with me. We searched the whole wardrobe."

The dealer, a young Hispanic man whose name tag read "Carlos" looked pointedly at Judith.

Renie, who had won the hand, nudged her cousin. "The seat's not free. In fact, it wouldn't be empty if that same old bat who tried to steal my chair at the slots hadn't just left in a huff because I spilled Pepsi in her lap. Give Carlos a couple of twenties."

Clumsily, Judith dug in her purse, then took out a fifty-dollar bill from her wallet and handed it to Carlos, who smiled and thanked her. Carlos gave her eight red five-dollar chips and ten silver dollars. "Do I have to bet a red one?" Judith whispered.

Renie nodded. "That's the minimum."

Judith had lost the first three hands by the time her Scotch arrived. She placed a silver dollar on the cocktail waitress's tray and thanked her. As she took her first sip, she looked across the pit area to the opposite table. Manny Quinn was playing with a stack of hundred-dollar chips.

Judith nudged Renie. "Manny's betting five black chips on one hand. How can he gamble like that when his wife is lying in the morgue?"

Renie scowled at Judith. "How should I know? Wake up, it's your turn."

"Oh." Judith smiled apologetically at Carlos, then waved her hand to indicate that she didn't want a card.

Renie got a ten on one ace and a queen on the other. "All right," she murmured. "Hey, coz, flip your cards over. Carlos wants to pay you. He's only got seventeen."

"Oh." Embarrassed by her gaffe, Judith showed her hand. She had a five and a six.

Renie held her head. "You didn't even look at your cards, did you? If you had, you could've gone down for double and gotten one of my ten cards for twenty-one. Maybe you should quit while you're behind."

Judith sighed. "Maybe you're right. I think I'll just walk around for a bit and then go to bed. Here, take my chips. We'll settle up later."

Renie didn't quibble. She was already examining her new hand. Judith wandered past the other blackjack tables. There was an open seat next to Manny Quinn. Judith wished she could afford the twenty-five-dollar minimum. Playing next to Manny would give her an opportunity to get better acquainted.

Instead, she'd just decided to see if she could find Joe when a huge cheer went up from one of the nearby craps tables. The big crowd surrounding the table was hugging, kissing, and slapping high fives. She paused for a moment, enjoying the sight of so many people—all ages, all races, all classes—sharing in the communion of craps. Maybe there was more to gambling than just the desire to make money. Maybe it was the true democracy, where the dice didn't care who you were, rich or poor, black or white, foreign or native born.

Still musing on her insight, Judith almost didn't hear the PA system call her name. Startled—and somewhat anxious—she marched over to the nearest house phone.

"A Mrs. Grover has been trying to reach you, Mrs. Flynn," said the operator. "Shall I connect you to her room?"

"Please," Judith said as her anxiety built up. What could have happened to the two old ladies that would necessitate Gertrude's using the telephone?

But it was the other Mrs. Grover who answered. "Judith, dear," Aunt Deb said in her pleasant voice. "Your mother insisted I try to reach you. You know how she abhors the telephone."

"Yes, I know that. What's wrong? Are you both okay?"

"Of course we're fine," Aunt Deb replied. "Your mother is watching TV and I'm doing the crossword puzzle. How are you?"

"Fine, great, good. Why did Mother want you to call me?"

"How's Renie? Is she warm enough? I think there must be draughts in a place this size. Is she wearing a warm, woolly sweater?"

"She is," Judith answered, truthfully. Of course the wool was cashmere and, if anything, Renie was probably too warm in the controlled temperature of the casino. "So why did—"

"You two are sticking together, aren't you? I know this is a very nice place, but some of the people who gamble could be white slavers. You read in the paper all the time about those poor Chinese girls being sold into bondage. It's terrible."

There was no point in reminding Aunt Deb that her daughter and her niece were not girls anymore, had never been Chinese, and would be lucky if some old duffer even winked at them.

"We're just fine," Judith said, her patience fraying. "Please, why did Mother ask you to page me?"

In the background, Judith heard Gertrude griping at Deb. "Say what you have to say and hang up the damned phone before I pull it out of the wall! I can't hear a word the Golden Girls are saying!"

"They look like Olden Girls to me," Aunt Deb retorted, away from the phone. "If you want to see a crabby old lady, go look in the mirror."

"Crabby?" Gertrude shot back. "If I'm crabby, it's because you're gabby! How would you like me to put that phone someplace where the sun don't shine?"

"I'd like to see you try it," Aunt Deb said in an unusually heated tone. "Go on, wheel yourself over here and strut your stuff!"

"My wheelchair's tougher than yours is!" Gertrude shouted. "I can take you out anytime!"

"Aunt Deb!" Judith yelled into the phone. "Please! Tell me why you called!"

A sudden silence fell at the other end. Judith closed her eyes, envisioning the old girls facing off in their wheelchairs. Maybe she should hang up and hurry to their room to prevent another homicide.

"It's your contractor, Mr. Bednarik," Aunt Deb finally said in her normal voice. "He called earlier this evening and we've been trying to page you, but you haven't responded."

Judith realized that the pages must have been announced while she was backstage or in the basement and out of hearing range. "I'm sorry. What did Mr. Bednarik want?"

"He said he found your countertop and he'll put it in tomorrow," Aunt Deb said. "It's the biggest he could find and has the right number and size of burners."

"That's great," Judith said with enthusiasm. "I'll call and tell him I'm pleased."

"That would be very nice of you," Aunt Deb responded. "You have such nice manners, Judith. Oh—there was one other thing. Mr. Bednarik says that in checking to make sure all your appliances were compatible with the fuse box, a carbon dioxide leak was discovered in the furnace. It's quite dangerous, and he feels you must replace the furnace. You'll have to do it now because otherwise the city won't approve of the renovations. He wants you to come into town tomorrow to get this straightened out or he can't proceed. Of course, you'll have to check with your insurance company, because they'll have to sign off on it as well. They may offer you a discount for the updates. Isn't that nice?"

Judith leaned against the wall. Aunt Deb's years as a legal secretary had given her the training to be precise about details, particularly where the law was involved.

"So I have to go into town tomorrow?" Judith asked in a woebegone voice.

"Mr. Bednarik was most insistent," Aunt Deb replied, not without sympathy. "He's afraid of an explosion. Of course, I'm sure he's sorry for the inconvenience."

"Damn!" Judith breathed. "Sorry, Aunt Deb, I shouldn't swear."

"Don't fuss, dear," Aunt Deb said. "I was married to your Uncle Cliff for well over forty years. There isn't much I haven't heard."

Remembering her manners, Judith asked in a listless voice how the conference had gone.

"It was wonderful," Aunt Deb replied warmly. "I can't understand why Renie doesn't want to be with these people. They're so very nice. And they make such a fuss over me! One of the big design firms wants to hire me as a consultant! Isn't that incredible?"

"Really?"

"Yes, but I don't know . . . I'll have to think about it," Aunt Deb said. "The money would be welcome. They've made a generous offer. And I could work at home, like Renie. Still . . ."

Gertrude's voice cut through, in the background. "Don't forget about my moving-picture deal! I'm going to make more than you are, you crazy old coot!"

"We'll see about that," Aunt Deb snapped. "I should go now, dear," she said, speaking again to Judith. "I think your dear mother's cigarette just set fire to her housecoat."

Aunt Deb hung up.

Judith found Joe—along with Bill—at the baccarat table. So absorbed were both men that she didn't know how—or when—to interrupt them. Standing a foot or two from Joe's chair, she hoped he'd look up and notice her.

He didn't. Judith surrendered. It was after eleven. Joe would be coming up to the room in about an hour. In the meantime, she'd try to find Renie.

Despite the approach of the witching hour, action in the casino continued. A dazzling young woman in a gold minidress had a box of cigarettes, cigars, chewing gum, breath mints, and stomach aids draped around her slim neck. Her red earrings lighted up and she fingered what looked like a yo-yo that flashed on and off. Another young woman in a long green gown carried a camera and asked if guests wanted their picture taken. Two keno runners in matching red cocktail dresses collected wagers and paid out winnings. It could be any time of day, Judith thought. Inside the casino, seven in the morning probably didn't look much different from seven at night.

Making a circle of the blackjack tables, Judith couldn't see her cousin anywhere. But Manny Quinn was still seated in the same place. His stack of black chips was down to about a half dozen. Judith watched as he shoved all of them forward.

"Boom or bust," he said before lighting a cigarette.

There were only two other players at the table, a chubby Japanese man and a man Judith guessed might be a Texan, judging from his dungarees, ten-gallon hat, and leather boots. Both players had two good-size stacks of chips in reserve.

The dealer showed an ace and asked if anyone wanted insurance. All three men shook their heads. The dealer flipped over a ten. Manny jumped up from his chair and swore.

"That's the tenth blackjack you've had!" he roared at the dealer, a balding man in his thirties who retained a stoic expression. "What do you do, slip 'em up your sleeve?"

The dealer said nothing. Neither did the Japanese man or the Texan, who both looked bemused.

Manny glared at the dealer. "I'm reporting you. You'll be out on your ass in ten minutes." He slammed his chair against the table and started to stomp off.

A man in a silver-gray suit executed a graceful move out of the pit area. "Mr. Quinn? Let's talk."

"I'll talk," Manny said in a surly voice. "I'll tell everybody that you run a crooked casino!"

The pit boss pointed to a smooth, round globe above the blackjack tables. "That's one of our eye-in-the-sky cameras. Would you like to come back to the surveillance room and watch the replay of the hands?"

"To see what?" Manny snapped. "You're all in this together!"

The pit boss smiled sadly. "No, we're not. And the cameras don't lie. Would a free steak dinner make you feel better?"

Manny threw his hands up in the air. "Oh, swell! Like a hunk of meat would help my bankroll just after I lost ten grand with your cheating dealer! I've been losing ever since I got to this half-assed place! I'm down almost forty Gs!"

"I'm sorry," the pit boss said, still keeping his voice low and polite. "You're obviously having a run of bad luck. Perhaps you'd like to speak to Mr. Green."

Mr. Green was already there. He had come up behind Manny and put a hand on his shoulder.

Manny jumped. "Don't touch me! I'll sue!"

Pancho's grip was firm. He stood toe-to-toe with Manny. It would have been difficult to put a five-dollar chip between them. The casino manager's voice was so low that Judith couldn't hear him from ten feet away. But whatever Pancho said, it made an impression on Manny. She watched the belligerence fizzle out of him like air from a burst balloon.

"Okay, okay," Manny finally said. "I'll suck it up." He turned and walked away, toward the Summer Bar.

Pancho exchanged a few words with the pit boss and the dealer. The Japanese man and the cowboy remained at the table, waiting with remarkable patience.

Judith had moved just enough so that Pancho couldn't help but see her when he began walking away from the blackjack tables.

"Mrs. Flynn," he said in surprise. "How are you this evening?"

"Better than Mr. Quinn," Judith said pointedly. "Does he always take a great loss so hard?"

Pancho's smile was thin. "I don't know him that well. But he's lost quite a bit of money, as I'm sure you just heard. It's natural for someone to get upset. Most high rollers can afford the occasional bad run, but some can't."

Judith's expression was quizzical. "I wasn't referring to just the blackjack game. I meant the loss of his wife, Sally."

"Oh. Of course." Pancho's swarthy skin grew even darker. He cleared his throat. "I suppose that gambling is a way for Manny to forget. Like drinking or drugging. In losing, his loss is felt even more keenly."

"Yes, that could be true," Judith allowed.

But somehow, she didn't quite believe it.

Chapter Fourteen

Judith needed to clear her head. And despite the late hour, she had to call Bart Bednarik about the blasted furnace. When she went out through the front entrance, she noticed that the rain had stopped and that a slight breeze was blowing the clouds away. Stars speckled the sky. The tall firs and cedars swayed gently, as if they were bowing to the half-moon rising above Mount Nugget.

But most of all, it was quiet. Only one parking valet was on duty, sitting in his small kiosk reading a magazine. Judith walked down to the driveway, then continued along the walkway that wrapped around the building. For the first time, she noticed the landscaping. All the plants were native to the area. There were trilliums, bleeding hearts, salmonberries, avalanche lilies, and the sweet yellow violets called Johnny-jump-ups. A dozen varieties of ferns were sprouting at the tips of their pale green fronds.

The night air smelled sweet, redolent of evergreen branches and damp spring earth. As Judith strolled along the north side of the complex, she could hear the river some fifty yards away. Some of her favorite memories from the family cabin were the smells and the sounds. She'd wake up in the morning to hear the river's ripple, the crow's call, and the wind whispering in the trees. She'd sniff the wood smoke from the old stove and the aroma of trout frying in a cast-iron skillet. Those were the days of peace and pleasure—simple, homely, precious.

At last, she came to a halt on the path and got the cell phone out of her purse. It would serve Bart Bednarik right if she woke him up. Not that it was his fault that the furnace had sprung a leak, but because the interruptions to her so-called vacation were getting out of hand.

Bart's phone cut over to his voice mail. Judith left a terse message saying she'd meet him at the house at ten o'clock. Just as she clicked off, she heard a noise that sounded like a growl.

It was too late in the year for a bear or a cougar to be so close to civilization. Maybe it was only a dog. But something moved on a narrow dirt track off to her left. Judith peered into the darkness. The figure was a man, not an animal. But she heard the growling sound again.

Moving to the edge of the dirt track, she watched the man walk slowly but purposefully toward what looked like small buildings near the edge of the lake. There was something familiar about the shadowy figure. *Dignified* was the word that came to mind. Judith realized it was Bob Bearclaw.

She followed at a discreet distance. Bob finally stopped by one of the structures Judith had thought were buildings. They were actually trailers like those used to transport circus animals. In a shaft of moonlight, she saw a tiger behind the bars. Bob was looking at the tiger, which no longer growled. In fact, he was speaking to the animal, though Judith couldn't hear what he said.

Yet there was something so compelling about the communion between man and animal that Judith was rooted to the spot. She lost track of how long she stood on the soft ground. But there was a chill in the air, so she decided to head back inside. Before she took more than a step, Bob, with his back still turned to her, called out.

"Wait, please." He finally moved away from the trailer. "I'll walk back with you, Mrs. Flynn."

Fascinated, Judith didn't budge. "How did you know I was here?" she asked as Bob joined her.

"I heard you. It sounded like your step." He smiled. "The old ways of our people don't always desert us. You shouldn't be out alone at this time of night."

The thought hadn't occurred to Judith, and though Bob didn't mention danger, she knew he referred to the fact that a killer was lurking somewhere around the resort.

"I needed some fresh air," she explained. "Do you enjoy animals?"

"Enjoy?" Bob looked skyward. "I admire and respect animals. They should not be in cages. They should roam free, as nature intended. I come to console them."

"That's very moving," Judith declared. "I imagine they appreciate your concern."

"Perhaps."

"They didn't growl after you spoke to them," Judith pointed out.

Bob shrugged. "It's the least I can do. Unfortunately, it's also the most I can do."

They had approached the casino entrance. "What time do you get off work?" Judith inquired. "It's going on midnight."

"Oh—it depends. I enjoy the night. The quiet. The feeling that the sky is so much closer. Sometimes, especially in winter on a clear, crisp night, you feel as if you could almost touch the Great Spirit." He stopped at the foot of the stone steps. "We speak of the sun going down, the moon coming up. That isn't right, you know. It's the earth that moves, not the sun or the moon. But we humans are so bound to our world that we speak of it as the center of the universe. It's not. We need to understand how small we are in the Great Spirit's plan."

Judith was silent for a moment. "That's true. I don't know if I've ever thought of it that way myself."

Bob's smile was gentle. There was something in his dark eyes that Judith didn't fathom. Pity? Compassion? Encouragement? A challenge? He tipped his cap. "Good night, Mrs. Flynn."

Judith didn't know what to say. But for a few moments, she felt as if she'd regained her sense of well-being.

Potentially explosive furnaces and deficient fuse boxes weren't what Joe wanted to hear about at two minutes after midnight.

"It's your house, it's your B&B, it's your problem," he declared, unceremoniously dumping the contents of his pockets on the dresser. "I'm supposed to be on vacation."

"So am I," Judith shot back. "And it's *our* house. You live there, too, unless you'd like to move into the toolshed with Mother."

"Come on, Jude-girl. The house is in your name. Your mother"—he winced at the word—"deeded it over to you years ago. Though, as I recall, not without threatening to burn it down first."

"Somebody did try to burn it down, which is why we're in this mess," Judith countered. "Not to mention whatever is going on at the family property on the river."

"That was your idea," Joe said with a wag of his finger. "I tried to talk you out of it. Jeez, we're at an age where we should be doing less, not more. And in case you haven't noticed, I'm actually working on this vacation. I may not win a giant jackpot, but I *will* get paid."

Judith took a deep breath. Joe had a point. Several, in fact. He *was* on the job at the casino. Maybe building a second innkeeping establishment wasn't wise. Hillside Manor was their home, but it was also Judith's business.

"Okay," she said in a tired voice.

Joe scowled. "Okay what?"

"Okay, let's not argue. I'll leave here a little before nine tomorrow. With any luck, I may be back before Easter."

Joe paused in the middle of undressing. "How much does a new furnace cost these days?"

"A lot," Judith replied. "I'm guessing, but around four or five grand. Maybe we can pay it off on the installment plan. Aunt Deb also mentioned something about a discount."

"Is there any way our insurance will cover it?"

Judith shook her head. "Not unless it actually blows up."

"Hmm."

"Don't even think about it!" Judith cried. "Not after all the work we've put into the house so far."

Joe shrugged. "It was just a passing idea."

Judith needed more than a doughnut and coffee to start her arduous day. When she rose at seven-thirty, Joe was already on his way out the door. She asked if he'd like to join her for breakfast in the coffee shop, but he couldn't. His first meeting was at eight, and breakfast would be provided in Pancho's office.

Knowing that Renie wouldn't be awake at least until ten and that Bill had probably gotten up at the crack of dawn, Judith decided to go it alone in the coffee shop. For a fleeting moment, she considered eating with her mother and Aunt Deb. But the equivalent of the Battle of the Bulge was no way to start her day. Solitude would serve her better.

There was a short line of guests waiting for breakfast. All signs of the evening's mayhem were gone except for the rest room area, which was still out of bounds. To Judith's surprise, the person in front of her was Inga Polson.

Judith considered whether or not she should approach Inga directly. The woman seemed very fidgety, shifting her weight from one foot to the other, scratching her hands, and looking this way and that. Except, unfortunately, at Judith.

But opportunity arrived when Inga got to the front of the line. The hostess apologized, saying that at present there were no small tables available. Singles were being seated at the counter. Would that do?

It would not, Inga asserted in no uncertain terms.

Judith came to the rescue. "Ms. Polson, remember me? I'm Judith Flynn. I'm alone, too. Do you mind sharing a table?"

Inga's raisinlike eyes scrutinized Judith. "Oh. You're that detective's wife. Yes, we've met." She hesitated, perhaps trying to recall if the meeting had been satisfactory. "Very well." She snapped her fingers at the hostess, apparently signaling that she wished to be seated.

"How's Freddy this morning?" Judith asked after they'd been seated toward the rear of the restaurant.

"Not so good," Inga said, disdaining the menu. "He had a very bad night. I hardly slept at all. Griselda's sitting with him now. I just had to get away for a bit. It's so difficult to watch him suffer."

"Emotionally, you mean," Judith said, wearing her most sympathetic face.

"Yes, of course. Freddy's so sensitive." Inga paused as a waitress whose name tag read "Greer" poured coffee and asked for their orders. "See here," Inga said, tapping the table, "I want a three-egg omelet with Gruyère cheese and porcini mushrooms. Whites only, no yolk. I'd like the leanest hamburger patty you have, well done. Seven-grain toast, two slices, no butter. And a glass of goat's milk."

Greer, who had iron-gray hair and looked as if she served herself nuts and bolts for breakfast, glared at Inga. "I'll see what I can do."

"Yes, you will," Inga asserted. "And you'll do it with haste."

"I do what's possible," the waitress retorted. "Yesterday you wanted quail eggs. We couldn't do that."

Inga shook her head. "Nonsense. I had quail eggs. Four, to be exact. Of course it took forever to be served."

"Ha!" Greer cried in derision. "How many eggs do you think we could squeeze out of those canaries your brother has stashed back in his zoo? Most of those birds are males."

"What?" Inga exploded. "Don't you dare tell me—"

"Honey," the waitress interrupted, "I wouldn't try to tell you anything. You know it all. And you'll get what we got." She turned to Judith. "How about you? Grilled lamb kidneys, maybe?"

"No," Judith replied, "I don't eat lamb kidneys."

"Well," Greer replied, "some goofy woman around here does. She ordered them yesterday from room service. What kind of nut eats innards?"

"That nut would be my cousin, Renie," Judith murmured, then meekly asked for the number three special of ham, toast, hash browns, and two eggs.

"How would you like your eggs?" the waitress inquired.

"Any way the cook wants to make them," Judith said, handing over the menu. "Thanks."

The waitress started to walk away, but Inga had one more request. "Separate checks. You hear me?"

Nodding, the waitress kept walking.

Inga reached into her purse to take out what looked like a paperback book, but was a reference guide to theatrical bookings. As she flipped through the pages, she kept shaking her head. She also scratched her hands, which seemed less blotchy than Judith remembered from the previous day.

"Do you have allergies?" Judith inquired politely.

Inga looked up over her half glasses. "Yes." Her eyes went back to the guide.

"I do, too," Judith said. "Especially this time of year. The pollen bothers me quite a bit."

Inga ignored the comment.

"I admire the way you take care of your brother," Judith said after a lapse of at least two minutes. "Particularly when he's so sensitive and such an outstanding *artiste*."

Inga not only looked up, but closed the book. "Our parents died young. Being somewhat older than Freddy, I virtually raised him. Make no mistake—I was more than willing. Freddy's such a special person."

Having struck the right note, Judith nodded sympathetically. "You've done a wonderful job. I'm sure you've been a large part of his success."

Inga shrugged. "The talent is his. I've merely encouraged him and tried to give him guidance in his career."

"Your participation must ease Mr. Fromm's responsibilities as well," Judith remarked.

"Well." Inga put a hand to her bosom and made a futile attempt to look modest. "Mr. Fromm handles the business side mostly. But it's true—not that I like to flatter myself—that I make many of the artistic decisions. For example," she went on, pointing to the guide, "I select certain venues for Freddy and submit them to Mr. Fromm with a strong recommendation. He then follows my instructions and takes care of the actual arrangements." She tapped the guidebook. "It occurred to me that Freddy should get away for his next engagement. Europe, perhaps. He's never been there, and the change might do him good. Too many sad memories for him now in the States."

"Remarkable," Judith murmured. "I don't see how you do it, especially after Freddy has suffered two terrible losses. You must have known Sally and Micki extremely well. I'm sure you're grieving, too."

"Of course." Inga turned in the direction of the serving area. "What's taking that waitress so long? Did the cooks all go on their break at the same time?"

"The restaurant's quite busy this time of day," Judith said, "not to mention filling the room-service orders. I'm sure our food will be up shortly." Without missing a beat, she sang another verse of Inga's praises. "It's wonderful to see such devotion of a sister to her brother. I hope you're not wearing yourself out, Ms. Polson. If you'd like me to spell you for a while later today, I'd be happy to sit with Freddy."

Inga eyed Judith with suspicion. "Now why would you want to do that?"

Judith held up her hands. "Because I like to help people. Because you must need some relief. Because I'm kind of at loose ends around here. I'm not much of a gambler."

Inga was musing on Judith's reasons when their orders were delivered. Judith thanked the waitress while her companion inspected the items as if she were doing scientific research.

"Where's the salt substitute?" Inga demanded.

"You didn't ask for it," Greer replied. "If I were a mind reader, I could be part of your brother's act."

"I asked for it yesterday," Inga retorted. "You should pay more attention to your customers."

"You should pay a bigger tip," Greer shot back. "Try to hold yourself together while I go to the substitute-salt mines out back."

"You have to watch these people every second," Inga declared after Greer had wheeled away. "You have to watch everybody. I'm not a trusting person, which is good."

"With your keen eye," Judith said, "not to mention your intuitive sense, you must have some idea of who killed Sally and Micki."

Inga, who hadn't waited for the salt, paused with a forkful of omelet almost to her mouth. "What makes you think that?"

"You said as much when we spoke at the casino entrance yesterday," Judith replied. "You were upset because Joe—my husband—didn't seem to take your ideas about the case very seriously."

"Oh." Inga glared at Greer, who had returned with the salt substitute.

The waitress slapped the shaker down on the table. "Was that fast enough or should I have had it flown in by bald eagle?"

"You're very cheeky," Inga declared. "I should report you to my dear, close personal friend, Pancho Green."

"Go ahead," Greer responded, one fist on her hip. "He's my

dear, close brother-in-law. Pancho always likes a good laugh." To underscore the point, Greer added a facetious, "Har, har," and clomped away.

"Really," Inga huffed. "That woman is impossible. How do the other customers put up with her?" Not waiting for an answer, she scratched her hands and stared into space. "What was I saying?"

"That you knew who killed Sally," Judith replied.

"Oh. Yes." Inga took a big bite of toast, chewed, swallowed, and resumed speaking. "I wouldn't want to make any accusations just now. Not after Micki was murdered, too."

"Micki told me she knew who killed Sally," Judith said.

Inga stared. "She did? Who?"

"She never got a chance to say. We were interrupted."

"Hunh." Inga looked puzzled. "That's very strange."

"Why is that?"

"It just is." Inga stuffed her face with more omelet.

"Do you know who this Marta woman is? The blonde who was holding the saber?" Judith asked.

Inga shook her head. "No idea."

"She must be a suspect," Judith pointed out.

"I suppose," Inga allowed. "But I can't think why. She's a complete stranger."

"I'm sure the police are checking her out thoroughly," Judith said. "She might have been brought back to the hotel by now."

A slight shrug of Inga's shoulders seemed to dismiss Marta Ormond Flax. "If I become too fatigued this afternoon, I may call upon you. Where can you be reached in the meantime?"

Judith explained why she wouldn't be at the casino until later in the day. "It's a nuisance," she complained, "but necessary. Home improvements take more time—and money—than you could ever imagine."

"Maintenance is all I worry about," Inga asserted. "We're on the road too much to worry about whether we have the latest furniture style or the fanciest washing machine."

"Do you still live in Idaho?" Judith inquired.

"Yes, but not in Shoshone," Inga replied. "We bought a house in Boise some years ago." Having eaten every morsel put before her, she brushed off some crumbs from her navy blue dress and stood up. "I must go. Griselda is probably anxious to get to work."

"What," Judith asked, "does she do when Freddy isn't performing?"

"She tends to the wardrobe, for one thing." Inga snatched up her purse and the guidebook. "She's a very good seamstress. You wouldn't believe the wear and tear on the costumes. I'll be in touch."

Judith was drinking her last sip of coffee when she realized that the waitress hadn't yet presented their bills. Seeing her at a nearby table, she gave the server the high sign.

"Where's your friend?" the waitress asked when she reached Judith.

"She had to leave," Judith said with a little grimace. "Actually, we're not friends, we just—"

"Don't bother to explain," Greer interrupted with a tired smile. "You got stuck with her. It happens all the time when we get busy in the morning." She fingered the two bills. "Do you know her room number? I can put her order with the other charges."

A flash of generosity passed over Judith, but she dug in her heels. People who had to buy new furnaces couldn't afford to treat people they barely knew.

"She's the Great Mandolini's sister," Judith said. "I don't know the room number, but she should be registered under 'Polson.'"

The waitress smirked. "She should be registered under 'Poison.' Maybe she thinks she can make the bill disappear. That crew has made some real people go away permanently." She glanced at the table. "No tip, either. I guess that disappeared, too."

To compensate, Judith doubled her usual gratuity on her credit-card slip. It was nine o'clock on the dot when she reached the casino entrance and asked a valet for her car. There was no sign of Bob Bearclaw.

Or so Judith thought until she saw him walking out of the underground parking garage. Just as he reached the driveway, a black Volvo pulled up. Bob went directly to the car.

Judith watched as Dr. Engelman got out of the driver's side. Bob had opened the passenger door and was helping someone who seemed to be having a problem.

"I'll give you a hand," Engelman called to Bob. "She's still a little woozy."

Bob called for a wheelchair. The two men carefully eased a woman out of the Volvo and held her up until the wheelchair arrived. She looked dazed and very shaky. It took Judith a moment to realize that the fragile arrival was Marta Ormond Flax. The blond hair was gone, and in its place were tufts of brown hair about an inch long.

She spoke, but with such difficulty that no one, least of all Judith, who was standing twenty feet away, could hear her.

Engelman looked at Bob. "What was that?"

"I think," Bob replied, "she asked for Fou-Fou."

"Oh." Engelman nodded, then lowered his head to speak into Marta's ear. "Fou-Fou's fine. You'll see her in just a few minutes."

Marta uttered a sigh, apparently of relief. The wheelchair arrived just as Judith's Subaru appeared from the garage. Judith passed the little group on the sidewalk. Bob smiled; Doc nodded; Marta stared into space.

Judith was shocked by Marta's appearance. During much of the drive into the city, she wondered if extreme drunkenness could cause such a dramatic change. Of course, the missing wig made a big difference. Still, it was Marta's demeanor even more than her looks that disturbed Judith. She couldn't help but think that the woman might have been drugged or even poisoned.

Bart Bednarik was already at Hillside Manor when Judith arrived at ten-fifteen. "Here's the deal," he said, leaning against the kitchen counter. "The gas company doesn't lease or sell furnaces anymore. They have a list of subcontractors they recommend. I've worked with a couple of them. I'd go with Fuddmeister. They've been around a long time."

"Okay," Judith said. "What do I do?"

"I'll take care of it. Let me get their number." Bart took a well-worn notebook out of his back pocket. "Here we go." He used his own cell phone to make the call. Nothing happened. "Hunh. They don't answer. Let me check the phone book. They might have moved."

While Judith waited, she gazed around the kitchen. A large carton sat in the hallway, near the back door. Moving closer, she saw that it was the countertop stove. At least it had arrived on the premises.

Bart was still looking through the yellow pages. "Has the electrician been here yet?" she asked.

"What?" Bart looked up from the phone book's furnace section. "The electrician? Oh, no, not yet. It'll be Artie Chow after all. His collarbone wasn't broken. He should be here around noon." He went back to his search of the listings. "That's funny. I can't find Fuddmeister in here."

"When was the last time you worked with them?"

Bart looked vague. "Oh—four, five, maybe six years ago."

Judith looked annoyed. "Have you considered that Fuddmeister might have gone out of business?"

Bart looked befuddled. "Gosh. That could be." He put the phone book down and scratched his head. "Now what?"

"Surely," Judith said in a barely controlled voice, "you've worked with other furnace companies in the past six years. Think fast, Bednarik," she ordered, one eye on her cutlery block. "I'm reaching for the carving knife."

Bart started to laugh, then quickly sobered. "You did have some guy pop off in your sink, didn't you?"

"That's how all of this started," Judith replied. "Now come up with a name. Quick."

Bart retrieved the yellow pages. His eyes darted through the listings. "Here—Hugo's Home Heating. I did a job with them last fall. They were okay. As far as I could tell." He grabbed his cell phone and dialed the company's number.

Dreading what debacle she might overhear on Bart's end of the conversation, Judith went out to the back porch. Sweetums was sitting in the garden, swiping at a stone bird in St. Francis's left hand. Except that the statue of St. Francis had never held a stone bird in that hand. The bird was real. Judith screamed at the cat. The bird flew off and Sweetums snarled at Judith.

Grabbing a broom, she waved it with menace as she started after the cat. But if Sweetums wasn't quick enough for the bird, he could easily outrun his human. In a flash, he disappeared behind the toolshed.

"Hey!" Bart called from the house. "I got them! They'll be here tomorrow." He seemed surprised by his coup.

Judith put the broom aside. "Tomorrow?" she echoed, going back to the kitchen. "Does that mean I'll have to come back to sign off on the damned furnace?"

Bart rubbed the back of his head. "I guess so."

Judith thought hard for a few moments. "I'm not doing that. The electricity's still off, right?"

Bart nodded. "Until Artie gets here."

"Okay. Here's what we're going to do." She picked up the phone book. "Hugo will fax me the contract at Heraldsgate Hill Mail &

Dispatch. I'll sign it and fax it back." She flipped through listings. "Call Hugo, then have them call the store. I'm leaving now and I won't be back until my vacation is over." She shoved the directory at Bart. "Got it?"

For once, Bart looked a bit sheepish. "I got it. I'll call right now."

"Good." Judith grabbed her purse and started for the door.

"Hey," Bart called after her, "did you want to go through your mail? I've been saving it in that pile by the computer."

Judith glanced at the foot-high stack that looked mostly like catalogs. There would be bills, of course, and perhaps some reservation requests. But they'd have to wait. For once, Judith couldn't stand being in Hillside Manor for another minute. The lack of electricity and water, the disarray in the kitchen, the furnace that could blow up at any moment, the absence of furniture to replace the pieces that had suffered damage in the fire, even the late stages of winter debris that Judith hadn't yet cleared away in the yard—all made her want to get away. It was like being with a once-healthy, robust loved one wracked by disease. Even though improvements had been made, Judith's cherished home wasn't the same. The warm feeling she'd experienced the previous day had evaporated into an imaginary cloud of lethal carbon dioxide fumes.

To her surprise—and relief—the fax process at the mail and dispatch store went smoothly. Judith got back into the car and headed for the freeway. An hour and a few rain squalls later, she was almost to the turnoff for the family cabin. On a whim, she pulled into the open area that had once been a playing field for family baseball and badminton games. At present, it was full of heavy-duty equipment, most of which Judith didn't recognize.

What was more surprising was that the workers seemed to be concentrating on the area near the highway rather than the building site another twenty yards closer to the river. It looked to Judith as if the men were using a dredger. She spotted Dale Armstrong in an orange hard hat and tried to make herself heard over the noise of the machinery.

He didn't turn around until Judith was within five feet of him.

"Mrs. Flynn!" he exclaimed in surprise, moving farther away from the work area. "What are you doing here?"

"The question is," Judith said, "what are *you* doing there?" She pointed to the bog.

Dale steered her back toward the open gate that led onto the property. "We're concerned about the ground around here. Too much spring water. That's what's caused the delay in laying the foundations for the inn itself and the adjacent cabins."

Judith was puzzled. "The plan shows the inn as being where our original cabin was. The four new cabins are all along the river, two on each side of the inn. I don't get it. Why are you concentrating on this part of the property?"

Dale gazed up through the budding vine maples that provided a canopy over the drive. "It's how we do these tests. We start where the ground seems most unstable. It's pretty complicated."

"Oh?" Judith was still puzzled.

"That's right," Dale replied, a bit blasé. "Say, we're about to break for lunch. Do you mind?"

"Mind what?"

Dale smiled in what he probably thought was his most charming manner. "Mind if we take off. We're running a little behind. It's almost twelve-thirty." He tapped his watch.

Judith hesitated. Like Bill before her, she felt she was getting the brush-off. "I do mind," she finally said. "I'd like to have you show me exactly what you've accomplished so far. Except, of course, for dredging the bog. I can see that for myself."

Dale looked pained, but agreed. "I'll show you around." He waved and shouted to his workmen. "Five minutes. I'm taking Mrs. Flynn on a quick tour."

They walked up the gentle dirt track that led to the river. There, on the relatively flat ground where the four original cabins had stood, they had a picture-perfect view of Mount Woodchuck. The twin crests still sported snow down to the three-thousand-foot level. Judith stopped at the edge of the riverbank to admire one of her favorite sights.

What she saw when she turned around was far less pleasing. A large hole had been dug where the main cabin had once stood. Except for a couple of pieces of machinery, the cavity was empty.

"In other words," she said angrily, "there *is* no progress."

"I told you," Dale said, looking mulish, "we can't do anything until we're completely satisfied about the ground's stability."

"Then get satisfied, quick," Judith snapped. "When I come back from the resort casino this weekend, I want to see that the foundation is laid. If it isn't, you're fired."

"Come on, Mrs. Flynn," Dale shot back, "be reasonable. You're building a much heavier structure than what was here before. This property's been flooded at least twice, we live in earthquake country, you don't want us to rush . . ."

But Judith wasn't listening. She was stomping back up the dirt road and refused to look back. Without another word, she got into the Subaru, reversed in a reckless manner, turned the car on two wheels, and roared off and onto the highway.

It wasn't until she got out of the car and was waiting to hand her keys to a parking valet that she glanced down at her black suede loafers.

A small speck near the toe of her right shoe caught her eye.

It shone in the sun.

It looked exactly like the gold glitter she had brushed from her hands and off G. D. Fromm's suit coat.

Chapter Fifteen

JUDITH took a Kleenex from her purse, carefully removed the gold fleck from her shoes, and wrapped it in the tissue. Gingerly, she tucked the small packet into her purse's zippered pocket. The tiny speck probably meant nothing. Although there had once been precious metals in the area, the granite rocks were full of various shiny particles, such as feldspar, quartz, and mica.

Inside the lobby, she decided to stop at the front desk to see if there were any messages. What she feared was a call from Hugo's Home Heating, saying that despite the contract, they couldn't install a new furnace at Hillside Manor because . . . Judith couldn't think of a reason, but for all she knew, Hugo's sister's aunt by marriage had once stayed at the B&B and had found a grasshopper in her cornflakes.

There was a message, but not the one she'd dreaded. Inga had left a note saying that Judith's presence was required in the Polson suite at four o'clock. Pleased at being invited into the inner sanctum, Judith used the house phone to call Inga and let her know that she'd be there on the dot.

It was Griselda Vanderbehr who answered the phone, however. "Inga told me you offered to sit with Freddy," Grisly said in a disgruntled voice. "She had to go into Glacier Falls to see the doctor, and since she didn't have an appointment, and she's already been gone for almost three hours, I don't know when she's coming back. I'd like to get away, if only for a little while, so I can have lunch in the coffee shop instead of calling room service."

"I'd be glad to come up right now," Judith said, noting that it was going on one o'clock. "What's the room number?"

"We're in the Wild Ginger Suite, top floor, the actual room number is 1806. I'll be waiting."

But not patiently, Judith thought, judging from the edge in Grisly's voice.

The Wild Ginger Suite, with its white double doors, was at the end of the hall. Judith rapped softly. One of the doors opened almost before she could lower her hand.

"Come in," Grisly said. "Thanks. I'll see you in an hour or two." She rushed out of the suite so fast that Judith felt a breeze.

Grisly's flight was understandable. She looked haggard, disheveled, and even thinner than when Judith had last seen her.

Freddy was nowhere to be seen in the elegantly appointed living room. To her right, Judith noticed that one of the doors was ajar. She walked across the plush beige carpeting and knocked once.

"Mr. Polson?"

There was no response. Judith knocked again and spoke Freddy's name a bit louder.

"What?" The reply from the other room was faint.

Judith opened the door. Freddy was propped up in a king-size bed with a compress over his eyes. He looked very small and very weak. Judith's heart went out to him.

"Mr. Polson?" Judith said, taking a few steps closer to the bed. "I'm Mrs. Flynn, Joe Flynn's wife. You've met my husband in the course of the . . . investigations." She couldn't bring herself to use the word *murder.*

Freddy moved the compress a bit higher on his forehead so that he could see. "Flynn? Oh. Yes."

"Did your sister mention that I might be staying with you for a while?"

Freddy hesitated. "Ah . . . yes. I think so."

Judith moved to the side of the bed. The headboard was painted with clusters of wild ginger. The shy, purple orchidlike flowers peeked out among the lush green leaves. The comforter and one wall carried out the same motif.

"Can I get you anything?" Judith inquired.

"No. Thank you."

A comfortable armchair sat next to the bed, probably a convenience for Inga while she watched over her brother. There was also a settee on the other side of the room. Perhaps, Judith thought, Inga slept there, though it would have been a tight squeeze for her ample figure.

"Do you mind if I sit?" Judith asked, indicating the armchair.

"Please."

Judith sat, then waited for a few moments before speaking again. "I have the greatest sympathy for you, Mr. Polson."

"Call me Freddy. Please."

Judith nodded. "Then you must call me Judith. In a small way, I understand what you're going through. I lost my first husband when he was still fairly young."

"Was he stabbed, too?"

"No." For a fleeting moment, Judith recalled the Thanksgiving Day when Dan had grudgingly permitted her to have dinner with her relatives. He wouldn't attend, of course, and insisted that she prepare him a turkey dinner with all the trimmings. Judith had complied, but upon her return from the Grover gathering, she had found the turkey, trimmings and all, in the gutter outside their shabby rental home. Judith had been so angry that when an explosive argument ensued, she had picked up the carving knife and stabbed Dan in the rear end. Since Dan had weighed over four hundred pounds, he'd scarcely felt the slight wound. Judith, however, had suffered from guilt for years. "No," she repeated, "he wasn't stabbed to death. He died of natural causes." Assuming, of course, that eating Ding Dongs by the case and drinking enough vodka to float the Pacific fleet was natural.

"That's different," Freddy murmured. "Natural causes must be easier. For the survivor, I mean."

"Perhaps," Judith said. "But losing a loved one is difficult no matter how it happens."

"True." Freddy moved fretfully in the bed. "But at least nobody thought you'd killed your husband."

"That's not so," Judith replied, surprised by her own candor. "I've always felt that I killed him with kindness." But she'd never said it to anyone but Renie. "The morning he died, before I went to work, I ran to the store and bought him a gallon of sweet grape juice. He had diabetes by then. I've always wondered . . ." Her voice trailed off. She was annoyed with herself for baring her soul to a stranger. With Judith, it usually worked the other way around.

"That's different, too," Freddy asserted. "You didn't force him to drink the juice. He asked you to buy it."

Judith sighed. "Logically, I know that. But it still bothers me." She wanted to get off the subject of Dan's unhappy demise. "Are you saying that people really think you're . . . guilty of such violence?"

"Some people do. Maybe the police think so, too."

"Why?"

Freddy removed the compress and set it down on the nightstand. "Because of the sabers, I suppose. I mean, they belong to me."

"That's ridiculous," Judith declared. "Anyone could have used them. Maybe," she went on as if she'd thought of it for the first time, "they don't understand why you wouldn't notice that it wasn't Sally in the saber segment."

Freddy gazed blankly at Judith. "But I wouldn't."

Judith cocked her head. "You wouldn't? Why is that?"

"Because," Freddy replied, "I'm so focused on the illusion itself. A polar bear could have come onstage and I wouldn't have noticed."

Not knowing enough about the art of illusion to question Freddy's statement, Judith frowned. "Well . . . okay, if that's how it works."

"It is. Think about the great magicians and illusionists. Consider the concentration it takes to pull off the kind of performance that the audience demands. Or that we demand of ourselves, for that matter."

Freddy's voice had gained strength and his features had become more animated. Apparently, just talking about his profession had improved his mental and physical health.

"What do you remember about the night Sally was killed?" Judith asked as gently as possible.

Freddy rubbed at the middle of his forehead. "Not much. An hour before I go on, I sit in my dressing room and meditate. It helps me become focused. Nobody interrupts me, except Inga when she comes in about fifteen minutes before curtain time with a cup of herbal tea. But she never says anything. She brings the tea, makes sure I look as if I'm almost ready, and then leaves." He paused. "I do remember the power failure. I also recall the segment where I spoke about the great prestidigitators of the past. I stay focused, but in a different way. I have to become more engaged with the audience." Freddy took a couple of deep breaths, as if talking so much had tired him.

"So what you're saying is that you're in a virtual trance during your act?" Judith asked.

Freddy nodded. "Exactly. It's almost a form of self-hypnosis."

"Did Sally have to do anything like that?"

"To a lesser degree," Freddy said, looking sad at the mention of his former wife's name. "But Sally—or any other person who takes part in the performance—doesn't have to concentrate as much."

"I know Lloyd Watts plays his instrument," Judith said, "but he's the only other person besides Sally who actually appeared in the performance. Do you ever use other people?"

"Occasionally." Freddy reached for the glass of water on the nightstand. "During some engagements, we've had a guest hypnotist or even another illusionist. We've done some things with marionettes where we've hired a puppeteer." He shrugged. "It depends upon the city, the available talent. G.D. doesn't think the act should get too static."

"What about illness?" Judith queried. "What happens if you get sick?"

"We cancel," Freddy replied. "Luckily, I'm usually pretty healthy."

"Can't Lloyd step in for you?"

Freddy grimaced slightly. "Lloyd's not quite ready for prime time. Don't get me wrong—he's a great idea man, very innovative. But he's not at the point where he can perform in front of an audience."

"What about Sally?" Noting the pained expression on Freddy's face, Judith spoke more rapidly. "Did she ever need someone to fill in for her?"

"Almost never," Freddy said. "She was in good health, too." He hung his head and bit his lip. "About six weeks ago, when we were in Vegas, Sally turned her ankle. Micki took over for two or three performances."

"Micki must have had the routine down pat," Judith remarked.

"She did." Freddy's expression grew even more distressed. "Micki had watched it so many times and sat through many of the rehearsals. She knew the drill. So much so that she had to take the oath."

Judith was curious. "The oath?"

"It's not really an oath," Freddy explained, "it's a sworn statement that you'll never reveal any of the illusionist's secrets. If you do, you can be sued or even brought up on criminal charges."

"I didn't know that," Judith admitted. "Does everybody in your group have to sign the oath?"

"Of course," Freddy replied, regaining a bit of color in his face. "Not to mention the stagehands and techs and such who work with us at different shows."

"So," Judith said, ticking names off on her fingers, "you, Inga, Mr. Fromm, Lloyd, Griselda, and both Sally and Micki know all the secrets. What about Manny Quinn?"

Freddy shook his head. "Not Manny. We haven't known him that long. And not G.D. He's totally uninterested in the performance aspect. He and Manny seldom come to the performances, let alone attend rehearsals or concept meetings."

"Concept meetings? Is that where you come up with new ideas?"

"Yes." Freddy took another sip of water. "Usually, it's only Lloyd and Inga and me. There's no point in the others wasting their time listening to us toss around bits that we might never use."

Judith's curious nature couldn't help but make her wonder what went on at such meetings. It would be fascinating to sit in on just one of them to hear how illusions were created and executed.

Executed was the word that brought her back to reality. "I know this is a painful question," she said quietly, "but can you think of any reason why someone would want to kill both Sally and Micki?"

Freddy's chin quivered and his eyes grew moist. "No. Honestly, I can't. And you can tell your husband that I'd be the last person to harm either of them."

"Homicide is often about gain," Judith murmured. "Not necessarily monetary gain," she continued, speaking louder. "Gaining prestige, position, love—there aren't many motives for killing in cold blood." She tried to ignore Freddy's shudder. "Are you certain that you don't know anybody who would fall into that category?"

Freddy wiped at his eyes. "No. I mean, yes, I'm certain I don't know anybody who would do something like that to Sally or Micki."

Judith switched gears. "By the way, do you know Marta Ormond Flax?"

"Who's that?" Freddy asked with a frown.

"The woman who was found holding the saber last night."

"No." He shook his head, his expression morose. "I've never heard of her. Do the police think she's the killer?"

"I don't know," Judith said frankly. "I think they're still checking on her background. I assume you wouldn't have noticed if she'd been in the audience Monday night?"

"No." Freddy looked rueful. "I may appear to make eye contact with the spectators, but I actually don't. I don't even see the people I know. Except Inga. I can always see Inga. Of course, she usually has a table at the front."

Recalling Inga's removal of the Flynn party from their ringside seats, Judith nodded. "I thought maybe if Marta Ormond Flax had her poodle with her, she might have caught your eye."

"A poodle?" Freddy shook his head. "Pets aren't allowed in the cabaret. That's because of the animals in the act. They might get spooked."

Judy heard only fragments of Freddy's response. She was thinking back to what Inga had said when she'd barged in on the Flynns and the Joneses. "Do you know who was supposed to sit with your sister Monday night? Besides Mr. Fromm, that is."

Freddy looked perplexed. "No. Was someone else joining her?"

Judith explained about the mix-up in the seating arrangements, and how Inga had mentioned that other people might be sitting with her. But Freddy still looked blank. "It was a table for four, right?" he asked. "If G.D. was there, the only other person I can think of who might have been sitting with them would be Manny Quinn."

"He wasn't backstage?"

"No. Manny has seen the show a couple of times, just to please Sally," Freddy said. "But usually he gambles during the performances when we're playing a casino. It's his thing, you know."

"So I've heard," Judith remarked. "Does he win?"

"He's pretty lucky," Freddy replied. "At least according to Sally. I wouldn't have wanted her to marry some guy who was going to fritter away her money."

"You were still protective of her, I gather," said Judith.

"Oh, sure," Freddy said, his eyes again growing misty. "Just because people split up, they don't have to hate each other. I don't understand why there are so many ugly divorces. If you loved somebody for years and years, how could you suddenly stop?"

"I really don't know," Judith said, wondering how to tactfully handle the issue of a loving couple who had divorced. "Perhaps Sally felt differently. That is," she added hastily, "she still loved you, but maybe working and living together made her feel . . . suffocated?"

Freddy, however, shook his head. "No, it wasn't like that at all. You know how some people have to get married?" He waited for Judith's acknowledgment. "For Sally and me, it was the opposite. We had to get divorced. We couldn't work *and* live together. It was too much."

An incredulous Judith was about to probe deeper into the problem when Grisly entered the room.

"I'm back," she announced, slightly out of breath. "Thanks, Mrs. Flynn. You can go now."

"I can stay longer," Judith insisted. "Maybe there's something else you'd like to do. Freddy and I are getting along fine."

Grisly shook her head. "No." She came to stand by Judith's chair and made an impatient gesture. "I'll sit with Freddy."

Having no choice but to get up, Judith smiled weakly. "If you need me again, just call."

"I might do that." Grisly lowered her voice. "There are arrangements to be made. G.D. and Inga can't do everything."

"Arrangements?" Judith put a hand to her cheek. "Oh! Of course. Arrangements. Yes, I'd be glad to help." Bidding Freddy farewell, Judith left the Wild Ginger Suite.

In the elevator, she wondered what she should do next. She wanted to learn what the police had found out about Marta Ormond Flax. She also wanted to tell Renie about the lack of progress at the family property on the river. Most of all, she wanted something to eat. It was going on two and she was famished. But she didn't want to waste time on a sit-down lunch. Reaching the casino floor, she headed for the snack bar that she'd spotted earlier. It was located outside the sports book and the area for off-track betting on horse races. Judith got into the short line and ordered a hot dog with sauerkraut, a small bag of potato chips, and a diet soda.

The section for horseplayers was decorated like a New York bar and grill, with plenty of brass fittings, polished oak, and plush green upholstery. Judith decided to eat her meal and watch the races. Maybe she'd even place a bet. One of the things that she had enjoyed with Dan was going to the track. Occasionally, he won. More often—especially when he took his rare paycheck instead of Judith with him—he lost.

Bettors were lined up at a half dozen windows, placing their wagers. Five separate big TV screens showed the various stages of races and race preparation from all over the country. Judith picked up a list of the upcoming events at the counter next to the wagering windows. She was about to take a seat when somebody poked her in the back.

"Coz!" she exclaimed, after turning around and looking straight at Renie. "What are you doing here?"

Renie held a large paper cup of Pepsi in one hand and a twenty-dollar bill in the other. "I was checking on Bill in the sports book next door. March Madness, you know. He's scouting some of the college basketball games. He often places a bet on the NCAA finals. Then I remembered I was supposed to make a futures bet for Tom on the Kentucky Derby. You know how much he likes horses."

Bill and Renie's son had always been an animal lover. But it was his Great-uncle Al who had taught him how to make a buck off the horses. Uncle Al was that rare creature, a lucky gambler. He was also a bit of a con artist, but in a lovable, rascally sort of way—or so the Grover clan liked to describe him. Tom had been going to the track with Uncle Al for years, and while they'd never won huge amounts, both the younger and the older man usually came away with a profit.

"Are you sitting?" Renie inquired, nodding at Judith's tray. "I'll join you, but I've got to get a futures sheet from the rack on the other wall."

Renie returned before Judith was able to open her bag of chips. "I heard you had to go back home to straighten out Boob Bednarik's latest screwup," Renie said, sitting down next to Judith on the green velvet banquette.

"That's not the half of it," Judith said with a sigh. By the time she'd finishing relating the whole of it, Renie was looking mystified.

"Bill thought something fishy was going on at the cabin," Renie declared. "What are they doing in that bog? Digging for buried treasure? Maybe they'll find your old sandals."

"Maybe." Judith sounded vague.

"What now?" Renie asked, slurping up Pepsi.

"Buried treasure." Judith's expression was thoughtful.

"In the bog?" Renie frowned. "Didn't we run into something like that when I went with you on your honeymoon?"

Judith smiled faintly. Her honeymoon with Joe had been very odd. Shortly after the couple's arrival on the Oregon coast, Judith's groom had broken his leg in a freak dune-buggy accident. The payment for the week-long stay at a cottage above the Pacific Ocean had been nonrefundable. While Joe recuperated in a local hospital, Renie had come down to Buccaneer Beach to keep Judith company. The cousins had enjoyed themselves right up until they found their landlady strangled with a kite string.

"As you may recall," Judith said, "the buried treasure wasn't exactly pieces of eight."

"I recall it all too well," Renie replied. "Nor would I expect a chest of doubloons at the family cabin. The only pirates who ever went there were those so-called chums of Uncle Corky's who stole two heirloom German beer steins, most of the silverware, and Auntie Vance's girdle."

"I'd forgotten about them," Judith remarked. "But the concept of buried treasure gives me an idea." She reached into her purse and took out the Kleenex that was wrapped around the gold fleck from her shoe. "What does that look like to you?"

Renie put on her much-abused glasses. Judith could never understand how her cousin could see anything through the smudged, scratched lenses. The frames were always bent or cockeyed, since Renie had a habit of stepping as well as sitting on her glasses. "A shiny, tiny fleck of . . ." Renie looked up from the tissue. "Are you saying gold?"

Judith recounted the incidents involving similar gold flecks, including those she'd brushed from G. D. Fromm's suit coat and the small scattering she'd discovered on her slacks the previous evening in the coffee shop. "Do you remember how when we were kids Great-uncle Chuckie used to pan for gold in the river? Every once in a while he'd find some."

"Of course," Renie replied as a loud cheer and a few groans went up when one of the TV monitors showed a field of charging thoroughbreds crossing the finish line at Santa Anita. "But the mines on Mount Nugget had long since been cleaned out. Anyway, they were a good fifteen, twenty miles from the cabin."

"I know," Judith agreed. "But Grandma and Grandpa Grover and the rest of them bought the land during the Depression. Who did they buy it from? A private party, a timber company? I never heard any of the relatives mention it."

"I didn't, either," Renie said. "But they bought it before we were born. Judging from the size of the trees when we were kids, I'd guess that if it had ever been logged, it was early in the last century. There were no full-scale reforestation programs back then. That's probably why there are so many different kinds of trees on the river site."

"That's right," Judith concurred. "The more recent clear-cutting in the area didn't start until we were teenagers. But my point is that whoever owned it back in the thirties probably had it while gold mining was in full swing on Mount Nugget."

"Ah." Renie set her Pepsi down on the table. "You're saying that someone who mined around there might have found gold and stashed it. But in the bog? That's crazy."

Judith added more sauerkraut to her hot dog. "Yes, it is. But something's very wrong at the cabin. I wonder if Bart Bednarik knows what's going on with his brother-in-law."

"I wonder what it's got to do with G. D. Fromm," Renie remarked, looking at one of the screens where a fractious horse was kicking up a storm in gate number four at Hialeah. "That is, how did he get gold dust—if that's what it is—on his coat? And how did you get it on your slacks, for that matter?"

Judith grew thoughtful. "I noticed it after the second power failure, when I'd been sitting with Lloyd Watts. People went by me during the outage. In the dark, someone—possibly Fromm—bumped into me. It was such a weird situation. And then we found Marta Flax with the saber."

Renie shook her head. "I'm trying so hard to have a good time. I'm really working at not getting too caught up in these murders." She nudged Judith with her elbow. "Why am I being sucked in by you, just the way I was when I rescued you from what we called the quicksand?"

Judith smiled. "Because you can't resist?"

"Because it's you," Renie replied. "I have a problem letting you go it alone." She glanced at the futures sheet in front of her. "I have to find the horses that Tom picked as possible bets for the Derby. Why don't you put some money on a race and let me concentrate?"

Judith studied the racing cards. At first, nothing caught her attention. Then she found the perfect horse. "Iron Dan's Pants is running in the third at Churchill Downs. The odds are fifteen to one. Dare I?"

"You have to, since Dan's pants were always the size of Old Ironsides's sails," Renie declared. "Why not?"

"That race is coming up next," Judith noted, looking at the screen from Churchill Downs. "I'll bet two dollars to show."

"Chicken," Renie said, and went back to her list of Derby eligibles.

Judith got into the shortest line, but after a minute or two, it seemed to be moving the slowest. She studied the other horseplayers, wondering if Manny Quinn was among them. He wasn't. Her mind drifted back to Grisly's comment about making the funeral arrangements. Would Sally and Micki be buried side by side in Idaho? But Micki wasn't from there. She might have relatives who would want her remains closer to them, especially since she hadn't yet married Freddy. Manny might prefer having Sally buried in his family plot, wherever that might be. On the other hand, Manny seemed so cavalier about Sally's death. Maybe he didn't care. Maybe he never had.

Judith was next in line. As she took the money out of her wallet, she kept her eyes glued to the race program, lest she forget Iron Dan's Pants's post position. Tote tickets were never issued by name, only by number; in this case, Judith's pick was in gate number six. She memorized the drill: race number three, two dollars on number six to show at Churchill Downs.

She was at the window when she spotted Doc Engelman amble into the room. He stopped to gaze at the tote board, which was showing the latest results from Hialeah.

"Miss?" The balding man behind the window leaned forward. "Miss, are you placing a bet?"

"Oh! Sorry. Yes," Judith replied, then recited her request.

The man took her money, punched in her bet, and handed over the tote ticket. "Thanks," Judith said, and rushed off to see Doc Engelman.

Doc was turning away from the tote board when Judith reached him. "Hi," she said, smiling brightly. "I'm glad I ran into you. How's Marta Ormond Flax doing?"

"Better," Doc replied. "Being reunited with Fou-Fou seems like the best medicine for her."

"You know," Judith said even as Engelman began to walk toward the wagering area, "I can't help but think it's strange that she had such a violent reaction to a few drinks."

"Everybody's different," Doc said with a shrug. "You can't always judge capacity by size or weight. Some husky men can pass out from a single cocktail."

"But this seemed so unusual," Judith persisted. "I'm no expert, but I used to tend bar before I got into the innkeeping business. I never saw anything like what happened last night with Marta."

"You can't pigeonhole people's reactions to alcohol," Doc said. "Excuse me, I want to place a bet on the next race at Bay Meadows."

Judith refrained from tugging at Doc's sleeve. "Have the police found out anything about her?" she asked, trying to keep up.

Doc looked over his shoulder. "That's not my line. Ask your husband. He *is* the police, isn't he?" Doc continued on his way to the windows.

Frustrated, Judith rejoined her cousin. "I give up. People are like clams around here."

"Was that Doc Engelman you were collaring?" Renie asked.

"Yes. He wouldn't tell me squat about Marta Ormond Flax." Judith took a vicious bite out of her hot dog. "I'll have to track down Joe."

"Speaking of track," Renie said, "how much did you win on your show bet?"

"Win?" Judith looked at the tote board. "Ohmigosh, Iron Dan's Pants showed! I got twelve dollars and forty cents!"

Renie patted Judith on the back. "Good for you. Go collect your winnings. That'll cheer you up."

Judith got in line at the same window where she'd placed her wager. She could see Doc Engelman just a few feet away, waiting in line and stroking his goatee while he studied the *Daily Racing Form*. Judith didn't believe the man for a minute. He was concealing the truth about Marta Ormond Flax. Of course, Judith realized, that was probably because of doctor-patient privilege. Nevertheless, she was still irked.

"Miss?" The balding man behind the window sounded a bit weary. "Miss?"

"Oh! Excuse me! I wanted to turn in my winning ticket."

"Fine." The man took the ticket, placed it in the machine, and began counting out Judith's money. And counting and counting. "There you are, miss. Fourteen hundred, ten dollars and thirty cents."

Judith gaped at the bills before her. "No! That can't be! I only bet two dollars to show."

The man cocked his head at Judith. "I don't mean to be impertinent, but that's not the case. I remember it well, because you seemed a little . . . rattled. Not to mention that you picked the horse with the longest odds. You said you wanted the number two horse in the third race for a six-dollar combo. Number two—ItsNobody-AtAll—went off at twenty-to-one odds."

"B-b-but I only g-g-gave you t-t-two dollars!" Judith exclaimed. If she'd been rattled before, she was practically a gibbering idiot now.

The man smiled and shook his head. "You gave me two twenties."

Judith clapped a hand to her head. "I don't believe it!"

"You better. It's true. I guess this is your lucky day." He nudged the money toward Judith. "Do you want to place another bet?"

Frantically, Judith shook her head. "No! No, I mean, not now. Gosh, thanks!" With trembling hands, she scooped up the money and hurried off to tell Renie what had happened.

"You're lucky even when you're stupid," Renie teased after Judith had finished her tale. "Write down that horse's name. When Bill and I go to the track at home, I like to bet on the out-of-town races."

Picking up a hotel notepad, Judith scribbled the name of her winner. She still felt dazed. "I don't see how I could have gotten so mixed up. Or given the guy two twenties instead of two ones."

"You probably had your mind on the murders," Renie said. "Or you were people watching."

"I was, at that," Judith confessed. "I'd just seen Doc Engelman come into the betting parlor. He wouldn't tell me anything about Marta Ormond Flax except that she loves her dog."

"I think we knew that," Renie said dryly. "Speaking of mysteries, I'd like to know what I got on the back of my taffeta skirt."

"The one you wore to the magic show Monday night?"

Renie nodded. "When I was getting dressed this morning, I was going through the closet to find these beige slacks behind the outfit I wore Monday night. The sunlight hit the skirt just so. The back of it looked odd, but with that bronze taffeta, the color changes with the light. But this didn't."

"Is it more gold flecks?" Judith asked.

"Nothing like that," Renie replied. "It's a big smudge just below the skirt band. It's crusty, too. In fact," she went on with a worried expression, "it looks a lot like dried blood."

Chapter Sixteen

THE "Inquiry" sign was flashing on the tote board from Bay Meadows. Apparently a possible foul had been committed during the race. But the lights going on in Judith's brain were what kept her eyes riveted on Renie.

"You'll have to show the skirt to Joe," Judith asserted. "Are you sure it could be blood?"

"As sure as I can be," Renie said. "Dried blood looks like rust, so on bronze fabric, it's not so obvious. Which is why I didn't notice it before. I haven't worn the skirt since Monday night."

Judith rested her chin on her hands. Vaguely, she recalled seeing the back of Renie's skirt when her cousin was leaning over the roulette table to place her bets. Judith didn't recall anything odd about the skirt, but maybe she wouldn't, given the color and fabric. Besides, she reminded herself, she had just discovered that Sally had been murdered. The shock might have dimmed her powers of observation. "How could it have happened?" Judith asked. "And when?"

Renie looked uncertain. "You're assuming it's Sally's blood?"

"Did you notice anyone else bleeding profusely?"

"No," Renie replied. "But then I didn't notice Sally bleeding profusely, either. Besides, during the power outage, someone could have gotten hurt and brushed up against me."

Judith's expression was droll. "Do you recall that happening?"

Renie made a face. "Of course not. I . . ." She stopped, raising a finger. "Wait. Do you remember when we were coming out of the rest room and groping our way through the dark? Somebody *did* bump into me."

"You didn't feel dampish?" Judith inquired.

"No. The skirt has an underskirt. You know, in case I win a big jackpot and wet my pants. Ha, ha."

"At our age, that's not so funny," Judith remarked. Making sure her purse was securely shut, she stood up. "I'm going to put this money in the hotel safe. Why don't you come with me and then we'll get your skirt so we can turn it over to Joe."

"Okay," Renie agreed, tucking the futures list into a huge purse that—appropriately enough—resembled a horse's feed bag. "I haven't exactly been raking in the money today."

Judith gave Renie a skeptical look. "In other words, you've exceeded your daily gambling allowance already?"

"Let's say that I've exceeded it through Friday," Renie admitted as they went out onto the casino floor. "Of course, I pointed out to Bill that you can't win if you're not gambling."

Dolly wasn't on duty at the cashier's window. Instead, an older woman with long silver hair stood behind the counter. Judith counted out the fourteen one-hundred-dollar bills. "I can't make up my mind what to do with this cash. Maybe I should put it in the safe with my other things," she said, feigning confusion. "Could you check to see what's in there now, please? It's under 'Fromm.'"

The cashier, whose name was Ella, didn't look surprised. But Renie did. When Ella had gone to the back room, Renie moved closer to her cousin. "What are you trying to pull now?" she demanded.

"I forgot to tell you about the gold nuggets," Judith whispered. "I don't know how I could have forgotten. Maybe, between homicide and home improvements, I have too much on my mind."

Ella returned, looking worried. "There's no Mrs. Fromm listed, ma'am, only a Mr. Fromm. I'm going to have to see your ID."

Judith slapped a hand to her head. "Of course! How stupid of me! Never mind." She paused, turning very somber. "As long as the gold nuggets are there, it's fine. There was a mix-up earlier. You wouldn't mind taking a peek just so I don't have to worry about them."

"They're there," Ella replied, though her concerned expression remained. "I checked on them earlier for Mr. Fromm. Have you decided whether or not you want a cashier's check, Mrs. Fromm?"

"Yes," Judith responded, yanking on Renie's sleeve, "but I'm making a gift of these winnings to my sister. Here, she can give you the information. The name is Jones, Serena Jones."

Renie opened her mouth to protest, but Judith enfolded her in a bear hug. "You deserve it, darling! After all the money you raised to send me to Lourdes for my miraculous cure!" Under her breath, Judith added, "Do it and shut up."

In a wooden manner, Renie went through the required motions. When the cousins were a good thirty feet from the cashier's cage, Judith explained why the ruse was necessary.

"I took a chance," she said as they strolled toward the elevators. "A mistake had obviously been made. What would be most likely? The boxes in the safe are filed alphabetically. So the gold nuggets in my box probably belonged to somebody else whose last name begins with F. *Ergo*, the man with the gold dust on his coat, G. D. Fromm."

"You could be arrested for fraud," Renie pointed out, poking the Up button for the elevator. "What if Ella is suspicious?"

"I'll deal with that when and if it happens," Judith said, though she looked a bit grim. "The usual cashier is Dolly, and I think we may have bonded. She'll figure I just got mixed up."

"Maybe I should keep the money in case I have to bail you out of jail," Renie said as they got into the elevator.

"The important thing is, where did the nuggets come from?" Judith mused as they arrived at their floor. "Is it possible they were found on the family property?"

"I can't imagine," Renie said. She stopped in front of their mothers' room. "Should we?"

"Isn't your mom at the conference?"

Renie shook her head. "This was to be a free afternoon. The conferees could do what they pleased—skiing, hiking, gambling, trying to kill their roommates."

Judith sighed. "I suppose. We *are* dutiful daughters."

She rapped on the door. There was no response. She rapped again. And again.

"I can't hear the TV," Judith said, pressing her ear against the door. "Maybe they're taking a nap."

"Maybe," Renie allowed. "Have you got a key card to their room?"

"Yes," Judith said, digging into her purse. "I had them give me an extra, just in case."

The small green light turned on; Judith opened the door.

Gertrude was on the telephone; Aunt Deb was on a cell phone. Both seemed engrossed in their conversations.

"Goodness!" Judith breathed, standing in the doorway with Renie next to her. "My mother on the *phone?*"

"My mother on a *cell phone?*" Renie whispered.

"You bet your big bottom I want script approval," Gertrude was saying. "Who knows what he might write about me? I thought you weren't sure if Dade Costello was still on the A-list after that dumb-cluck producer's big flop. You're my agent, Eugie, you work it out. Just send the money in a big armored truck and make sure the nitwits driving it have guns."

"Yes," Aunt Deb said, "I do know quite a bit about the timber industry. My late husband and my father worked in it . . . A slogan? . . . That's not exactly a *design*, is it, dear? . . . Well, I suppose I could. What comes to mind, of course, is that only God can make a tree. What if you said only God *and* Wirehoser can make a tree? . . . You like it? . . . Heavens, it was just off the top of my poor old addled head . . ."

Judith quietly closed the door. The cousins exchanged bemused looks in the corridor.

"Do you really think either of them can make a buck in their dotage?" Renie asked.

"More power to them, if they can," Judith replied.

Renie opened the door to the Joneses's room. "Ooops!" She put a finger to her lips. "Bill's taking a nap. Stay in the hall, I'll grab the skirt."

It didn't take Renie a full minute to complete her task. "Now," she inquired, "how do we find Joe?"

"Good question," Judith responded. "We could page him, or go to Pancho's office where they all seem to sit around on their dead butts and not solve the case."

"Try the page first," Renie suggested. "You can do it from your room."

The cousins moved back down the hall. Judith slipped the key card in and opened the door. To her surprise, Joe was also taking a nap.

"Oh, good grief!" she exclaimed, backing out of the room and shutting the door, though not so softly. "Joe never takes naps at home!"

"Oh?" Renie looked amused. "What do you bet he does when he's on a surveillance job?"

"Well . . ." Judith stroked her chin. "Maybe that's why he sometimes takes so long to finish an assignment. Of course he *does* get paid by the hour."

A rumpled Joe Flynn in an even more rumpled blue bathrobe yanked the door open. "What now?" he asked in a groggy voice.

"Skirt," Renie barked, shoving the garment at Joe. "Dried blood. Check it out. 'Bye." She trotted off toward the elevators.

"Hey!" Joe called after her.

Renie didn't turn around. Judith put a hand on her husband's arm. "We didn't know you were asleep."

Joe's expression was defensive. "I was resting my eyes. We took an hour's break."

"That's fine," Judith said, smiling in an understanding, wifely way. "Renie discovered there's dried blood on the skirt she wore the night that Sally was murdered. We thought maybe the lab should check it out."

Joe made a grumpy noise. "Sheriff Costello moves with the speed of old glue. We haven't gotten a damned thing back from him so far. It's no wonder we're bogged down in this investigation."

Judith pointed to the skirt, which was draped over Joe's other arm. "It does look as if it could be blood. What do you think?"

Joe held up the skirt, which rustled softly as he turned it around to catch the light. "Oh. I see what she means. Hunh. It might be, at that."

"Of course we won't know whose blood," Judith noted, "except that it's not Renie's. Someone might have brushed up against her when we were in the rest room during the blackout."

"Okay." Joe folded the skirt over four times. "I don't have an evidence bag here. I'll put it in one of the hotel's laundry bags."

"Thanks." Judith wondered if she should tell Joe about the gold nuggets and the gold dust. Out of the corner of her eye, Judith could see Renie doing a graceless little dance by the elevators. It was a sign that her cousin was growing impatient. "Are we having dinner together?" Judith asked her husband as she retreated from the threshold and into the hallway.

"Sure," Joe said. "Let's live it up and eat in the salmon house. I'll meet you here around six." He started back into the room, but stopped. "How'd it go at the house this morning?"

"It went," Judith replied. "I'll tell you later."

"If," Renie said when they were in the elevator, "I was a betting woman—which I am—I'd give you two-to-one odds that Joe never leaves the room until it's time for dinner."

"I suppose he's tired," Judith said. "He expected a vacation, not a job. The last few months have been hard on us both. By the way, Joe wants to eat in the salmon house tonight. Could you and Bill join us?"

"Sure," Renie replied as the elevator came to a halt. "I'll wait tables and Bill can be one of the line cooks."

Judith made a face at Renie. "It can't be that bad."

"Well . . . Not quite. Sure, we'll—" As the elevator stopped and the doors slid open, Renie gave a start. "We're in the basement. Didn't you poke One?"

"No. I thought you did. One of us must have bumped B by accident." Judith stepped out of the elevator. "Wait a minute—this is the underground parking area. Is there a P on the elevator panel?"

Renie was still in the car. "Yes, there are two—P/1 and P/2. We're on P/1."

"As long as we're here . . . ," Judith began.

"Oh, no," Renie protested, "we're not going to search parked cars. Come on, coz, let's go back up."

Judith had to admit that there was no reason to look around the garage. "You're right," she said, starting back into the elevator. "I don't know what I was thinking of."

She had just stepped inside when shouts erupted.

"Rats!" Renie said under her breath. "What's that?"

Both cousins exited the elevator. Listening intently, they could make out the raised voices of a man and a woman. It sounded as if they were engaged in a fierce argument.

"It's coming from over there," Judith finally said, pointing to their left. "Dare we?"

"Offhand," Renie replied dryly, "I say we don't. Getting mixed up in other people's quarrels is definitely a bad idea."

"Define 'getting mixed up,'" Judith said softly. She began to move quietly in the direction of the argument.

"Damn!" Renie swore under her breath. "I won't let you go alone, you reckless fool!"

Judith and Renie ducked behind the cars as they approached the source of the noise. The concrete pillars were numbered with red paint. The cousins had advanced to 1 D. The loud voices seemed to be in the vicinity of 1 H.

By the time they reached 1 F, Judith not only could identify the combatants, but she could catch most of the heated exchange.

"You're slime!" Inga Polson shouted. "I want you out of here! I never want to see you again!"

"Listen, you old bat," G. D. Fromm roared, "if it weren't for me, that halfwit brother of yours would be doing card tricks on senior citizen bus tours!"

With Renie behind her, Judith reached 1 G and stopped, leaning against a steel-gray SUV. The cousins were separated from Inga and G.D. by only two rows of vehicles. They couldn't see either of the adversaries, but every word was loud and clear.

"You're nothing but a leech!" Inga cried. "You chased us down in Reno and practically begged us to let you manage Freddy! You were broke, your wife had thrown you out, you were practically living in a cardboard box! When I seize an opportunity to advance my brother's career, you don't argue, you go along—or you go, period." Inga paused for breath. "Now look at this other mess you've got me into!"

"That's not my fault!" G.D. shot back. "Don't blame me for your wretched personal problems! How was I to know about your aberration?"

"Aberration, indeed!" Inga was panting a bit, her deep voice growing hoarse. When she spoke again, it was more softly. "I'm going to my room now. I want your resignation by six o'clock."

The cousins stayed hidden behind the SUV as Inga's flat-footed steps came closer. Fortunately, she turned down the aisle instead of cutting across to the elevators. There was no sound from G. D. Fromm. Judith and Renie stayed put.

Inga's footsteps faded. "Elevator?" Renie mouthed at Judith.

Judith nodded. But G. D. didn't seem to budge.

Renie sank down onto the concrete floor. "How long, oh Lord?" she whispered.

Judith shrugged just before she heard G.D. walk rapidly away. A moment later a car door opened, slammed shut, and the engine was turned on. The vehicle's tires squealed as it roared out of the garage.

Renie struggled back to her feet. "At least I didn't sit on a grease spot," she said, checking out her slacks. "What do you figure that was all about?"

"Other than dissension in the ranks?" Judith shook her head as the cousins walked toward the elevators. "I'm not sure. But I can't figure out how two such strong personalities could work in tandem."

Renie didn't get a chance to respond. A mid-size sedan that apparently had just entered the parking garage suddenly picked up speed and hurtled in their direction. Judith lurched to her right; Renie leaped to her left. The car kept going, screeching as it made a sharp turn to avoid hitting the wall.

"What the hell?" Renie panted, clinging to the hood of a blue BMW. "That idiot came so close that I could almost feel it!"

"I couldn't see who was driving," Judith replied, also gasping for breath. She tested her artificial hip. Nothing seemed amiss. "The car must have tinted windows.

"Maybe," Judith continued, "it was just a valet showing off. It wouldn't be the first time I've been in parking garages where the tires squealed like a pig farm every time one of the guys brought out a car."

"True," Renie agreed, punching the Up button. "I know they have to be quick, but I always feel as if Cammy's being abused."

"I suppose," Judith said as the elevator doors opened, "we could check with Bob Bearclaw to see who's entered the garage in the last five minutes. But I wouldn't want to get one of those valets in trouble. They're just kids."

Arriving on the casino floor, the cousins couldn't believe their eyes. A full-fledged scuffle had broken out just a few feet away. Judging from the jeans and cowboy boots on one side and the long hair and flannel shirts on the other, a battle of the bands had erupted. Three security guards—Emily Dancingdoe, Amos Littlebird, and Ronnie Roughrocks—were trying to pull them apart.

"Good grief," Judith gasped. "What now?" Sheriff Abbott N. Costello and Deputy Dabney Plummer pushed their way through the melee. "Hold it!" Costello shouted. "I'm counting to three and then I draw my piece!"

Renie leaned closer to Judith. "I'm glad he's not counting to ten. As I recall, Costello's too dumb to get that far."

No one paid any attention to the sheriff. Bob Bearclaw came up behind Costello and tapped him on the shoulder.

"Let me take care of this," Bob said quietly. "I don't want a gun going off in here. Someone could get hurt."

"Hurt?" Costello shouted. "You don't call *this* hurt? Hell, they could kill each other!"

"No." Bob shook his head, moving straight into the fracas. "It's a matter of pride," he asserted, putting up a hand to block a fist aimed at someone else's face. "They represent two generations, two styles of music. They're defending their artistic honor."

"Bull!" Costello burst out. "They're just a bunch of brawlers! They need some time in the slammer to cool off."

"They need to become civilized," Bob declared, grasping the collars of two opponents who were locked in combat. "You're both victorious," he said calmly as he pulled them apart. "You've demonstrated stamina, bravery, and determination. And you're still standing up."

The melee began to subside. A few of the participants were regarding Bob with awe.

"See," he pointed out to Costello. "The fight is over. Well done, my friends," he said in salute. "You've shown your mettle." He turned back to the sheriff. "Let's step aside so the medics can attend to the injured."

Costello turned to Dabney Plummer. "Damnedest thing I ever saw," he muttered.

"Who won?" The query came from several onlookers.

Bob acknowledged the crowd. "Everybody won. They've proved their manhood. Would you please clear the area? Thank you very much." The cousins kept close to the wall, avoiding any of the fallen combatants. Eventually, they made it into the casino area, where clusters of guests were discussing the excitement and, in some cases, arguing over the nondecision.

"Now what do we do?" Renie asked.

Judith looked at her watch. "It's after five. I suppose we could have a predinner drink. The Summer Bar is closest."

Instead of music, the sound of the river was piped into the bar. The illusion was heightened by a small stream that rippled around the bar's perimeter. Judith admired the artificial cottonwood and alder saplings, along with the various replicas of Alpine flowers. What intrigued her most, however, were the salmonberries and huckleberries and thimbleberries that looked good enough to eat.

The summer mood upon them, Judith and Renie diverged from their usual Scotch and bourbon, opting instead for daiquiris. After they'd been served, Judith sat back in the white-pine Adirondack chair and sighed.

"I can't seem to get a handle on any of this," she declared. "It isn't as if I haven't been on the outside of an investigation before. But this one utterly stumps me."

"You've been stumped before and still come up with the who-done-it," Renie said. "Besides, you've had too many distractions, what with the B&B remodeling and what's going on at the cabin site."

"Which I also can't figure out," Judith said. "The cabin, I mean. I wonder if there really is gold somewhere on the property."

"Dubious," Renie said. "If it was buried after it was mined, the family would have found it. Don't you remember how often we used to have to dig a new privy hole?"

"True. But we hardly covered every inch of ground. What if—" She stopped speaking as Lloyd Watts entered the bar.

"Lloyd!" she called as he started to sit down at a nearby table. "Won't you join us?"

Looking at the cousins in surprise, he hesitated, then came toward them. "Sure. Hear about the fight?"

"We saw it," Judith responded. "Were you in the crowd that was watching?"

Lloyd shook his head. "I got there just as they were taking a few of the guys to the hospital."

"Was anyone seriously hurt?" Judith inquired.

"I heard one of the security guards say that somebody from Craven Raven got a nasty head cut. Another," Lloyd said, interrupting himself to give his club-soda order to the hovering waiter. "The Kitshickers' lead guitarist hurt his hand pretty bad." He paused again, apparently to recall who else was on the disabled list. "Oh—the Craven Raven drummer broke a finger and their bass player sprained his wrist."

Renie took a sip of her daiquiri before asking a question of her own. "Kitshickers was the band that replaced your act, right?"

Gazing at Renie's glass, Lloyd nodded. "Your drink's on fire."

Renie and Judith stared as flames erupted from the cocktail.

"Yikes!" Renie cried, attempting to fan the fire with her hand.

The flames went out immediately. Lloyd chuckled. "That's one hot drink, eh?"

Renie stared at the daiquiri. "Is it safe or will I die of sulfur poisoning?"

"It's safe," Lloyd replied in his laconic manner. "It's an illusion, that's all. You were watching my face, and not really seeing what else was going on."

"Whew!" Renie grinned and passed her hand over her forehead. "I'll have to trust you."

Lloyd shrugged. The waiter returned with the club soda. "That fight caused a problem." He sipped his drink.

"How do you mean?" Judith asked.

"For us. For Freddy." Lloyd looked worried.

"How so?" Judith persisted.

"Neither of the bands can play tomorrow night. Too banged up."

"Who's playing tonight?" Judith inquired.

"Tonight's a benefit for the local volunteer firefighters." Lloyd took another sip. "Kind of a talent show."

Renie had dared to sample her drink. It tasted just fine. "Can't the casino book someone else by tomorrow?"

"Pretty short notice," said Lloyd. "Pancho Green's upset." He paused to sip again. "Guess we'll have to go on after all, eh? It's just one show. It's the end of the run here anyway."

Judith was aghast. "How can you perform? I saw Freddy this afternoon and he's a mess. Besides, he has no assistant."

"Needs must," Lloyd said with another shrug. "I'll help." He stared off in the direction of a salmonberry bush. "The show must go on, eh?"

Judith and Renie followed his gaze.

A rainbow trout leaped out of the bush and jumped into the small stream by the bar.

Judith was beginning to wonder what was real and what was not.

Chapter Seventeen

JUDITH could hardly believe that Freddy would be able to perform in just a little over twenty-four hours. But as she and Renie headed back to the elevators to go upstairs and change for dinner, the hotel staff was erecting the signs announcing the Great Mandolini's farewell performance.

Joe was already dressed when Judith returned to their room. She assumed he'd resumed his nap, but there was no sign of the laundry bag containing the taffeta skirt. Maybe she'd misjudged him. He must have gone back to work, not back to sleep.

But her husband's siesta wasn't uppermost on her mind. "I'm amazed," she declared after informing Joe about Freddy's return to the stage on Thursday night. "I saw him this afternoon. He's a wreck."

Joe shrugged. "The show must go on. Besides, it might do him good. Lots of people submerge their sorrow in work."

"True," Judith conceded. "Oh, Joe," she continued, putting her hands on his shoulders, "I've so much to tell you. Do we have time to talk before we meet Renie and Bill? I told Renie we'd be at the salmon house by six-fifteen."

Joe grimaced. "It's five to six now. Can you change clothes and talk at the same time?"

"Of course," Judith replied, going to the closet and taking out a two-piece purple ensemble that was a perfect match for the amethyst necklace and earrings Joe had given her for Christmas. She began with the latest news from Hillside Manor.

With scarcely a pause for breath, Judith backtracked to breakfast with Inga, then moved on to Freddy's suite, in the afternoon. "It's strange, in a way," she said, slipping into her black suede sandals. "Freddy's just a shadow of himself. I've never seen anyone so prostrated by grief."

Joe looked in the mirror over the dresser to adjust his tie. "As Inga likes to say, her brother is very sensitive because he's an *artiste*."

"Freddy's suffered two losses," Judith noted, "so his emotional state is understandable. But he seems more disturbed over Sally's death than Micki's. He talks mostly about Sally, unless I'm imagining it. His behavior really puzzles me."

Joe shrugged. "He'd spent most of his life with Sally. From what I gather, he's known Micki for only a couple of years."

"I suppose," Judith allowed, standing in front of the mirror to apply her makeup. Briefly, she thought back to the years between Dan's death and her marriage to Joe. She couldn't recall speaking effusively or at length about her first husband. Maybe she'd been trying to forget, at least the bad times. Only in the security of her union with Joe had she begun to mention the better side of Dan, the rare virtues, the occasional joy, and especially his role as a father to Mike. For that, she would be ever grateful to Dan McMonigle.

"Then there was the brawl between the two bands," Judith continued, carefully putting on her lipstick. "Did you hear about that?"

"Uh—yes," Joe replied. "You actually saw it?"

Judith nodded. "We were getting out of the elevator. It was quite a fight, but Bob Bearclaw managed to end it. Anyway, Renie and I . . .

Oh! I forgot to tell you about the argument between Inga and G. D. Fromm in the parking garage."

At this point, Joe was leaning against the wall by the door. "What were you doing in the parking garage? You worry me. Are you actually *looking* for trouble, Jude-girl?"

"No. I guess we poked the wrong elevator button." Judith put her cosmetics away and gave her salt-and-pepper hair a vigorous brushing. "By the way, don't call me 'Jude-girl.' You know I've never liked that nickname. It makes me sound like a wind-up doll."

Joe looked hurt. "You don't think it takes us back to our youth?"

"It does," Judith replied. "You always called me that when we were dating, but after you dumped me for Herself, I never liked the nickname."

Joe moved away from the door. "I thought you'd forgiven me for that."

"I have. Of course I have," Judith reiterated. "But once in a while, 'Jude-girl' can still conjure up unhappy memories."

Joe looked perplexed. "What should I call you? 'Judith-woman'?"

"Hmm. I'll have to think about it."

"How about this?" Joe said, moving to the nightstand and picking up the message tablet. "You would never have brought up the subject if you weren't frustrated over the murder case. But it's not the first time you've beaten your head against a brick wall. And almost always, you finger the perp."

Judith stared at Joe to see if he was humoring her. "What's the point of all this?"

Joe gave Judith a quirky smile. "You started it, Jude . . . my dear." He handed her the tablet and a pen. "Just for the hell of it, I'll give you twenty-four hours to write down the name of who you think killed Sally and Micki. By that time, the police might have solved the case. If they haven't, the bet's off. But if they've fingered the perp, and you're wrong, you've got to promise to stop putting yourself in jeopardy by getting involved in every homicide that crosses your path."

"Are you serious?"

Joe nodded. He had not only turned serious, he looked downright solemn. She put the hairbrush back in her purse.

"I really mean it," Joe replied. "Your guardian angel must be about to submit his—or her—resignation. Eventually, your luck will run out, just like it does for any gambler. Do we have a deal?"

Judith was stunned. Her initial reaction was to refuse. But Joe had a point. There had been so many close calls, so many scrapes with danger, so many near-death experiences. Too often, she'd put herself—and sometimes Renie—at risk. Besides, she had twenty-four hours to identify the killer.

"Okay," she said with a tight little smile, "I'll do it." She pushed the pen and tablet away. "I'm not ready yet, but when I am, I'll write it down and put the name in the hotel safe."

"Good. Let me know when you do. I want to be there to see you hand it over for safekeeping. Better yet, let's say we'll go to the cashier's window at six tomorrow evening. Okay?"

"That's less than twenty-four hours," Judith pointed out.

"Only by a few minutes." He kissed Judith gently on the lips. "Are you ready for dinner?"

"Yes," Judith replied. "I'll tell you about Lloyd Watts in the elevator."

Heaving a big sigh, Joe opened the door. "You were in the elevator with Lloyd Watts? What did you do, find him in the parking garage?"

"No," Judith replied, exasperated. "We met up with him in the Summer Bar after the fight."

"You've had a busy day," Joe remarked as they headed down the corridor.

"Yes, I have." Judith watched Joe poke the elevator button. She hadn't yet mentioned her stop at the family cabin site. Maybe that could wait. Relating the conversation with Lloyd would take up the brief time before they got to the salmon house.

There was no waiting list for seatings this early in the evening. Bill and Renie hadn't arrived yet, so the Flynns decided to claim a table. The restaurant was officially called the Stillasnowamish Salmon House. The interior was modeled after the local tribes' wooden high-ceilinged longhouses. The tantalizing aroma of smoked salmon lingered in the air. Though the cedar furnishings looked rustic, the chairs were very comfortable. The walls were decorated with handcrafted masks, spears, and various animal hides.

Judith again ordered a daiquiri, but Joe stayed with his favorite Scotch.

"Lloyd sounds pretty clever," Joe remarked. "Why can't he stand in for Freddy if the show must go on?"

"Freddy says Lloyd isn't ready for big performances," Judith replied. "He can do the small stuff, but I suppose the big illusions, especially in front of an audience, are more difficult. Say, what have you found out about Marta Ormond Flax?"

Joe frowned. "She swears she doesn't remember anything after being in the bar with her poodle yesterday afternoon. The next thing she knew, she woke up this morning in the Glacier Falls hospital. The lab tests won't be back for a couple of days, so we have no idea what was in her system except for the booze."

"Does she admit to being a drinker?" Judith asked.

Joe chuckled as their own drinks arrived. "Marta allowed that she enjoys the occasional cocktail. As does Fou-Fou."

"Hey!" It was Renie, charging toward the table. "You started without us!"

"We wanted to be sure we got a good place," Judith replied. "You can watch them barbecue the salmon from here. Where's Bill?"

"He stopped to admire the trout tank," Renie said, sitting down.

"With sports fishing so lousy around here, he hasn't seen trout that size in years except at Falstaff's Grocery."

"Who has?" Joe remarked in sympathy.

Bill strolled over to the table. "I might play some baccarat tonight. How about it, Joe?"

"Actually *play*?" Joe feigned amazement. "Not just study and watch?"

"I'm ready," Bill declared, sitting next to Renie. "I won a hunsky at craps last night."

"Can I have some of it?" Renie asked, pleading like a puppy.

Bill ignored her.

Renie pouted.

Somehow, the dinner conversation managed to skirt the topic of murder. Everyone ordered the salmon, its delicious flavor enhanced by the smoke from the alder planks on which it had been cooked. Joe and Bill planned their baccarat strategy, which seemed to consist of how much money they could afford to lose. Judith fussed about the B&B renovations. Renie fretted over her children's weddings. At the end of the meal, Bill silently reached into the pocket of his brown corduroy vest, took out a small leather purse, and handed Renie a fifty-dollar bill.

"Stick to roulette," he advised.

"Oh, Bill," Renie cried, planting a big kiss on his cheek, "I love you so!"

As the men parted company with the women outside the restaurant, Judith asked her cousin if she really intended to stick to roulette.

"Sure," Renie replied. "That way, if I hit a couple of numbers, I can go play the slots. Come on, coz, join me."

Judith winced. "It's a five-dollar minimum for the numbers, right? That's a lot. I'll just wander around for a bit."

Renie shrugged. "Whatever." She moved swiftly toward the roulette wheels.

Judith kept alert for anyone connected to the Mandolini act. She hit her own version of pay dirt when she spotted Manny Quinn at one of the craps tables. The atmosphere was subdued. Judith assumed nobody was winning. Apparently, Manny felt the same way. He moved on.

A cheer went up from the next table. There was room for at least a couple of newcomers. Manny slipped in between an older man in coveralls and a clean-cut young fellow who looked like a college student. Judith waited a few moments before approaching the table. There was a spot open on the corner, between the college student and a petite blonde with a rose tattoo on her left hand.

Judith couldn't remember the protocol for craps. A row of black, blue, green, and red chips stood on end in the table's grove, where Manny stood. Judith leaned down to whisper to the blonde: "What's the buy-in here?"

The blonde shrugged. "If you want to go low ball, give them forty bucks. It's a five-dollar minimum here at night. Get some dollar chips, too."

Judith gulped, nodded, and obeyed. A bearded man next to the blonde held the dice. The stickman shouted, "Coming out!" Encouraging cheers rose from not only the players, but the employees working the table. Noting that everyone seemed to have placed chips on the line that read "PASS," she followed suit.

The man threw a three. Judith was puzzled when everyone else groaned. Her chip, along with the others, disappeared. The college student shook his head and walked away. Judith was now next to Manny Quinn.

"What's wrong with a three?" she asked.

Manny turned to look at her. "Oh. It's you." He didn't sound pleased but had the grace to explain the throw. "He threw a three on his first roll. He crapped out."

"I see." Everyone was putting chips on "PASS" again. Judith reluctantly did the same.

The blonde threw a two. "Snake eyes," said the stickman with a sad little smile. Again, all the chips were swept away. Two must not be any good either, Judith thought to herself.

With an angry motion, Manny put a black chip on the line. Judith remembered that black stood for a hunsky. With a little sigh, she set down another five dollars.

"Do it," Manny ordered in a gruff voice.

"Do what?" Judith asked.

He pointed to the stickman, who was pushing the dice at Judith. "You're up next. Throw the damned things. Make us some money."

"Oh, dear." She thought she'd seen other people pass the dice. But Manny made her feel as if she had to play. Nervously, she picked up two of the red dice. Shaking them as if they were a pint of heavy cream, she aimed for the far end of the table. The dice bounced a bit, but settled into a two and a five. Everyone cheered.

"That's the way," Manny said, grinning. "Do it again."

Judith did. This time she rolled a one and a six. More cheers, more applause, more encouragement from Manny as well as the stickman. On the third try, the dice turned up a four and a six.

"Ten's a tough point to make," Manny remarked. "Go for it."

Judith threw a six.

"Cover the six and the eight," Manny murmured.

"Huh?"

Handing over several blue and black chips, Manny requested that they be placed behind the row of numbers on the other side of the table. "Go on," he said to Judith, "do it. A five and a one."

Feeling stupid, Judith did as she was told. She threw an eight.

"Is that good?" she inquired.

"Yes, it's great," Manny said, then pointed to his chips and called to the stickman. "Press it."

Judith threw an eight, a six, another eight. The table was going wild. Everybody else seemed to be covering the six and eight, too.

"What's that?" Judith asked, pointing to a cluster of dice figures on the green baize table that said HARDWAYS.

"That's if you throw two fives to make your point instead of the four and six you threw the first time," Manny explained. "It pays seven to one. Try it. I think I will, too."

Aware that all eyes were upon her, Judith hesitated. Finally, not wanting the rest of the players to think she was chicken, she put a red chip on the pair of dice that showed two fives.

She threw an eight. "Drat!"

"No problem," Manny said amid the other gamblers' high fives and whoops of joy. "You made more money behind the line. The hardways bet stays until you crap out or throw a six and a four to make your point."

"Oh." With a full table now and several onlookers cheering her on, Judith threw again. A six, another six, an eight—and at last, two fives. The crowd went wild. Even the stickman, the dealers, and the boxman were applauding. Manny grabbed Judith in his arms and kissed her.

"You were great!" he exclaimed. "Keep rolling!"

Judith felt depleted. "I can't. I have to sit down." She smiled weakly. "I have a bad hip."

"Get her a chair!" someone yelled. "I'll hold her up!" another shouted. "You rule, babe!" cried a third voice.

The stickman proffered the dice again, but Judith shook her head. The whole table groaned.

"I'm buying you a drink," Manny announced. "Collect your winnings and let's go to the Spring Bar. This is the best run I've had in days."

"Did I win much?" Judith asked as Manny collected his chips.

"You did just fine," he replied. "You were smart to leave your original bets behind the line."

"I was?"

"Sure. Some people take them down every time they win," Manny said, sizing up his own windfall. "But neither of us did. That means we just kept adding on. I made close to two grand off you."

Judith received a black chip, a couple of greens, and some red. "I guess I got almost two hundred dollars."

"You should've bet up," Manny said as they walked away from the table. "I take it you're new at craps."

Judith nodded. "I've never played before."

"Beginner's luck, maybe," he noted as they approached the Spring Bar with its falling petals, drifting cottonwood fluff, and chirping birds. "I'd like to have seen you keep at it. You were literally on a roll."

"I decided to quit while I was ahead," Judith said. "I didn't want to lose the other players' money in case I pooped out the next time around. Then they'd resent me." She offered Manny her most charming smile. "This way, I'm Lady Luck."

Manny cocked his head to one side. "Why not? It beats being known as Fatso."

Judith stopped short of the bar entrance. "Where did you hear that nickname?"

Manny gazed up into a faux Japanese cherry tree where a mechanical robin hopped among the pink blossoms. "I don't know," he said with a wry expression. "Maybe a little bird told me."

Chapter Eighteen

Judith and Manny sat down at a table next to a small pond where real water lilies floated and live goldfish swam. She decided to let the "Fatso" comment pass. If Micki Mendoza had known about the Internet sobriquet, others in the group might, too.

"I understand," Judith said, wearing a sympathetic expression, "Griselda is making the arrangements for both Sally and Micki. That must be a relief to you."

Manny nodded even as he signaled to the waiter. "Grisly's a big help. Too bad she doesn't get paid for all her hard work. G & T for me," he said as the waiter arrived. "How about you, Mrs. F.?"

Judith stayed with a daiquiri. When their orders had been taken, she looked at Manny with a curious expression. "What do you mean, she doesn't get paid?"

Manny pulled a pack of cigarillos out of his inside jacket pocket. "Do you mind?"

Judith didn't. Joe enjoyed an occasional cigar, not to mention Gertrude turning the toolshed into a smoke-filled den.

"Grisly's a volunteer," Manny explained after lighting up. "She doesn't want to get paid."

"How does she survive?" Judith asked.

"She's rich," Manny replied, blowing a couple of smoke rings. "I guess her family owns half of Shoshone, Idaho."

"Hunh." Judith looked bemused. "I thought the Polsons and the Vanderbehrs were neighbors. Somehow, I figured that they all grew up in small, tidy houses in a small, tidy town."

"I've never been to Shoshone," Manny said. "But Grisly lived in a big house with hired help. She went to private schools, at least for most of the time. It was Freddy and Sally who were raised as neighbors. I don't know about tidy, but I got the idea their houses were small and kind of crummy."

The drinks arrived. Manny raised his glass to Judith. "To you, Mrs. F. You might have started me off on another winning streak." He took a big gulp, laid his head back against the white scrollwork patio chair, and let out a sigh.

"Good luck to you," Judith said, taking a small sip from her daiquiri. "You already seem in a much better mood."

Manny grinned broadly. There was charm, Judith thought, and a hint of danger. Maybe that's why Sally had found him attractive. But maybe she'd found more danger than she'd bargained for.

"Luck definitely runs in streaks," Manny allowed, growing more somber. "I consider myself a lucky person. Some people are. 'Born lucky,' they say. That's me. But even a lucky guy can have a run of bad luck. Like I've had here."

"Yes," Judith agreed. "It must be terrible to lose your wife and your luck at the same time."

"Maybe they were the same thing," Manny said with a frown as he took another deep swallow from his gin and tonic. "I was always lucky with Sally around. Maybe my luck's finally run out."

For the first time, Judith saw what might be genuine sorrow in Manny's expression. But whether it was for his wife or his money, she couldn't be sure.

"No point in talking about the past," Manny declared. "That's one of the things about gambling—you lose, you get another chance. You never know when you're going to hit the big one."

It was clear that Manny didn't want to discuss his personal life. Judith didn't want to talk about a gambler's life. She steered the conversation back to Griselda.

"I'm puzzled. Why would a wealthy young woman who could afford to attend a good college or university want to be an offstage assistant to a magician? I mean, an illusionist."

Manny chuckled. "You mean, why would Grisly run off and join the circus?"

"That's one way of putting it," Judith replied. "Does being associated with an illusionist's act have the same kind of attraction for young people as a circus does?"

Manny chuckled again, this time adding a leer. "If not the illusion, how about the illusionist?"

"You mean . . . ?" Judith paused.

Manny nodded. "Grisly's always had a thing for Freddy. Don't ask me why. But Sally did, too. Who's to say with women?" He shrugged. "What does a guy like me have in common with a guy like Freddy?"

"You're both risk takers," Judith pointed out.

"Huh?" Manny tapped his cigarillo into a petal-shaped ashtray. "Yeah, I suppose that's right. But we don't look or act alike."

"Men and women are both attracted to certain qualities beneath the surface," Judith said. "Love is as much about emotional needs as it is about sex."

Manny smoothed his silver hair. "I never thought much about it. You know—you see a babe who's really hot and . . ." He shrugged again. "Speaking of hot," he went on, taking a final swig from his glass, "I'd better go see if I still am. Of course, I was winning on your luck, not mine." He dropped a twenty on the table. "See you around, Mrs. F."

Judith had barely touched her drink. She scanned the other bar patrons, hoping to see someone she knew. But she recognized no one, except for a couple of faces she'd noticed around the casino.

She hated waste. As the daughter of parents who had lived through the Great Depression, and as the wife of a man who had been a poor provider, Judith had learned not to waste things. She didn't need the drink, didn't particularly want it, and hadn't even paid for it with her own money. But leaving the glass almost full was wasteful. Judith took another sip. She should see if Renie was still at the roulette wheel. She should check on Joe and Bill to see how they were faring at baccarat. She should—taking a bigger swallow—call on her mother and Aunt Deb.

Judith did none of the above. Doc Engelman entered the bar before she could make up her mind. To Judith's surprise, he had Fou-Fou with him.

The bar had become crowded since Judith had sat down with Manny Quinn. It was almost nine-thirty, perhaps the intermission for the cabaret's talent show. Engelman was looking around for a place to sit with the poodle. He didn't seem to be having much luck and was about to leave when Judith stood up to call his name.

"Mrs. Flynn," he said with a small smile. "How are you?"

"Fine. Won't you sit down?" She noted that the doctor stiffened slightly. "I'm about to leave," she added hastily. "It looks as if you need some room for Fou-Fou."

"Well . . ." He stroked his goatee. "I suppose I could."

Engelman didn't have much choice. Fou-Fou had already bounded onto the patio chair left vacant by Manny Quinn. The poodle sat up straight, tongue wagging and panting softly.

"Have you taken charge of Fou-Fou for Mrs. Flax?" Judith inquired.

"Yes," Engelman replied, sitting down between Judith and the dog. "Fou-Fou had to be walked. I checked in on Mrs. Flax a few minutes ago and she asked if I'd take the dog out for a while. We've just returned. Mrs. Flax insisted that Fou-Fou likes a nightcap after her walk."

"How *is* Mrs. Flax?" Judith asked as the waiter approached, bearing a bowl of champagne and what looked like a Gibson.

"Much improved," Doc said, thanking the waiter. Apparently, the staff knew not only Engelman's preferences, but Fou-Fou's as well. "She should be up and about by tomorrow."

"But does she remember anything yet?"

Engelman shook his head. "Sadly, no."

"Could she have been hypnotized?" Judith asked, trying to ignore Fou-Fou's loud slurping of the champagne.

"I'm a general practitioner," Doc responded. "I leave those matters to the psychiatrists."

Or psychologists, Judith thought, and wondered why she hadn't pressed Bill into service. "My cousin's husband might know," she said. "Dr. William Jones. Bill. You've met him."

"Yes," Engelman agreed. "Last night, when Ms. Mendoza was found murdered. He seems an able fellow."

"Very," Judith said. "Would it be okay if he saw Mrs. Flax and evaluated her?"

"That's up to Pancho Green," Doc said as Fou-Fou finished her champagne and began to pant again. "I believe he's been trying to contact Mrs. Flax's personal physician in Salt Lake City."

"Oh." Judith was disappointed. She might as well finish her daiquiri and be on her way, especially since Fou-Fou was becoming agitated, either from the lack of a refill or by the petals that drifted onto her long, nubby ears. "I should go," Judith stated, then to be polite, she asked Engelman if he'd lived in the area for a long time.

"We've owned our place up here for over forty years," Doc answered. "When I retired, we decided to make this our permanent home. It's very peaceful. Usually."

"Our family's had property in the area for almost seventy years," Judith said, then briefly sketched her plans for the new B&B establishment.

"I've noticed the construction," Doc said. "You must be right across the road from the Woodchuck Auto Court. We're about a quarter mile west, just beyond the big meadow."

Judith knew the spot. Indeed, she knew the house. "It's red, with white trim, isn't it?"

Doc smiled. "It is now, but we need a paint job. This summer, we may go green."

Judith wished she'd stayed with green for Hillside Manor. The more she thought about it, the less she liked the stark white. A deep blue with a touch of red, or olive and cream. She'd talk it over with Joe. Excusing herself, she left the bar and went in search of her cousin.

Renie was no longer at any of the roulette wheels. Judith headed for the nearest quarter slots in the Spring section. She found Renie at a console, looking content.

"Did you win at roulette?" Judith asked.

"I did," Renie replied, not looking up. "I won big, then lost three times in a row. I have a rule. When that happens, I quit. I walked away with four hundred and seventy-five dollars. Your money's in my purse, side pocket."

"Great," Judith enthused. "I've been drinking with Manny Quinn and Doc Engelman."

Renie shot her cousin a curious glance. "Are you drunk?"

"Of course not. It was the same drink."

"Doc and Manny were hanging out together?"

"I drank with them separately. Also," Judith added, "with Fou-Fou."

Renie thumped the Credit button. "This machine's not paying off and you're not making sense. I think I'll go see how Bill and Joe are doing."

"I'll go with you."

The cousins found their husbands at the far end of the table games. Joe and Bill sat as if they were carved out of clay. The only movements they made were to place their bets. They neither saw nor sensed their wives' presence.

"They both have chips in front of them," Renie noted. "That could be good."

Judith nodded and yawned. "I don't know why, but I'm really tired."

Renie snickered. "Surprise. With all your running back and forth to town and tramping around the resort tracking down homicide suspects, you've expended more energy on your vacation than you do when you're running the B&B."

"I suppose you're right," Judith allowed. "I think I'll stop by to see the mothers and then go to bed. It's after ten. If you see Joe when he's not zoned out, tell him I've gone up to the room."

"Will do." Clutching her bucket of coins, Renie waved Judith off and headed back to the slots.

As Judith tapped on the door, she realized that both mothers had been far less trouble than she'd feared. Or maybe it was too soon to pass judgment.

"It's me," Judith called, inserting the extra key card so that the old ladies wouldn't have to trouble themselves to admit her.

Gertrude and Aunt Deb were sitting in their wheelchairs, both reading what looked liked the *Wall Street Journal*. No TV blared, no telephones were in use, and the room was utterly silent until Judith walked in.

"What do you want now?" Gertrude rasped, peering out from behind her newspaper.

"Hello, dear," Aunt Deb said in cheerful greeting. "You look a bit peaked. Are you feeling all right?"

"I'm a little tired," Judith replied, plopping down in one of the armchairs. "How are you two?"

"Older than dinosaurs," Gertrude snapped. "And just as tough."

"I can't complain," Aunt Deb replied, though her tone hinted that she'd really like to. "Don't worry about me. Where's Renie? I haven't seen her since before she went to dinner."

Judith assured Aunt Deb that Renie was fine. "What are you reading?"

"The paper," Gertrude retorted. She rattled the pages. "What does this look like? Bedsheets?"

"We're studying investment possibilities," Aunt Deb explained a bit diffidently. "It may sound silly, but if we each receive a windfall, we should be prepared. The market is very uncertain these days."

"I don't like these high-techy things much," Gertrude announced. "Those companies don't even have real names. They all sound like some kind of skin disease—this 'ex,' that 'iva.' What next, St. Vitus Dance? I want to put my money in businesses with real names, like Ford and AT&T and John Deere tractor."

"What we need, of course," Aunt Deb said, "is a shrewd financial advisor. I'm sure that some of these nice graphic-design people will be able to point us in the right direction."

"That's very smart," Judith said, then turned to Gertrude. "You've heard from your agent, Eugenia?"

Gertrude nodded. "You bet. She's ready to pitch."

It was hard for Judith to understand how her mother could have picked up the movie jargon so easily. Ordinarily, it was a task to get Gertrude to say "vegetable oil" instead of "lard" or to stop referring to the refrigerator as the icebox.

"That's great," Judith said, patting her mother's arm. "How's the script coming?"

"Script?" Gertrude glowered at Judith. "We're at the pitch stage, then the treatment, and last of all, the script. Right now, Eugie doesn't know whether to use my First or Second World War bravery in the pitch. It seems WW Two is big right now."

Judith was taken aback. "Your world war bravery? Mother, you didn't serve during either of the wars."

"What are you talking about, dopey?" Gertrude huffed. "I served in the Red Cross during both wars. Not to mention that your father was an air-raid warden. And I suppose you were too little to remember how Auntie Vance and I chased the burglar out of Deb and Cliff's basement when we heard him trip over the sandbags they kept down there. Your Uncle Cliff was an air-raid warden, too." She glanced at Deb. "Am I right?"

"Yes, dear," Aunt Deb replied. "You and Vanessa were very brave. That awful crook might have stolen all my canned goods."

Judith decided to change the subject. She pointed to her aunt's copy of the *Journal*. "Does this mean you've decided to take on the job as a consultant?"

Aunt Deb did her best to look embarrassed. "Well, yes. In fact, Wirehoser has already offered me a handsome sum just because I came up with a little slogan for them."

"That's wonderful!" Judith exclaimed, with a pat for her aunt.

Gertrude harrumphed. "It's not as much as I'll get for my movie story."

"No," Deb agreed complacently, "but it's a start. After all, Gert, you only have one story to tell."

"What?" Gertrude shouted. "I've got a million of 'em! What about sequels? And prequels?"

"Dear me." Deb sighed. "I hadn't considered that. I guess," she went on with a sharp look at Gertrude, "that means I'll just have to add a few other large firms to my consultant's file."

"I think I'll be going now," Judith broke in before her mother could come back at Deb. "I'm off to bed."

She kissed each of the old ladies in turn, then scampered for the door. As she made her exit, she heard Deb say in her normal voice, "What about airlines, Gert?"

"They're in the toilet," Gertrude replied.

"Yes, but buy low, sell high," Deb responded. "We might think about that . . ."

It was wonderful, Judith thought, as she went into her own room, that two old women could be so optimistic about planning for the future. Maybe that was why Gertrude and Aunt Deb had survived so long. They wouldn't give up. And each of them was determined to outlast the other.

Judith, however, was giving in. She could hardly keep her eyes open as she took off the amethyst necklace and earrings. Unfortunately, fatigue made her hands unsteady. She dropped one of the earrings, which bounced inside the open closet. Cautiously, she bent down to see where it had gone. The stone caught the light from the hallway and winked at her as if it knew she'd dislocate her hip if she got down on the floor to retrieve it.

"Damn!" Judith swore, looking around the room for something that she might use to reach the stray bauble. Nothing seemed available. She glanced in the bathroom. There wasn't even a bath brush. Finally, she searched the closet itself. Sure enough, there was a broom just inside the near wall. Judith used the stick end to go after the earring. Still winking, it rolled farther away. She swore again. Bending carefully, she used the other end of the broom to sweep out the earring. On the first try, it moved even more, bouncing up against something solid. Judith pushed aside some of the garments that blocked her view.

The earring was resting next to a laundry bag. With one mighty thrust, she swept at the bag, which in turn propelled the earring where Judith could pick it up.

"Gotcha!" she said in triumph, holding her prey in her hand. Then, because she was curious as to why the laundry bag had been shoved so far back into the closet instead of in the room by the luggage stand, she peeked inside.

Renie's taffeta skirt lay before her. Joe hadn't given it to the cops. Judith wondered why.

Voices and laughter in the corridor woke Judith up. *Thoughtless morons. I'm still tired. I want to get back to sleep.* Turning over, she glimpsed the digital clock on the nightstand. The red numbers showed 11:04. Judith blinked. Had she just gone to bed? With the heavy draperies covering the windows, she couldn't be sure whether it was night or morning. She blinked again and focused on the clock. It was now 11:05 A.M. Judith couldn't believe she'd slept for over twelve hours. She hadn't done that since . . . She couldn't even remember the last time she'd been out for so long and awakened so late.

The people in the hall had moved on. Joe obviously had, too. Judith staggered into the bathroom where she found a Post-it note stuck to the mirror.

"Went to B&B. Furnace trouble. Back this afternoon."

"Oh, no!" Judith sighed. The phone must have rung earlier in the morning, but she'd slept through it. Joe must have taken the call. He'd be furious at having to deal with Bart Bednarik.

Still, Judith was secretly relieved. She couldn't bear to make yet another trip into the city. It had become a daily commute. No wonder she was tired.

Breakfast in bed—or at least in the room—sounded blissfully comforting to Judith. After showering and shampooing her hair, she perused the menu. Belgian waffles sounded good to her; so did eggs and link sausages. The room service operator informed her that breakfast would arrive in less than thirty minutes.

On a whim, she dialed Renie's room number. Her cousin always slept in when she had a chance. It was no surprise that Renie answered on the third ring.

"I finished eating half an hour ago," Renie said a bit ruefully after Judith explained her late rising. "I got up early to stagger out before

Mom left for the morning conference session. I had to let her know I was still alive."

"I assume she was convinced," Judith replied.

"Yes, but I wasn't. It was nine-thirty. Good Lord, the things I do for my parent."

"So you're headed for the casino?" Judith inquired.

"I was. Do you want company?"

"Well . . . It'd be nice."

Renie paused. "Okay. I'll drop in. See you in a minute."

Judith left the door ajar, then started to get dressed. Renie was as good as her word. "Hi," she called. "I brought the rest of my coffee. I can't believe you slept so late."

"Neither can I," Judith said, stepping into a pair of navy slacks.

"It's a good thing you did," Renie remarked. "Otherwise, you'd be the one heading down the road to Hillside Manor."

"I know," Judith agreed. "I feel guilty, though. But maybe Joe can be more forceful with Bart."

"As in threatening him at gunpoint?"

"Something like that," Judith said, pulling a red, white, and blue cotton sweater over her head. "However—and don't say anything until I finish—I think we should drive down to the cabin and try to figure out what's going on there with Bart's cohort Dale Armstrong."

Renie raised her eyebrows. "'We'?"

"Yes."

"Gee," Renie responded, "I don't know . . ."

"Are you up or down overall?" Judith asked.

"Uh . . . down."

"Then you should ease up, so you don't get further down," Judith advised. Seeing Renie start to open her mouth, Judith held up a hand. "I'm not done. Look outside." Her hand swept in the direction of the floor-to-ceiling windows where the drapes had been opened to reveal a beautiful March day. "Have you even been outside since you got here? Have you gone down to the lake or the river? Have you walked the woodland trails? *Have you breathed fresh air?*"

"What fresh air?" Renie's voice was a bit of a squeak.

"Come with me or I won't be your cousin anymore," Judith asserted.

Renie made a face. "Okay. I'll admit I'd kind of like to see for myself what they're doing. Or not doing."

While waiting for the Joneses' Cammy, Judith confided in her cousin about the bet with Joe.

"I don't know who to root for," Renie finally said. "But my money's on you."

"That," Judith said wryly, "isn't necessarily a good sign."

It was shortly after noon when the cousins left the casino. The sun was high in the sky, its shafts filtering through the tall evergreens that grew along the winding road that led to the family property. The river played hide-and-seek with the highway, its deep-green waters spilling over big boulders and forming quiet pools near the sandy verge. Though the river had changed course over the years, the cousins still recognized some of the family's favorite fishing holes. The Big Bend. The Deer-Fly Curve. Roy's Riffle.

Pulling off the road at the entrance to the cabin site, Renie came to an abrupt stop. "The gate's closed," she said. "Look, it's been padlocked."

"That's odd," Judith remarked. "What day is it? I've lost track. Thursday?"

"Right." Renie fingered her short chin. "It doesn't look like anybody's around."

"That's not surprising," Judith said, getting out of the car. "It's lunchtime. Maybe they all went up to the Green Mountain Inn or even into Glacier Falls."

The cousins went around the big wooden gate with its "No Trespassing" sign. On their left, they saw the so-called quicksand bog. Or what was left of it. The hole was fifteen feet wide and ten feet deep, large enough that it almost reached the slight bend in the highway.

"Good grief," Judith breathed. "They've certainly been digging. But to what purpose?" Suddenly, she whirled around. Something was missing. Everything, in fact. "The equipment's gone! They've pulled out!"

"You're right!" Renie was aghast. "*What the hell is going on around here?*"

Chapter Nineteen

This is an outrage!" Renie exclaimed. "We should call the sheriff!"

Judith looked askance at Renie. "Are you kidding? That would be Abbott N. Costello."

"Oh." Renie winced. "You're right. He's a boob."

The cousins stared at each other, then began tromping up the dirt track toward the site of the proposed construction. Excavation had begun on the old cabin spot, with another, bigger hole dug far into the ground. But there was no sign of a foundation.

"They've been on the job for a couple of months," Judith said in an angry voice. "What have they got to show for it? They've cleared away a bunch of trees and dug two big holes."

Renie was studying the excavation. "You must admit, there's been snow up here until recently."

"Not as much as usual," Judith pointed out. "This has been a mild winter." She looked up at Mount Woodchuck where the snow line was higher than in winters past. "It's been a bad year for the ski business."

"True." Renie walked over to the river's edge. "I miss this place."

Judith felt defensive. "What was left was falling down. Something had to be done with the property. I couldn't bear to sell it."

Renie stood quietly, apparently lost in memory. When she turned around, all traces of sentimentality were gone. "We have to take action. If not the sheriff, call Bub, Bill's brother, and have him sue the pants off old Armbuster. Bub represents builders, so he knows both sides."

"I'm in a pickle," Judith confessed. "With Dale and Bart related, I'm afraid to do anything to stop Bart's work on the B&B. Bart might get mad and walk off the job. The house is supposed to be finished by this weekend. If I stall a few days, I won't jeopardize the Hillside Manor project. That's my priority." Yet she couldn't turn away from the present dilemma. "What if there really is gold around here?"

"Get an assayer or some other expert up here," Renie said. "One thing's for sure—we're not doing any good standing around looking at a couple of holes in the ground."

Renie was right about that. With a big sigh, Judith started back to the car.

"I have to sleuth this afternoon," Judith said in a grim tone. "I have just five hours to figure out who did it or I'll lose the bet with Joe."

"You're under the gun," Renie remarked after the cousins were inside the Camry.

"I know." Judith sighed again as Renie turned onto the highway. "By the way, are you going to Mandolini's show tonight?"

"I'll see what Bill wants to do," Renie said, "though I'll admit I'm curious about how Freddy can manage an entire performance. With the bands so busted up, who'll open for the illusion act?"

"How about our mothers?" Judith said dryly. "They're as amazing as any magician."

"Yes, they are," Renie conceded, passing the entrance to Mount Woodchuck's ski area. "Oh—I forgot to tell you. The conference awards banquet and closing ceremonies are tonight, and Mom can bring a guest. She's taking Aunt Gert."

"Oh, my goodness." Judith shook her head. "If I could wangle an invitation, I'd almost rather see that than poor Freddy floundering around the stage."

"So you and Joe are going to watch the act?" Renie asked as they followed the curving course of the river for almost a mile.

"Yes. Pancho can get us comps. We'll get more if you and Bill go."

"I'll let you know," Renie said. "What kind of sleuthing do you plan to do this afternoon? You seem to have covered just about everybody."

"Then it's time to see Marta Ormond Flax," Judith said, opening her window just enough to let in the evergreen-scented air. "In fact, I'd like to take Bill with me. He can judge her mental state better than I can."

Renie slowed behind a large white truck. "I'll see what Bill's up to. He'll probably take a walk after lunch. Maybe we can catch him before he goes out."

Having Bill's casino routine down flat, Renie had no trouble finding her husband. He was in the sports book, finishing a bratwurst sandwich and studying the MLB futures for the upcoming baseball season.

"The Cubs," he said when Renie and Judith showed up. "They look good up the middle. I think they have a chance this year."

Renie kept a straight face. "Why not? That's what everybody says. Every year. Every decade. Every century."

Bill ignored the comment. He also dismissed Judith's request, though with reluctance. "She's not a patient and she hasn't consulted me. It would be unethical," he explained, "to barge in on Marta Ormond Flax. But frankly, I'd like to study her. She's an unusual subject."

Judith understood Bill's dilemma. Thanking him anyway, she tugged at Renie's sleeve. "We'd better be on our way."

"Huh?" Renie stared at Judith. "Oh—sure, Bill's going to take his walk." She kissed the top of her husband's head. "Good luck with those Cubbies. Maybe they're having spring training in Mexico this year. They could go to the Shrine of Our Lady of Guadalupe and pray for a miracle."

Bill didn't respond.

"Now what?" Renie inquired after they left the sports book.

Judith was moving through the casino at a brisk pace. "Just follow me, Dr. Jones."

"What do you mean, 'Dr. Jones'?"

"I mean you and Bill share a practice. You know all the jargon, you can pretend. If nothing else, you can report back to Bill and see what he thinks."

"But," Renie began, hurrying to catch up with Judith's longer strides, "I only parrot what Bill says. I'm not a psychologist, I'm a graphic designer."

"Not here you're not," Judith said with a smug expression. She picked up a house phone by the elevators. "Do you want me to blow your cover?"

"Aaargh," Renie groaned, putting both hands around her neck and feigning self-strangulation. "Never mind. Do with me what you will."

Judith asked the hotel operator to connect her to Mrs. Flax's room.

"Would you spell that, please?" the operator asked after a pause.

Judith complied.

"I'm sorry," the operator apologized. "We have no one registered under that name."

"You must," Judith insisted. "She was in the hotel this morning." A sudden thought occurred. "I can't imagine why she'd register under an assumed name."

"Unless you know what it is," the operator said, still polite and with a hint of regret, "I can't help you. Oh! Here she is—Mrs. Flax checked out shortly before noon. That's why I couldn't find her on the current hotel register."

"Really? Thanks." Judith replaced the receiver. "The bird has flown. So, I imagine, has the Fou-Fou."

"Does that mean I can gamble?" Renie asked.

Judith looked exasperated. "Can't you give it a rest for a few hours?" She tapped her watch. "It's almost two. I have only four hours before I have to come up with the name of the killer. I need your help."

"I have mixed emotions," Renie said, concern etched on her face. "If I'm an accomplice and you win, I'm helping you to continue risking your neck. And maybe mine."

"Don't be silly," Judith admonished. "Even if I figure it out and win the bet, that doesn't mean I have to be reckless if I ever get involved in another murder investigation. I'll take this as a lesson. No more chances, no more danger. Okay?"

Renie looked bleak. "I don't believe you."

"Please?"

Renie sighed. "I don't see what good I can do." She stopped suddenly. "Shoot—I forgot to ask about tonight's performance."

"That's okay," Judith said, poking the elevator button. "We might as well get the extra set of comps. Plus, I'd like to see how the meeting in Pancho's office is going this afternoon. I haven't seen Joe all day."

Emily was again behind the desk. She had three textbooks in front of her, and was taking notes.

"I'm working toward a master's degree in law enforcement," she explained, sweeping a hand over the texts. "How can I help you?"

Judith stated her request for more comps, then added that she'd like to speak to Joe if he was available.

The extra tickets were no problem, but when it came to Joe,

Emily shook her head. "They've all gone to the sheriff's office. I gather they're involved in getting some lab results. They should be back by five."

Judith tried to hide her disappointment. Indeed, she should have been pleased that the lab work was finally under way. "It's a half-hour drive from here to the county seat," Judith pointed out. "What time did my husband get back from the city?"

Emily considered. "It must have been around one. He was here when they all left together."

Maybe, Judith thought, *that meant that things had gone well at Hillside Manor. A quick trip might equal a successful trip.*

"You struck out on that one," Renie said after they left the office.

"Don't sound so gleeful," Judith snapped as she punched the elevator's up button.

"Hey, where are we going?" Renie inquired. "The opportunity for vast riches is down, not up."

"I want to know if G. D. Fromm really got fired by Inga," Judith replied. "We're going to the Wild Ginger Suite."

Renie shook her head in a hopeless manner. "To what purpose?"

"I don't know," Judith replied as they stepped aside for a couple who were getting out of the elevator. "I follow my instincts. Maybe we'll find out why Marta Flax suddenly checked out."

"At least we assume she didn't check out permanently," Renie noted as they began to ascend to the top floor.

"I hope not," Judith responded.

The elevator stopped three times to let guests on and off. When the cousins reached the Polson suite, Griselda answered their knock.

"What now?" she asked in her usual no-nonsense manner.

"Is it inappropriate to wish Freddy good luck for tonight's performance?" Judith asked.

"It's unacceptable," Grisly retorted. "First, you never wish a performer good luck. Second, he's in his room, trying to focus. This is going to be very difficult for him."

Judith and Renie had managed to inch their way inside the suite. Lloyd Watts was sitting at a desk, intent on what looked like a set of matchboxes. A pugnacious Inga Polson was standing by the window.

"You shouldn't be here," Inga declared. "These rooms are off-limits to everybody but the troupe."

"There's not much of it left these days, is there?" Renie shot back.

Inga recoiled. "What a dreadful thing to say!"

Renie shrugged. "It's true, isn't it? Who'll be Freddy's assistant?"

Inga turned to Judith. "Who *is* this person? Where did she come from and why?"

It dawned on Judith that Renie hadn't met all the Mandolini stage-family members. Quickly, she introduced the two women to her cousin. Inga looked affronted; Grisly was indifferent.

"Freddy doesn't need a female assistant," Grisly put in. "Lloyd can do it." She gestured at the young man behind the desk. "He conceived of the trick. It's utterly amazing. Which means," she continued, advancing on the cousins, "neither of you should be up here spying on us."

"Hey," Renie said, holding up her hands to fend off Grisly, "from the looks of it, Lloyd could be building a farm. All he needs are some pigs, chickens, and a lot of horse poop."

With a wave of her arm, Judith intervened before Grisly could verbally or physically attack Renie. "It was Inga I really wanted to see. Could she spare me a moment in her own room?"

Grisly scowled at Judith. "Why?"

Inga, however, seemed curious. "Can you be brief?"

"Oh, yes," Judith assured the other woman. "I can."

Inga nodded once. "Very well. Come along." She started to cross the room in the direction opposite to Freddy's lair. Judith followed, but Renie remained in place.

"Inga!" Grisly shouted. "If you're going to talk to Mrs. Flynn, take this other thing with you. In case she can't keep her big mouth shut, I don't want to have to rough her up. Lloyd's trying to concentrate."

Walking past Grisly, Renie smirked. "Want to take this out into the parking lot later?"

"Love to," Grisly retorted.

Inga's bedroom was a smaller version of Freddy's, but, with its wild ginger motif, just as elegantly appointed. The cousins were not invited to sit. Inga paced in front of the white-pine armoire, rubbing the backs of her hands.

"Well, what is it?" she demanded.

Judith took a deep breath. "Is it true that you fired G. D. Fromm?"

From the surprised look on Inga's face, it was obvious that this was not the question she'd expected. "Why is it any of your business?"

"Because," Judith said quietly, "I think he's making you sick."

Inga had stopped pacing and put her hands behind her. "What on earth are you talking about?"

"Your hands," Judith replied. "And other parts of your body that have a rash."

With a curious look at Judith, Inga flopped down on the bed and examined her hands. "They're better."

"I'd expect so," Judith remarked. "What is it about him that you're allergic to? Or does he give you a nervous rash because he's difficult?"

Inga looked bewildered. "That's what Doc Engelman said, but when I went into Glacier Falls the other day to see a dermatologist, she thought it was a contact allergy. There's no allergist around here, so I'll have to wait until we move on to make an appointment."

"I've noticed you don't wear jewelry," Judith said, leaning on a wild flower–covered chair. "Your watch is pinned to your bodice. Is that because you're allergic to gold?"

"Oh, very much so," Inga replied. "I've never been able to wear gold—or silver." She looked closely at Judith. "Are you saying this could be a metal allergy?"

"It'd be the first thing that would come to mind," Judith said.

Renie stepped forward from where she'd been standing near the door. "I'm allergic to nuts and peanuts," she said. "Especially peanuts, which aren't really a nut but a legume. I don't have to eat or even touch them to get a reaction. If peanuts or peanut butter are in the air, I start to wheeze and sneeze."

"Interesting," Inga murmured. "Do you think it's because women in casinos wear so much jewelry?"

"It's possible," Judith said, "but I don't think that's the reason. I'm sorry, I didn't hear you say if you fired Mr. Fromm."

"I didn't say," Inga responded, her usual hostility absent. "But I did. Fire him, that is. He and I simply couldn't agree on major business decisions. He's very pigheaded."

"I would guess," Judith said with a smile, "that with Mr. Fromm no longer in the picture, your rash will clear up."

"And the point of that was . . . ?" Renie inquired when they were out in the corridor.

"First," Judith replied, "to find out if G. D. Fromm had been canned. Second, to verify that Inga has a precious-metals allergy. And third, to see if she knows anything about the gold. Judging from her reaction—excuse the expression—I don't think she does."

Renie shot her cousin a quizzical glance as they entered the elevator. "The gold, as in the alleged lode on the family property?"

"I'm beginning to think so. Now how did G. D. Fromm find out about it?" Judith paused, then answered her own question. "Because

Dale Armstrong has done some work for the casino. I don't know how he hooked up with G.D., but he must have. Fromm is the one who seems to be shedding gold dust in his wake."

"You can't fool around with this, coz," Renie declared. "When Bart Bednarik wraps up the B&B renovation, you'll have to go to the cops."

"I know, I know," Judith replied. "I still have to tell Joe about it. I'm afraid he'll think I'm nuts."

The cousins got off on the casino floor. "So how does this gold thing tie into Sally and Micki's murders?" Renie asked.

"I don't know," Judith admitted with a nervous glance at her watch. It was two-thirty. "Damn! I'm stymied. There's no one to talk to. I don't even know what questions to ask. And I forgot to bring up Marta Ormond Flax's sudden departure when we were in the Wild Ginger Suite. This bet with Joe has got me rattled. Where's my usual logic?"

"What about learning how the original trick was done?" Renie suggested as they wandered aimlessly in the direction of the table games. "Do you think Lloyd would tell us, and if so, would it help?"

Judith shook her head. "Lloyd's sworn to secrecy, like the rest of the company. If he weren't, it might be helpful to—" Judith snapped her fingers. "G.D. Fromm! I'll bet he'd rat on the Great Mandolini crew. I wonder if he's still around. Let's go to the front desk and find out."

G.D. Fromm was indeed still registered. Judith turned to Renie. "I can't do this," she averred. "If he's in on the gold deal, then he may not want to talk to me. He doesn't know you. Can you handle it?"

Renie looked appalled. "So who am I supposed to be? The Middle-Aged Siren of the Stillasnowamish River?"

"That's not a bad idea," Judith said. "You clean up pretty good."

"Come on, coz," Renie protested, "even if I looked more like Janet Jackson instead of Andrew Jackson, I don't see how I could beguile the magic trick out of him. He's on the business side, he may not know."

"You're creative," Judith said. "Check out the bars. I've never seen G.D. gamble, but he enjoys a drink." She pointed to the Autumn Bar. "I'll stay near the table games. I might even play some blackjack."

"Swell." Renie stomped off to the designated watering hole.

Judith wandered around the gaming area, keeping an eye out for Manny Quinn. She didn't spot him, however, and finally sat down at a five-dollar blackjack game. Even as play began, she was rubbernecking for any sign of Doc Engelman. If anyone knew why Marta Ormond Flax had checked out of the resort so abruptly, it would be the doctor.

Engelman wasn't around, either. Perhaps he was following the horse races in the sports book. Or maybe he didn't visit the casino every day. Judith was down thirty-five dollars before she stopped gawking.

Half an hour had passed since Renie had gone off on her quest for G. D. Fromm. Judith was growing more anxious by the minute. She could swear that she heard her watch ticking like a hammer. She put down her last five-dollar chip and promptly lost it. Getting up from the table, she paced the floor. It was after three o'clock. Maybe she should just try to think. Logic. Reason. How many times had she solved a murder case by applying her knowledge of people and her listening skills? Why couldn't she do it now?

"*Must kill cousin.*" The words came from behind Judith, along with two hands digging into her shoulders.

"Coz!" Judith cried, trying to turn around. "What happened?"

Renie let go. Her hair was more tousled than usual, there was a large wet spot on the front of her lime-green sleeveless sweater, and a small cut was still bleeding on her left arm.

"I found G.D.," she announced, taking a Band-Aid from her

purse and applying it to her wound. "He was in the Winter Bar, drunk as a skunk."

"Did he attack you?" Judith asked in alarm.

Sitting down at a closed roulette wheel, Renie shook her head. "I attacked him. Well, not really. It was a series of accidents."

"Oh, dear." Judith felt guilty. "What happened?"

Renie took a couple of deep breaths. "I first saw G.D. in the cabaret, when he joined Inga at what should have been our table. So that's how I approached him—being funny, as in, 'Aren't you the man who sat at our blah-blah? Yuk, yuk.' Since he wasn't there when we got usurped, he was befuddled. And since he was wasted, it didn't matter."

"So were you able to hold a conversation with him?" Judith asked.

"Sort of," Renie said, taking a hairbrush out of her purse. "I felt obliged to order a drink. While I waited, I made small talk to see if he was tuned in. I mentioned things like I'd won a million dollars on a quarter machine and the casino was being sold to a group of penguins and my feet were connected to my arms. No reaction." Without using a mirror, Renie brushed her hair. "My screwdriver arrived just as G.D. was trying to relight his cigar. He knocked the drink over, which resulted in this." Renie pointed to the stain on her sweater.

"Did he notice?"

"Nope. Before I got a replacement, he hit the empty glass and it broke." Renie pointed to the cut on her arm. "I helped the bartender pick up the pieces. Meanwhile, G.D. dropped his cigar, burning a hole in his pants. 'Your pants are on fire!' I shouted. That got his attention, especially when I dumped his drink in his lap to put out the fire."

"Goodness." Judith shook her head. "I won't ask about your hair."

"I think I was trying to pull it out in frustration," Renie said. "But I did find out about the illusion. More or less."

Judith's eyes widened. "You did? Tell me."

"It was kind of a muddle," Renie began. "G.D. was never sworn to secrecy because he worked exclusively on the business side. He said that if he hadn't taken over the act, Freddy would still be pulling canaries out of his pants in Shoshone, Idaho."

"How did you get him to open up?"

"After I dumped the drink on him," Renie explained, "I mentioned that if I were a magician I could wave a wand and fix the hole in his trousers. Then I added that speaking of magic, the Great Mandolini stunk. That's when G.D., who now thought I must be smart, came into focus and began railing against the Mandolini troupe and how badly they'd treated him, particularly Inga."

"Ah!" Judith smiled in approbation. "Nice work."

"Anyway," Renie continued, "even though he didn't work on the artistic side—which is why he didn't sign an oath—most of the illusions were standard fare. The saber-and-cabinet act involved a trapdoor. After the cabinet was shut, Salome—I mean, Sally—dropped a few feet below the stage. Sawing somebody in half involves the person's torso being lowered into a cavity on the table. The saw cuts through whatever is on top—fabric, usually. It's all about diverting the audience's eye."

"Interesting," Judith murmured. "But not very helpful when it comes to solving the murders. Did he say anything enlightening about the individuals?"

"Mostly that they're all a bunch of hard-hearted idiots," Renie said. "G.D. thinks Freddy is using Lloyd, who has the real creative talent, and that Lloyd, not Freddy, should be the star. Grisly was wildly jealous of both Sally and Micki because she's always been in love with Freddy. Furthermore, Grisly put up the money to get Freddy started. Manny Quinn isn't a very good gambler, but he's an outstanding moocher who's living off Sally's money." Renie paused to catch her breath. "Oh—one other thing. Inga isn't Freddy's sister. She's his mother."

Chapter Twenty

JUDITH stared at Renie. "Inga is Freddy's *mother*? Why the charade?"

Renie shrugged. "G.D. insisted that Inga wants to seem younger than she really is. Vanity, I guess."

Judith made some calculations in her head. "Freddy's not much over thirty. I figure Inga for early, mid-forties. Let's add another five years for her. Yes, that'd work. Inga could have been a teenage mother."

"So who was Dad? Or," Renie added, "does it matter?"

"It would to Dad," Judith replied.

"Maybe not," Renie put in. "Maybe Dad ran off. Maybe Dad never knew about Freddy-to-Be. Maybe Freddy made Dad disappear."

"Whoever Dad is," Judith said slowly, "I doubt that he's part of the troupe or the hangers-on. That would be too much of a coincidence."

Renie gazed at her cousin. "Would it?"

Judith sighed. "It would. Still, I understand what you're saying. It wouldn't be the first time we've run across that type of coincidence. Which is seldom a coincidence at all, since the connection often has had a direct effect on the murder investigation."

"In other words," Renie said, "if someone is out to kill someone else, they don't necessarily present their ID at the door."

"Exactly." Judith crossed her arms over her breast. "Which gives me some ideas."

"Such as?" Renie inquired.

Judith grimaced. "I have to let everything get arranged in my brain. Let's go outside and sit by the lake. Or maybe the river. I've always found the river peaceful."

Renie stood up. "So I'm supposed to sit and watch you think? With all these fortune-making opportunities before my very eyes?"

Judith took umbrage. "I thought you wanted to help."

"Hey—I know how it works when you're in your thinking mode," Renie responded. "You just sit for ages, and when you come up with a solution, you don't always tell me because you're not one hundred percent sure." She looked at her watch. "It's a quarter to four. If you're not back by five, I'll come looking for you."

Judith knew Renie was right. Sometimes a solution could be reached by bouncing ideas off her cousin. Other times—and this seemed to be one of them—Judith had to go it alone. Her logical mind demanded that she get her thoughts lined up like ducks on the lake.

Which was exactly what she was looking at ten minutes later. She'd gone to the river first, but the sun was out and a dozen or more children were playing along the bank. Their happy shouts would have pleased her at another time, but she needed quiet. There were a few boats on the lake, but she found a peaceful place in the picnic area. Despite the sunshine, the March temperature remained in the upper forties. It wasn't yet spring; it wasn't the season for dining al fresco.

So Judith watched the mallard ducks swim and dive in the emerald-green waters. The lake was small, and its far rim nestled against the craggy slope of Mount Nugget. Patches of snow clung in deep crevasses halfway up the mountain. Two waterfalls tumbled down into the lake that fed, in turn, into the Stillasnowamish River.

It was quiet, a perfect setting for concentration. The only sounds were the occasional chatter of a chipmunk or the caw of a crow.

Grisly Vanderbehr was rich, and in love with Freddy. Inga was Freddy's mother, not his sister. G.D. Fromm might or might not have been responsible for Freddy's success. Either way, he had been fired by the dictatorial Inga.

The sun scooted behind a cloud. Judith kept thinking. Manny Quinn had been living off Sally. Had he killed the goose with the golden egg, or was Sally highly insured? The latter, most likely. Show-business personalities were often insured by their employers. Was Lloyd Watts so frustrated with playing second banana that he was willing to sabotage the company? Lloyd was the quiet type, to Judith, always a dangerous sort. And where did Micki figure into all of this? Where had she come from? Had she hoped to become not only Mrs. Polson, but Freddy's new stage assistant?

And then there was Marta Flax. She was the real mystery woman. Judith could hardly believe that Joe and the rest of the investigative team hadn't learned more about her background. Or had they? Maybe Joe wasn't talking because he didn't want to endanger his wife.

Judith kept thinking. Personalities, situations, connections—all tumbled around in her head. A picture was coming into focus, not unlike Mount Nugget's mirrored image in the lake. When she discarded theories, studied suspects, delved into relationships, there was only one person left. She knew who'd killed Sally and Micki.

Feeling confident, Judith stood up, turned around, and let out a yelp. "Coz!" she exclaimed. "You scared me! Why do you keep creeping up on me like some demented stalker?"

"I don't," Renie said, put off by the accusation. "I've been standing here for five minutes, waiting for you to come out of your trance."

"Oh." Judith uttered a foolish little laugh. "Sorry. But I've got it."

Renie grinned. "You do? Great! Whodunit?"

Judith opened her mouth, but stopped. "I'm not sure I should tell you. I mean, it's because of the bet between Joe and me. Anyway, you'll know soon enough."

Renie kicked at some pebbles. "Damn, damn, damn! See? It's exactly what I said. What's the point of me hanging around and watching you think? Instead, I won four hundred dollars on a Beaver machine."

"Good for you." Judith checked the time. "It's five-twenty. I lost track. But I'll make the six o'clock deadline."

"I had to line up three beaver dams," Renie said. "I figured the machine would be lucky because kids made fun of my big teeth in grade school and called me Bucky."

"It's been a handicap," Judith asserted, "being almost completely out of the loop on this case. Plus, I haven't had that many opportunities to talk to the suspects. The more they say, the more they reveal."

"I'd already won fifty bucks by getting three beaver tails in a row," Renie recalled. "That's when I really sensed that Bucky could be hot."

"The thing is," Judith said as they started up the trail, "that after I considered the personalities and the possible motives, it all came down to one person."

"I hit the dams just before five," Renie said, "and the machine pays out only the first four hundred of the sixteen hundred quarters. I had to wait to get the rest in cash. That's why I was late coming to get you."

"Now what should I do?" Judith muttered as they approached the casino's rear entrance. "Go up to the room and see if Joe's there, or just hang out in the casino and meet him by the cashier's window at six?"

"One of the employees told me that the machine was fairly new and nobody had hit the jackpot until I did," Renie remarked as they went inside. "I drew quite a crowd."

"The other question is, should I notify someone, like Jack Jackrabbit?" Judith wondered. "He'd have to promise not to tell Joe, but at least Jack would be on guard in case there might be another victim."

"I remember," Renie said as they passed a couple coming from the resort's gym, "years ago when we were in Reno, I was the first one to get a jackpot on a San Francisco machine at Harrah's. I lined up the three sections of the Golden Gate Bridge."

"Coz!" Judith barked. "You haven't heard a word I've said!"

"Huh?" Renie blinked at Judith. "I have, too. Besides, you weren't listening to me. In fact, you weren't talking to me. You were talking to yourself." She took Judith by the arm. "Go write down your solution and have it ready to put in the safe. Then call up to the room to see if Joe's there. If not, we'll wait. How's that?"

Judith stopped in the hallway that led to the lobby. "Okay."

She found a notepad at the front desk. Huge placards advertising Mandolini's return seemed to be everywhere. Motioning for Renie to back off so her cousin couldn't see the paper, Judith wrote down the killer's name and slipped the single sheet into her purse.

"Five thirty-five," she stated. "Let's wander over to the cashier's."

By chance, they walked past the yellow Corvette with its smiling blond mannequin. Judith shuddered. Then she took a second look. Next to the blonde behind the wheel was a figure in the passenger seat—a pretty woman with stunning red hair.

The redhead bore a remarkable resemblance to Micki Mendoza.

Shaken, Judith sat down on a chair across the aisle from the 'Vette display. Renie had turned pale. "Gruesome," she declared. "Is that part of the promotion for tonight's performance or somebody's idea of a joke?"

"Either way, it's ghoulish," Judith said, feeling both upset and angry. "Let's get out of here. We can wait by the cashier's cage."

They didn't have to wait long. At five to six, Joe appeared, looking uncommonly jaunty.

"Hey," he called to Judith, "you ready to bet your life?"

"I feel as if it's more like 'bet your wife,'" Judith retorted. She didn't smile; she was still disturbed by the mannequins in the

Corvette. But she reached into her purse and took out the slip of paper. "I've got it."

Joe's face fell a notch. "You have?" He shrugged. "Okay, let's get an envelope and put it in a safe place. Do you want me to fill out the forms?"

"What forms?" Judith asked.

Joe waved in the direction of the cashiers' windows. "You have to sign up to get a box in the safe."

Judith's face was stiff. "I already did."

"Oh?" Joe shrugged again. "Go ahead. I'll watch."

To Judith's relief, Dolly wasn't on duty. A young Asian man whose name tag identified him as "Sidney" was behind the window. At least Judith would avoid having Dolly ask if she'd won another bonanza. Joe didn't need to know about her earnings just yet.

Joe, however, was curious. After he'd watched Judith put the killer's name into an envelope and sign for it, he asked why she already had a box.

Judith never minded telling a fib for a good cause. "Mother didn't feel secure about wearing her engagement diamond in a gambling establishment," she replied, ignoring Renie's incredulous look, "so I put the ring in the safe for her." Joe wouldn't have noticed or remembered that Gertrude hadn't worn her engagement ring for some time because of arthritis.

"Okay." Joe rubbed his hands together. "Let's go upstairs and change." He turned to Renie. "I almost forgot. I ran into Bill and asked if you two would like to attend the show tonight. He said it was up to you, but he wouldn't mind seeing how Freddy performs under great duress. A case study, I suppose. We'll have to postpone the free dinner in the Johnny-Jump-Up Room. Anyway, are you in? I already got you comps."

"Sure," Renie said. "Same time, same place? Drinks in the Winter Bar at seven?"

"You got it," Joe said as he put his arm around Judith. "You going up now?" he asked Renie.

She shook her head. "Not quite yet. I'd sort of like to hit the beavers again."

The Flynns parted company with Renie. When the elevator doors opened on their floor, they were confronted by Gertrude and Aunt Deb in their red and yellow wheelchairs.

"Move it, twerps," Gertrude ordered. "We've got places to go and chicken to eat."

"We can't be late for the social hour," Aunt Deb said with a smile. "It'd be rude."

Judith and Joe edged around the wheelchairs. "Have a wonderful time," Judith said to the old ladies, who were racing each other into the elevator.

"Break a leg. Or a hip," Joe called out as the elevator doors closed.

"Joe! That's a terrible thing to say!" Judith scowled at her husband. "Deep down, don't you find them incredible?"

"As in I can't believe they're real?" Joe snorted. "I guess so. In a weird kind of way."

"You're awful," Judith said as they went into their room.

Joe glanced at Judith to see if she was kidding. She wasn't. "Well, there goes my chance for a passionate preprandial rendezvous."

"Your chance for that went out the window with your wager," Judith declared. "I'm still irked. Besides, I want to hear about what happened at Hillside Manor this morning."

"Everything went off on schedule," Joe replied, obviously disgruntled by Judith's rejection. "Furnace, countertop stove, rewiring—I don't know why you have such problems with Bart Bednarik. He seems pretty easy to deal with as far as I'm concerned."

"Male bonding," Judith muttered. "That's great," she added in a louder voice. "So everything will be ready when we get back Saturday?"

"It looks that way," Joe said, heading into the bathroom. "Unless you figure out how to screw it up again." He slammed the door behind him.

Judith happened to glance in the mirror over the dresser. She looked tired, irritable, and unattractive. The evening was getting off to a bad start.

Even after Judith and Joe had readied themselves, the icy atmosphere between them seemed fitting for a meeting with Renie and Bill in the Winter Bar. Indeed, the Joneses, who had arrived first, sensed the chill immediately.

"If either of you has bruises," Renie stated, "don't show them to me. I'm in a good mood. Bucky Beaver pooped out on me, but I won another two hundred bucks on a Wild Bird machine. I lined up three cedar waxwings."

"Great," said Judith.

"Terrific," said Joe.

"Franz Kafka," said Bill.

"Huh?" chorused the Flynns.

"Kafka," Bill repeated. "Gloom. Doom. Total despair. That's what you both act like."

"Sorry," Joe said, summoning the waiter. "My lovely bride seems to have overextended herself. She forgot she was on vacation." He shot Judith a dirty look.

"I'm not prone to argue," Judith retorted.

"You're not prone to do much of anything," Joe shot back.

"Kiddies!" Renie cried, waving her hands. "Stop it! We're supposed to be having fun." With one hand, she picked up the candle that illuminated their table. With the other, she held the bar menu. "Kiss and make up or I'll set the goodies list on fire."

Judith and Joe stared at each other for a long time. Renie ignited the menu's corner. Bill, with the expression of a man who has suffered greatly for the cause of marriage, remained stoic. But Judith snatched the menu out of Renie's hand and dipped the burning corner in her cousin's glass of ice water.

"You idiot!" Judith cried as the fire was doused. "Leave the burning tricks to Freddy and Lloyd." She glared at Renie, then turned to Joe. "Okay. Let's be nice."

The Flynns exchanged pecks. Judith tried to smile; Joe gave their cocktail orders to the waiter, who had a wary eye on Renie.

The tension remained, however, even after the drinks were finished and the foursome headed into the cabaret. Judith—a true Libra—could see both sides of the quarrel. She knew why she was angry, she knew why Joe was mad. But she wasn't ready to give in. Not until she proved that she'd identified the killer.

The rest of the audience was in a much better mood, exuding an air of anticipation. Once again, the Flynns and the Joneses were given a ringside table. Apparently, it was theirs to keep. Inga Polson and Grisly Vanderbehr sat a half dozen tables away, accompanied by Pancho Green and Doc Engelman. During the entrée, Judith spotted Manny Quinn, sitting toward the back. He was at a table for two with a woman Judith didn't recognize. Only G. D. Fromm seemed to be absent from the gathering. There were, however, a number of familiar faces Judith recognized from the previous performance as well as from the casino. The hasty but grandiose advertising campaign for the Great Mandolini's farewell appearance had obviously paid off.

Twenty minutes later, when the dessert plates had been whisked away, the houselights dimmed. Pancho left his seat and went up on the stage, waiting for the crowd to quiet.

"Good evening, ladies and gentlemen," Pancho began. "This evening you are in for an unprecedented experience in the art of illusion. Despite the terrible losses suffered this week by the Great Mandolini, he is a veteran performer who truly believes that the show must go on."

A murmur of high anticipation passed through the audience. Judith shifted uncomfortably in her chair. Joe and Bill kept their eyes fixed on Pancho. Renie brushed crumbs and other debris from her wine-colored evening ensemble.

"There will be no opening act tonight," Pancho continued. "Instead, let me present a real trouper, the Great Mandolini."

Houselights down. Drum roll. A hush throughout the room. Renie choking on a sip of water. Bill slapping her hard on the back. The curtain slowly rising. The empty stage. The eerie sound of Lloyd Watts's theremin in the background. A single spotlight.

A rabbit dashed out of the wings, made a complete circle, and sat in the spotlight. The stage went dark for the blink of an eye. The lights came back on. The rabbit had disappeared. The Great Mandolini stood in its place. Excited applause burst from the onlookers.

"Ha!" Renie said under her breath. "I can figure that one out from what G. D. Fromm told me. The spotlight was moved. Freddy was there all along."

Bill scowled at his wife. "Keep it to yourself. Everybody else had to pay to get in."

"Tough," Renie retorted, but she shut up.

Maybe it was Judith's mood, but the next series of illusions didn't strike her as very innovative. Almost all of them were variations on objects disappearing and reappearing or birds and small animals showing up in unusual ways. Lloyd Watts seemed to be an able, if uncharismatic, assistant. The audience seemed restless, exchanging whispers and moving about in their seats.

As for Freddy, Judith thought he looked much better than when she had visited him in his suite. Of course, he was wearing heavy stage makeup. But there was nothing tentative or unsteady about his demeanor. Freddy's ability to focus completely on his performance undoubtedly carried him through.

After about an hour, there was a brief intermission. Waiters roamed the tables, taking after-dinner drink orders. Judith twisted around in her chair to observe Inga and the rest of her party.

"Fifty, if she's a day," Judith whispered to Renie. "I misjudged her age, probably because I assumed Freddy's so-called sister couldn't be too much older than he is."

"They all look a bit grim," Renie responded. "Of course Grisly always does. Even Doc seems off his feed. Only Pancho is acting like his usual suave self."

Judith turned in the other direction to look to the rear of the cabaret. Manny Quinn and his female companion sat in stony silence. Judith wondered who the woman was. From such a distance, it was difficult to make out her features except for her short dark hair and a high-necked black dress.

As the houselights dimmed, Pancho returned to the stage. "What you are about to see is an illusion never before performed anywhere in the world. This is a truly death-defying act. The Great Mandolini and his assistant, Lloyd Watts, will lock themselves in separate cages, each containing a fierce leopard. In the wilds, the leopard's favorite food is the wild monkey. Our two courageous gentlemen have been sprayed with a monkey scent that will make them vulnerable to the fierce leopard's taste buds. This is not an illusion for the squeamish. If you'd prefer not to be a spectator for this first-time event, feel free to leave the cabaret."

Pancho stepped down as another murmur raced among the audience. Five people—two women, two children, and a man—rose from their seats and made their exit.

"Yuk!" Renie exclaimed. "This sounds kind of terrible. Maybe I should get out of here. The only time I don't mind seeing real blood is when it belongs to one of my graphic-design competitors."

"Come on, coz," Judith urged, "you know that Freddy and Lloyd aren't actually going to get eaten alive."

Renie moved closer to Bill. "I'll close my eyes." She clung to her husband's arm. "Tell me when it's okay to look, just like you do at the movies."

The curtain went up to reveal two steel cages. Each held a prowling leopard some six feet long. As the stage lights struck their eyes, they let out deep, frightening growls.

"Real teeth," Renie said, moving even closer to Bill. "Bigger than mine."

"But not as scary," Bill murmured.

After a pause, Freddy and Lloyd emerged from opposite sides of the stage. They were no longer dressed in tuxedos, but costumes made to resemble monkey fur. Slowly, they moved toward the cages. The audience was completely quiet. Even Renie kept her mouth shut.

In unison, the two men opened the cage doors with keys on large silver rings. They stepped inside and locked the cages before tossing the keys out through the bars. The leopards continued to growl.

Freddy and Lloyd did a little dance, as if to taunt the beasts. Both leopards drew back to survey their prey. The men made shrieking noises, imitating monkey cries. The big cats crouched, snarled, and narrowed their eyes. Then, with lightning movements, they pounced.

The stage was plunged into darkness. The audience came alive with voices of fear, excitement, and a few nervous giggles. Judith couldn't help herself. She grabbed Joe's hand and held it tight.

The stage lights came on again.

The leopards were gone. Freddy and Lloyd stood in the locked cages, now wearing their tuxedoes. Each man had a beautiful woman on his arm.

One was Sally. The other was Micki.

They smiled and waved at the crowd.

Judith fainted.

Chapter Twenty-one

AMID the applause and cheers, Judith numbly accepted a sip of water from Joe's glass. Slowly, she turned to look at the stage. Apparently, she had blacked out for only a second or two. Freddy, Lloyd, Sally, and Micki were taking curtain calls in response to the thunderous ovation. All four of them looked hale and hearty.

Judith stared coldly at Joe. "I hate you," she said. Without another word, she rose from her chair and stalked out of the cabaret.

Apparently, word of the unique illusion—and resurrection—had already leaked onto the casino floor. Small groups were clustered near the slot machines, laughing and talking. The word passed among the blackjack tables, the roulette wheels, the craps games. *No doubt,* Judith thought bitterly, *the news had spread to the sports book.* Instead of the latest NBA victory, the board probably read "Mandolini 117, Fatso 0."

Judith finally reached the entrance to the casino. It had started to rain, but she didn't care. She marched down the stone steps, almost colliding with a couple of newly arrived guests. Or *suckers,* she thought angrily. She'd certainly been played for one.

Bob Bearclaw was in the driveway, giving one of the valets instructions about a luggage cart. Judith charged toward the doorman, then slowed her step. No matter how irate she felt, Bob Bearclaw wasn't someone to approach in anger.

"Mrs. Flynn," Bob said, doffing his cap. "You seem agitated."

Judith faced him squarely. "Do you know why?"

Bob looked as if he might be trying not to smile. "I have an inkling."

His response made it hard for Judith to repress her outrage. "Does that mean you were in on this so-called practical joke, too?"

Bob motioned for Judith to move closer to the valet kiosk. "It didn't start out with you in mind," he replied, now very serious. "It was something that the Mandolini troupe felt would be a sensation, and great publicity. Mr. Polson thought it was time to make a major leap in his career. It was only after your husband and Pancho Green got together after your arrival that they decided to use the opportunity to deceive you as their stepping-stone. Mr. Flynn felt you'd be bored at the casino. I understand you chose our resort because one of your relatives was attending a conference at the same time that you had to vacate your home. Your husband said you're not much of a gambler. Except when it comes to murder," Bob added meaningfully.

"Who all was in on this devious plan besides the Mandolini bunch?" Judith asked, keeping her temper at bay.

Bob started ticking names off on his fingers. "Mr. Quinn. Doc Engelman. Our security people, as well as the local sheriff. Your cousin's husband, Dr. Jones."

The enormity of the deception overwhelmed Judith. "Not Mrs. Jones?" was all she could say.

Bob shook his head. "No. Your husband felt that the two of you are so close that somehow Mrs. Jones would give it away."

"But what about the other guests?" Judith asked. "Was it fair to fool the visitors?"

Bob sighed. "That bothered me a bit. But it was entertainment, after all, and that's what people pay for. Mr. Fromm, however, was very much opposed even though he went along with it in the beginning."

"Was his disapproval why he got fired?"

Bob shrugged. "The company's relationships and personalities aren't an illusion. What you've seen of them is real."

Judith considered Bob's words for a moment. "What about Marta Flax? She wasn't real, was she?"

Bob shook his head. "Marta Flax doesn't exist. She's Martha Engelman. Martha's very shy and rarely drinks. The only way she would take part was to become inebriated. It was very brave of her. Being unused to alcohol, she didn't realize she'd end up in such a state. Luckily, she's recovered quite well. Without the blond wig, you probably didn't recognize her sitting with Manny Quinn, toward the rear of the cabaret."

"Don't tell me Fou-Fou was an illusion," Judith retorted.

Bob smiled. "Fou-Fou is Fou-Fou. A rather spoiled animal, but Mrs. Engelman's pride and joy. I believe Fou-Fou is a show dog."

"Great." Judith paced a bit. "I still can't believe it." She paused, a hand to her cheek. She no longer felt faint or weak, but she was still fuming inside. "Could you send someone to get my car?"

Bob stared briefly at Judith. "Of course." He cleared his throat. "I trust you're simply going for a drive to clear your head."

"That's right," Judith replied. "I have to get out of here for a while."

"Then drive carefully," Bob cautioned. "These mountain roads can be dangerous at night."

"I'll be safe," Judith promised.

Motioning to a valet, Bob went into the kiosk to fetch Judith's keys. "Excuse me," he said, "a limo is pulling up. I should greet the newcomers. I believe it's our next headliner, a well-known rap star." Bob shuddered slightly. "Their music is worse than our tribal chants. Whatever happened to ballads?"

Judith murmured her thanks. For a couple of minutes, she tried to stand still, forcing herself to regain her composure. The Subaru roared out of the garage and came to a stop.

"Thanks," she said as the valet held the door open.

As she started to get into the car, she heard a sound in a nearby cedar tree. It was the cry of a flicker. Judith snorted in contempt. The previous cries had sounded shortly before the supposed deaths of Sally and Micki. For all of Bob Bearclaw's local folklore knowledge, the flicker's calls hadn't forecast anything dire—unless they were intended to make her look like an idiot.

Which they certainly had, Judith thought grimly. Pulling onto the highway, she automatically headed in the direction of the family property. The rain had stopped, but except for the intermittent yellow divider, the highway looked—and felt—like slick black satin. Judith slowed down as a pair of taillights appeared after she had turned a sharp corner. The vehicle was a rusted red pickup, traveling well under the speed limit. There were cars coming from the other direction. Judith had no choice but to hold steady at forty miles an hour.

The old truck left the road when they reached the Green Mountain Inn. Judith, however, didn't press down on the accelerator. She, too, was going to turn off in another three hundred yards. Sitting by the river, she'd seek peace in a place that had always provided sanctuary.

Judith stopped at the gate. It would be locked, of course. She'd have to walk the rest of the way. Going to the narrow opening past the gate, she felt the soft, damp earth under her feet. Rain dripped from the evergreen branches overhead. Without bothering to look at the excavated bog, she walked up the dirt drive, coming out onto flatter ground near what she hoped would be the future site of her country inn.

The clouds were moving swiftly to the east, allowing glimpses of the half-moon. Judith could see the outline of Mount Woodchuck against the night sky. Downriver, to the west, she could see a handful of stars.

It was peaceful on the riverbank. Judith sat down on an old hemlock stump. Her father and Uncle Cliff had sawed down the tree forty years ago because it blocked the view of the mountain. Just before the final cut, Uncle Cliff had pointed to his left, and yelled, "Timber!" The tree had crashed to the right, almost crushing Auntie Vance and Aunt Ellen. Fortunately, everyone had laughed. That was typical of the Grover clan. They could laugh their way through almost anything.

The memory improved Judith's mood. She'd never sought out danger. She'd never come near a homicide until after she'd opened Hillside Manor. In the years that followed, she'd run into situations where she could—in retrospect—have predicted violence. Guests such as opera stars, members of the mob, a movie company—all were fraught with the potential for murder. And when she was away from the B&B, the chain of events that led to homicide were already in motion before she came upon the scene.

Of course, there was her curiosity. But that stemmed from her interest in people, along with an innate sense of justice.

Maybe Joe was right. Certainly she had encountered some close calls along the way. Her luck could be running out. Maybe the speeding car in the hotel's parking garage had meant to run her down. Or the falling sandbag had been intended to crush her. Maybe somebody thought she was a nuisance—somebody like G. D. Fromm. Judith should be grateful to her husband for his concern. He only wanted to protect her. And that was because he loved her. She might feel foolish, but she shouldn't be angry.

The sound of the river and the quiet of the night had eased her mind. She wasn't quite ready to look back on the events of the past few days and laugh. But eventually, she would. She'd laugh with Joe.

A noise behind her broke her reverie. Judith swiveled around on the stump. Perhaps a deer was coming down to the river for a drink. Or an owl was flying among the trees.

But the figure that appeared out of the shadows was human. Judith squinted to identify the newcomer. It was a man. It was, she realized as he drew closer, Doc Engelman.

"Hi," she said in a puzzled voice. "What are you doing here?"

"I often walk the river at night," Doc replied, looking equally surprised. "After all, I live only a quarter mile down the road."

Judith stood up. "You must have left the casino just before I did."

"Maybe so." Doc shrugged. "My wife and I came in separate cars. She headed home right after the final curtain. She never likes to leave Fou-Fou alone for long."

"Of course," Judith said, taking a last look at the mountain. "I should go back to the casino. Joe must wonder where I am."

"I'll walk you to your car," Doc offered. He turned quickly, as if he were suddenly in a hurry.

"Thanks," Judith replied as they headed for the drive. "Will you go home by the road or back along the river?"

"I may walk a bit farther," Doc said. "The rain's stopped. It's a decent night."

Judith agreed. "We could use some good weather around here. I can't understand why Dale Armstrong's crew virtually walked off the job. As soon as I get home, I'm going to take legal action, if necessary."

"Contractors can be temperamental," Doc allowed as they reached the clearing near the road. He stiffened slightly at the sound of an oncoming car. "You'd better be on your way. It's getting late."

Through the trees, Judith could see the vehicle's headlights pass by. "Yes." But she began to walk toward the bog. "I still don't understand why Dale started digging this close to the road if he wanted to test the ground. I don't plan on building so near the highway."

Another car was coming closer. Doc pursed his lips, head cocked. Again, the car kept going. "What? Oh—who can say? But I wouldn't go any farther. It must be very soft around the edges. The rain, you know."

"I'll be careful." Judith took a couple of steps closer. In the dark, she could see nothing but a black hole. "That's another thing—why dig so deep? If they want to test the stability of—"

The moon broke through the clouds, shining down into the trees. Judith saw three mounds barely poking through the ground. They could have been the lids of treasure chests, she thought, before her gaze roamed closer, to the bog's perimeter. What she saw there wrenched a scream from deep in her throat.

G.D. Fromm was lying faceup, tongue protruding, blank eyes staring skyward. His body was already partially submerged in the swampy ground.

Trembling, Judith faced Doc Engelman. "Look! It's terrible!"

Doc didn't move. Judith assumed he was stunned. Then she saw the cold look in his eyes and the tightening of his jaw. Despite the shock, her brain was still functioning. Doc didn't need to look. He knew what was in the bog. He was the one who had put G.D. Fromm there.

"You should have listened to me," Doc said in a weary voice. "There was no need for this."

Judith felt that "this" had a double-edged meaning. "Those are real treasure chests, aren't they?" she said in a rapid, high-pitched voice. "But why? I mean, why kill Fromm?"

Doc sighed. "Your family's land originally belonged to the Stillas-nowamish. I've known about the gold and silver deposits around here for some time. I've even found a bit of gold at my place. When Dale Armstrong was working on the casino construction, he heard a story about how the Native-American miners had hidden their caches in the ground. It seems they became finicky about the whole mining process. When the railroad was built and an entire town sprang up on Mount Nugget, the tribe felt that nature was being savaged. There were even quarrels, among the tribe, over the gold. The old chief stopped the mining and decreed that they offer their treasure back to nature. They chose this particular site because it was an unusual type of ground for the area. The Stillasnowamish considered it sacred. The gold was sunk where it supposedly would never be unearthed by anyone else."

Judith held up a hand. "Wait a minute. Are you saying that the Indians hid their gold in the swampy place we call the quicksand bog?"

Doc nodded. "Yes. Who would expect quicksandlike ground in such a place? Dale Armstrong was amazed. Of course, I've known Dale for some time. I offered him twenty percent of whatever we found." Doc grimaced. "Unfortunately, that meddlesome Fromm overheard Dale and me talking in the bar a few days ago. He tried to horn in on the deal. He came down here to see if there was any sign of gold. By chance, there was some dust and even a few nuggets."

Judith was trying to stay calm. She noticed that Doc's head swerved when he heard another vehicle approach. But it didn't stop, and he resumed speaking. "Dale's crew knew nothing about the gold. He and I performed some tests the other day with metal detectors. We knew the chests were about to be uncovered. I had Dale suspend the digging operation. He came by earlier to make sure we'd judged correctly. Now he's on his way back with a four-by-four and a winch to remove the chests."

"I thought you were waiting for someone," Judith said, her voice still sounding strange. "What happens to Dale after he gets the chests out? Does he end up with G. D. Fromm?"

"I never look too far ahead," Doc replied. "It's like practicing medicine. I perform one procedure at a time." With a quick motion, he took Judith by the arm. His grip was firm, but not painful. "There was no bloodshed," he said quietly. "Not that I'm squeamish about blood. I can't be, in my profession. By tomorrow, there will be no body. There's still enough suction in the bog to make sure no one ever finds a corpse."

Judith didn't take in all of Doc's last few words. She was standing by the very spot where she'd almost lost her life a half century earlier. Surely she wasn't going to die in her family property's quicksand bog.

"How did G. D. get here tonight?" she asked. "I didn't see his car."

"I brought him earlier this evening," Doc answered. "He wanted to make sure the chest had been exposed. When I walked from home now, I was startled to find you here. I hoped you'd cooperate and leave."

Judith assessed Doc's physical condition. He was at least seventy, but appeared to be in excellent shape—certainly better than she was with her artificial hip. It would be useless to run. Panic overcame her.

Doc recognized the change. He had pulled something out of his jacket pocket, but Judith couldn't see what it was. "Enough," he said, sounding gruff. He twisted Judith's arm behind her, turning her back to him. His other arm wrapped around her neck. As pressure was applied, Judith began to gasp for breath. Then she felt a plastic bag being slipped over her head. The kicks and scratches she aimed at Doc glanced off harmlessly. She couldn't see. She couldn't breathe. She could taste the plastic on her tongue. She was going to die.

"Greed," said a nearby voice, "breeds violence. And murder is the ugliest of sins against nature."

Judith felt Doc's grasp on her neck ease off ever so slightly.

"You don't understand," Doc said, his voice lacking its usual calm. "It's a game. It's part of the joke we all played on her. Everything's been a joke, hasn't it?"

"No, no." The pitying laugh came from Bob Bearclaw, who was standing a few feet away. Through the filmy plastic, Judith could see that he was unarmed, yet his very presence exuded power. "This is no joke," Bob said. "Please remove that bag. The poor lady can't breathe."

After a moment's hesitation, Doc obeyed. Judith staggered, holding her throat and gasping for air. She stumbled as far as she could from Doc, finally bracing herself against a young alder tree.

Doc put the plastic bag into his pocket. "It doesn't matter what you see, really," he said, regaining some of his composure. When the hand came out of the pocket, it held a gun. "I swear, Bob, I don't want to do this. But I must."

Bob shook his head sadly. "No."

From the shadows of the salmonberry bushes and sword ferns, Jack Jackrabbit and Emily Dancingdoe appeared from their hiding places near the gate. They each held a Colt .45 semiautomatic.

"I hope," Bob said, "that Jack and Emily will only wound you. But they're in law enforcement, and duty bound. Please drop your weapon, Dr. Engelman. Don't turn this into yet another tragedy."

From six feet away, Judith swore she could hear Doc's teeth grinding. By chance, she glanced from Engelman to Bob Bearclaw. Judith didn't see Doc aim at Jack and pull the trigger.

The bullet grazed Jack, who sank down on one knee. Before Doc could fire again, Emily shot him through the heart.

The noise and the flashes sent Judith sprawling on the ground. She could smell the damp earth, but it was marred by a more acrid odor. *The gunfire,* she thought. Maybe she should stay where she was and wait for everything awful to go away.

As if from a great distance, she heard movement and voices. Emily was on a cell phone, requesting emergency vehicles. There was no rush, she added.

Judith felt someone touch her shoulder. She looked up. Bob Bearclaw was kneeling beside her. "Are you all right?" he asked gently.

"I'm a wreck," Judith admitted. "You followed me?"

"Emily and Jack followed Doc," Bob replied. "They parked across the road, at the auto court. We'd heard about Dale Armstrong's work crew pulling out. We've been aware of what's been going on here. Mr. Fromm wasn't very discreet, especially when he'd been drinking. We thought something was going to happen here this evening. When Jack and Emily saw your car, they alerted me, so I drove down. I arrived just as Doc tried to smother you, though you were never in any real danger. Jack and Emily were hiding by the gate. They were waiting to see if he'd make a move that would incriminate him."

"Goodness. I wish I'd known that," Judith said as Bob helped her sit up. "Did you believe G. D. Fromm had been killed?"

Bob surveyed Judith to make sure she hadn't suffered any serious physical damage. "Not necessarily. We believed the treasure chests would be removed tonight before the construction crew started asking questions. Their pay would stop with the job incomplete."

Judith allowed Bob to help her stand up. Except for a very sore neck, she felt almost human. She gazed at the bog, though avoided looking at Fromm's body. "I can't believe there's gold on our property."

Bob smiled. "There isn't."

Judith turned swiftly. "There isn't? You mean those chests are empty?"

"No, no." Bob's smile became ironic. "They're full of gold. But they're not on your property. They never were."

Judith was flabbergasted. "What do you mean?"

"Have you ever noticed how the highway takes a slight bend by the bog?" He saw Judith nod, though she still looked confused. "The road was built around it because of the swampy ground. The Stillasnowamish owned this land, and when it was sold to your family, it was surveyed in a straight line, allowing for six feet on each side for future highway expansion. You may recall that when you were

young, the road was gravel. After the war, it was widened and resur-
faced. Thus, the bog has always been owned by our tribe. We knew
it was unlikely that the Grover clan would ever dig in that swampy
area. It was a dangerous place. But last week, when we heard that
something odd was going on, our tribal attorney wrote you a letter to
inform you that the bog was off-limits as far as your building plans
were concerned. I gather you never received the notification."

Judith thought back to the mail that had piled up since she'd left
for the resort. No doubt the letter was in the stack on the kitchen
counter.

"Oh, dear." she sighed. "You're right. I was so involved with the
renovations at home that I didn't open Saturday's mail. And Monday's hadn't come before we headed out of town."

Bob shrugged. "No matter. Now you know."

"So what are you going to do with the gold?" Judith inquired, still
trying to sort through Bob's revelation.

More vehicles were pulling up alongside the road. Judith could
see that one of them was an ambulance. Bob glanced in that direction, then turned back to Judith. "We also own a hundred feet of
property next to you, upriver. I considered leaving the treasure
where it is. After all," he added with a droll expression, "the resort
casino is our real gold mine. But other tribes aren't so fortunate. We
can help them with our long-buried treasure. In exchange, we'll
deed you the property that includes the bog and the other hundred
feet from river to road."

"Oh!" Judith smiled a bit tremulously. "That's very generous. But
are you sure?"

Bob nodded. "Yes, quite sure."

Judith stared briefly at Bob. "You seem to have a great deal of
influence around here. And not just with the members of the Stillasnowamish tribe."

"You mean," Bob remarked wryly, "for a mere doorman?"

Judith was caught off guard. "Well—not exactly. That is . . ."

Bob smiled. "I *am* a mere doorman. I'm also the tribal chief."

Dale Armstrong and his four-by-four arrived just as Bob was about to escort Judith back to the hotel. Abbott N. Costello showed up a minute later and promptly arrested Armstrong.

"Do you think Doc would have killed Dale after they got the gold out?" Judith asked Bob as Costello put the cuffs on the contractor.

"I'm afraid so," Bob replied. "Doc didn't seem to want to share."

A decision was made that Emily would drive the Subaru back to the resort. Bob felt it best that Judith didn't get behind the wheel until she'd had more time to recover. G. D. Fromm's body would be removed as soon as possible. Judith avoided looking at the bog as they started for the gate. But she couldn't ignore Doc Engelman's body. It had been covered with a Native-American blanket depicting eagles and elk and rainbow trout.

Judith admired the tribe's respect for the dead. But the beautifully crafted blanket didn't seem right. As far as she was concerned, Engelman should have been covered in cheap plastic.

When Bob Bearclaw showed up with Judith on his arm, Joe couldn't believe his eyes.

"What happened?" he asked in astonishment as he rose from his place next to Bill at the baccarat table. "Did you fall down again?"

"Sort of," Judith replied in a lame voice.

Renie, who had been watching the husbands, scrutinized her cousin. "You look terrible. And your clothes are a mess."

Bob suggested that they all go up to Pancho's office. When the whole story was unraveled, Joe was aghast, Renie was incredulous, and even Bill's usual stoic facade was severely cracked.

"I should have known," Joe declared, holding his head. "You just had to come up against a killer and damned near get yourself whacked." He stared hard at Judith. "But no more. You've lost the bet."

For now, Judith didn't care. "I just want to go to bed and sleep until noon. We'll sort everything out tomorrow, including Bob's offer."

Joe agreed. After offering more thanks to Bob, the Flynns headed up to their room. When they got into the elevator on the second floor, Gertrude and Aunt Deb were already there. Neither of the old ladies had any idea of what had happened at the family property. Nor would they have to know, at least not now.

"Say, Toots," said Gertrude to her daughter, "you look like the pigs ate your little brother. What did you do, walk into a wall?"

"Now, Gert," Aunt Deb reprimanded, clutching a crystal trophy with the words "Most Outstanding Participant" etched on it, "don't be so hard on Judith. She's just a bit clumsy, like her poor old auntie."

"Yeah?" Gertrude snapped. "That's how you ended up in a wheel-chair, isn't it? At least I never broke *my* hip."

"You still can't walk very well," Aunt Deb replied in an amiable tone, "or else you wouldn't be riding around in a wheelchair, too. We should thank the good Lord that we're still around."

The elevator stopped at their floor.

"Maybe the good Lord doesn't want us," Gertrude said. She glanced at Deb. "Race you to the room."

"You're on," Deb responded.

The two old girls went charging down the hall. Judith smiled. Joe merely shook his head.

It was almost eleven o'clock before Judith and Joe woke up the next morning. They had breakfast in their room and were just finishing when the phone rang.

It was Pancho Green, asking if Judith would be willing to attend a press conference in about an hour.

"Who called it?" Judith asked with a frown.

Pancho made a grumbling noise at the other end of the line. "Not us. Not even the Mandolini bunch, although they're certainly going to use the staged murders as publicity."

"Then who?" Judith persisted.

"You can't expect a murder, a shoot-out with a killer, and a treasure trove *not* to make the news," Pancho reasoned.

"Come on, don't be coy," Judith retorted. "Who?"

Pancho's sigh was audible. "Sheriff Abbott N. Costello."

Judith held her head. "Why am I not surprised?"

"He claims it all happened under his jurisdiction," Pancho said.

Judith tried to ignore Joe's inquisitive expression. "Tell Sheriff Costello that I'm indisposed. Tell him I've got mumps. Tell him good-bye."

"But he told us he'd like to meet the famous Fatso," Pancho said.

"He already has," Judith replied and hung up.

The rest of the day passed in a haze. Joe insisted that Judith stay in bed and recover from her ordeal. She'd objected at first, but finally gave in. She was worn out, and her hip was bothering her. She wasn't surprised that she took two long naps during the afternoon. When she finally woke, it was after seven P.M.

Joe was watching a basketball game with the TV sound off. He got up from the armchair when he heard Judith call his name.

"How are you?" he asked, sitting on the edge of the bed. "Would you like to eat here or join Bill and Renie in the Johnny-Jump-Up Room? They have seven-thirty reservations, and we have a free meal, remember?"

Judith waited a moment to clear the fog of sleep from her head. "It's our last night. We've got to do something festive. It won't take me long to get ready."

The Flynns arrived in the restaurant by seven-forty. Renie and Bill were already there, seated away from the windows, which offered a panoramic view. Bill didn't like heights. And Renie apparently couldn't see. She was wearing dark glasses and a glum expression.

"Oh, no," Judith exclaimed, "has your chronic corneal dystrophy come back?"

Every couple of years, Renie suffered a recurrence, but she usually wore an eye patch to speed her recovery. "No," she snapped, yanking off the glasses. "That awful woman I keep running into gave me a black eye."

Judith sat down and put an arm around her cousin. "Good grief! What happened?"

Renie sighed. "Since it's our last day here, I thought I'd try the Black Leopard dollar machines. They were really paying off, so it was hard to find one that was open. I finally did, and on the first try, I hit a three-hundred-dollar jackpot. My nemesis was right behind me, claiming it was her machine and that she'd just gotten up to get change. That's when we got into it."

"She had her jacket over the back of the chair to reserve the machine," Bill pointed out, no doubt for the third or fourth time.

"I didn't see the damned jacket," Renie retorted. "Besides, it's a no-no to do that in most casinos."

"Who won?" Joe asked.

"I did," Renie said with an air of satisfaction. "Security came over, in the form of Amos Littlebird. I guess after all that's happened with our party, he has a soft spot for us. Anyway, he broke up the fight after I busted the old bat's glasses, and now she's going to get charged with attempted homicide."

"What?" Judith was incredulous.

Renie, who had put the sunglasses back on, smirked. "On a crazy whim, I accused her of trying to run us down in the parking garage and dropping that sandbag from the catwalk. She admitted it, and said she was damned sorry she missed me. Bill figures her for a nutcase. I think she's just a jerk."

Joe raised his glass of Scotch, which had just arrived. "To Serena Jones, world featherweight champ."

"Here, here," Renie echoed, then paused. "Hey—what about my taffeta skirt? Was that really blood on it?"

"Fake blood," Joe replied. "It'll come out. You must have run into Grisly. She impersonated Sally in the first part of the saber illusion. They had to wrap Sally in the cape to move her into the Corvette. Grisly couldn't impersonate Sally for the conclusion. She doesn't have the figure for it, so they put one of the mannequins in the cabinet and brought the curtain down fast. They also had a mannequin of Freddy and one of Micki, in case she had to stand in for Sally."

"So," Judith mused, "the redheaded mannequin was placed in the 'Vette just to add to my confusion?"

Joe nodded. "They didn't need a power failure for that. They did it in the wee small hours when the casino was virtually empty."

Judith's dark eyes narrowed. "What about that threatening note in my purse?"

Joe looked sheepish. "I did that."

"No!" Judith burst out. "That wasn't your handwriting!"

"It looked odd because I wrote it when the lights went out in the coffee shop and put it in your purse while you were sitting with Lloyd Watts."

"You twit," Judith said, but she lacked the energy to be angry. "It certainly was an elaborate hoax."

"Lloyd thought up most of the plan," Joe said. "The Mandolini gang loved doing it. They really threw themselves into their parts."

"Indeed," she noted archly. "So what were you all doing at the sheriff's office yesterday?"

"We weren't at the sheriff's office," Joe replied, the gold flecks dancing in his green eyes. "We were playing poker in one of the meeting rooms on the second floor. I won two hundred bucks. Speaking of winning, when do you want to show me who you thought killed Sally and Micki?"

"Uh . . ." Judith grimaced. "Is that necessary? It was all a big joke, right? The bet's not a real bet."

"A bet's a bet." Joe was adamant. "With all your experience, you could have figured out that the so-called murders were a prank. Let's face it, from what I could tell, you never ever had a handle on the case. Coming up against all those dead ends should have made you think twice about what was real and what was not."

Judith's mouth was in a tight line.

"The main thing," Joe went on, "is that by not guessing correctly, you've agreed to stop getting mixed up in murders. Recent involvement notwithstanding."

Judith got up from her chair. "All right. Let's get it over with. If we don't, I'll lose my appetite."

Joe also rose from the table. He glanced at Bill and Renie. "You coming?"

Renie shook her head. "I want to try to read my favorite literature—the menu."

Bill said he'd stay with Renie to help her.

Five minutes later, the Flynns were at the cashier's window on the casino floor. Dolly was on duty, agog when she recognized Judith.

"Oh, sweetie, I heard about what happened to you last night!" Dolly exclaimed. "Are you sure you're okay?"

"I'm fine, thanks," Judith replied, handing over her receipt.

Dolly leaned closer, looking at Joe. "So this is Mr. Flynn?"

"It always has been." Joe smiled.

Dolly let out a gusty laugh. "Okay, be right back."

Judith and Joe waited in silence. She looked grim; he seemed smug.

Dolly returned, holding four envelopes. "This morning, Mrs. Jones asked me to put her envelope with yours. I assume you wanted everything out of the safe?"

"Ah . . ." Judith winced. "Yes, I guess so. We're checking out tomorrow."

Joe eyed the envelopes. "Don't tell me you made four guesses. That's cheating."

"No," Judith replied, then thanked Dolly, who wished the Flynns good luck. "I had some windfalls," Judith remarked as they walked away. "Shall I show you the name now?"

Joe suggested that they return to the Johnny-Jump-Up Room. "You should do it front of the Joneses," he said, heading for the elevators. "That way, if you lose your mind over the bet, Bill can help you."

"Very funny."

"What about those other envelopes?" Joe inquired as they waited for the express elevator that went straight to the penthouse restaurant.

"They're a surprise for after we get home," Judith replied. "A good surprise."

Joe looked curious, but didn't badger Judith further. By the time they rejoined Renie and Bill, a waiter was serving various appetizers.

"Well?" Renie asked. "Did she or didn't she?"

"We'll soon find out," Joe said, sitting down again.

Judith handed the envelope to Joe. "You open it."

"Okay." His movements were deliberately slow. When he finally read what was on the slip of paper, his jaw dropped. "I don't believe it. You win."

Judith stared. "What?"

"I don't know *how* you did it. You seemed as amazed as anyone when Sally and Micki were restored to life."

"I was," Judith answered with a frown. "But what has—"

"Stop the suspense. Either read it aloud or give it to us." Renie lunged at Joe.

He held the slip of paper just out of Renie's reach. "Okay." Joe cleared his throat. "My lovely bride has written, 'It'sNobodyAtAll.'"

Judith looked as stunned as Bill and Renie. "I did? I mean, I *did* write that down." Feeling her cheeks grow warm as she remembered making a notation of the long shot that had won her big bucks, Judith turned to Renie. "You wanted me to . . . er . . . ah . . . mmm . . ."

"Yes," Renie intervened. "I wanted you to do that. You win."

Joe was shaking his head. "I can't believe it."

Judith was rummaging in her purse. "I need lipstick," she said in a strained voice. Sure enough, when she delved deep enough she could see another slip of hotel paper. She left it in her purse, but she could see the name she'd written: "Freddy Polson." As she took out her lipstick and compact, she couldn't believe she'd put the wrong note in the safe. Except for Renie, nobody would ever know of the mistake. Judith couldn't resist smiling into the compact's mirror.

Joe and Bill were herding the old ladies and the luggage. Judith and Renie were checking out. Judith looked over the room charges and shook her head.

"I'm sorry," she said to the desk clerk whose name tag identified her as "Willow Windrush," "but there's a mistake for the Grover room. What's this eight hundred and fifty-six dollar charge for?"

Willow examined the bill. "It's for keno games," she said. "See the symbol next to it? HTVK stands for 'House Television Keno.'"

"Good grief!" Judith cried. "I forgot all about Mother playing keno!"

Willow again pointed to the charge. "She won a few. There's a thirty-dollar credit."

"Great." Judith signed off. At least her winnings of $5,800 would cover it, though she knew she needed every cent to pay for the new furnace and the overrun costs at Hillside Manor. At least the keno games had kept her mother occupied.

It was drizzling as Judith and Renie went out to meet their husbands and mothers. The old ladies were being loaded into the Camry and the Subaru. Judith decided not to say anything to Gertrude about her gambling losses. What was done was history.

Bob Bearclaw was wishing the old girls a safe trip. He turned when he saw Judith and tipped his cap. "You're a brave woman. May the wind always blow in your favor. But," he added, taking Judith's hand, "be careful. Evil exists."

"I know," Judith said, squeezing Bob's fingers. "Thank you. You saved my life."

Bob didn't respond. Instead, he looked into Judith's eyes as if he were trying to impart some of his own wisdom to her.

As she walked away to get into the Subaru, she heard the sound of a bird somewhere in the trees. It wasn't the flicker, but a songbird. Judith glanced up into the branches of a tall hemlock. She recognized the bright yellow coloring and black wings. The bird was a goldfinch.

Then she saw Joe standing by the car. There was love in his green eyes with their golden flecks. Magic eyes, Judith always called them.

Not everything in life was an illusion.